$\mathcal{P}R$/

MW01487702

"Ava's story is witty and charming."
—Barbara Freethy #1 *NYT* bestselling author

Selected by *USA Today* as one of the Best Books of the
year alongside Nora Roberts' *Dark Witch* and
Julia Quinn's *Sum of all Kisses*.

"If you like Nora Roberts type books, this is a must-read."
—Readers' Favorite

Country Heaven
"If ever there was a contemporary romance that rated a 10
on a scale of 1 to 5 for me, this one is it!"
—The Romance Reviews

"*Country Heaven* made me laugh and cry...I could not
stop flipping the pages. I can't wait to read the next book
in this series." —Fresh Fiction

Country Heaven Cookbook
"Delicious, simple recipes... Comfort food, at its best."
—Fire Up The Oven Blog

The Bridge to a Better Life
Selected by *USA Today* as one of the Best Books of the
Summer.

"Miles offers a story of grief, healing and rediscovered
love." —USA Today

"I've read Susan Mallery and Debbie Macomber...but
never have I been so moved by the books Ava Miles
writes." —Booktalk with Eileen Reviews

The Gate to Everything
"The constant love...bring a sensual, dynamic tension to
this appealing story." —Publisher's Weekly

More Praise For Ava

The Chocolate Garden
"On par with Nicholas Sparks' love stories."
—Jennifer's Corner Blog

"A must-read...a bit of fairy magic...a shelf full of happiness." —Fab Fantasy Fiction

The Promise of Rainbows
"This is a story about grace, faith and the power of both..."
—The Book Nympho

French Roast
"Ms. Miles draws from her experience as an apprentice chef...and it shows...I loved {the} authenticity of the food references, and the recipes...looked divine." —BlogCritics

The Holiday Serenade
"This story is all romance, steam, and humor with a touch of the holiday spirit..." —The Book Nympho

The Town Square
"Ms. Miles' words melted into each page until the world receded around me..." —Tome Tender

The Park of Sunset Dreams
"Ava has done it again. I love the whole community of Dare Valley..." —Travel Through The Pages Blog

The Goddess Guides Series
"Miles' series is an **exquisite exploration** of internal discomfort and courage, allowing you to reclaim your divine soul and fully express your womanhood."
—Dr. Shawne Duperon, Project Forgive Founder, Nobel Peace Prize Nominee

"The Goddess Guides are a **world changer**. Well done, Ava." —International Bestseller Kate Perry aka Kathia Zolfaghari, Artist & Activist

Also by Ava Miles

Fiction
The Love Letter Series
Letters Across An Open Sea
Along Waters of Sunshine and Shadow

The Dare Valley Series
Nora Roberts Land
French Roast
The Grand Opening
The Holiday Serenade
The Town Square
The Park of Sunset Dreams
The Perfect Ingredient
The Bridge to a Better Life
The Calendar of New Beginnings
Home Sweet Love
The Moonlight Serenade
The Sky of Endless Blue
Daring Brides

The Dare River Series
Country Heaven
Country Heaven Song Book
Country Heaven Cookbook
The Chocolate Garden
The Chocolate Garden:
A Magical Tale (Children's Book)

Fireflies and Magnolias

The Promise of Rainbows

The Fountain of Infinite Wishes

The Patchwork Quilt of Happiness

Dare Valley Meets Paris Billionaire Mini-Series

The Billionaire's Gamble

The Billionaire's Courtship

The Billionaire's Secret

The Billionaire's Return

The Goddess Guides to Being a Woman

Goddesses Decide

Goddesses Deserve The G's

Goddesses Love Cock

Goddesses Cry and Say Motherfucker

Goddesses Don't Do Drama

Goddesses Are Sexy

Goddesses Eat

Goddesses Are Happy

Goddesses Face Fear

Other Non-Fiction

The Happiness Corner: Reflections So Far

Home Baked Happiness

The Sky of Endless Blue

The Dare Valley Series

Ava Miles

ISBN-13: 978-1-949092-05-9
www.avamiles.com
Ava Miles

DEDICATION

To my great-great grandfather, George, who inspired Arthur Hale—for his wisdom and sense of justice, using both words and grit to get the job done.

And to my divine entourage, who continues to help me find my happily ever after every day.

The Grand Mountain Hotel

Emmits Merriam University
The Hale School of Journalism

Washington
Elementary School

The Western
Independent

Dog Park

Dare Valley General Hospital

Barber Shop

OAK ST.

Sleek Lines

Hairy's Pub

Fire Station

Don't Soy
With Me

Smith's Hardware

PONDEROSA ST.

N
W   E
S

Hot Cross
Buns
Bakery

Don't Wedge
Me In

Brasserie Dare

ASPEN ST.

MAPLE ST.

MAIN ST.

Community Center

The Chop House

Justice Center

DARE VALLEY, CO

Population 21,777 Elevation 9400 ft.

Thorn's Peak

CHAPTER 1

Rome, Italy

February

J.T. MERRIAM HATED HAVING TO HOLD TIGHT ON THE RO-mance reins. He couldn't wait to start the new chapter of his life, and he already knew he wanted to start it with the captivating Caroline Hale.

"I can't believe you rented out the whole restaurant!" she was exclaiming, standing at the edge of the rooftop terrace boasting one of Rome's most brilliant views of the Vatican. "It's the Hotel Raphael, for heaven's sake."

The candlelight cast a warm glow on her glossy brown hair, the waves as beautifully defined as if created by an oil painter's brush. Watching Caroline in a setting like this was akin to seeing a masterpiece come to life. He took a moment to soak in the sight of her, then came up behind her, wishing he could put his arms around her and smell the citrus and flowers always present on her skin.

Not yet. You're not free yet.

"It was your last night in town," he said. "Like I told you when we first met again at your art gallery, 'welcome to my world.'"

"I thought you were crazy then and I still do." She looked over her shoulder and flashed him a bright smile. "But I love it."

It wouldn't be the first time someone had thought him crazy for following one of his impulses. Caroline had brought out the long-dormant romantic in him.

He hadn't walked into the famed Leggett Art Gallery in Denver weeks ago expecting to be bowled over by her beauty and wit. He certainly hadn't expected to fall so hard or so quickly for someone he hoped to work with on his new venture—an art museum at the university his great-grandfather Emmits Merriam had founded in Dare Valley. But her professionalism and taste had impressed him, and something about her had reached in and grabbed his heart, giving it a healthy shake. He'd flown Caroline to Rome for the weekend because he wanted her help evaluating the family art collection, but if he was being entirely honest with himself, he had also wanted to see her.

It felt appropriate for them to work on this venture together. Caroline was the great-niece of Emmits' best friend, Arthur Hale, a man J.T. called Uncle Arthur. Indeed, it was Uncle Arthur who had suggested he talk with Caroline about the museum, and he suspected his honorary uncle had played matchmaker, though the older man would likely never admit it.

Now, watching her hair whip in the wind and her eyes widen in delight, he couldn't be happier things had worked out the way they had. There was only one thing left to settle...

"Are you cold?" he asked. "I made sure they brought out patio heaters for our dinner."

"After living in Denver, this feels refreshing," she said, grinning at him. *"You're* the one who's going to have the wake-up call once you move to Dare Valley. You're going to freeze your butt off."

"I'm eager for a new challenge," he said, staring down at the city he loved. "And some butt freezing."

She chuckled, looking down at the view with him. Taking in the gold-lit Santa Maria della Pace and the Church of St. Mary of the Soul. Then she turned serious. "You'll miss it, though. How could you not?"

How indeed. And yet, he'd meant every word. He *would* miss the golden city, but it was time to start over.

His old life had ended. He'd just resigned from his position as head of Merriam Oil & Gas' Africa and Middle East division, something he'd done to prevent his shares of the family company from falling into the hands of Cynthia Newhouse. He'd lost three years of his life fighting her for a divorce from a marriage that had only lasted two years.

J.T.'s older brothers, Connor and Quinn, had bought his shares in the Merriam conglomerate, something they'd arranged with his other siblings. All of them had shared in his regret.

He was the first of his six siblings to strike out on a solo venture, but to his mind, the museum was still a family enterprise. Opening it—something he'd gotten the university's board of trustees to approve in complete secrecy two months ago—would be his second chance at life. The fresh start he'd fought so hard for.

Caroline Hale would be a part of that new life too, in his museum and hopefully in his arms.

"Maybe I'll buy some long underwear to keep me warm," he joked, signaling to the waiter to bring forward the champagne he'd requested. "When I was a kid, we only visited Dare Valley in the summers, but the mountaintops were still snowy some years."

Those summers had been precious to him. He and his siblings had played with the Hale children, including Caroline. One day he'd accidentally slung dirt on her pretty dress, earning himself the nickname of Mud Slinger.

It was funny to think of them then, young children with no idea their lives might one day lead them to each other. He rather liked that thought.

She turned and looked at him, her mouth twitching. "I'm trying to imagine you wearing winter underwear under a Fendi suit. Nope. Can't see it."

The thought of her imagining what was under his suit made him feel things better left buried for the moment. He cleared his throat. She stilled, seeming to sense the change in his mood, something she'd excelled at all weekend.

They'd acknowledged the attraction between them but agreed to put the romance on hold. He hadn't yet told her his primary reason for making that request, fearing she'd step away if she knew about Cynthia and the divorce drama that had driven his life for years. Early on, he'd discovered that people who learned about his protracted divorce fell into two categories: the flight or fight types. His twin brother, Trevor, was the fight type. He'd stood by his side for the entire divorce, working with him and the lawyers to block Cynthia's every money-grubbing move. But some of his siblings had opted to stay out of the fray. He couldn't blame them, but he'd grown careful about telling people, something made easier by the fact that they'd kept it quiet. He and Caroline needed more time to grow, and with the divorce's end finally in sight, he'd concluded he wasn't in the morally wrong department. That mattered to him.

Call him old-fashioned, but he wanted to be completely free and clear before dating again. He just hadn't thought it would take this long.

God, he needed it to be over. He couldn't take any more.

"Is that Armand de Brignac Brut Rose?" she asked as the waiter opened the bottle. "J.T., seriously, doesn't that vintage cost *ten thousand dollars*?"

She would flip if she knew what he'd paid to rent out the restaurant.

"We're here to celebrate our new venture. Let's drink some bubbly and watch the sunset," he said, handing her a glass. "To new horizons."

When their glasses clinked, he felt the charge shoot all the way to his heart.

"Is it terrible to say this?" she asked, lowering her voice. "I can't tell why this should cost ten thousand dollars. Not that I'm not grateful, J.T., but you need to stop being so... grand with me."

"That's like telling the stars to stop shining." He loved that money didn't motivate her, and it was another reason he was so affected by her. Not only was she beautiful and interesting, but she had integrity, something more valuable than any fortune.

"Caroline, you make me want to be grand again. I'm excited about the museum. I have been since the idea first came to me. But working alongside you—being with you— is going to make it spectacular."

"I like you too," she said, ducking her head. "Why else would I come to Rome like this?"

"Why else?" He raised his eyebrows theatrically. "Because Rome is awesome. Come, let's feast. I took the liberty of ordering the chef's tasting menu. I hope that's okay."

"Okay?" She made a face. "I'm still full from lunch, but I'll find a way to do it justice. I wouldn't want the chef's feelings to be hurt."

Yet another sign of the goodness in her heart. He couldn't help smiling. After spending years being circled by vultures, it was nice to socialize with someone sweet...like a koala. He wasn't going to share that compliment, though. What woman liked being compared to a marsupial?

"You're saving him from complete culinary depression, no doubt," he said, pulling out her chair and waving off the waiter who'd stepped forward to attend to them.

Rather than sit, she put her hand on his shoulder. Even through his clothes, he could feel the heat of her fingertips somehow, each perfect oval searing into him. Their eyes met, and he held his breath. Then she was sitting down and looking at the view. He took a moment to sip his champagne and calm his racing heart.

Tonight the only view he was interested in was her.

They talked of art and family as they supped on a golden beet salad with fresh peas, the finest carpaccio this side of heaven, a mushroom and leek risotto, monkfish stewed in fennel, and then figs sautéed in cinnamon and red wine. They shared their dreams as the sunset turned to twilight. In the candlelight, her eyes seemed to wink out at him, and all he wanted to do was kiss her hand.

He told himself to wait. She deserved to know the truth before they deepened their relationship, and he still wasn't ready to tell her.

The candles were sputtering by the time he finally stood. "We should get you back to your hotel so you can sleep for a few hours."

The plane he'd chartered for her was supposed to take off at eight. Of course he could delay it, but she wanted to arrive back in Denver with enough time to prepare for work the next day, something he respected.

"I can sleep on the plane," she said softly, standing as well. "Can't we…"

She gestured toward the view, and he waited as she found her words.

"J.T., I want to walk the streets with you and talk about art and life and…well, everything. I don't want to waste a moment."

This time he felt it was safe to take her hand. "Neither do I. Prepare yourself, Caroline. I plan to lay Rome at night at your feet."

And he did.

Sure, they didn't continue to hold hands as he took her down streets lit with golden light or coaxed her into throwing a coin and making a wish in one of the many fountains. But they found frequent excuses to brush against each other. He told himself it was enough. For now.

As the sun rose, he surprised her with hazelnut gelato, a flavor he'd discovered was her favorite.

"I never want this trip to end," she said, leaning her head against his shoulder as they studied the view of the Colosseum from Palatine Hill.

"Me either, but we'll have more trips. Remember, you still need to see the rest of the Merriam collection in Napa." He planned to ask his parents to clear out of the house for their visit. It was way too early for them to meet her again in this new context. Knowing his mom, he'd probably get teased, but he could take it.

Caroline laughed as she spooned up the last of her gelato. "Oh, *Napa*. I don't know how I'll manage it."

"I'm glad I won't have to work so hard to convince you this time."

Leaning back, she plopped the spoon in her mouth and made a humming sound, one he found very arousing. "I'll pretty much go anywhere with you. Not only are you interesting, J.T. Merriam, but you're fun. Who else would stay up all night and have gelato for breakfast with a view like this? I thought being a responsible adult was the thing to do, you know. Have a great career. A nice place to live. You're opening up all sorts of new possibilities. I like being in your world."

"Music to my ears," he said, savoring it all. "You're opening up my world too, you know."

She was quiet for a moment. "I like hearing that."

He planned to tell her much more—when he was free.

The drive to the airport was pure torture, every mile punctuating the distance that was about to open up between them. In the car, he told himself he would be able to take her in his arms soon. At the plane, he fought the urge to cup her face and tell her how important she'd become to him in such a short time. Instead, he took her hand again and squeezed it, the safest gesture he could make.

"I'll see you soon," he said. "I'm not sure exactly when, but time will go by in a blink. Trust me."

"I do," she said, forcing a smile. "Well, I'd better go. Can't have them waiting for me."

He loved that she cared about that. His soon-to-be ex-wife never had. Suddenly, holding her hand wasn't nearly enough for him. "I'm going to send you off like a good Italian," he said softly.

"Two kisses on each cheek," she said, a red flush staining her cheeks. "Just like you greeted me."

He stepped forward, feeling the heat of her body. Lowering his head, he kissed one cheek and then the other, inhaling her perfume, fighting the instinct to gather her up in his arms. He realized she wasn't breathing, and he stepped back.

"Well... Thank you for one of the best weekends of my life."

"That was my line," he said. "This is only the beginning, Caroline."

She nodded and reluctantly walked off while he stood there, watching. His heart dipped a little as she waved to him from the plane. All he could think about was starting his new life with her free and clear of the past.

After she took off, he turned his phone on. Trevor had texted him, and the message sent shockwaves through him.

Her lawyers say you resigning from Merriam isn't

going to make them back down. They still want the lion's share of your money. They're pushing the community property bullshit big-time. Same song, different day. What do you want to do?

He looked up in the blue sky, searching for Caroline's plane, and thought of the endless blue sky awaiting him in Dare Valley. Nothing was going to stop him from taking the next step of his new journey.

There was only one more play available to him if he wanted the judge to give him the freedom he craved more than anything.

He was going to have to give away the majority of his fortune to finalize his three-year-long divorce.

Welcome to his world, indeed.

CHAPTER 2

March

Dare Valley, Colorado

HIS DIVORCE WAS FINALLY DONE.

J.T. Merriam stared down at the decree that had made it so on his phone, something he'd done twenty times since the decision had come in two days ago. Personally, he thought someone else telling him that his marriage was over—and on a piece of paper, no less—was pure crap. But the legal system played a role in people's private business in ways he'd never imagined. He was finally free of Cynthia Newhouse, and he almost wanted to weep in pure relief.

Some might say he'd paid an insane price. The press release outlining his donation of five hundred million dollars to Evan Michaels' new energy company in Dare Valley had gone out yesterday. The world finally knew about his decision, but he didn't care. It was over!

Now it was time to tell Caroline and make his move.

"That's one hell of an apology picnic," Trevor said, surveying the contents of his basket. "I've never seen so much girly food."

"Caroline likes salad," he said, covering the basket

with his hands. "You can't have the champagne. Is it too much?"

"Depends," Trev said, trying not to laugh. "Are you planning on telling her your tragic tale of divorce before or after you eat?"

Tragic tale of divorce. Sometimes Trev really had a way with words. "Before. After. I don't know. I'm nervous."

"That's why I'm here, brother." Trev patted him on the back. "How could I stay in Dublin when I knew you had this on your conscience?"

He'd rented the house his friend, Chase Parker, had just vacated to move in with his fiancée, Moira, Caroline's sister. His great grandfather's place—the man they all simply called Grandpa Emmits—was ancient, having been built in the 1920s. When winter was over, J.T. planned to walk the Merriam land and find a spot to build his dream house. In the meantime, he and Trevor were roommates like they had been at Stanford.

"I told you I was good," he told Trev. "You can head back to your life."

"I think Caroline will thank you for saving her the worry," Trev said, ignoring him completely. "I personally can't wait to say goodbye to my acid reflux. I told Flynn he should have his people come up with something better than what's on the market."

Their brother was famous for coming up with new ideas, some of them off-the-wall. "Flynn said he's thinking of turning the pharmaceuticals over to Connor again because he's bored with drugs." He leveled his brother a look. "You're evading. I know you're here because you're worried Cynthia's going to cause more trouble."

Trev was truly the best brother in the world. Not that J.T. was going to tell him that. They had a policy on mushy stuff like that.

"I'm also here to celebrate your divorce, moron," Trev said, not debating him. "The fam wants to throw a big shindig in Napa."

He cringed. "I don't want this to be a deal. I only want to move on with my life."

"Fine! I'll tell Mom and have her put out the word. Now get going. Your woman and your 'salad' picnic awaits. Oh, and take your phone in case you get attacked by bears."

"It's winter, Trev," J.T. muttered as he picked up the basket. "They're hibernating. And stop making fun of my picnic. If I'm not back for the party at Natalie and Blake's later..."

"I'll assume you've been eaten by some large animal," Trev said. "Man, I hope I won't see you for other reasons."

That was assuming his talk with Caroline went well. And he thought it would—once he laid everything out and explained his reasoning. Then he could kiss her for real, and court her the way she deserved to be courted. Okay, so he'd lowered his guard and kissed her once, when he'd flown in for Evan's fundraiser a few weeks after her trip to Rome. He'd come back to see *her*. Evan hadn't needed him there. Then he'd had to pull back from her again, citing the museum and their professional relationship. He'd felt like crap, but today he was going to set the record straight for good.

"I'll try not to cry myself to sleep if you don't come home," Trev said. "Oh, go have fun. You deserve it."

Yes, he sure as hell did.

His Ferrari FF, chosen for its style and ability to handle snow, purred to life. Just because he didn't live in Rome anymore didn't mean he had to drive an SUV.

Caroline was staying with her mother this weekend since she was still working in Denver at the gallery. Pretty soon, she'd be able to resign and move to Dare Valley to work full-time on the museum. Many people would shrink from the prospect of starting a (hopefully) long-term relationship with someone they'd also be working with, but he couldn't wait. They shared the same dream, and there was no better foundation for a future together.

He headed toward downtown, delighting in the sight of Main Street's colorful shops like Don't Soy With Me, where he could get a pretty decent espresso, thank God. When he arrived at April Hale's house, he didn't go to the door like usual. No, he was too eager to get going, and while he loved Caroline's mother, they'd end up talking for twenty minutes. Living in a small town meant talking to people whenever he met them, either out at the bakery or the store. He liked that normally. Not today.

Caroline ran out of the house before he could text her, a treat for the eyes in a red winter jacket, white ear warmers, and bright blue winter pants.

"Hi there!" she said when she opened the door and jumped in. "Oh, I'm so excited. I can't wait to see where we're going."

All he'd told her was to dress for the outdoors. "Hey. Come here." He made himself kiss her Italian-style, but he let his mouth linger on her cheek.

So did she.

The urge to dip his lips down to her mouth was so strong, but he made himself wink at her and pull away. Her shoulders seemed to sag, and there was the familiar confusion in her eyes that gutted him.

"Let's get going," he said, revving the engine.

He drove them to Black Lake, and she bounced in her seat as they parked. "This is my favorite place in Dare Valley."

"I know," he said, unable to fight a smirk. "I asked your sister. Moira. Not Natalie."

"How sweet!" she said. "Oh, I'm so happy, J.T. While I loved dashing off to see you in Rome and Napa, I have to admit, it's much nicer now that you're only two hours away."

He couldn't agree more. "And pretty soon you'll be moving here once we make the announcement about the museum."

"Now that your donation to Evan's new company is out, it shouldn't be too much longer," she said. "Boy, you're going to be racking up goodwill points with all this generosity."

His conscience reared up, knowing his decisions hadn't just come from a place of pure altruism. "I don't know about that. Come on. Let's get our picnic stuff. I've never had a snow picnic before, but your cousin Jill tells me they're awesome."

"Jill is game for anything," she said. Her cousin was known for antics as wild as her curly red hair. "Brian told me the last time they went for a hike, she danced disco to make a moose go away."

He laughed uneasily. "God, I hope we don't run into any moose today." While Trev's mention of bears was unfounded, moose were dangerous. Mac Maven, the owner of The Grand Mountain Hotel, had horrified him with a story about what a moose had done to his sports car when he and his now-wife were inside.

"Don't worry," Caroline said as they exited. "I'll protect you."

He might bring some pepper spray along next time just in case. After grabbing the basket and a waterproof blanket, they walked on a path plowed by the park service. The sun was blinding, and J.T. was glad for his shades.

"Can you ice skate on the lake?" he asked. After all, it wasn't a big lake and it looked completely frozen.

"Never ever ice skate unless there's a sign with conditions posted," Caroline said seriously as they spread the blanket out by the water and sat down. "Sorry, that sounded like a PSA. But you're new to town, and I'd hate for someone to punk you. Like my brother, for example. They don't call him Matty Ice only because he's a tough guy."

"Good to know." If things didn't go well with Caroline this afternoon, he could look forward to a hypothermic outing with her brother.

"I mean, you probably wouldn't die, but it would be cold. Really, really cold."

He laughed. He loved her sense of humor.

"Oh, you brought salads. How fabulous! Darn it, J.T., I told you to stop buying us the Armand de Brignac. Especially now that you've given away most of your money."

He almost rolled his eyes. "Caroline, you know I still have millions from the trust my parents created when I was born. It's not like I'm hurting. Besides, I wanted this to be special." He needed her to know he could still stand on his own two feet financially and treat her right.

"It's special because we're together," she said, "even though you've been acting a little weird lately. I imagine giving away that kind of money must be...an adjustment."

"Caroline, there's a reason I've been acting weird. I wanted to tell you before, but I thought it would be better to wait until—"

His "Gold Digger" ringtone sounded in his coat pocket and stopped him short. Shock rolled through him. No, it couldn't be. Not Cynthia. It was like she had satellites watching him.

Pure terror followed. Why would his now ex-wife be calling him?

Don't you dare pick up that phone, he could almost hear Trev hiss in his head. But he had to find out why she was calling. If he didn't, he'd think of nothing else until he found out.

"That's an interesting ringtone," Caroline observed.

"Ah...Trev added it. He said to bring my phone with me...for the bears, and I...ah...forgot to put it on silent. Excuse me for just a moment."

He trudged through the snow, bypassing the path, hoping to get out of hearing range. "Cynthia, you shouldn't be calling me. We're divorced, remember?"

"I hoped you were going to pick up, J.T.," Cynthia said in her perfectly pitched boarding school voice. "You didn't think it was over simply because a judge stamped a piece of paper, did you? Oh, darling, you used to be so intelligent."

God, at one time he'd thought she was as beautiful and charming as Grace Kelly. Her polished manners and style had pleased and impressed him. What a fool he'd been.

He wanted to grind his teeth. "What do you want, Cynthia?"

Her husky chuckle raised the hairs on the back of his neck. "What I've always wanted since you left me and the life I'd planned for us, darling. To make you *suffer*. I told you no one ever walks away from me. I do the walking if and when I choose. You humiliated me, J.T., and you're going to keep paying for it."

Keep calm. It's spoiled grapes now. "I paid for three years, and it's finally finished. We both get to move on with our lives."

He glanced over to where Caroline was sitting, her back to him, as if she were giving him privacy. He would have found it sweet if he hadn't been sweating bullets.

"No, you don't. You finally showed me your new playbook. How nice of you. Then again, you always were a nice boy."

Frustration raced through him, and he kicked at the snow. "This has to stop, Cynthia. I gave you more than you deserved, and I told you that was the end of it. The judge agreed."

"Oh, J.T. Of course that wasn't the end. I've heard rumblings about a Merriam art museum at various social engagements—you know art experts can't keep their mouths shut even when you pay well."

And he had paid well. If he found out who'd talked...

"I've wondered where it would be for some weeks, and now I know. That press release about Evan Michaels' new company put the pin in the map. Of course you would want it to be at the university your great grandfather founded. You adore the man. It didn't dawn on me before because it's in some podunk town in Colorado. And not even somewhere with class like Aspen or Vail, darling, but Dare something."

He told himself there was nothing she could do. This was harassment at best. She was acting out after receiving the final decree. Unfortunately, knowing that didn't stop him from wanting to be sick. "Let it go, Cynthia, will you?"

"Do I hear a 'please' coming? Darling, you know me better. Once I set my sights on something, I go after it with everything I have at my disposal. When I saw you across the drawing room in that Lake Como villa, I decided I had to have you."

Talking to her again, something he hadn't done much of during the divorce proceedings, brought it all back. He'd fallen into her clutches just like everything else she'd decided to have. He'd been so charmed by the elegant, classy blond woman in the cream silk one-shoulder dress, the rich tones of her voice wrapping around him like the diamonds on her wrist. Cynthia Newhouse was interested in art. She was a noted philanthropist and socialite, praised for her charity fundraising. He'd thought they could do incredible things together in the world and have a rich personal life.

It was all a lie. The shiny image was only skin deep. Underneath the veneer was a ruthlessness and cruelty he hadn't seen.

Two years into their marriage, he couldn't take it anymore. He'd asked for a divorce, and she'd sworn to make him pay over and over again.

Moron that he was, he'd married her at her parents' Hamptons estate in New York, a state with some of the most prohibitive divorce laws on the planet, giving her a huge leg up. Since they were both as rich as Croesus, he hadn't suggested a pre-nup, another mistake. Her money wasn't the only reason he'd held back. He'd been a romantic then, thinking that two people who loved each other enough to pledge to spend a lifetime together would never knowingly hurt or take from one another.

Cynthia and her lawyers had given him a cold, hard lesson in divorce. It wasn't like they'd been married long, but family law didn't seem to care about that. He'd paid for everything during the marriage, trying to be the "man," and in so doing, he'd opened himself to her lawyers' argument that she should be allowed to maintain the lifestyle she'd enjoyed while married to him.

"I've divested myself of all my money except the trust, which was created way before you and I got together," he said, clenching his fist. "Talk to my lawyers if you want confirmation. They'll tell you what I'd like to in *nicer* terms."

"Oh, J.T. is displeased," she said, speaking to him like he was a child. "How tragic. Darling, this was never about the money, and you know it."

"You could have fooled me."

"You still don't understand? I went after your holdings because you value them, because the great and mighty Emmits Merriam entrusted them to you. Now you've given me something even more valuable. No one loves art quite like you do, and those paintings in your family collection are your pride and joy. Oh, darling, you're making this too easy. I'll be in touch."

The line went dead, and he stared at the phone. Surely he'd finally checkmated her. They'd finally settled the terms of their divorce, for Christ's sake.

What could she do to hurt him now? His so-called donation to Evan's new company, Infinity Energy, should be untouchable, and Emmits Merriam University was a tax-exempt private university. He'd insisted admission to the museum would be free in his proposal to the trustees. If he hadn't gone that route, Cynthia might have tried suggesting J.T. had gotten the idea for the museum during their marriage and, as such, was entitled to some of the money it generated. God, it was messed up that someone could claim ownership of another person's dream.

Trev was going to have a fit when J.T. told him. Then again, wasn't Trev here in Dare Valley because he'd expected something like this might happen? Hell, all of J.T.'s siblings had been against his marriage. If only he'd listened to them.

"Dammit!" he whispered, kicking more snow.

He'd need to alert Evan Michaels and Chase Parker about the call. While he didn't think Cynthia could do anything about the money he'd donated, it wouldn't hurt to be on guard.

But there was something he needed to do first. He headed toward Caroline, unable to stop the litany in his ears.

He'd be damned if he'd let it start all over again.

CHAPTER 3

CAROLINE STOOD UP AS SHE WATCHED J.T. TROMP through the snow back to her. He was clearly upset, and she was having a hard time keeping herself from dwelling over who'd called him. She'd never heard that ringtone before. Could it be an enterprising ex-girlfriend? It seemed like the kind of thing Trev would find funny.

"All right, let's hear it," she said when he reached her. "Something is obviously wrong."

He took her hands. "You know how much you mean to me, right?"

The girlfriend line of reasoning was looking more plausible. "Yes, J.T., but frankly, I'm a little worried right now."

He helped her sit back down and cuddled close. "Me too, if I'm being completely honest. Remember how I told you that I...needed to put the brakes on our relationship until some secrets were out in the open?"

"Like the big announcement in the press release yesterday? It hurt me that you didn't think you could trust me with that. I would never have told anyone."

"That wasn't completely the reason." He paused, as if searching for the right words.

This was sounding worse and worse. "Who were you talking to, J.T.?"

"My ex-wife."

"Your ex-wife!" Caroline shouted back. "You were married? Wait! How did you not tell me something this important?"

She couldn't have heard him right.

"I wanted to wait until the final decree came through to tell you everything, and it did a couple days ago, thank God."

"Then why are you talking to your ex now? Are you thinking about a reconciliation? Oh, God. This can't be happening." She'd fallen for him in the freaking gallery. Gone to Rome. Daydreamed after he'd taken her walking through the vineyards in Napa. Imagined their families getting together for the holidays. He'd swept her off her feet, and now she realized it had left her with a long way to fall.

He shook her hands as if to grab her attention. "It's not what you're thinking. If she fell off the face of the earth, I'd pop open the most expensive champagne I own—just like I did with Trev when the judge finally granted me a divorce."

She sagged against him. "Sorry, my mind went to a dark place. I expect you have a good reason for keeping this to yourself. You've always struck me as an honest man."

He shook his head. "Thank you for that. I try to be— despite how this situation seems. Let me start at the beginning. It's a long and depressing tale, and I really wanted it to be behind me before I started something with you. Caroline, the relationship ended three years ago, but I didn't feel it was right..."

"To begin something with me," she finished. "Okay, I see your point."

"Trev said I spared you a lot of worry," J.T. said,

taking his sunglasses off. "It's hard to convey how hard the last three years have been. I didn't want it to touch you, especially when we'd only just—"

"Reconnected," she whispered, studying his beautiful green eyes. "And fallen for each other."

"I was so into you," he said, gripping her hand. "I didn't want to taint what we might have."

The sincerity with which he said it made her heart swell and took some weight off her shoulders. "Okay, let's get through the particulars. How long were you married? What's her name?" She really didn't want to hear it, but this was part of his personal history, and that made it important to her. Plus, it seemed to be affecting the situation between them, and knowing more might help her better understand.

"Thank you," he said, releasing a deep breath. "We were only married for two years. Her name is Cynthia Newhouse, and she...wasn't the woman I thought she was. Everyone thinks she's this beautiful, generous philanthropist, but she's..."

"A gold digger?"

"Actually, her family is extremely wealthy, but she's pressed for things...like a gold digger might. Trev programmed the ringtone one night when we were drunk. It was supposed to be a joke."

Some joke. God, it sounded like a celebrity breakup.

"Some days I thought I'd never be free of her. I resigned from my old job and sold my company shares when she pressed for them. They could have given her a controlling interest. I thought that would stop her..."

"But you were only married two years. How could she—"

"Take me to the cleaners like that?" he asked. "We were married in New York and didn't have a pre-nup. A mistake on my part, but honestly, my lawyer said even if we'd had one, she would have tried to break it.

Apparently it's easier to do than you'd think, especially in New York. There are lots of wily divorce lawyers who like to challenge everything that's decent and good about the law. And she's represented by one of Manhattan's best firms."

Her head was swimming. "I still don't fully understand."

He ran a hand through his wheat-colored hair. "I know... I didn't at first either. I had no framework for the way people could manipulate family law to suck a person dry. I tried over and over again to give her a fair settlement, but it was never enough. I finally gave the bulk of my money away. It was the only play I could see. Thankfully, the judge finally granted our divorce."

Goodness, she couldn't imagine anyone being that greedy. Or bitter. "Then why is she calling now?"

He shrugged. "She said she's not done making me pay, and...she thinks I've given her an opening—"

"With Evan's new company?"

"She mentioned the museum."

She reared back. "The museum? But how could she? You're donating all of the paintings to the university."

And as his art consultant, Caroline had gone over the entire collection with him. The provenance was solid, she knew, as was his vision for sharing the Merriam art collection with the world.

"I don't know," he said. "I want to think she's gone bat-shit crazy in response to the final decree."

She could hear the quaver in his voice. "And yet she tied you up for three years."

He nodded. "When you put Cynthia and her lawyers together, even the titans would tremble. But don't worry. Our lawyers are the best too, and they've helped me look at every loophole. I've done what I can to protect myself and those assets from her."

But would it be enough? Suddenly she was as worried

about their dream as he appeared to be. "Oh, J.T."

"See! This is why I didn't tell you before. I didn't want to see you tense up like this. Today was supposed to be a celebration for you and me, moving forward."

Yeah, the champagne didn't seem appropriate anymore. "Did she say what she plans to do?"

"Other than skewer me alive and turn me on her great fire pit? No, nothing specific. But I'll know soon. She moves fast."

That certainly didn't make her feel any better. "Do we need to talk to the university?"

"The new university president might not be the one who originally green-lit the idea, but he's completely on board about the museum. The trustees approved it."

And yet, the light that had always shone in his eyes when he talked about the museum just wasn't there. His vision for the art gallery had so charmed her that she hadn't thought twice about agreeing to leave her job in Denver to help set up the museum. While her logical mind had suggested it might be a bad decision to work for the man who had her heart, the strength of their connection and the quality of his art collection had overridden it. Oh, to be a caretaker for those remarkable works of art, working side by side with this man...

The romance and beauty of the idea had swayed her, but now she had to wonder if she'd been foolish. What if she ended up marooned in Dare Valley without a job? While being back here with her family was tantalizing, the town didn't yet have a gallery capable of competing with any in Denver.

"J.T., I need you to tell me the truth." She took off her sunglasses so she could look him in the eye. "Do you think she'll try and stop the museum somehow? Should I hold off on quitting my job?"

He heaved a weary sigh. "As much as I wish it were otherwise, let's give it a little more time. I should know more soon. Then we can decide on the best course."

"I think that's smart," she said, her stomach turning sour.

She sure as heck didn't want to burn any bridges, and her boss was not going to be happy when she handed in her notice. She feared Kendra might not act professionally, so she'd been practicing her resignation speech in the mirror, trying to decide on the best way to frame her decision. The art scene was like a small town—everybody knew everybody, and gossip was rampant. If she made it known that Kendra's mentoring had prepared her for an opportunity of a lifetime, curating the Merriam art collection, it would look like a win for both of them. Even Kendra would have to acknowledge that. But if she left her job and the museum didn't come to fruition, well, that same gossip mill could turn against her easily enough. At least this happened before she'd quit.

"I hate this," J.T. said. "That spark of light in your face when we talk about the museum is gone, and it's my fault. Dammit! I didn't want this to touch you."

She'd noticed the same thing about him, of course, but she didn't want to mention it. "Did she live in Rome with you?" she asked, wondering how much she could ask about this woman.

"No, she never liked having a permanent residence. She was one of those wealthy socialites who goes from house to house, party to party."

Caroline had sold art to such people, but it wasn't her world. She couldn't imagine being so rootless. She loved traveling, sure, but there was no better feeling than coming home and sleeping in her own bed. And she loved spending time with her family.

"But you worked in Rome," she said. "How—"

"I'd fly out to join her for long weekends if I could get away or conduct business wherever she was calling home. Sometimes she came to Rome, but not often. That arrangement didn't work for me, which is one of the reasons it didn't last long."

"Did she cheat on you?" His posture straightened, as if her question had physically jolted him, and she put her hand over her mouth. "I'm sorry. That was a terribly nosy question."

His mouth tipped up on the right, and his dimple appeared. "But a fair one, I suppose. No, not to my knowledge."

Silence grew between them, a little uncomfortable now that she'd brought up his former sex life.

"I'm glad you put the brakes on due to something this serious," she felt compelled to add.

"I told you in Rome I wanted you," he said, his voice pitched low. "Yes, we'd only just met as adults, and yes, we'll be working together, but that wasn't the reason I held back. I'm glad you know I'm finally free. I just wish…"

"She hadn't called and ruined our picnic?"

He closed his eyes, his face drawn. "I'll make it up to you somehow," he said. "Are we okay? I mean, despite the fact that I may have a shark coming after me."

"I know what this means for my job." She paused, looking him in the eye. "What does it mean for us?"

He took his time answering. "Let's see how this week goes."

A week? She didn't like it, but she could do a week. "I'm here for you, J.T. Whatever comes."

"Thank you," he said, opening his eyes and gazing at her. "I wanted to protect you from this. Her."

His tone held the kind of defeat she'd only heard in movies about the Alamo. "I want to punch her…in the face or something for hurting you. For hurting what you love."

What I love.

He lifted a hand and caressed her face. "Finding you has given me a future to look forward to. So has the museum." His eyes got a far-off look. "The idea came to me while I was sitting in front of my favorite painting in my parents' house in Napa, nursing a few whiskeys. I'm not sure what I would have done otherwise."

She knew the painting he was referring to. He'd first shown it to her when he'd brought her to Napa. Now it hung in his den here in Dare Valley. The sight of it had made Uncle Arthur teary-eyed. "The one of Emmits Merriam at his first oil well."

It showed him as a young man dressed in work clothes with oil on his rough brown boots. His hands stretched out to the big blue Oklahoma sky and his eyes held the rapture of someone who'd just struck it rich. Literally. That oil had changed Emmits' life, and he'd done a lot of good in the world with his money. Fortunately, so had the generations after him, and J.T. was one of them. Or had been.

"Spending time with that painting reminded me of how much I loved art. Musing over my Grandpa Emmits' life, I remembered one of his sayings that always stuck with me. *You can do anything you want. You just have to decide to do it and give it your all.* That's when I realized I could make something new with art, and I knew it had to be a museum, so everyone could see the art our family has collected over the years. What better place to bring it than here, to the university he started."

But he wouldn't be bringing all of it because his aunt had a portion of the collection in her hands. He'd briefed her on the family feud between his father and his aunt. His dad hadn't liked the guy she'd married, and they'd had a row because her husband, a trust fund dick, had tried to insert himself into Merriam Oil & Gas. Reinhold Allerton hadn't really wanted a job—his interest in the company was limited to a title and a paycheck. J.T.'s grandma had told Reinhold to back off and leave the family company to J.T.'s father. Clara hadn't liked that much, and so it had begun.

Plucking up all the paintings from the family house in the Hamptons had been her revenge. She and J.T.'s dad hadn't seen each other since their mother's funeral.

Even so, Caroline figured it would be worth asking the woman again—this was years ago and it was for a good cause—but J.T. hadn't come around. Secretly, she hoped his Aunt Clara would hear about the new museum and want to contribute her portion of the Merriam collection, either out of conscience or the fame it would bring her. Caroline didn't care which.

"It's no wonder Emmits and Uncle Arthur were such good friends," she said. "I wish I'd known him."

Some of the light returned to his eyes. "Me too, but in a way I feel like I do, never more so than when I look at his painting or walk through this town. God, I love this place." He stared at her with the intense focus that came so naturally to him. "And even though I've kept something so important from you, I hope you can forgive me."

She felt the corner of her mouth tip up. "Just this once."

"Funny. I don't suppose you'd still like to pop this champagne and munch on some of your favorite greens before we head over to your sister's house."

She could tell he needed some reassurance too, so she forced a smile. "Of course."

Even to her ears, her voice was flat. The pop of the champagne cork seemed to echo her sentiments, and for once neither of them toasted. They mostly ate in silence, and it galled her to realize their outing had fallen short of both their expectations.

The secret that had held him back might be out, but it hadn't brought them any closer together.

CHAPTER 4

ARTHUR HALE HATED WAKING UP WORRIED, BUT HE feared the Merriam legacy in Dare Valley was in jeopardy. Trevor had pulled him aside at yesterday's shindig to give him the news. He'd been wondering about J.T.'s prune-like face and the worried looks he kept darting at Caroline.

Cripes, that woman! Cynthia Newhouse didn't know what she was up against this time. A fight was brewing, and he needed to get ready for it, both for J.T. and for the memory of his long-lost friend and mentor, Emmits Merriam. Emmits had fought for what he believed in until his last breath, and Arthur intended to do the same.

Still, there was no denying it was getting harder to crawl out of bed these days. He was turning eighty this May, and some mornings he felt every day of it. He rubbed his right hip, which hurt like a bitch, and watched the sun rise through the large windows in his bedroom. The pink and orange tones seemed to spread flame across the sky. The sunrise always inflated his spirits. There was another day to do what needed doing, and he was grateful for the chance. After his beloved wife, Harriet, had died, he'd ripped off the curtains so he could take in this daily spectacle of creation. It wasn't like he was worried someone was going to see him parading around naked. His house was remote, and the only unexpected visitors he had were animals. And really, was a wild turkey or an elk going to pause and stare at his old, scrawny body? Not in a million years.

He eyed the clock. Waking up at six fifteen wasn't bad after going to sleep late last night. His extended family had partied until after ten, when Caroline had finally announced that she needed to drive back to Denver so she'd be ready for work in the morning. God bless J.T. He'd offered to drive her back, but no, his niece had turned him down. That worried Arthur some, but who could blame the poor girl for needing space after J.T.'s ex-wife had interrupted what should have been a romantic picnic? Arthur hadn't liked Caroline not knowing about the infernal divorce proceedings, but he'd understood and respected J.T.'s desire to keep it a secret until it was over.

Regardless, those kids belonged together. Cynthia Newhouse might try to wreak more havoc, but Arthur didn't intend to let her ruin things for J.T. and Caroline. And that wasn't the only thing he had to sort out before he left this world.

Of course, at his age, he thought about death. Not in the weird coffin kind of way—like whether his dead body would be surrounded in white silk or some such nonsense. He could care less. No, he thought about what he was leaving behind and making sure the future was secure for those who came after him—exactly as Emmits had done before him.

Sure, Arthur's dream had come true when his granddaughter Meredith left New York for Dare Valley and re-joined his newspaper. Even better that she'd wed a famous journalist, Tanner McBride, and brought him on board too. He'd danced more than a few times with his cane when no one was looking. *The Western*

Independent was stronger from an editorial point of view than ever. Arthur didn't even write every Sunday op-ed anymore, granting that prize spot to Meredith and Tanner whenever they pitched him something worthy.

But financially, the paper was going through the same crunch every other paper from *The Washington Post* to *The New York Times* was experiencing. Technology had changed the landscape forever, but Arthur had resisted changing with the times. He didn't want to offer his paper for a free trial on some decked-out website or post part of an article, only to bribe earnest readers—forcing them to either become an online subscriber or forever wonder how the story ended. Meredith had put her foot down, insisting they had to have some sort of digital presence. Both of them had caved some.

The three-million-dollar loan he'd taken out to go digital wasn't paid off yet and the interest was killing him. Bah! Meredith was battling with him more and more about trying new online tricks while Tanner watched all creepy quiet from the corner. That man could give lessons in active listening and watching. Right now, Arthur was going to have to hold the line on rejecting more tech improvements. Paying his loan on time was important, especially since he'd put the newspaper's building up as collateral. Adding to it would only extend things, and Arthur didn't like the idea of leaving Meredith and Tanner with a load of debt should he up and die.

Plus there was the damn advertising... Courting new and old clients was more competitive than ever, and none of them liked that part of the business.

Arthur scratched the scruff on his face as he stared out the window. Shaving had gotten harder as he'd grown older. Hell, his secretary sometimes pointed out that he'd missed part of his face or under his chin. Like he could see that well anymore. Even his glasses weren't that good, and it pissed him off. He'd thought about growing a beard in his older years, but it didn't seem professional to him. In his generation, men were expected to be clean-shaven. Male facial hair was a bit baffling when you stopped to think about it. Why in the hell didn't it give out like the rest of the body? Why did hair stop growing on a bald man's head and sprout from his nose instead? Did God chuckle every morning at such male inconveniences?

Getting old was for the birds.

He gathered himself to roll over and winced as he heard four pops in his back. Some days, it sounded like someone was popping off gunfire back there. But at least he had his mind. His mind and the paper, digital inconveniences aside.

People kept asking why an almost eighty-year-old needed to work from eight in the morning until six at night. He usually barked his response. Because he fucking loved it, and yes, he'd said "fucking." Sometimes it was the only word to get the job done. He loved what he'd created with the paper. Loved the buzz of the newsroom. Loved shaping words with the intention of changing opinions or opening minds to a subject or issue. It was in his veins, like the black ink he joked about. How did a man walk away from what pumped in his heart?

He was trying to secure his own legacy as best he could—and now he was going to have to protect the Merriam legacy too. J.T. needed a pep talk but good. Arthur sat up and reached for his cane, feeling the weight of re-spon-si-bil-ity. Some called it a dirty word, but not him. He had the strength to do what was needed, and he tapped his trusty cane on the floor for good measure. He was going to call that boy right now and leave a message. Yesterday's party hadn't been the place for them to talk. Plus, he'd wanted to stew over matters, much like he knew Trevor would be doing. That boy was downright scary sometimes, but he was a good ally in this fight against the woman he called Sin City. Heck! Now that was some nickname. The boy was right. Never get involved with a woman whose first name had "sin" in it, even phonetically. Big mistake.

He pushed off the bed to stand up, and his back popped a few more times in response. "Bah! You're not stopping me from getting up, dammit," he told his body.

Reaching for the phone, he realized he'd forgotten to put on his glasses so he cursed again. Then he dialed J.T.'s number.

"Uncle Arthur! Is everything okay?" the young buck immediately said when he picked up after two rings.

"Why are you up this early?" Arthur barked.

"Why are you?" J.T. fired back.

He laughed despite the ache in his back. "Because old men like me wake up at the butt crack of dawn, especially when they're worried. Since you're up, why don't you come over for coffee before I go into the office?"

There was a pause. "Something on your mind?"

So Trevor hadn't mentioned spilling the beans. Good. "Since I haven't lost it, you bet your ass there is. Be over here in fifteen minutes. I don't care if you aren't your normal pretty self."

He hung up and toddled over to the bathroom. He'd make himself as presentable as he could in the time he'd allotted. It wasn't like he'd win a beauty contest or anything.

Fifteen minutes later on the nose, he was ambling down the stairs when he heard the purr of a Ferrari engine in the driveway. Now that was an unmistakable sound. If Arthur had ever had that kind of spare money, he would have gotten himself a fast car. But all of his extra money went into the paper, and he wasn't sorry for it.

When he heard a loud knock, he opened the door.

J.T. was dressed in one of his fancy suits, minus the tie. Well, good for him. Arthur had barely managed to dress in pants and a sweater.

"You bang like that on everyone's door or only on an old man's? My hearing is fine."

"You're punchy this morning," J.T. said, holding up a big brown bag. "I brought my small Italian espresso machine and two cinnamon rolls from Margie's bakery. She says hello, by the way."

"You made a run to Hot Cross Buns Bakery? You must have broken speed records."

J.T. followed him into the kitchen. "I was already shaved and dressed when you called, so I simply grabbed my keys and headed out. Honestly, I was happy to leave. Trev was snoring like a mother—uh, sorry."

"For cursing? Please. I've been known to drop the f-bomb on plenty occasions." He studied the young man as he unpacked the sleek Italian coffee maker. "I remember when we used to boil coffee grounds in a pan on the stove."

"Don't make me cry," J.T. said. "Coffee is an art."

As he watched the man work, Arthur had to agree. "Emmits loved him a cup of strong black coffee with—"

"A buttload of sugar if he had it," J.T. finished. "I know all the stories."

Arthur harrumphed. "I doubt that. So were you up early because you slept like shit? Did Sin City—man, I like that name—mess up your night? She sure seemed to mess up Caroline's."

"I'm going to kill Trevor for saying anything," he said slowly.

"Of course he told me! I'm your uncle in spirit if not blood. Emmits would want me to look after you, and if that woman is coming back, you're going to need help."

J.T. pulled out two espresso cups from the bag he'd brought. Boy was prepared.

"Thank you for that. I'm still a little in shock, honestly. I thought it was over."

"We'll make it over," Arthur stated, hoping to offset that kicked-puppy look on the boy's face.

"When you called, I thought you were mad at me for messing up things with Caroline," J.T. said, filling the cups with the dark brew.

Arthur took the small cup from J.T. "Might as well be a guest at the Mad Hatter's party with this cup. No, I'm not mad. I'm sure it was a shock to both of you. In the end, there's only one question that matters. Are you going to keep dicking around or are you ready to move ahead?"

J.T. snorted. "Everyone who's married in the Hale extended family has warned me about your relationship advice."

He was proud of his track record. "What's there to warn about? Aren't they all happy as clams? Heck, now they're popping out babies. Natalie's up, and I have a hundred-dollar bet with Rhett that Jane is going to be up next." That poker player would bet on anything, Arthur had found out to his delight.

"You're betting on who's going to get pregnant next? That's kind of weird and awesome at the same time." J.T. raised his cup in salute and then slowly sipped his coffee. That first taste was followed by a gusty sigh of pleasure.

Arthur couldn't help but say, "Do you need a moment alone with your coffee or can we continue this conversation?"

That grin was back. "Man, you're fun. I always remembered that from being here for summers. Over the phone, you were always...starchy. But in person... Uncle Arthur, you defy convention in the best way possible. I can see why you and Emmits got along so well. Everyone says he could be starchy too."

Yes, he had been, Arthur thought warmly. If Emmits were here, he'd have called J.T. at six in the morning as well to shake him up some. A downright happy thought if you asked him. "You're evading my question."

"Was it a question?" J.T. asked, pulling out the cinnamon rolls. "Got any plates?"

"I don't live in a barn. Top shelf to the right." Of course, he should move those to a lower shelf. His bony arms couldn't lift like they used to, but he was too proud to admit it. Unloading the dishwasher took forever these days. He'd thought of shifting to paper plates, but it would raise questions.

When J.T. set the roll in front of him on the kitchen counter, he gave in and led the way over to the kitchen table. "Might as well sit down like civilized people."

"Because we don't live in a barn," J.T. said, picking up Arthur's coffee before he could say anything.

"Don't repeat me, kid," Arthur told him. "Makes me think you're the one with the memory issue."

J.T. laughed. "You want to have breakfast with me every morning?"

That was good news. "You'd do better to stay in Denver with Caroline. Don't turn down a beautiful woman for an old man. Ever. That's free advice."

He could see the boy's shoulders shaking. "If you're going to start charging me, I'll happily open my wallet. I've probably got a thousand in cash on me. That should last me a couple hours."

"You young people," Arthur barked, not sure how to respond. J.T. *would* pay him, and that would be embarrassing. He didn't take money from anyone. Never had. Never would.

"It strikes me, Uncle Arthur, that you talk about helping everyone around here, but you never mention how anyone can help you. Well, except when you ask

Jill to shut it or stop dancing like a stripper."

"That Latin dance class will be the downfall of us all." Arthur shuddered. "Wait, the Calendar Girls' calendar the ladies shot in their birthday suits might be worse." Even though the proceeds had gone to a good cause, he hadn't needed to see people he'd known most of his life, including his crazy granddaughter, Jill, posing with strategically positioned bananas and melons. He hadn't been able to eat fruit for a month.

"I still need to get a copy," J.T. said, munching on his breakfast.

Arthur had one upstairs, but he didn't plan on mentioning it. "Of course, no one asked me to pose in it. Now, stop talking and let me eat my roll."

Maybe he could evade J.T.'s question much like the boy was evading his. The first bite of the cinnamon roll was sheer heaven like always.

"Do you need a moment alone, Uncle Arthur?" J.T. quipped.

"You're cheeky, but I like you," he said before he took another bite. "Of course, your coffee sucks."

"Sucks! These are prime Italian espresso beans, my friend. When was the last time you were in Rome?"

Arthur thought about it a moment. "1982. It was a dark time in politics."

More laughter from wonder boy. Notes of Emmits' laugh could be heard in J.T.'s, and it was bringing back more good memories. He'd never stopped missing his friend after he'd passed. Heck, he missed him almost as much as he did Harriet.

"You probably don't like espresso," J.T. said. "Some say it's an acquired taste. Do you want me to make you regular coffee?"

"I have instant in the drawer by the sink." Arthur laughed when the boy's eyes bugged out in horror. "No, it's fine. I'll have some at the office."

"I admire you for continuing to work, Uncle Arthur," J.T. said slowly.

"I can hear the 'but' coming a mile away," he growled. This was the last thing he felt like discussing. "Did someone ask you to talk me into stepping down?"

"No!" he said, unconvincing.

Arthur gave him a look designed to shrink a man's balls. This wasn't supposed to be about him. *He'd* called the boy over.

"Okay, some people have expressed a thought about you cutting back some. I thought you might hear me out as the new guy in town."

"Really? You read minds now? Tell me what I'm thinking."

"You might kill me and leave my body out back for the wolves."

"Wolves are endangered," Arthur said. "I would fear the coyotes more. They roam the hills looking for prime white flesh like yours."

Another chuckle. Good. He'd at least gotten the boy's mind off that Sin City woman.

"Seriously, if everyone's telling you to cut back, you might want to consider it. I remember the kind of stress I was under when I was running the Africa and Middle East Division of Merriam Oil & Gas. And I'm only thirty-five. I can't imagine what it's like for you. Now, before you growl again, hear me out. Please."

Arthur took an aggressive bite of his cinnamon roll. Emmits had never eased back or retired, and he certainly wasn't going to do so either.

"When we talked from time to time during my divorce, you never tried to sugarcoat things or pat me on the head. Not that Trev did, but you were outside the situation and gave me some sound advice. That meant a lot to me."

The boy coughed, and Arthur found himself temporarily unable to swallow his bite of cinnamon roll, the burst of emotion as sticky as the sweet bread.

"You told me to find something else that I loved and make a viable pursuit out of it. Continue with my life."

Arthur finally managed to swallow. "I told you to make a list."

"Art was at the top," J.T. said. "I'd like to think Grandpa Emmits helped me figure out the rest as I sat in front of his painting night after night."

Damn if that didn't make Arthur's eyes water. "Maybe I should be charging you for advice for real."

This time J.T. gave a slow smile. "Your words are worth their weight in gold, and we all know it. Everyone loves you like crazy. They just want to make sure you let us...well, give back to you, is all. You can't keep being the giver all the time, Uncle Arthur. You're turning eighty."

"Back in my day, that's just what the elder generation did. It's what Emmits did for me. If he hadn't helped me start the paper, it wouldn't have gotten off the ground."

"He knew a good idea when he saw it. My dad said he believed in what you were doing. Trying to be the voice of the west at a time when the only real national news was coming out of the East Coast."

"Emmits was from Oklahoma, and even if it's technically not in the west, it's in the middle of this fine country of ours. He understood how little people in powerful positions in Washington and New York knew or cared about what was going on in places like Tulsa or Dare Valley."

"And you changed that," J.T. said, setting his espresso down. "Maybe now it's time to give yourself more time to do the other things you love."

"Bah! Like what? I don't have any real hobbies."

"Maybe *you* should make a list."

Arthur's look made the boy shift in his chair. "Hell, I only play bingo on Wednesday nights to be up on my local gossip. Couldn't stand people calling me on the phone, jabbering about this and that. I have eaten, drunk, and slept the newspaper business since my first job, and that's over sixty years now. Old dogs like me don't learn new tricks. We just get slower. That's why I have Meredith and Tanner. But don't tell them that. And this cane, of course."

"What about a girlfriend?" J.T. asked. "Have you ever thought about getting married again?"

"At my age? Please. I had a girlfriend for a while, but it wasn't for the long-term." He'd gone out with Joanie enough to call her his girlfriend for a while, but they'd kept their lives and families separate. He'd been happy to have a companion from time to time for dinner or other comforts, but they hadn't seen each other lately. Ultimately, he knew she wasn't over her husband.

"Been there done that, huh?" J.T. asked.

"*You* ever think about marrying again?" he deflected.

The boy tensed up. "After what I went through? Honestly, I want to find a life partner, but I'm not sure about marriage. There are too many legal issues around matters of the heart."

Arthur could understand his position. It still saddened him, both for Caroline and J.T. "Perhaps someone will change your mind."

J.T. waggled his brows. "And perhaps someone will change yours."

Not likely. Only one other woman had touched his heart before Harriet, and she'd been a brat. Speaking of which. "You'll forgive me for changing the subject, but you should call your Aunt Clara and ask her about donating the rest of Emmits' paintings to the museum."

J.T. shrugged. "It's like I told Caroline. Aunt Clara and the family haven't spoken since she took those paintings from Grandma's house in the Hamptons after she died."

Arthur didn't know the specifics, but he knew it had

been some kind of a petty revenge on Clara's part. Maybe her husband had put her up to it. He hadn't seen her since 1962 when she'd married a rich guy with a stick up his butt. Heck, who knew what was in Clara's mind? She was as changeable as the sunrise he'd watched this morning.

"I still think you should try," he pressed. "Emmits would want the whole collection back here at the university he founded."

"Perhaps I'll call her when you think about retiring," J.T. added with a wink.

"When pigs fly, like Trev says."

"Okay, I did my part. Seriously though. If you need anything, I'm here for you."

"What! Are people worried I'm about to kick the bucket?"

J.T. finished off his espresso. "You've been talking about dying a lot, I hear. Jill and a few others are worried."

He waved his hand in the air. "That's age talking. Only a stupid man doesn't think about what he's going to leave behind or what it's going to be like...after. These are questions man has been asking since the dawn of time. Speaking of which, you've sidestepped me pretty good, but that ends now. I know your relationship with Caroline is your own, but I'm going to say it again. Don't let Sin City's potential return stop you from having a normal, happy relationship." He'd let the marriage thing go for now.

The joy of their discussion faded from J.T.'s face. "After I got home and Trev tried to give me a pep talk, I went to bed early. But I couldn't sleep...I just can't figure out what I did to deserve this kind of revenge. Hearing her talk yesterday, she's still out to hurt everything I love. It's like the divorce hasn't changed a thing for her!"

Arthur heard the undercurrent of self-pity and wasn't going to pat him on the back and tell him not to feel it—or not to worry. "That's not the thing to focus on. You have a lot of good things happening. Being back here. The museum. Caroline."

A slow smile spread across his mouth. "I didn't expect Caroline, truthfully. I don't want her hurt."

"From what I can see, you've fallen for her. Hard-like. And she you. That's a fact. Sometimes, you just have to hold on to each other. There will always be storms, J.T. It's how you meet them together that counts."

"Were you always this wise?" J.T. asked, picking up their empty plates and taking them over to the sink.

"The only people who can argue with me are dead, so I'm sticking with, 'of course.' I know you're waiting to see what move Sin City is going to make next, but a real man doesn't sit around waiting for a snake to strike. Surely you've come across plenty of snakes in the oil business."

"I have," J.T. said in a serious tone.

"Then you're an old hand at this," Arthur said, rising and grabbing his cane.

Suddenly he was tired, and it was good to lean on it in moments like this.

"Cynthia isn't like any snake you've come across, Uncle Arthur," J.T. said. "A divorce doesn't seem to have stopped her."

Arthur had to acknowledge his point. "You know what Emmits used to say in cases like this."

J.T. met his gaze. "What?"

"You just have to study the snake longer and closer then. *Everything* has a soft underbelly, J.T."

And Arthur was going to help the young man find it if it was the last thing he did.

CHAPTER 5

GOING BACK TO WORK AT LEGGETT GALLERY WAS DE-pressing, especially now that Caroline's dream job seemed to be just that: a dream.

Working with J.T. to create the Merriam Art Museum in her hometown was supposed to be her next great adventure. Moira had teased her about having senioritis when it came to her current job, and there was some truth to it. She came into work every day with an internal countdown in her head about leaving. Sure, there'd never been a fixed date, but she'd thought it would come and soon.

Now she wasn't so sure. Heck, she wasn't even sure of her relationship with J.T. His ex-wife still seemed to be looming large. They'd gone together to the family gathering at her sister's house, but he'd immediately peeled away to speak with Trevor, who'd turned downright ferocious. J.T. had offered to drive her back to Denver at the end of the night, but she'd declined, thinking some space might help them get over the shock of things. Besides, the last thing she'd wanted was another platonic hug goodnight or chaste kiss. The fact that he'd kissed her goodbye Italian-style, like usual, told her she'd been right to turn him down.

She decided to make herself a strong cup of coffee and focus. Four new paintings were arriving at the gallery today, and there was a lot to do. This was her job now, and maybe for a while; she was going to make the best of things.

Her stomach was rumbling hours later as she finished unpacking the last painting. The front door chimed, and she grabbed her keys to lock up the workroom per their security policy.

When she entered the gallery, she spied an elegant blonde in a white fur coat standing in front of a painting by one of Colorado's finest.

"Layla Martigue is incredible, isn't she?"

The woman turned and took off her designer sunglasses. Caroline didn't remember seeing her before, but the woman clearly had money and taste. The bag slung casually over her arm was a Hermès Kelly Rose Gold purse worth two million dollars.

"Welcome to Leggett. I'm Caroline Hale, the gallery's manager. Let me know if I can be of any help. Would you like some coffee?"

"I'd love some," the woman said. "But first, tell me more about this painting."

Her skin tingled like it did whenever she felt a big sale coming on. "Layla doesn't simply paint landscapes. She creates them. This painting is of a meander of the Colorado River called Horseshoe Bend located outside Page, Arizona. Her impressionistic style is meant to convey—"

"An actual metal horseshoe," the woman finished, opening her purse and pulling out a sunglasses case. "*Interesting.*"

Caroline didn't know what to make of the edge in her voice. "Please look around. I'll get you that cup of coffee."

The woman wasn't going to be an easy sell, but Caroline had dealt with difficult rich clients before. She'd watch the woman for a while and see what paintings drew her in. When she returned with the coffee, she couldn't help feeling like the blond woman was studying her as much as the paintings lining the walls. Again, not unusual. She'd had other clients try and size her up. Usually it meant they were the kind who negotiated hard on a price. She fought off a wave of irritation. When you had a two-million-dollar purse, why dicker over a few thousand?

"You seem young to be the manager of a gallery with this reputation," the woman commented.

Caroline gave her best fake smile. "What can I say? I've worked hard and do a wonderful job because I love what I do."

"So Kendra told me," she said, opening her fur coat finally like she'd grown warm.

"You know Kendra?" she asked. "Then you know how serious she is about this gallery and the art we show."

"Yes, which is to your credit," the woman said, finally sipping her coffee. "Oh, European beans, thank God. I don't care if it makes me a snob, but coffee from anywhere else isn't in the same class."

Caroline knew it wouldn't be wise to point out that the actual beans were always from somewhere other than Europe. They might roast beans, but they didn't grow them.

"What is your favorite painting right now?" the woman asked.

"That's a tough one since I select most of the paintings in our collection," she replied honestly. "Right now, I'd say it's the one by Marlo Hap. It's the—"

"Oil painting of the deconstructed male body captured as metal spikes," she finished for Caroline.

"Yes, you certainly know your art," she said. "How is it you've never visited us before? Are you new to Denver or only visiting?"

"Visiting," she said, extending her empty cup to Caroline. "Do you have anything in the back? I love seeing the paintings no one else has laid eyes on yet."

Of course she did. Many rich clients felt the same. "Let me lock the front first, and then I'll show you them one at a time."

This woman was obviously not a burglar, but Caroline made a point of upholding their security protocols. She could afford closing the gallery for a possible sale. It was a Monday, after all.

"If you're nervous, you can call Kendra," the woman said.

"No, of course not. I'm only following our policies. I'll be right back."

When she brought out the first one, the woman barely gave it a glance. "Next."

Okay, that was dismissive, Caroline thought. She brought out the rest, one by one, but the woman didn't like any of them.

"If you could buy any painting in here for your personal collection, which would it be?" she asked. "Because I don't think it's the Marlo Hap. You admire the sentiment, but you wouldn't hang it on your walls."

While the woman wasn't wrong, Caroline didn't like her personal speculation. "As I said, I select all of the paintings here, so that's a hard choice."

"Indulge me," the woman said with a pointed look, one that conveyed she was used to getting her way. "I'm always curious about the kind of painting someone like you would buy if you had the money."

Now that was downright insulting. Caroline thought about being contrary and selecting a painting she'd never hang on her walls, but better sense bore out. This woman didn't give a crap about her. She was another rich person trying to prove she was bigger than someone else. Caroline took a breath and pointed at the one she'd choose.

"Henry Farve has a wonderful Impressionistic style. His use of light and brushstrokes is second to none, if you ask me. I love the way he represented the Colorado prairie. Most people think it's all mountains out here, but we have a diverse geography."

The woman studied the painting. "Indeed. How much is it?"

Okay, here we go, Caroline thought. "It's twenty thousand."

"No wonder you like it," the woman said. "It's probably on the low end of your stock, isn't it?"

She ground her teeth and smiled. *Bitch.*

"I'll give you eighteen for it," the blond woman said, taking out her wallet and pulling out a gold credit card.

Caroline thought about haggling with the woman, but honestly, she only wanted her gone. They'd still make a good profit for the artist, and if the woman knew Kendra like she said, Caroline would be wise to play nice.

She took the card. "I'll run this for you and then pack up the painting."

"You can send it to my hotel," the woman said. "I can't be weighed down with it today. I have a lot to do."

"Of course," she said. "There's an extra charge for the courier service."

"Fine," the woman said, giving Caroline her back as she looked back at the paintings.

She ran the card—and then nearly dropped it when she noticed the name. Cynthia Newhouse.

Holy shit!

"So you know who I am," she heard the woman say.

Looking up, she noted Cynthia looking back at her over one shoulder, a sly smile on her face.

"You didn't come here to buy a painting," she said simply.

"No, I didn't," the woman said, turning and sauntering toward her, her fur swaying with each step. "Kendra was bragging to some people I know about J.T. Merriam buying a painting from her gallery last month. I keep tabs on the poor man, you see. Even though we're technically divorced, I can't seem to stop myself from being concerned about his life choices and the people he surrounds himself with. It's a wife thing, and I'm afraid he's fallen prey to some really poor advice these past years."

Since he'd decided to leave her, no doubt. God, this woman was even worse than she'd imagined yesterday.

"You were in Rome with him for a short time, I hear."

That stopped her short. "How did you—"

"Like I said, darling...tabs. You'd be wise to remember that. Oh, and thank you for sharing your personal choice with me. Every time I look at the painting you love, I'll enjoy knowing I took it out of your reach."

Cynthia extended her hand for the bill of sale and card but didn't take the pen Caroline handed her.

"I never use other people's pens, darling. You never know where the ink has been."

Caroline thought about poking her in the eye with said pen.

Cynthia scrawled her bold signature at the bottom of the receipt and handed it back. "You can deliver the painting to The Grand Mountain Hotel in Dare Valley. I'll be staying there for a while."

"What?" Caroline blurted out. Her imagination had run wild, but this wasn't a possibility she'd considered.

The woman pulled out her shades. "You know it, of course, having been born in that *quaint* town."

If this woman hadn't known Kendra, Caroline would have shown her "quaint."

Cynthia slid on the glasses, her sly smile firmly in place. "Be sure to tell J.T. I'll see him soon."

Hadn't she told him as much yesterday? "Wait! Why are you doing this? I mean, J.T. said you're divorced now. What's the point of all this?"

The smile disappeared, and the woman lowered her glasses a touch before ramming them back in place. Caroline could have sworn she'd seen a flash of vulnerability in her eyes, but the glasses had handily hidden it.

"Have you ever been in love? The kind of love that makes you believe everything is possible, the kind that changes your life?"

She'd been in serious "like" before, sure, and while she'd had glimpses of such a feeling with J.T., his withdrawal had made her doubt herself.

"Not really," she answered honestly.

"Then don't judge me," Cynthia said in a hard tone. "I opened my heart up to J.T. Joined myself in *marriage* to the man. Hell, I even bought an ugly set of china he liked. And what did he do? He walked out on me. Me! Cynthia Newhouse!"

The force of her words shook Caroline, almost like thunder rattling a window pane.

"No one does that and gets away with it."

Cynthia gave her one last look and spun around, stalking out of the gallery.

Caroline had the urge to sag against the wall again. Goodness, the negative emotions emanating from J.T.'s ex were powerful. No wonder he'd been so shaken after his call with her. She'd heard about bad breakups, but Cynthia seemed to be taking a line from the whole "hell hath no fury like a woman scorned" cliché.

Caroline looked at her phone with dread. His ex was coming to Dare Valley, clearly on the war path like he'd suspected.

She had to tell him about this awful encounter—even if it made him withdraw further from her.

CHAPTER 6

"I SHOULD HAVE HUNG WANTED POSTERS ALL OVER THE STATE of Colorado with the caption, *Cynthia Newhouse. Female Killer. Armed and dangerous. Approach with caution.*"

J.T. still couldn't believe she'd shown up bold as brass at the gallery where Caroline worked. And that she was coming here! To Dare Valley.

"Wouldn't have helped," Trev said, throwing a basketball up in the air from his position on the couch. "She'd have shown up anyway. Crazy-ass gold diggers do that. Caroline was smart to call you."

While she'd been calm on the phone, he'd heard her voice tremble. It had just about killed him to know his messy baggage had done this to her. The deflated picnic had been bad enough.

"The Grand Mountain Hotel should bar her or something."

"It's a hotel," Trev reasoned, reminding J.T. he was getting dramatic. "They don't discriminate. At least we know she's coming for sure."

Trev hadn't been surprised to learn Cynthia had made her move, although neither of them had expected she'd physically show up in Colorado.

"Will you quit it with the whole basketball MVP

fantasy?" J.T. said, marching over and catching the ball Trev had once again tossed in the air. "She knows about Caroline, Trev. This is bad. Really bad. I'm already having fantasies about wrapping Caroline up in a blanket and whisking her off to safety."

"Very romantic of you," Trev said. "Again, it was only a matter of time before Cynthia found out about her. You're hoping to start dating her, after all."

He tightened his grip on the ball, wanting to throw it through the window. "But Cynthia and I are *divorced*... She isn't supposed to be keeping tabs anymore."

"You have a real tantrum coming on, don't you? Should I burp you or something?"

"You're a real dick sometimes."

"And you need to get a hold of yourself," Trev said, sitting up and swinging his legs onto the floor. "I'm glad Uncle Arthur called you over this morning. My pep talk clearly didn't make a dent."

J.T. had felt better after their talk. Mostly. But that call from Caroline had brought him low again.

"Personally I'm glad Sin City is coming *here*," Trev said. "It gives us a home field advantage, of sorts. Everyone in town loves the Hales, and they have warm fuzzies about the Merriam line too because of the university. They'll look out for us. She won't be able to do anything without us knowing about it. Hell, Jill works at The Grand and so does Natalie. We have a built-in Hale security force."

"Maybe you're right," J.T. said, the first hint of mirth cutting through his fear. "I wouldn't put it past Jill to sneak into Cynthia's room and plant a snake under her pillow along with a nighttime chocolate." The image made him think of Arthur's comment about looking for a snake's underbelly.

"J.T., as your older brother and genetic superior, I'm always right," Trev said, grabbing the ball from him.

He'd never let J.T. live down the fact that he was his elder by two minutes. "Now go see Caroline."

"Huh?" His mind was spinning a mile a minute. "But Cynthia is coming here."

His brother jammed the ball against his chest. "Yes, and we'll watch her. Right now, you need to get your ass up to Denver and reassure Caroline. I know you're in shock, but let me repeat back your side of that brief conversation."

His brother mimed a cheesy smile.

"Caroline. Hi. I've been thinking about—" The smile turned to an over-blown face of horror. "What? When? You're fucking kidding me! *Oh, my God!* I'm so sorry. Thanks for calling me. Don't worry. I'll look into it. Okay, I've gotta go."

"You should have gone into comedy instead of the family business," J.T. said, slamming the ball back against his brother's chest. "I wasn't that bad."

"Yes, you were," Trev told him as he tossed the ball on the couch. "Now listen to your older brother."

"Like the two minutes you have on me has given you such a wealth of wisdom," J.T. drawled.

Trev tapped him on the side of the head before he could blink. "Listen to me!"

"Hey!"

"I mean it, J.T. I've been by your side for three years over this, and I've seen every permutation. The *Fast and Furious* binge watches. The long sprints until you can't breathe. The sad hours of drinking whiskey from the bottle."

Depression settled over him. "It's never going to end. She'll never back down."

"It already has ended," Trev said. "You're divorced, and that's a fact. You've handled the past shit as well as you can and you and the rest of us will keep handling Sin City this time. But I'm with Uncle Arthur. Don't you dare let her ruin your possible future with Caroline. J.T., I like her, like her in a way I've never liked anyone you've ever dated. Okay, except that flight attendant from Alitalia. She was—"

"I get it! Okay!" He pushed Trevor back, but his brother held his ground.

"No you don't," Trev said. "You're letting Sin City undermine your chance with Caroline. Now, get your ass in your car before I clock you. Don't make me call Mom."

"You're bluffing." Usually Trev kept their mom out of things.

"You know what Dad says. You can take the girl out of the Southside of Chicago, but you can't—"

"I know the rest," he said, kicking the couch. "She'd probably tell me one of Grandpa's war stories or talk about the sacrifices Grandma made during the war."

His mother's parents had met writing letters to each other after her brother had died in WWII. Theirs was one of those epic romances you only expected to see in movies and books, and it had filled him with a romanticism his siblings sometimes teased him for.

"She might make you read their old letters again," Trev said. "Mom always said it helped build character."

Their mother hadn't come from money like their father had, and she'd felt it was important they had a sense of hard times, even if they never experienced them. Of course, J.T. now felt he could lay claim to some.

"You only talk this tough when you're worried. Big W worried."

His brother only stared him down.

"It's no wonder we hired you to deal with the Russians. I'm afraid of you too when you get like this."

"That's why I'm your older brother," Trev said, grabbing him in a man hug.

"Yuck. Did you have to put your meaty arms around me?" But he squeezed him back with all his might. Damn he was a good brother.

"You're just jealous you're not this buff."

"In your—"

"Out! And tell Caroline that if you act like a moron again, I'll beat you into shape for her." Trev made a show of kicking him in the backside as J.T. walked over to the side table and pocketed his key fob.

"Thanks, Trev."

"I've always got your back, little bro," he said.

"It was only two minutes," J.T. said, grinning at him over his shoulder as he left. Trev had already found the basketball and was once again tossing it into the air.

Two hours later, J.T. walked into Leggett Gallery. Caroline was working at her sleek white desk, her laptop open. She looked up. He couldn't help but notice her smile took a while to develop.

"I'm sorry I wasn't more...comforting on the phone," he said, strolling over. "Blame it on shock."

"Join the club," she said, not rising from her position.

He pulled out one of the chairs in front of the desk and joined her. "I didn't expect her to...mess with you."

"It's not surprising, I suppose," Caroline said, closing her laptop. "Kendra bragged about selling a painting to you, which wasn't very professional of her."

"And yet so common in the art world when it comes to big art fish like me," J.T. said. "I've always found it annoying. I'm sorry. What can I do to make it better? Have you had lunch yet? I know it's late..."

"Cynthia told me why she's intent on messing with you," Caroline said, kicking back in her chair with an aloofness he wasn't used to from her.

He remembered how easily they'd laughed together over their dinners in Rome. Right now, those seemed ages ago. "Did she now?"

"I've had a while to think about it."

Those words seemed ominous. "And what did you decide?"

"You broke her heart," she said quietly. "Somehow I hadn't expected that. Not after what you'd told me yesterday."

He knew it was true, to some extent, but he also knew Cynthia had a remarkable ability to manipulate people and garner sympathy.

"She asked me if I'd ever been in love, and I honestly couldn't tell her I had. She said she'd pinned all her hopes and dreams on you, more or less."

That was classic Cynthia. "Not all, perhaps, but some, of course. One has to pin some of them to consider marriage. It wasn't a commitment I took lightly. I loved her too, you know."

Caroline looked him in the eye, her gaze intent. "Then what happened?" she asked.

He'd hoped what he'd shared with her yesterday would be enough, but if she needed to know more about the breakup to understand, he'd give it to her.

"She was beautiful and elegant, of course. That struck me right away. We had a lot in common, and, well, I thought she was a good person. Trev says I got snowed in by all the philanthropy she does."

"So what helped you see her differently?" she asked, crossing her arms.

His brow wrinkled at her sign of discomfort. Heck, he couldn't blame her. He wasn't comfortable either.

"When I suggested she join me for a goodwill tour to some terrific charities in the Middle East and Africa that I was visiting as a representative of Merriam Oil & Gas, she balked. It was beneath her, she said, and suddenly I realized she only wanted to...raise money like a socialite might. Not get her hands 'dirty,' so to speak. She didn't care to meet the real people she was helping."

For the first time, he'd recognized the look of calculation in her eyes. Cynthia had apologized and tried to fix it with sex, but he'd started to realize his wife wasn't the woman he'd thought he had married.

"Then it was a bunch of little things that didn't feel so little to me. I caught her dressing down the coat check person after I went outside to give the valet our ticket. I was appalled. The woman had only misplaced her fur. It certainly wasn't a reason for Cynthia to question her intelligence and make her feel like shit.

"It went downhill quickly after that. I caught her being rude to one of our custodians at the office, and I mean ugly rude. I didn't want to be with someone like that."

"I'm glad you find that type of behavior upsetting," she said. "Not everyone would."

Sad but true. "We Merriams might have money, but we've never believed we're above anyone. We always try to treat people with respect and kindness. I honestly don't understand why anyone would do otherwise."

"So you left."

"There was more to it," he said cautiously, not sure how much detail to give. "I thought she'd settle down with me in Rome, but she was constantly trying to talk me into taking time off. She didn't think I should work so hard. I was rich. Why did I need to toil and sweat every day? There was this party she wanted us to go to in Milan, but I had a big meeting the next day. She tried to persuade me to send an 'underling' in my place, saying that was what important people did. You get the picture. When I told her I loved what I did, she was baffled."

"You weren't who she thought you were either," Caroline said, pushing aside her laptop.

The weight of his past seemed to extend the divide between them. He wanted to curse Cynthia yet again.

"No, I wasn't, and when I told her that we weren't

right for each other, she went kinda crazy. She said no one left her—and a whole bunch of other stuff not fit for anyone's ears. I...didn't let it sway me. I thought it would be a simple divorce. We hadn't been married long. We both had our own money."

"But that wasn't how it went," she finished for him. "You were smart to get out when you did. More time wouldn't have helped, I don't think."

He wanted to reach out and touch her. To stroke her cheek. But he didn't dare, not until he finished. "No, it would only have made it worse. She said she wanted kids, but I quickly realized she didn't mean it the same way I did. She planned to hire a nanny to raise the kids and then ship them off to boarding school like her parents had done with her."

"I'm trying to summon some compassion for her, but I just can't," Caroline said. "Everyone has something in their past they need to overcome, but it doesn't justify hurting other people."

"I couldn't agree more," J.T. said. "It worries me that she came to see you. Part of me wants to tell you never to contact me again."

"That's dumb," she said and then slapped her hand over her mouth. "Oops. Did I say that out loud? The Hale gene sometime kicks in when I'm feeling vulnerable."

J.T.'s mouth twitched. "You don't look anything like Uncle Arthur, thank God, but you sounded like him right then. He chewed my butt pretty good this morning, but he followed up with a good dose of his proverbial wisdom."

"Sounds like Uncle Arthur," she said. "I'm glad he talked to you."

"Me too. He was right. I don't want Cynthia to ruin what I have with you, but I'm not going to lie, the thought of her visiting you, harassing you, made me break out in a cold sweat. It's not right. What did she do, by the way?

I was so shocked, I...didn't ask many questions or say anything to reassure you. I'm sorry about that."

She looked down, as if contemplating how much to share. Oh, they were on a conversational tightrope now, dammit.

"We talked about the paintings in the gallery for a while, and then she asked which painting I would purchase. If I could afford it, of course." She gave him a fake smile.

He cursed.

"Perhaps I shouldn't have told her, but I've dealt with people like her before, and I hate to lie. I figured why not tell her."

J.T. was already shaking his head. "Let me guess. She bought it."

"How did you know?"

Shrugging, he said, "I've seen her pull that kind of power play before with people she doesn't like."

"I don't much like power plays," Caroline said.

"Neither do I," J.T. said. "I want to protect you, but I'm scared I can't. If she knows you were in Rome with me, she'll likely surmise you're helping me with the museum. I told you she moves fast. Did she say anything about that?"

She shook her head slowly. "No, not explicitly."

But you could feel the silent elephant in the room.

"That makes you a potential target," he said softly. "I'm...really upset about this, and I'm really sorry."

"A target?" she asked, gripping the edge of the desk. "What do you think she'll do?"

He rubbed the back of his neck. "I wish I knew. You seem to be in her sights, and the fact that she's staying in Dare Valley is honestly terrifying. I might have to buy a crucifix and garlic on the way back."

"I'll go with you," she said, trying to joke. "Vampire Busters is right around the corner."

"Caroline..."

Something in his tone caught her attention. "Yeah?"

"I don't think she knows how I feel about you yet, but she will if we keep seeing each other."

"Then we should...shack up together in Dare Valley this weekend for sure!" she blurted out.

Her words shocked him silent, but then he started to laugh. Her ability to laugh at herself and life—even some of the paintings she loved—always lifted his spirits. It was one of the things he loved best about her.

"My filter clearly is gone," she said. "It's like nervous Tourette's or something."

"Cynthia has a way of pushing everyone to their breaking point. But honestly, this is an important decision. I can't predict what she's going to do. If you want out, I'm totally cool with it." He almost managed to say the words in an easy tone. Almost.

She studied him. "But you aren't. I can see the fire in your eyes. I appreciate you for saying this and giving me the choice. But honestly, there is no choice. I won't let her intimidate me. I want to work with you on the museum. It's a great career move for me." She held his gaze, then added, "And I want to be with you. None of that has changed."

"Are you absolutely certain?"

She nodded decisively. "Yes."

He blew out a harsh sigh. "I'll ask you again if things get rocky, but I'm..."

She laid her hand on the desk, as if reaching out to him. Giving in to his need to touch her, he took it and clasped it firmly.

"Relieved," he finished after a long pause. "Also, please feel free to say I'm being 'dumb' anytime. Maybe it's because I grew up in a tough-talking family, but oddly I respond pretty well to that kind of talk." Uncle Arthur had his number too, thank God.

She tried to fight the smile, but it won out, he was relieved to see. "Noted. I'll tell you when you're being dumb anytime. You don't have to ask me twice."

"Have any plans tonight?" he asked, quirking his brow at her. "I thought I might stay over in Denver tonight. I'm officially divorced, remember?"

They'd walked this infernal tightrope for too long. Not together but not *not* together. They needed to know if they worked as a couple before Cynthia tried to tear them apart. The way Caroline was standing by him—professionally and personally—meant the world to him. Loyalty mattered, and anyone who said otherwise hadn't been betrayed by someone they loved.

"I was hoping you'd remember that." Her thumb stroked the back of his hand. "It just so happens my dance card is free tonight."

"Seems my luck is improving."

He got to his feet and circled the desk, not wanting any separation between them. Taking her into his arms, he spun her around in a circle, bringing her close enough for him to hear her rapid breathing, feel the heat of her body. Something between them had shifted. Cynthia had no doubt intended to scare Caroline off with her gambit, but instead she'd brought them closer together.

They were finally going to dance like they both wanted to.

CHAPTER 7

THE DAY TODDLED ON FOR CAROLINE AND HER CONSTANT surveillance of the clock didn't help. It was as if the day's hourglass had gotten clogged, slowing down Father Time.

J.T. told her to text him when she was finished, and she was out the door at six on the nose, her cell phone in hand. She was punching in her message to him when she heard his unmistakable laugh. Swinging around, she spied him across the street, leaning against his Ferrari.

He held an entire bunch of colorful balloons. "I thought you might finish on time today," he said, checking both directions before walking toward her. "You should have seen me trying to fit these in my Ferrari."

She realized she should meet him halfway, but her feet couldn't seem to do it. Since he'd left the gallery earlier, all she'd thought about—heck, fantasized about—was him. Some of her worry about Cynthia hadn't gone away, so she'd overridden her fears with thoughts about his hands running all over her naked body. She'd gotten so overheated, she'd had to prop the front door open for a while. If any passersby had thought it odd, well, too bad. Spending weeks around J.T., on the brink of a relationship but not quite there, had driven her crazy with wanting.

He'd finally stepped forward! She could feel it. About damn time, she wanted to say.

"How about an early dinner?" he asked when he reached her. "I have a restaurant rented out for your complete enjoyment. Oh, and I have a clown on standby if they don't freak you out."

She'd had time to think about how she wanted things to go. And dinner didn't figure into her plans just yet. She didn't want to give him time to change his mind again.

"Not that I don't enjoy the gesture—and clowns don't freak me out FYI—but how about you follow me home?"

The heat in his green eyes made her want to sigh right there on the street.

"Dinner would be a safer place to start," he said in a quiet voice.

"And you said let's wait a week to see what your ex would do." She planted her feet. "Well, now we know. Forget about the week."

His mouth parted as if he were surprised at her directness.

"Do you still have reservations about me and how I feel?" she asked. "Or how you feel?"

He reached out to caress her upper arm, the touch sending a shiver through her. "Never you, and I know how I feel about you."

"Then let's get a move on. J.T., I want you to follow me home."

"Yes, ma'am," he said, sweeping his hand out grandly. "After you."

"And hurry," she added.

He let go of the balloons in his hand immediately, his gaze blazing with desire. "Your wish is my command."

Music to her ears. She strode off to where she'd parked and checked to make sure he was behind her. Behind her? Suddenly, she had an image of him standing behind her, his hardness pressed against her, kissing the back of her neck as she...

Goodness, she was going to implode on the way home if she didn't get herself under control. She drove slowly even though he knew where she lived. She went through all the reasons she shouldn't sleep with him, but the only one that came to mind was that she hadn't shaved her legs last night. Did she have stubble? Moira and Natalie always said men didn't care, and right now, she was inclined to believe them. Heck, she wasn't thinking clearly. Maybe she needed an outside perspective.

She called Moira first, and her sister picked up on the first ring.

"Hey! I was just thinking about you. Are you calmer after what happened yesterday?"

"My hormones are out of control at the moment," she replied. "I'm thinking about having sex with J.T. tonight. Any concerns? I can't seem to come up with a negative except I didn't shave my legs last night."

"I told you men don't care," she said immediately. "I could have hair like a mountain man and Chase would still do me. Right, hon?"

Caroline heard Chase bark out a laugh in the background.

"Thanks for that image," Caroline said. "Seriously, Mo, am I going too fast?"

"Has J.T. finally picked up the pace?"

"Yes, he's on the uptick. And wait until you hear this. His ex-wife paid me an unpleasant visit at the gallery today." Of course, she'd told her siblings everything about his ex after the family party.

"She did what?" her sister yelled. Then she could hear the sound of Mo's muffled voice at the other end of the line, and she knew her sister was filling in Chase.

"Yes, seems she knows I was in Rome with J.T.

Anyway, I'll tell you more about it later. Right now you need to help me. J.T. drove up to Denver after his ex visited—long story—and we talked. He tried to give me an out after meeting his ex, but I didn't bite."

"Of course you didn't. We don't let crazy people dictate our actions. If J.T. is up for it, you should go for it. You've wanted him since Rome, Caroline. And we both know how rare that is. I was the same way with Chase and look how that's worked out."

After Rome, Caroline had secretly wondered if J.T. might be "The One." Heck, when he'd flown to Colorado to see her a short time later, under the guise of attending a corporate party for Evan's new ventures, she'd walked on air for days. But he'd held back, and now she understood why—he hadn't wanted them to get serious before she understood the situation with Cynthia, and he hadn't wanted to explain it before they got a chance to know each other.

The invisible wall that had stood between them was finally gone.

"Thanks, Mo," she said. "I'm almost home. If you don't hear from me—"

"I'll hope it's because you're too exhausted to pick up your phone. Have fun, babe."

Leave it to Moira to be practical. Her sister had always been good at breaking things down. She thought about calling Natalie just to cover bases, but she was making the left to her street and there wasn't time. Plus, shouldn't she be confident enough to make such a choice on her own? She snorted aloud at the thought. She didn't call her sisters in moments like this because she needed reassurance—or at least that wasn't the main reason. Mostly she called them because they were her sisters and she loved them.

She parked her car in the space closest to the sidewalk that would take her to her apartment. J.T. pulled in next to her. Caroline checked to make sure the lipstick she'd applied before closing the gallery was in place. Then she laughed at the impulse. It wasn't going to last long if she had anything to say about it.

J.T. was waiting by her car door, and when she opened it, he helped her out and closed it like the gentleman he was. "Too bad about the balloons."

"Collateral damage. Did you call one of your sisters?" he asked, the streetlights casting shadows on his face.

"How did you guess?" she asked, stepping back a moment.

"I have siblings too," he said. "We do the same thing."

She tilted her head to better see his face. "So did *you* call anyone?"

"Nah," he said. "I already knew what Trev would say."

Taking his hand, she led him down the path to her apartment. "What's that?"

"Go for it," he said. "He's been at me for weeks to stop letting the past hold me back."

She liked the man Trevor had become. He was big and tough, and no one with sense would want to mess with him, but he'd cracked joke after joke with them. He seemed to belong with the extended Hale clan as much as J.T. did. Of course, now she understood why Trevor was spending time in Dare Valley—J.T.'s twin had his back.

"I'm glad you decided to take his advice," she said, fighting the urge to rush down the sidewalk.

She had her house key ready when they reached the door, and she waved his hands away when he offered to open it. No, it was faster this way. The moment the door closed, she locked it and leaned against it.

"I'm not normally this bold—"

"Caroline, I've wanted you from the first moment I saw you in the gallery," he said, shrugging out of his overcoat. "Come here."

She felt the flutter of relief in her gut. "Whew! I was hoping you hadn't changed your mind on the way here."

He chuckled, but it was a husky sound, full of pent-up longing. "Not a chance. Do you remember how it was in Rome? I asked you where you'd been my whole life, and I meant it. Caroline, this isn't casual for me. That's why I needed the divorce to be final. What I feel for you is wonderful and raw and joyous."

She felt a wave of awe flood through her. Of course she had known the connection between them wasn't casual—at least it had never *felt* casual—but this...

"Dammit, you've really been holding back! That might be the sweetest thing anyone's ever said to me."

He tugged off his tie and shoved it in his suit pocket. "I'm only getting started now that we've put the turtle pace behind us. You're overdressed."

She still had her coat on, but when she tried to shrug out of it, she caught the right sleeve on her purse. "Oops. I forgot."

He took the bag from her and walked around to help her out of her coat. "Let me help."

She leaned back against him as he slid an arm around her waist. "Oh, J.T., I've been thinking about this all day. Well, if I'm being honest, I've been thinking about it since Rome."

His lips brushed the side of her neck, and she felt him move her hair to the side. The kisses were gentle, but oh so hot, and she angled her head to give him better access.

"I'm glad we didn't go to dinner," he whispered.

"I hope the clown wasn't crushed when you gave him the night off."

He laughed. "Forget about his feelings. Sweetheart, I plan to savor you all night."

She loved that idea. And that word... No one had ever *savored* her before, not that she was all that experienced. Her first had been in college, and she'd been intimate with a few men she'd met in professional circles. None of the relationships had become serious. That line of thinking reminded her that she was cautious by nature and there were practical considerations to address.

"I'm not on the Pill right now," she said, "but I bought some condoms a few weeks ago, hoping…"

"It was my first post-divorce purchase," he said, laying his head against hers for a moment in what felt like a comforting embrace. "And I'm clean. Caroline, you can trust me."

"You can trust me too, J.T."

"I know that, and for someone who's developed serious trust issues the past couple of years, you have no idea how much that means to me."

But she was starting to understand that. It seemed important to face him, so she turned around and looked him in the eye.

"I'll never betray you," she said.

His face tensed up and then he took her in his arms. "I know that too."

They held each other for a moment, and she knew he was battling something. She gave him time. When he leaned back and looked into her eyes, she knew he'd found solid ground again.

"Kiss me," she whispered.

His head lowered, and their mouths met. They both took their time, letting the passion between them build. Then he tugged on her bottom lip, and she could stand it no longer. She opened her mouth and welcomed his tongue. The kiss turned hot and carnal, and her hands gripped his back.

Pulling away, she reached for the buttons on his suit jacket. He took her hands in his.

"Caroline, part of me wants to just take you on the floor, now, but it's our first time. Plus, it's cold in here, and you tend to get chilly easily."

She remembered how he'd made sure their outside dinner in Rome had patio heaters. His insight and his attentiveness sliced straight down to her heart. "Come with me."

They took the stairs and walked hand in hand into her bedroom. She'd completely forgotten in the heat of the moment, but her bed was unmade, and she had work clothes and shoes from last week still on the floor in the corner.

"It's a mess. I didn't...ah...expect company," she stammered. "I mean, I was gone all weekend."

"I kinda like seeing this," J.T. said, gesturing with his hand. "Makes you seem human like the rest of us. I'll confess something to you as well. If I didn't have someone come twice a week, my place wouldn't be inhabitable. And I haven't made a bed since I moved out from under my mother's eye. Bad habit perhaps, but I figure I'm only going to—"

"Crawl back in later so why bother?" she finished for him.

He smiled at her. "We're a match made in heaven. I've...never had anyone finish my thoughts before."

She rested her hand on his chest. "And no man has ever paid close enough attention to realize I get chilly easily."

He caressed her cheekbone and pushed her hair back behind her ear. "You pay attention when you care about someone. Let me show you what else I plan to pay attention to tonight."

As he undid her silk blouse and opened it, she kept her eyes on him. J.T. knew how to make a woman feel like she was his whole world.

"You're so beautiful," he said, tracing a line from her collarbone to her belly button. "But I'm really going to have to buy you some special lingerie."

She pushed him playfully. "What's wrong with it?"

He was chuckling under his breath, and she knew he

was teasing her. "Nothing, but breasts this perfect should be cupped in Italian lace."

When he reached behind her and unhooked her bra, her skin tingled. "No one has ever said my breasts are beautiful."

He edged back. "Those guys were dumb. These are works of art. For a while, I thought the best depiction of breasts was in Dominique-Louis-Féréa Papety's painting *The Temptation of Saint Hilarion*. Then I saw René Magritte's *Philosophy in the Boudoir*. Talk about... Never mind."

Caroline had to admit those were some great breasts. "You've thought about things like this?" she asked, not sure if she should laugh out loud.

"I was a boy who loved art," he said. "Of course, I thought about it. Trev says seeing naked women is the only good reason to support the arts, but that's his philistine side showing."

Okay, this time she did laugh. "So that's why you have a huge section of nudes!"

He snorted. "Grandpa Emmits bought most of those. What can I say? A love of beautiful breasts runs in the family. You should hear my brother, Flynn, wax poetic about them. Never mind."

And yet she understood. "When I spent that summer in Rome in college, I finally saw the beauty in the human body. Male and female. Before that, I was embarrassed by the whole thing."

"Did you lose your virginity in Rome?" he asked in a teasing tone.

"That is none of your business!"

She made a show of pulling her shirt together, but she rather liked that they could talk so openly in such an intimate moment. Somehow it made them feel closer. She didn't want J.T. for his body alone, although he really did have too many clothes on.

"Isn't it time for you to get undressed?" she asked.

"Not yet. Come here, Caroline Hale." He grabbed her and made a show of lifting her off the floor and twirling her around like he'd done in the gallery.

"What are you doing?" she asked, trying not to start laughing again.

"Distracting you," he said with an exaggerated huff. "You were starting to get nervous."

She slid down his body as he lowered her, and her laughter subsided. "It's our first time, so yes, I am a little nervous."

He framed her face in his hands. "I'm nervous too. It's been...a long time since I've...put my heart out there. And I haven't been with anyone since..."

He'd left his wife, she realized. "It's going to be all right," she said, lifting her hand to touch his.

His smile was slow and sensuous, and her belly fluttered once again. "Oh, it's going to be better than all right. You have my promise on that."

When he moved in to kiss her, she edged back. "You know what I mean, don't you? J.T., I'll be careful with you. You have my promise on that."

He pressed their foreheads together. "That...moves me. More than you know. Come. Let me make love with you."

With you. Not *to* you. She liked the difference.

He shrugged out of his jacket and then started unbuttoning his dress shirt. She knew this act was somehow a show of trust even though she didn't fully understand it yet. Instead, she simply watched as he bared his chest to her. When he crossed the short distance between them, he took her hand and placed it over his heart.

"It's yours," he whispered, "along with the rest of me."

She touched his jaw with her other hand. They stayed

in the moment, merely gazing at each other. Words were unnecessary. She knew what was in his heart, and in the silence, she let him see what was in hers.

Pulling back slowly, her eyes linked to his, she shrugged out of her blouse and let it fall to the floor. Once she was free of her top and her unhooked bra, she wrapped her arms around him and stepped forward until their skin met, his hot against hers. Her breasts suddenly felt heavier, and when he shifted his hands and held them, her head fell back. With that first touch, she let her eyes close. And when his mouth covered her nipple and started to suck, she was sure she was experiencing heaven on earth. He took his time like he'd said he would, and she caressed the long line of his back, luxuriating in the muscles there.

When he walked her backward toward the bed, she smiled at him, reveling in the moment—and in the realization that this was already the most sensual experience she'd ever had.

When the backs of her legs touched the edge of the bed, she undid the rest of her clothes and let them fall away. His face grew flushed, looking at her. Then he undid his pants and slid them to the floor, removing the rest of his clothes in their wake.

God, he was beautiful, his body a union of perfect, graceful lines of muscle and bone. This was the kind of male beauty that had inspired some of the ancient greats.

"You're so beautiful," he said in a hushed voice, his finger tracing a line across her belly. "And I want you. God, how I want you."

"I was thinking the same thing," she whispered. "Come here."

When he took her mouth in a kiss again, the preliminaries were gone. Heat rolled through her, and she closed her eyes and simply fell into the moment. His lips rubbed against hers, and then his tongue was seeking entrance again, and oh, how delicious it all felt.

Her hands gripped his hips and he moved against her, sending shockwaves through her body. Suddenly all she wanted was him. On top of her. Inside her. All around her.

She lay back on the bed, and he followed, covering her. Pressing her lips to his skin, she savored him as well, delighting in the change in his breathing and the tension in his body. He was hers for the taking, and she wanted every bit of him.

When he slid his hand between her legs, she moaned and surged up to meet it. God, this was good. So good. His clever hand knew just where to touch her, and she came hard and quick. She was still crying out in pleasure when he caught her cry with his mouth. A new feeling of urgency built in her core, pulling another moan from her, and this time he edged away. She heard the tear of a condom's foil packet. Forcing her eyes open, she watched him position himself between her legs. He was hard and hot, and she reached out her hand to him.

He slid over her, and their hands entwined as he came into her. The fit was tight and hot and wonderful.

"God, you feel good," he hissed out, pressing deep.

She moaned when he reached the hilt. "J.T."

"Yeah, babe?" he whispered, slowly withdrawing and then sinking back inside her.

"Don't ever stop," she said, and caught his smile before she closed her eyes again.

And so it went. The slow entry and the smooth withdrawal. Over and over again, until his breathing shuddered out and he picked up the force of his thrusts. This time he moved rapidly and with less finesse, but it was perfect because she didn't want finesse now. She wanted madness and heat and all of him, moving inside her as though driven to the very edge.

They crossed that edge together, and she held him

when he fell onto her, not minding the weight or the sheen of sweat on his body. No, he was exactly where she wanted him, exactly where he was supposed to be.

When he rose up and stared into her eyes, she noted the dampness in his hair and the look of awe on his face.

"You," he whispered. "Just you."

Her heart gave an answering cry in response. "Yes. You."

CHAPTER 8

J.T. AWOKE OUT OF A DEEP SLEEP TO HEAR HIS PHONE buzzing. Caroline mumbled in her sleep and rolled onto her stomach as he left the bed to grab it, stooping to pick up his pants on the way out. They'd stayed awake for most of the night, talking and making love, and he couldn't blame her for being tired. He was feeling it himself although he couldn't complain. It had been one of the best nights of his life.

"Trev, you'd better have a good reason for calling me," he said as he closed the bedroom door.

"You know I do," his brother replied. "I decided to do a little reconnoitering to confirm some suspicions. Interested in hearing who Cynthia is meeting with right now for breakfast?"

Holding the phone against his ear with his shoulder, he pulled on his pants and eyed the clock. It was after nine. "I should take you to task for the spy work, but hell yes, I'm interested."

He walked down the hallway and took the stairs back to the kitchen. He might need a cup of coffee to get him through this call.

"You aren't going to like it. Hell, I don't like it, and you know I've had some pretty dark thoughts toward her."

His siblings all loathed Cynthia for treating him as she had. He appreciated their concern and certainly understood such thoughts. He'd been okay if suddenly a piano fell on her, after all.

"Give it to me straight," he said, looking in Caroline's cabinets for coffee.

"She's meeting with the new president of the university," Trev said.

He almost dropped the phone. "What? Shit!"

"Yeah," Trev said. "Right in The Grand Hotel's restaurant. It's like she wanted you to know."

His mind spun. He'd suspected she'd go for the lawyer route again. It wouldn't have been easy now that the papers were signed, but it certainly would have been aggravating.

"You're right. She would have been discreet otherwise. You think she's planning on talking him out of the museum? I mean, can she? The board approved it—even if he wasn't president at the time."

"Seems like the horse I'd bet on," Trev said. "It's total bullshit, but that won't stop her. The question is how she plans to do it."

Now that made his belly churn. Cynthia would know he had all the I's dotted and the T's crossed. What was her play? Cause more havoc in his life? Delay the process? Talk badly about him to his new partners of sorts?

"President Matthau doesn't know me well, and he's—"

"Young and ambitious," Trev said. "Who knew universities could be such political hotbeds?"

"Maybe that's why Dad resigned from the board when we were kids."

J.T. had hoped to regain their family's connection to the university his great grandfather had started.

"I suppose I'd better make up an excuse and call Matthau then," J.T. said. "We need to head Cynthia off."

Trev snorted. "You can't head off Calypso."

An apt comparison, J.T. thought. In the Greek myth, Calypso detained Odysseus for seven years on her island, hoping he'd become her immortal husband.

"What do you think she's up to?" J.T. asked. "We've been playing the Cynthia guessing game for three years now, and you're a pro."

There was a pause. "What you said. Smear you and maybe our family. We'll have to see. Of course, she might be volunteering her fundraising for all we know. She does have a hell of a track record at it, but I can't imagine why she'd volunteer to help with the museum. She's never had a day job, and I doubt she wants to stay in Dare Valley for longer than it takes to torment you. Besides, it would look really weird if the university let that happen. She's your ex-wife for God's sake."

"She likes to circle around and wait for the right moment to attack," J.T. said.

"Pisses me off," Trev said, his voice rising. "All right, I'm getting worked up. I won't give my power away like that. Neither should you."

"No, she's controlled way too many of my moods in the past three years," J.T. said. "Last night, I turned a new corner in creating the life I want. I'm not going to let Cynthia fuck that up."

"Good," Trev said. "Are you still with Caroline?"

"Yes," he said, "but she doesn't seem to have any coffee."

"You should dump her right now," Trev said without missing a beat. "I mean, your children might end up liking tea instead."

The thought gave him a jolt. He wasn't ready to think about kids. Hell, even the M word made him break out in hives after what he'd been through. He hadn't lied to Uncle Arthur. He wasn't sure he ever wanted to get married again. People in Europe lived together all their lives without traipsing down the aisle and bringing in all the legal shit. He was leaning that way.

"Tea's not so bad."

"Right," Trev said. "But you'll only drink the kind that doesn't come in bags. You're a beverage snob, but I love you. Don't come back here right away. I'll keep my eyes and ears out. Do you want to call Uncle Arthur and get his sources working for us?"

He thought again of what Uncle Arthur had told him the previous day. The Hales had a bead on everything that happened in Dare Valley—they were the best allies he could have. "Good idea."

"That's why I'm watching over you, little brother. Have fun with Caroline. And remember. Don't let Sin City get to you. See ya when I see ya."

"Unless I see you first," J.T. said, making Trev laugh before they ended the call.

He set the phone down and leaned back against the counter, trying not to let himself worry. He'd done *everything* he could to ensure the museum was safe. But clearly Cynthia had a plan, and he had little choice but to wait for her next move. God, he was so tired of this shit.

Once, and only once, he'd asked her what it would take to make her stop. They'd just crossed into year two of the proceedings with no end in sight. Her response had devastated him. *You can come back. On your knees.* He'd hung up immediately and gotten drunk. It wasn't an option, and after all her subterfuge, he couldn't believe a word she said.

"Good morning," he heard Caroline say in a jovial voice. "Were you talking to someone?"

He turned to her, and a new calm settled over him, almost like a cool wave in the ocean on a hot day. "God, you're beautiful in the morning. I should have expected it."

She ducked her head. "Thanks. My sisters tease me

about it. What can I say? My hair stays in place."

Yeah, the dark brown curls rested on her shoulders, an array that would have made Da Vinci rush to his easel, but it wasn't only that. Her skin was luminous without makeup, and sure enough, her lips were a little red and swollen from all their kissing last night.

"Sorry if I woke you," he said, crossing to take her in his arms.

She laid a hand on his chest and lifted her face. Last night had changed things between them, and he wanted her to know just how much. He cupped her cheek and kissed her slowly, as if the outside world didn't exist, something he very much wanted to believe right now.

Her sigh was audible when she laid her head on his bare chest. "I'm so glad it's not weird between us."

Yeah, he'd had those mornings too. "No way. Caroline...I've never felt like I did last night."

"Me either. J.T., I know this is early, but I need to tell you...I might be in love with you."

Everything inside him seemed to still. His heart expanded, and he wanted to punch the air and yell *yes* to the heavens. Maybe the gods or whoever was up there were looking out for him, after all.

"That's music to my ears," he said. "I might be in love with you too."

She beamed, and his heart grew larger yet—until the remaining walls he'd built around it tumbled. Filled with awe and gratitude, all he could do was stare at her, like she was the moon or a supernova or something even more beautiful and spectacular.

"Actually, no it's not a might or maybe," he said, his voice becoming stronger with each word. "I have... complete certainty about this."

He'd never been one for half measures. She was blinking at him, and he finally smiled at her.

"I felt...something huge for you in Rome, but I didn't

want to say anything. I had…baggage. I didn't completely trust myself. I mean, we barely knew each other, and I didn't want to…"

He trailed off when he realized he was babbling.

She touched his cheek, as though trying to tell him it was okay.

Then he caught sight of his phone lying on the counter. He still had baggage, he realized, in care of his ex-wife, who was meeting with the president of the university where he'd planned to stake his future.

Caroline's future was at risk too.

Then he looked into her eyes again, and the love he felt for her helped settle the seething feelings. She loved him and he loved her. Uncle Arthur was right.

They would face whatever came together.

CHAPTER 9

CAROLINE HAD TO SPEED A LITTLE TO ENSURE SHE GOT TO work on time.

Thank goodness the gallery opened at eleven. J.T. had teased her about her lack of coffee and the random tea bags stuffed in the back of one of her kitchen drawers. Upon learning she usually had her coffee at work, he'd pressed his hands to his face in horror and told her he just couldn't love her anymore, which had made her laugh. Then he'd stopped her mirth by opening her robe and taking her on the granite countertop.

She'd finally had kitchen sex! Oh, she couldn't wait to tell her sisters, especially Moira, who was always bragging about her sexual escapades with Chase. Natalie was a little more reserved, although she'd told them about the Highlander kilt Blake used to role-play Jaime in *Outlander,* one of Natalie's favorite heroes.

A wave of giddiness made her want to skip to the front door of the gallery. She and J.T. were in love, and despite his ex's intrusion into their lives, she was happy. Happier than she'd been in a long, long while.

When she reached the gallery, the lights were already on inside. Weird. She could have sworn she'd turned them off last night. That worry was easy enough to swat away, but the door was also unlocked, and when she opened it, the alarm didn't beep. She scanned the gallery in a panic, relieved to see that all the paintings were still on the walls.

"Caroline," she heard and looked over to see her boss standing in the doorway of the break room decked out in leather gaucho pants and a cashmere sweater.

"Kendra! Whew! I didn't know you were coming in today."

While Kendra didn't always tell her when she was going to pop in, she usually had a reason for coming by, like a meeting with an artist or a high-rolling client. The kind of thing Caroline scheduled. They didn't have anything like that today.

"For a moment, I was afraid someone had broken in or something."

"With the door unlocked and the alarm off, I don't think so," Kendra said dryly.

Who got up on the wrong side of the bed? Well, not everyone could be as sexually satisfied as she was this morning. "Have you had coffee yet? I was going to make some."

"No," her boss said, her frown firmly in place. "Caroline, let's sit down."

A frisson of worry went through her as she walked to where Kendra was standing. "Sure. Let me put my things in the break room."

"That won't be necessary," Kendra said, taking her by the elbow and steering her to the sleek white desk in the corner where they conducted client business.

Okay, now she was really getting upset. "What's wrong, Kendra?"

Her boss sat behind the desk Caroline usually occupied and pointed to the chair across from her. "Sit down."

She complied, her coat still on, her purse still in hand.

"Caroline, I've had a bad report about you, and I'm sorry, but I'm going to have to let you go."

Caroline's stomach dropped like she'd taken an unexpected plunge on a roller coaster. She'd never considered the possibility of getting fired. Kendra had never been anything but satisfied with her work. "What? But that's crazy. You know how hard I work to make clients happy."

Kendra cleared her throat. "Yes, I do, but it seems you might have had personal reasons for being rude. I was surprised, of course, but—"

"Personal reasons?" Her brain clicked, and suddenly she knew the answer. "Did Cynthia Newhouse say bad things about me?"

"Yes," Kendra said, pulling out a cigarette and lighting it.

Caroline had never seen her smoke inside the gallery—it was prohibited, after all—and she coughed when her boss blew out a few puffs of smoke.

"I was a complete professional, Kendra, and between us, she didn't make it easy, but—"

"She said you asked her reasons for divorcing her husband, whom you apparently spent time with in Rome," Kendra said with a pointed look. "I thought you were on vacation, but Cynthia said you're working with J.T. on a proposed museum to house the Merriam collection at Emmits Merriam University in your hometown. Is that true?"

Her diaphragm felt like a boa constrictor had wrapped around it. So this was how Cynthia Newhouse worked. God, she felt like she needed to take a shower. "My great-uncle asked me to help him out as a family favor." That was true, at least.

"So you aren't going to quit working for me when this museum gets further along?" Kendra asked, drawing on her cigarette hard.

Caroline stared at the line between the fire and ash. That was pretty much where she was standing right now. "Kendra, I'm still here, aren't I?"

"You didn't answer my question, Caroline," Kendra said, stubbing out her cigarette.

Caroline looked her in the eye. She'd always believed it best to be truthful, but oh, this was going to hurt. "Yes, I've been strongly considering it, but the museum hasn't even been officially announced yet and—"

"But there are rumors," Kendra said, leaning forward. "I made a few calls last night. When you told me J.T. Merriam had bought a painting from us, I was over the moon. Now I realize he was poaching my manager. In my very own gallery."

"That's not how it was," Caroline said, wanting to defend J.T. "He was in town on business and decided to swing by after my great-uncle told him I was open to helping him."

Her boss' brow knit. "So he didn't try and talk you into working with him?"

Oh, this was bad. He had, she realized, but not in the way Kendra was thinking. "Well, he might have mentioned it and—"

"Bullshit!" Kendra said, standing up. "He was poaching. I've heard a lot of rumors about J.T. Merriam from people close to Cynthia Newhouse. I'm starting to believe some of them."

"It wasn't like that," Caroline said, lurching to her feet. "He isn't like that. She's the one who's a..." She cut herself off before she let the word slip.

"A bitch?" Kendra finished for her, crossing her arms. "Talk about personal. Caroline, you've been a good manager for me, but that ends now. You're fired. I want you to leave. Someone will pack up and deliver any personal effects to your house along with your final check. I have to say, I'm disappointed in you. This is something I would never have expected."

She felt tears burn her eyes. *Disappointed?* Kendra wasn't the only one. "And I never expected *you* would listen to idle gossip and be influenced by someone like Cynthia Newhouse. Talk about personal. No one else has said a bad word about me. I did a good job for you here, Kendra."

Kendra's mouth twisted. "Yes, you did. That's what makes this whole situation so hard. Goodbye, Caroline."

She thought about attempting to reason with her, but why bother? Kendra had made her decision, and it was clear she wasn't interested in continuing the conversation. She probably wouldn't believe her anyway. God, this shouldn't have happened. Not like this. She'd loved this gallery and everyone she worked with—especially the artists—and while Kendra could be challenging, she'd found a way to create a rewarding professional relationship with her. Or so she'd thought.

Score one to Cynthia Newhouse.

CHAPTER 10

As far as Arthur was concerned, everything was going to hell in a handbasket.

"Meredith! Tanner! Get in here."

He knew he shouldn't bark, but this was a newsroom dammit, and there should be some perks to being the editor. Hadn't Ben Bradlee at *The Washington Post* barked at Woodward and Bernstein back in the day?

"Grandpa, we're right next door," Meredith said, her tone the verbal equivalent of an eye roll, as she appeared in the doorway with Tanner.

"Sometimes that's the way it's gotta be," he told them. "Close the door. We have a shit storm on our hands."

Tanner didn't say anything—he just took Meredith's elbow and led her inside. They both took a seat in front of his desk. If Arthur weren't so upset, he'd have been tickled by the gesture. Meredith had sure as shooting picked a good one, and after he was gone, he knew Tanner would take care of her. Not that she needed it. But everyone deserved a good partner, and he was happy his granddaughter had found one, especially after the asshole she'd married the first time around.

"We have a new story we need to start pulling on," he said, leaning back in his chair, the faithful squeak a comfort. Like his old bones, it was showing its age, but it came through in a pinch.

"What's got you riled up?" Meredith asked, as sassy today as her red hair, it would seem.

"Cynthia Newhouse," he said, pushing his glasses down on his nose to make the point. "J.T.'s ex-wife."

Meredith's brows shot to her forehead, but Tanner simply sat back in his seat, all cool like. Someone else might have misinterpreted his attitude as disinterest, but Arthur knew he got as still as a panther waiting to pounce when he was preparing for a new story. Oh, and he could pull together an article so beautiful it would make a grown man weep.

"I just heard from a first-hand source at the university that the new president, that Matthau fellow from California, met with J.T.'s ex-wife at The Grand Mountain Hotel, where she's staying, it seems."

"At The Grand?" Meredith asked. "Are you sure?"

"Woman, I just called reception and asked to be connected to her room."

"Did you talk to her? Good God, what did you say?"

"Nothing. I hung up before she could pick up. I wasn't trying to interview her. Only confirm her whereabouts. Good gracious, Meredith, have I taught you nothing?"

She leveled him an arch look, and he knew he needed to dial it back. It wasn't like she was a rookie reporter.

"Then Jill did that whole text thing with me. Caroline was fired from Leggett Gallery this morning. Again, because of this Newhouse woman, it seems. I can see why Trevor calls her Sin City. She could drive a saint to sin with all her shenanigans."

"Wait!" Meredith said, sitting up straighter. "Caroline got fired? Why didn't I hear that?"

Arthur pushed his glasses up. "Apparently your sister calls me first in family emergencies."

Poor Natalie had come into Jill's office in tears. Of

course, Natalie wasn't normally this emotional, but she was pregnant, and Arthur knew pregnancy hormones sometimes affected women like that. His wife had been the same way.

"That's dirty business," Tanner said in his scary voice.

"Yes," Arthur said, "which is why we need you to start looking into this woman. I know we have a personal relationship to some of our subjects here so we'll do our best to be objective, but this is just going to be local news, I expect. My source doesn't know what that Newhouse woman is up to quite yet, but you can bet it has something to do with undermining J.T. and the museum. This museum was approved by the board of trustees, and messing with that is serious news."

Tanner nodded.

"I'll call some of my old contacts in New York and see what I can find out about her," Meredith said. "God, I feel so bad for Caroline."

Arthur did as well. Even though his grandniece had planned to leave, no one wanted to leave a long-time job on such a sour note. "You can get the full story from Caroline when she comes home with J.T. Apparently he's driving her back now so she can be around her family."

Arthur had gotten a little emotional hearing that. The boy had listened and gone to Denver yesterday, it seemed. He was glad Caroline hadn't left the gallery to go home to an empty house. Everyone needed support in a crisis, and now she was coming back to her family. He was grateful for that.

"How do you want to handle asking about Cynthia's meeting with President Matthau?" Tanner asked. "The museum's not yet public, so it would seem odd if we called and asked for an interview."

"Let me talk to J.T. about it," Arthur said. "I have a few close friends on the board I can talk to when the time comes. But I like the idea of asking Matthau right to his face. I'm still testing his mettle. I want to make him tell us straight out, but we need to approach him with some delicacy."

"Which puts you out of the running for the interview," Meredith said, a half smile on her face.

Had he said sass earlier? Yeah, she was sassy. Just the way he preferred. He didn't want any of his family members to be milquetoasts.

"Let me do some digging," Tanner said, "but if we decide to go straight to J.T.'s ex for an interview, maybe I should do the interview."

"I hate to agree, Grandpa," Meredith said. "Tanner is relatively new to the family and can project more objectivity."

Objectivity. Arthur mulled that over. Investigating this woman wasn't very objective, but she was bringing trouble to Dare Valley—and that made her and her plans news. He'd have investigated her even without the connection to J.T. But they would have to be careful like they'd agreed.

"We've dealt with exes effectively in the past," Arthur said, catching Tanner's eyes. "I seem to recall we gave Meredith's ex the runaround."

"But not before he caused us plenty of trouble," Tanner said.

The couple shared a look, and Arthur knew they were remembering that difficult time. "But we got through it," he said. "You two got hitched and now I have a great-grandbaby who I pray every morning and night has the black ink in his veins Jill seems to have missed."

"Jill would have made a terrible reporter, Grandpa," Meredith said with a laugh. "Like she says, she makes news."

"Makes news indeed. I've never seen such a nut, but that's why we love her. Let's get cracking on what we can dig up on Cynthia Newhouse. I'm going to talk to Trevor in person. Sometimes pulling the threads in a conversation—"

"Helps you understand what to look for," Meredith finished for him.

He tossed her a red hot. "Okay, hot shot. Why don't you come with me? We can interview Trevor together."

Tanner stood and nodded. "I'll get started. We can brief each other when you guys return."

Meredith ducked out, but he knew she was just grabbing her steno book and her purse. He tugged his coat off the rack and slapped a hat on his head. Damn if this cold wasn't chilling his bones.

"You ready, Grandpa?" Meredith asked, crunching on the candy as she came back in.

He grabbed his infernal cane and walked toward her, happy to feel his legs were solid. "Always."

She took his elbow. "Just like old times."

As they walked out, he memorized the moment, from the way the newsroom buzzed to the touch of baby powder Meredith had on her, likely from changing his great-grandson.

Yes, it was just like old times, and he hoped he and Meredith would have many, many more of them together. He remembered J.T. asking him why he refused to cut back on his hours or step away from the paper.

This is why he came to work every day.

CHAPTER 11

J.T. WISHED HE'D NEVER HEARD THE NAME CYNTHIA NEWhouse.

After Caroline had left, he'd gone to the closest Sur La Table intent on buying her some fine coffee. He'd found the coffee, but he'd also come back with a top-of-the-line Breville Espresso machine along with some hazelnut gelato. Maybe they could eat it for breakfast tomorrow as they'd done in Rome.

Then, to his shock, Caroline had come home. Her story had come out in a few gushes, and his hand had tightened around his coffee cup so much, it was a miracle of engineering the thing didn't shatter. His worst fear had come true. Caroline had gotten hurt because of him. More than hurt, she'd been fired. From the sound of it, her reputation might suffer, but he pledged that her career would not. No, she was going to be the curator for a museum as acclaimed as the Met or the MoMA if he had anything to say about it.

"I'm sorry," he said. The words sounded so piteously small, he added, "I know it doesn't seem like much, but I swear I'll make this up to you."

She shook her head, her face ashen. "It's not your fault. Much as it galls me, some of it is mine. I wasn't completely honest with Kendra, and I kinda got caught in a lie."

He wasn't buying that. "I don't think—"

"Of course, I realize most people don't tell their bosses they're scoping out new jobs, but none of that matters now. Regardless, it sucks."

That was putting it mildly. "Big time."

"I don't want you to feel guilty," she said, touching the back of his hand. "You were sweet to buy me coffee and this machine, but it's too much, J.T."

"Why wouldn't I feel guilty?" he said, not willing to let her change the subject just yet. "My ex-wife just got you fired!"

"But she was the one pulling the strings—not you." She went over and poured herself a cup of coffee. "I didn't have any at the gallery. Maybe I would have been more...with it or something if I'd had coffee. Oh, crap, this is just... I'm a little shell-shocked. All the way home I kept thinking, *I just got fired. How in the hell did that happen?* Then I'd be like *what are you going to do now?* Honestly, J.T., this isn't how I expected today to go."

Last night had been so wonderful for both of them, and Cynthia had found a way to infiltrate it. To sour the day they'd first pledged their love to each other. "Me either. I don't know what to say to you. What can I do? Did I tell you I bought some hazelnut gelato too?"

"Crap, that's going to make me cry. I think I need to get out of here. Go to my family. But I'm shaking too much to drive. Moira said she'd come get me, but you're here—"

"Of course I'll take you home."

And so he was. He spent the whole drive trying to think of some way to make it right, but he just couldn't. As they drove into Dare Valley, the endless expanse of sky somehow failed to raise his spirits like it usually did.

Calypso had brought the storm.

"Do you want me to talk to Kendra?" he finally asked. "I don't know that I can convince her to give you your job back, but if it's what you want, I'll move heaven and earth to make it happen."

She didn't turn and look at him. In fact, she'd been downright quiet, and he'd let her stew.

"No," she said, "I don't think that will do any good. Besides, Kendra won't ever trust me again. What you can do is get this museum going. When do you expect to put out the announcement?"

Shit. Double damn shit. J.T. continued to swear in his head. He hadn't told her about Trev's call earlier, not wanting to spoil their first morning together. Cynthia had struck twice today, and given the catastrophic fallout of her first attack, he had a bad feeling about the game she was playing with President Matthau.

"There's something I need to look into, and then I can tell you more," he said, cruising down Main Street.

She darted him a nervous look, and he had to lock his jaw not to spill everything. But she had enough to deal with right now, and his news would only make her feel worse.

The city streets were freshly shoveled, it looked like. They must have had a dusting of snow last night. The day was cold, but the sun was out. Some people were bundled up in winter coats while a few brave—or crazy— people were running around in nothing but long sleeves and shorts.

"We haven't had lunch," he said, eyeing the time. "I know it's close to three, but maybe we should grab some takeout. I could call that clown again and have him juggle while we have a sandwich. What do you think?"

She made a soft sound before replying, "I couldn't eat anything."

"Okay," he said, hoping his stomach wouldn't grumble.

His body always let him know when it needed to be fed, whether he had an appetite or not. He wanted to mother-hen Caroline, but he didn't want to push her. Not now.

"Do you want to come back to my house?" he asked. "Trev will make himself scarce. Unless you want him to express his outrage for you."

"I'll have plenty of that since I called both of my sisters on my way home from work. I told them to spread the word."

"I hope they kick my ass," he said, wishing it would make him feel better if they did.

"I told you that it's not your fault," she said. "Now, why don't you drop me off at my mom's house? I think…"

Her voice broke for the first time all day. Her numbness was wearing off. Man, he felt like shit.

"Your mother's it is," he said, turning off the main drag for Aspen Street.

He knew where everyone in the extended Hale clan lived, and they'd been great to him. Would they feel differently now that he'd hurt Caroline, even if inadvertently? Then he realized Jill Hale would know. They called her the town crier in the family, and for good reason. She liked to talk, but since she was so funny and cheerful, no one seemed to mind.

When he pulled into April Hale's driveway, he gripped the wheel, trying to control his emotions. They'd just become intimate, and here he was, dropping her off at her mom's house to get some TLC because his ex-wife had gotten her fired. What a bunch of—

"Hey," she said softly. "Your ears are red, and you look about to explode."

He wanted to gulp in air, but that would be obvious. "It's you I'm worried about. Caroline—"

"No," she said, putting her hand on his arm. "Stop the self-recriminations and guilt. I…can't take it right now. I don't blame you, and you shouldn't blame you. I'm going to go in. I'll...ah...call you later. Okay?"

When she leaned over to kiss him on the cheek, he got a hold of himself and took her in his arms.

"I love you," he said against her hair. "Remember that."

"And I you," she said, forcing a smile when she pulled away and exited the car.

He helped her with the suitcase she'd packed and almost jumped out of his skin when he felt a hand on his back.

Turning, he saw April Hale standing there with sad blue eyes, her other hand on her daughter's back. Then the two were hugging, and he stood silently watching, letting the cold wind blow over him.

The scene made him think of his own family. His marriage and divorce had hurt some of his most treasured relationships. His father was still disappointed in him while a couple of his siblings were angry he'd let a woman they disapproved of get close enough to hurt everything they'd worked for. Trev was his only constant, likely because he was so mule-headed.

He'd hoped to forge a new life here in Dare Valley, to leave all of the old hurts behind, but they'd followed him as surely as his shadow.

"I'll see you later," Caroline said, and then she and her mother went inside together while he stood there, helpless, and watched.

He got back in his car and sped all the way home, needing to open up the road a little to expend some frustration.

When he pulled into the garage and went into the house, he pulled out his phone and saw that Uncle Arthur had called him. Had he heard the news too? Of course he had.

Trev was waiting for him in the kitchen when he

came into the house. "You look like someone sucker punched the everlasting crap out of you."

"You should see the other guy," he joked and then pinched the bridge of his nose. "I got her fired."

"No, Sin City did that," Trev said, planting his giant feet in front of him. "I knew you were going to take this on. Man, this is not your fault. It's hers. I'm not saying this doesn't suck colossal balls, but you need to keep your chin up."

He rose and looked at his brother. "Trev, we just slept together! And it was wonderful. The best night of my life. And now this! How is Caroline going to be able to...trust me now? Everything around me gets hurt."

Trev shook him. "Stop this! You and I have had some pretty bad days, and this is certainly one of them. But what do we always do?"

He'd always appreciated his brother using "we" when he talked like this. "We get back up."

"And we fight back," Trev said in a hard tone. "Go hit something for a while or go for a run or whatever, but get it out. Look, Caroline was planning on leaving her job anyway. Does it suck that it was like this and earlier than planned? Yeah. But let's keep our eyes on the prize. We need to figure out what Sin City is up to with the university president and stop her."

"I love her, Trev. I told her this morning. From the moment I laid eyes on her at the gallery... I told Grandpa Emmits she was the one." Somehow he'd known he could tell his grandpa his most secret thoughts.

"You've been talking to ghosts?" Trev said, looking over his shoulder in the direction of the den, where the painting hung. "That creeps me out. How long has this been going on?"

"I've been talking to his *painting,*" J.T. said, feeling compelled to point out the difference. "You know how much I admire him. And when I was...depressed during the divorce and visiting the house in Napa, I'd get drunk in the office and talk to him. It...made me feel better."

Trevor went scary still.

"Do you think that's weird?" he asked.

"No, I think that's just the kind of thing you'd do," his brother said slowly. "You always used to imagine what the people in portraits were thinking, what their lives were like."

Sensitive, his mother had said at times. Maybe she was right. "The museum was my new dream. Then I met Caroline—"

"And you hoped to ride off into the sunset with her," Trev said. "I get it, J.T. Although you suck on horseback. Remember that time we were supposed to go riding in Napa?"

"The horse licked me. What can I say?" He pointed to his suit. "I was particular about my clothes even then. Didn't want horse spit all over them. Good of you to remind me."

His brother smiled. "Just keeping it real."

No, Trev was trying to keep him afloat, just like he always did. A wave of gratitude helped displace some of his despair. "Thanks."

"All right, enough of this walk down horse-spit lane. We have a problem, and we need some help. Have you called Uncle Arthur yet?"

"No, I didn't have the time. But he called me."

"He showed up here too, with Meredith, but I told him the four of us should talk together. I suggested he run an errand or get some coffee at Don't Soy With Me until you got here. Do you know what he said?"

J.T. expected it was a doozy.

Trev smiled. "He didn't like froufrou coffee laced with raspberries and topped with whipped cream like a fruit salad. He's a hoot. Why don't you call him, J.T., or do I have to do everything? Maybe you need to confer with Grandpa's painting?"

He snorted. "I guess cleaning up isn't on your to-do list," J.T. said, pointing to the kitchen counter. "Couldn't you throw away your pizza box?"

"At least I got rid of all the strippers I had over," he said deadpan. "Call him and put him on speaker."

J.T. shrugged out of his jacket and did just that. Uncle Arthur picked up on the first ring, his growl audible.

"It's about damn time," he barked. "Did you have high tea with the queen or something?"

"I was driving Caroline back," he said. "She—"

"Got fired because of your punk-ass ex-wife," he finished, causing Trevor to laugh. "Why do you think I showed up to talk to Trevor?" He mumbled something J.T. couldn't make out. "Meredith said to ask if we could come over, now that we've finished twiddling our thumbs. You took long enough that Tanner's free to come too."

"Are you planning on dressing me down in front of witnesses?" He was joking. Kind of.

"Dress you down? Boy, I'm trying to help you with this Sin City woman."

"Come over then. Bring a guillotine if you like."

"Guillotine, my ass," he heard the older man growl and then the line went dead.

"I love him," Trev said, shaking his head in apparent delight. "I want to be that spry and ornery when I'm that age."

Thirty minutes later, the trio of reporters was standing in the kitchen while Trevor made everyone coffee. Well, everyone except Uncle Arthur, who'd complained he'd never sleep if he had another cup of joe.

J.T.'s stomach grumbled, and Uncle Arthur lowered his gaze to stare at it.

"You swallow some wooly mammoth in Denver?"

he asked, pulling out a handful of red hots and passing them around. "All right, feed your monster while I tell you what Meredith and I learned."

Trevor threw him a banana, and since J.T. had noticed Uncle Arthur was leaning heavily on his cane, he suggested they all sit down in the den. The older man grumbled, but J.T. heard him sigh when he sat down and rested his cane by his knee. His eyes tracked to the painting of Grandpa Emmits hanging above the fireplace, and his gaze lingered there for a moment before he shifted it to J.T. There was fire there.

"You have any paintings stolen by the Nazis in this collection of yours? Can't say I imagine Emmits would ever buy anything fishy, but from what I understand, folks don't always know what they have. Forged bills of sale and the like are common enough."

J.T. had to choke down the last of the banana. "That's her line?" he asked, throwing the peel on the coffee table because he needed to throw something. "Of all the—"

"No need for antics, boy. A simple yes or no will do."

J.T. crossed his arms. "Sorry, it's been a bad day. No, we don't have any stolen Nazi paintings. Give me some credit."

Uncle Arthur narrowed his eyes. "You sure? There's never been any accusation or—"

"We had one, we discovered," he said. "I had our lawyers locate the family, and we returned it. So she's making accusations, is she? What have you been hearing?"

"It's early yet, and I've only been on this for a little over an hour, but it's not good," Uncle Arthur said, looking over at Meredith, who was standing next to her husband with her arms crossed.

"I don't have any first-hand information, mind you," Arthur said, "but it seems President Matthau has asked a couple of art history professors I know to look into the provenance of the paintings in the Merriam collection to see if any were stolen by the Nazis."

J.T. stood up. "This is incredible! I would never, *ever* keep a painting I knew belonged to someone else. Certainly not a stolen one. We returned that painting the minute—"

"Calm down, J.T.," Trev said, kicking out his feet. "This is how she works. She probably suggested you got caught and *had* to do the right thing. And if there was one dirty painting, maybe there are more. Would the university want to take the chance? It's bad press and all that."

Oh, how the spider spins her web. Trev was right. He could almost hear her boarding school accent laying it on thick, so cultured and so very convincing. "But I have the provenance! Doesn't President Matthau know she's my ex-wife? Obviously she's interested in frying my balls."

"Eww," Meredith said. "Thanks for the image. Yes, I imagine President Matthau knows exactly who she is. Certainly the art professors Grandpa visited are aware. I imagine she's telling Matthau she's privy to secrets no one else knows."

"Exactly," Tanner agreed. "She probably claimed she spilled the beans out of a guilty conscience, because she's a philanthropist and art lover herself. Blah-blah-blah."

"You don't even know her, and you're already onto her game," J.T. said.

"Dirt is dirt," Tanner said.

Yeah, it sure as hell was. He sank back onto the couch. "Why not ask me for the provenance directly? The board of trustees never asked for it under the old president."

"Because this Matthau fellow doesn't know or trust you," Uncle Arthur said. "This museum wasn't his baby, you see. He's inheriting it from his predecessor, one he didn't like, mind you."

"They didn't get along?" J.T. asked. "I didn't know that."

"It's not openly talked about," Uncle Arthur said. "They were at Oxford for a summer at the same time, I heard, and things didn't go swimmingly. They've had a long-time feud over faculty tenure positions and grant money. Some say President Matthau only took this job as a FU to his old rival when he left. Petty, if you ask me."

"But it's done all the time," Tanner said gravely. "Arthur thinks I should interview you about this. As a former war correspondent, I've written about stolen art before. That way, it'll be on record, and we start to head off some of the crap she's saying on the back end."

"Happy to go on record," J.T. said.

"Any other thoughts on what she might say?" Tanner asked.

"If it's vile, she'll say it."

Uncle Arthur growled. "She won't say you hit her or anything, will she?"

The words physically jolted him. That possibility had never occurred to him. "God, I..."

"She hasn't attempted anything like that since J.T. filed for divorce," Trev said, "so no, I don't think she'll go that far. There wouldn't be a lick of evidence, and we'd sue the hell out of her for defamation."

"You've thought about this?" he asked his brother.

Trev's mouth was hard. "Of course we did. We had to think of every way she could hurt you, and unfortunately, this is one of the ways some people try to malign a former spouse in a divorce."

"Pisses me off since domestic abuse is such a serious problem," Meredith said. "When people falsely accuse others, they... It's not right. It's just not right."

"So she's making me out to be a war profiteer instead?" he asked. "Lucky me."

"It's codswallop," Uncle Arthur said, "so we'll do our part to print the truth. Even if we can't directly call her a liar, you'll look noble, above reproach, and that is needed right now. When are you going to make the formal announcement about the museum? Hard to print the article before that happens."

"I'm supposed to get back in touch with the university's public relations office," he said. "We agreed the announcement shouldn't be too close to the one about my donation to Evan Michaels' company."

It was ironic, really. He'd given away five hundred million dollars, his payout for his Merriam shares and holdings, and it didn't seem to matter. Cynthia just kept coming.

"J.T.," Meredith said softly. "How are you doing really? It must have been horrible, hearing what she'd done to Caroline."

He squeezed his eyes shut for a moment, unable to speak.

Someone else cleared their voice, and he thought he recognized Uncle Arthur's cough.

"Don't go blaming yourself," the older man rasped. "It's wasted energy."

"That seems to be the consensus," J.T. said, "and I know it."

"But it still feels like shit," Tanner said simply.

"Yes," he said honestly, "yes, it does." He opened his eyes and rubbed them with his hand. "I...really appreciate you helping me. I..."

"Well, of course we are," Uncle Arthur said, standing up. "You're family, and we circle the wagons and fight until our last breath if that's what it takes. Emmits would have done the same for any of us."

When the older man dropped his hand on J.T.'s shoulder, he could feel himself getting emotional. Man, it was good to have people care about him. Rally around him.

"I don't want you to get hurt, Uncle Arthur," he said, looking at everyone. "Or any of you."

Uncle Arthur tapped his cane on the ground. "We don't give in to bullies. Now, before everyone starts to blubber, we're going to leave. I have a few more calls to make, and Tanner and Meredith need to wrap up so they can get home to their son."

Tanner crossed the room, and J.T. rose and shook his hand. "Thank you."

"Like Arthur said, we circle the wagons."

Meredith kissed his cheek. "You keep your spirits up, okay?"

"Trying," he said. Maybe he should call the clown for himself. Hah.

Uncle Arthur looked at him. "Don't make me pat you on the head and kiss your cheek. But if you need something, you call me. I'll keep digging."

"I have a pretty big shovel out back," Trev said, putting his arm around the older man in a way J.T. knew was designed to support his weight without looking like it.

"Mine's bigger," Uncle Arthur said, "as is something else."

Trev barked out a laugh. "You still make dick jokes?"

"Oh, good Lord," Meredith said. "I'll be in the car."

"Back when our knuckles dragged on the ground," Uncle Arthur said, grabbing his cane, "poor guys with small winkies were eaten by buffalos or something while big guys like me were the ones who got the girl and made fire."

"You aren't that old, Uncle." J.T. found himself laughing, a miracle. "Did Grandpa Emmits and you used to joke like this?"

Uncle Arthur's gaze tracked to the painting again, an amused smile touching his lips. "Wouldn't you love to know?"

Yes, he certainly would.

Somehow the thought of Uncle Arthur scheming

with his great-grandfather lightened his mood. He looked back at the painting, wishing he really could talk to the
man.

Surely Grandpa Emmits would know what to do now.

CHAPTER 12

CAROLINE WAS GOING TO TEAR IT UP A LITTLE TONIGHT, AND she was glad Moira and Jill could join her last-minute at Hairy's pub.

All her life, she'd played it safe. Worked hard. Smiled in the face of grouchy and entitled clients. And for what? She'd been fired after faithfully serving her boss for five years. Tonight she was going to get a little crazy. It wasn't like she had to get up in the morning to go to work. Hairy's was the place to be if you asked her. Besides, the St. Patrick's Day decorations were still dangling from the ceiling, and some of the banners were amusing.

Okay, the one right in front of her was gross—*Don't fart in an Irishman's direction or he'll fire one back at you*—but the crazy-eyed leprechaun to her right appealed to her. *When you can't find a rainbow, don't blame me*, he proclaimed. *Paint your own.*

Self-help from the little people. Why not?

"Let's do something different tonight," she called out, going for bravado over the aching regret in her heart. "Tequila for everyone."

"You're a lightweight in the *wine* department, Caroline," Moira said, studying her face like she was their doctor brother, Andy, checking out a patient. "Do you think shots are a good idea?"

"I like where she's headed," Jill said. "I just need a responsible ride home. Yo, barkeep! Three tequilas. Lime. Salt. The whole setup."

"Jill, you've known me my whole life," the bartender said when he appeared in front of them. "Stop calling me barkeep."

"Okay, Mikey," she drawled, blowing him kisses. Mike rolled his eyes, but Caroline didn't miss the grin that went along with the dismissive gesture.

"I don't know about this," Moira said. "What's Mom going to think when you stumble home? I'm so going to get busted."

"Nah," Jill said, dancing in place like she was wont to do. "There are some occasions where shots are appropriate. Encouraged even. It's not every day your boyfriend's ex-wife gets you fired."

True that.

"Besides, this way, we can get away with dancing on the bar. Just watch."

Dancing on the bar? She'd never done that before, but what girl hadn't watched *Coyote Ugly* and secretly dreamed?

"I need those shots," Jill said, slapping her hand on the bar. "It's Mommy's night out. We're going to cheer you up, Caroline."

Mike finally laid out their spread. After one shot, Caroline was feeling downright cheery. Who wanted to work for a witch like Kendra anyway? Much better to be here, in Hairy's, humming along to the dirty Irish ditty Jill was belting out about a red-haired lass with a bowlegged frame.

"Another round of shots!" Jill declared.

Caroline had leaned forward to grab one when she felt a tap on her shoulder and looked around to see her two brothers, Matt and Andy.

"You let her drink shots?" Andy asked her fellow partygoers.

Caroline hugged them. "Hey! I didn't think you guys could come tonight. Mike, my bros need shots."

"No, we don't," Andy said. It struck her that he didn't seem very invested in the spirit of things. In fact, he looked downright worried. His expression reminded her a little bit too much of what J.T. had looked like earlier.

"Mo, what were you thinking?" Matt added, going full Matty Ice.

"Caroline wanted to," Moira said, clutching Andy's jacket playfully. "And then Jill ganged up on me."

Jill crossed her eyes and downed her second shot of tequila. "Oh, be a good girl and own up to your own decisions, Moira. Caroline wanted tequila, so we're having tequila. It's the drink of breakups and getting fired."

Which was why Caroline had suggested it even though she wasn't much of a drinker. According to country music, tequila *was* the go-to for tough times. "I wanted the shots, boys," Caroline admitted and then burped. "Oh, my goodness. I didn't know shots could do that."

Mike was laughing as he pulled a Guinness for another customer. Well, at least someone was entertained.

"Probably because your stomach lining isn't used to hard liquor," Andy said, picking up the second shot and taking a whiff. "Well, at least it's the good stuff."

"I'd never give someone who got fired the bad stuff, Andy Cakes," Moira said, poking him in the chest. "Oh, might as well. Down the hatch." She took the shot from Andy and downed it in one go. Jill applauded. Caroline joined in. Oh, this was fun.

"Yay!" Jill called out. "We're starting to have a party!"

Yes! A party! That was what she wanted. "This is a... celebration," she said, lifting her second shot in the air. "Of my freedom from tyranny and oppression. Kendra was a big...poop in the end." She felt a splash of liquid on her hand and realized part of her drink had sloshed out. "Oops. Down the hatch."

"Oh, good Lord," Matty Ice mumbled. "Caroline, you're already wasted, and it's only seven."

He was such a fuddy duddy. She wondered if his wife knew. Where was Jane? Oh, who cared? This floating feeling was so nice. She leaned back on her barstool and felt someone strong come up behind her. Oh, she knew that body. And that cologne.

Turning on her barstool, she wrapped her arms around J.T "Hi there, big boy! I can't wait to get you naked again," she murmured.

Oops. Trevor was standing right beside him with a grin as wide as the Cheshire Cat's.

"Big boy?" Trevor said, his shoulders shaking.

Ignoring him, she grinned at J.T. "I kinda like that name. From now on I will call you Big Boy instead of J.T. Did you bring the clown?"

"Ah, no." He only grimaced a little before leaning in to kiss her cheek. "You went with tequila, eh? Well, if that's the way you want to go, I'm all in. Trev?"

"Only if I can call you Big Boy too," he said, earning himself a glare. "I'll ask about the clown later."

Caroline laughed, soaking in the fun. "We should do this more often. And I can because...hey, I've got no job. I'm unemployed. I'm—"

"Headed for the loony bin," Matty Ice said after putting a finger over her lips. "Maybe Big Boy and I should step outside for a minute."

"*Matt...*" Andy said, placing a hand on their brother's shoulder.

"If you guys want to deck me for sleeping with your sister or getting her fired," Big Boy said, "we can go outside right now. I'll probably be able to get up easier before I do shots."

She shifted in her stool. "Why would they hit you?

I wanted to sleep with you, Big Boy. Haha. Anyway, it's *so* not your business, Andy Cakes and Matty Ice. I'm an adult."

Then she burped again and laughed. Well, mostly an adult.

Her brothers exchanged a look, and she wanted to sock them for putting a damper on the night. Again. "Don't be so serious. If I'm not mad, you shouldn't be."

"We'll save that talk for later—should it become necessary," Matty Ice said, never breaking that frown of his. "Oh, Jesus, Jill, please don't get on the bar. I love you, but you're a bad influence."

Mike held out his hands as she crawled up from her barstool and stood. "Jill, you get down from there!"

She shook her head emphatically. "Time to dance," she said, starting to shake her booty to the delight of the other patrons, who started whistling and clapping. "Come on, Caroline. Are you a liberated woman or not?"

"Totally liberated!" she said, disentangling herself from J.T. "What happened to your lips? You look like you're biting them."

"He's trying not to laugh, sweetheart," Trevor said, holding out a hand. "Here. Let me help you up onto the bar so you can dance too."

J.T. elbowed him.

"What?" Trev asked. "Sometimes you have to get it out of your system."

Strong arms helped her up, and then Jill was grabbing her hands and twisting her hips. "What ya got, Shorty?"

She didn't know who this Shorty was. How drunk was Jill? "I'm Caroline, and I've got plenty."

Someone barked out a laugh—a really nice one—and she looked down to see Trevor giggling like a school kid, his arm around J.T. Ah, they loved each other. It was so sweet.

The Irish music continued to blast from the speakers, and then the barkeep Mike was next to them, yelling for them to get down.

"Mike!" Jill said to him. "Come dance with us. We need a man up here."

"That's enough," the barkeep called. "Harry is going to bust my balls for letting you pull this."

"Not finished with my *Coyote Ugly*," Caroline said, letting go of her hands and turning to face the crowd.

"You want more?" Jill called out. "Come on, give it up for Mamacita and Carlita."

People called out colorful responses, making Caroline laugh. "Am I Carlita?" she asked.

Jill nodded as she did the salsa. Caroline—no, *Carlita*—matched her steps, pausing for just look enough to reach out a hand to her sister. "Come on, Mo. You can tell your grandkids about this someday."

Her sister gave Andy and Matt a look before hopping onto the stool and joining them on the bar.

"Yay! Oh, I love you guys," she said.

Mo gave a good wiggle of her hips, and she followed suit.

"Now, that's what I'm talking about," Jill, aka Mamacita, said. "Okay, ladies, lock arms and kick those legs."

She watched as Jill started to imitate the Rockettes, and soon she and Mo had fallen into a rhythm with her. J.T. seemed to be hovering as she kicked, his hands ready to catch her if she fell.

"I've already fallen," she told him. "Head over heels for *you*, Big Boy."

Trev turned to his brother and fitted his hands into a heart. Her big boy shoved him, but there was a little smile on his lips.

The music stopped mid-beat, and Mike clapped his hands. "All right. Show's over. Ladies, if you'd get down now, please. You don't want my boss to fire me, do you?"

"Oh, Harry would never fire you," Mamacita said, hopping down with Andy's help. "I would talk him out of it. Besides, my doctor cousin here is married to his daughter."

"You're trouble with red hair in the best way," Trev said. "I think I'm in love."

"Too late," Mamacita said, holding out her left hand. "Already hitched. Have a family."

He was laughing, and it was so contagious Caroline started laughing too. Soon they all were. Well, all except for her wet blanket brothers and J.T.

"Mamacita is a catch for sure," she told Trevor as both of the Merriam brothers helped her down. "But she's already been caught."

"Then I'll have to settle for friendship," Trevor said. "I need someone like you around to lighten things up."

Mamacita dug into her purse. "Here's my card. Call me any time."

Caroline burst out laughing again. "But you already *know* each other."

"But we've moved on to the uber stage of our friendship," Mamacita said. "Trevor, my darling, since you appear quite sober, could you take me home to my one and only?"

"Be happy to," he said, linking their arms. Turning to the Hale brothers, he asked, "You guys got Moira?"

Matty Ice dug out a coin and flipped it. "Heads or tails, bro."

"Tails," Andy called.

When Matty looked at the coin, he cursed. "Okay, I'll see her home. J.T., I assume you have Caroline?"

"Oh, he has me," she purred, nuzzling into his warm body. "And our names are Carlita and Big Boy, remember? Maybe I can stay with you tonight, honey. My mom's going cluck like a hen when she sees me."

J.T. and Trevor were both trying not to laugh, but her brothers still had their fuddy duddy hats on.

"Oh, will you stop looking at each other like I'm crazy? I had some fun and danced on a bar. I feel great. Really."

"I'll bet," Andy said. "Hopefully, you'll feel the same way in the morning. If not, take an aspirin and drink lots of water. I'm going home. Good luck with Mo, Matt."

"I'm totally fine," her sister insisted, a claim that was immediately debunked when she stumbled as she reached down for her purse. "My tequila was defective or something."

"At least you're not as bad as Natalie," Andy said. "Good thing she's pregnant or she would have been out here drinking and dancing 'til Hairy's closed. Later, Merriam."

"Should I really take her back to your mom's?" J.T. asked Andy. "Like this?"

"Why are you asking him?" she said, pushing away from him. "I told you. I want to go home with *you.*"

He gazed at her for so long she started to see two of him.

"Hang on. I know what this is about."

She climbed onto the barstool again and felt strong arms supporting her.

"Everybody! Hey, everybody."

The bar went quiet. There were so many faces, two of each in some cases.

"I know this is a small town and people talk, so let's cut to the chase. I've slept with Big Boy here. That's J.T. Merriam to those of you who don't know him. And I plan to do it *a lot more.* You have a problem with that, that's your problem."

Strong hands pulled her off the barstool. "I can't believe you just did that," Big Boy said. "We are so out of here."

"And you say you're cos-*mo*-politan," she said as he led her through the crowd to the front door. "Stuffed shirt more like it."

"Way to go, Caroline!" someone called out.

"Good for you, honey," another woman said. "He's prime meat."

"I'm standing right here," J.T. mumbled, opening the door. His cheeks had turned an adorable red.

"He's sensitive," she told them, pointing to her nose. "I didn't know. Oh, you have your car. Man, I can't wait to sleep with you in your bed. We slept in mine so it's only fair. How is Trevor getting home? Gosh, I really like him."

"Trev and I thought I might be staying longer so we both drove," he said, leading her to it. "Okay, we'll head to my place. That way I can take care of you."

"Ah...sensitive and sweet. No wonder I love you."

He helped her into the passenger side, and she cuddled into the soft leather. After he clicked on his own seatbelt and helped her with hers, he gave her a look and started the engine.

"You're a constant surprise."

She was? Awesome. "It smells so good in here," she said, the floating feeling surrounding her like a warm blanket. "Like leather and musk and you. Thanks for coming to my *I got fired* celebration, Big Boy."

"Celebration, my ass," he muttered. "It's my fault this happened."

"Not entirely," she said. "But having that bitch of an ex-wife *certainly* isn't helping anything. Is she ever going to go away?" Her eyelids were getting heavy, so she leaned back into the seat more, trying to get comfortable. "God I hope so. Because I would hate to have her around all the time, trying to ruin our happiness."

He laid his hand on her leg and rubbed it. "Me too. Close your eyes, Carlita. I'll drive you home."

Home. "I like that word. Never had one with a guy before."

"Me either."

She laughed at his joke. "I hope not, Big Boy, but with that name..."

"Oh, good Lord... Take a nap, Caroline."

"Okay," she muttered, too tired to tell him that wasn't her name tonight.

She closed her eyes and saw a picture of her and Big Boy walking together in the sunshine, holding the hands of a little girl between them.

Yeah, home.

CHAPTER 13

THE SUN WAS SHINING BRIGHTLY THROUGH THE BAY window in the kitchen nook, and all J.T. wanted to do was mope.

Caroline was still sleeping, but he couldn't shake the thought that she'd gotten wasted and acted out of character last night, and it was all his fault. Given the small-town gossip circuit, he would wager everyone knew about them. Normally that wouldn't bother him, but he'd hoped to share the news in a more dignified way. Big Boy hadn't been it. It would serve him right if she woke up angry and full of regret.

Surely there was something he could do to cheer Caroline up. Heck, cheering wasn't enough. He needed to do something grand. Trev had teased him but good about the balloons and clown, saying no movie hero worth his salt would have gotten the girl with that. What would? He wracked his brain. Poetry? God, he sucked at making things rhyme. Then he found himself thinking again of his grandparents' letters. Man, those two could write. Their letters were practically poetry, if you asked him.

Wait!

He could ask his mom to send the original letters. They were as cherished to the family as Grandpa Emmits' painting. He reached for his phone on the kitchen table and texted his mom since it would stave off other questions.

His mother's reply was freaky. She'd always had a sixth sense, likely from her Irish roots. *Caroline Hale must be some girl for you to ask for them. I'll overnight them. Next time you bring her to Napa, your father and I won't be giving you space, FYI. In fact, come soon. I miss you, kiddo.*

Crap. He missed her too. *As soon as things settle here. Love you.*

Her reply was immediate. *Don't let Cynthia mess things up anymore. Remember who you are. Love you.*

He squeezed his eyes shut. So she knew the latest. Heck, hadn't he known Trev kept everyone informed on some level? Shit! His life before Cynthia had been so much less complicated.

"Damn, these cinnamon rolls are good," J.T. heard Trevor say as he came in from the garage carrying a pastry box. "Evan's Margie has a good thing going with that bakery. It was already packed. Has *Carlita* made an appearance yet? Man, she and Jill were hilarious last night. I'd pay weekly for a show like that."

He thought about asking his brother how the rest of the family had reacted to the news that Cynthia was still coming for him, but he didn't have it in him. "You're not making me feel any better."

His brother slapped him on the backside of his head.

"Hey!" he said, rubbing the sting.

"Stop moping! You look like you put your dog to sleep. What happened to Caroline was a shock, I'll grant you that, but I need you in fighting shape. Sin City has come with her A-game. What ya got, Big Boy? From where I'm standing, she's already put you down."

"Call me Big Boy again and I'll put *you* down." He scowled. "Give me one of those cinnamon rolls."

"That's what I'm talking about. Why do you think I got all pretty and went to the bakery? I had to get my bro some special carbs."

"Ha. Ha. You know, Trev, sometimes you're a pain in the ass."

His brother laughed and then popped another bite of cinnamon roll in his mouth. "Only sometimes. Besides you know I'm right. *Big Boy*."

"You're a dead man," he said, rising from his chair.

Trevor darted back like he was about to run. J.T. had every intention to chase him, only a discreet cough stopped him. He turned and saw Caroline standing in the doorway of the living room, yesterday's clothes good and wrinkled, her cheeks a fetching pink.

"Morning, sunshine," Trev said.

J.T. shot him a look. All he wanted to do was sweep her up in his arms, but he was hesitant. Surely she had to be having second thoughts about him. Them. Any normal person would after what she'd been through.

"I couldn't be more embarrassed," she said, pressing a hand to her temple.

"Oh, please don't be," Trevor said, crossing the kitchen and pouring her a cup of coffee. "J.T. and I once woke up in Rome with a whole gaggle of women in togas and didn't know how we'd ended up with them."

J.T. made a cutting motion to his neck—*seriously, Trev?*—and finally let himself walk over to her. She wouldn't meet his eyes. Not a good sign.

"Ignore him," he said. "My mom swears she left him at the edge of the forest, hoping the wolves would take him like Mowgli, but even they were too smart for that."

Trevor shook his head as he sauntered over and handed Caroline the cup of coffee he'd poured. "That's a good one, man. All right, I'll leave you two alone for a while. Caroline, if you want me to make you a hair of the dog, give me a shout. I have a never-fail recipe that has gotten me through a lot of vodka matches with our Russian colleagues."

J.T. led Caroline over to a chair at the kitchen table. He closed the shades so the sunlight wasn't beaming down on her like a spotlight, then sat opposite her. "Sun and hangovers don't mix."

"I can't believe I did shots," she said, gripping the handle of her coffee mug. "It seemed like such a good idea at the time."

"Usually does."

"I feel like I'm on a boat during a storm on the Atlantic or something. Everything inside is wobbly."

"At least there are no icebergs in sight," he said, wanting to reach for her hand. "Bad joke. Sorry. What can I do to help? Although Trev's right. He does make a better hair of the dog than me."

"Does it involve a raw egg?" she asked, sipping her coffee tentatively.

"At least one," he said, not wanting to tell her the rest of the ingredients. She already looked sick at the thought.

"Then no thank you," she said politely. "Where did you sleep? Because I think I woke up in your bed. It smelled of you."

It warmed him to hear she knew his scent. He'd known hers since Rome, that alluring mix of citrus and flowers. "I bunked in the third bedroom. Trev offered the other side of his bed for old time's sake, but I still have nightmares from family vacations when he'd grind his teeth most of the night."

"The more I get to know him, the more I like him," she said. "He's a good brother. Do I remember him taking Jill home?"

"Yeah. Jill cranked his rap music all the way up in the car and sang her heart out the whole way. He would have paid for the performance, it was so funny."

"That's Jill," she said, shaking her head and then wincing. "She's what we call an instigator. Now I can check off dancing on the bar from my bucket list. Oh, God, what will my mother think? I'm never going to live this down. At least Moira was an accomplice. That's got to count for something. But it would have been better if Matt had participated. He has the longest memory of all my siblings."

So did his oldest brother, Connor, who managed the entire Merriam conglomerate now that their dad had retired. He'd thought J.T. negligent in his duty to protect the company, and they hadn't spoken much since he left his job. God, he'd hoped to mend fences once his divorce was done. Cynthia was upsetting his plans on that front too.

Now he had the Hale brothers to contend with. J.T. took a drink of coffee, remembering the way her brothers had looked at him, like they were trying to decide if he was good for her. The jury was still out if you asked him.

"I think the highlight was you announcing to the whole bar that we'd slept together and you planned to get me naked again."

She grimaced. "Yes, and me calling you Big Boy. God, I'm so sorry about that, J.T. It struck me as funny for some reason."

He tried to keep from laughing. "At least it was a flattering nickname. Personally, I can't wait to hear what Uncle Arthur says when I see him. Knowing him and his ability to find sources everywhere, I'm sure he's already heard about it."

"And yet, I awoke in my clothes," she said, gesturing to herself. "Thank you for that. I found it...sweet."

She'd called him that last night. He'd thought about undressing her to her underwear so she'd be more comfortable, but it had seemed...presumptuous, especially when she was in such a vulnerable position.

Sure, they'd been intimate, but only for one night. He felt like he was walking on eggshells.

"No guy should take advantage of a woman who's indulged a little too much. My dad raised us right." But his dad was still probably wondering what he'd done wrong with J.T. on other fronts, he thought cynically.

She gulped down her coffee, and he rose to pour her another cup. Her pallor could use some improving, and maybe the caffeine would help her head. He'd convinced her to swallow an aspirin last night, and hopefully that would help too. Of course, he'd had to send Trevor to go to the drugstore to buy some, because seriously, other than Dr. Andy Hale, who had aspirin in their medicine cabinet anymore? It wasn't like he had a heart condition.

Caroline stared into her cup. "Did I embarrass you last night? I mean, my behavior was—"

"Completely innocent and understandable," he said, setting the coffee carafe on the table between them. "Think nothing of it."

He'd already had two cups this morning, waiting to hear more news about Cynthia's plans, but there was no more information. Trev had urged patience, but he found he didn't have much left. Part of him wanted to march into The Grand Mountain Hotel and demand to see her. Have it out. Not just for him but for Caroline too. But that would be the worst thing he could do. It would only give her more ammunition.

Then he realized he was thinking about his ex and not the beautiful woman in front of him. Like Trev—and now his mother—kept telling him, he needed to stop focusing on the past, even though Cynthia kept trying to beat him in the face with it.

"Are you feeling as awkward as I am?" he asked, deciding to call it out there.

Her lips tipped into a slight smile. "Yes, because I really need a toothbrush, and I didn't want to use yours."

He was silent for a moment, and then he reached his hand out to her. "You can always use my toothbrush, Caroline."

She looked up. Finally. Her eyes were bloodshot, but at least she was looking at him. She didn't hesitate to take his hand, thank God. "Why does that make me want to cry?"

"Trev would say it's probably because a monkey wouldn't use my toothbrush, but—"

She smiled. Sure, it took a moment, but it was like the sun appearing. "Ah, there it is."

"What?"

"A smile," he said. "I feel like shit too, but for different reasons."

She turned her coffee cup in a half circle before saying, "I know. I could see it on your face when I stopped at the doorway. Is there a hair of the dog to cure guilt?"

He laughed despite himself. "Trev probably has one with bitters in it. Nothing says guilt like bitters. Shit, I'm babbling. Are we okay? I honestly—"

"Gold Digger" started to play, interrupting him. His whole body tensed, and Caroline's hand jerked in his. Their eyes met, and the look in hers—like a wounded animal—made him want to hit something. Dammit!

"You should take that," she said slowly. "Maybe she'll tell you her coordinates so you can send in some really scary clowns."

"Why hadn't I thought of that?" he asked, making himself laugh at her attempt at humor.

He grabbed his phone from the table. Trev suddenly appeared on the stairs, his supersonic hearing clueing him in. His mouth was grim, but he didn't say a word. Yeah, he knew J.T. had no choice but to pick up her call.

Part of him wanted to leave the kitchen—he didn't know how the call would go, and the last thing he wanted to do was upset Caroline—but he didn't want her to think he had anything to hide either, so he walked over to the doorway, still in view.

"Cynthia," he said. "I hear you're in Dare Valley. How nice, but honestly, I can't say that you're going to like it here. Too...ah...what's your word for it? Provincial."

Her laughter sounded like the tinkle of breaking glass. "Oh, but I'm loving my stay here so far. And I'm learning so much about small-town life. You know, Julian, I had a feeling you might be interested in Caroline Hale when I met her the other day at Leggett. She's your type, isn't she? Elegant. Nice. Likes art. I suppose she's...beautiful in a way, although she's nothing like me, of course."

Word travels fast, he thought. Well, it wasn't like they'd set out to hide it. He was proud to be with Caroline, and he wouldn't pretend otherwise.

"No, no one is like you. Cynthia, you need to stop this. I mean it."

"When I have you so on edge and protective? Oh, darling, no. The fun has only begun. I have to say, Caroline's boss became such an easy ally. All I need to do was drop a few hints."

Hints were her insidious way, he knew. She had a gift for charming people into doing and saying whatever she wanted. "You're going to pay for that." He knew it was the wrong thing to say, but he couldn't help himself.

"Ah...I have your protective side kicking up again, don't I? Don't make it too easy for me. Please, you know how I like a challenge."

Yes, she had in bed. She'd only acted interested in sex as a game, a power struggle for control. He hadn't recognized that in the beginning, but it hadn't ever worked for him. She hadn't liked that.

"I know you met with the university president, Cynthia. He's going to be unhappy when he realizes you've led him on a merry chase and wasted his time and his resources checking provenance that is well vetted."

"You think I don't have a game plan for all of this? Oh, my love, you're playing checkers and I'm eight moves ahead of you in chess. I heard Ms. Hale announced she's sleeping with you to a whole bar last night after doing shots. Goodness, shots! I thought she had more breeding than that, but then again...she was born here, wasn't she? J.T., even with her art background, you must know you're slumming."

You cold-hearted bitch. He thought again about leaving the kitchen, but one look at Caroline rooted him to the spot. "That's enough of that. I'll ask you again. Why are you calling?"

"To tell you that you made me very angry," she said, her voice almost a whisper. "I wondered who you would find after me. I knew it would upset me, but somehow I didn't realize how much. To think I loved you. I can't believe I married you. Gave myself to you—"

"On that we agree," he said, lowering his voice. "We've both hurt each other, but this needs to end."

"No," she said, her voice hard. "You haven't suffered enough."

He heard Trevor's loud boots slapping on the stairs. His brother was coming down to offer his support.

"And you're just continuing to stir up your own hurt," he said to Cynthia. "How is that a smart thing?"

Trev stood in front of him, arms crossed. He looked about ready to grab the phone and lob it across the room.

"My parents started sending me to a psychiatrist when I was ten, Julian," she said. "Panic attacks at boarding school were frowned upon. Trust me. Therapy doesn't give us the sense of wholeness we're all searching for. Revenge does. Oh, I should write a self-help book."

He knew her sob story. At one time, he'd felt compassion for the little girl who'd battled anxiety and then anorexia after being shuffled off to boarding school at six. "I'm sure it will be a bestseller. I'm hanging up,

Cynthia. When you call like this, I sometimes think it's only to hear my voice."

Trevor's brows flew to his hairline. Yeah, it had been a risky thing to say, but she was the one talking about emotions. Silence hung over the line. He knew he'd struck a nerve, but he felt no sense of victory.

"I'll be seeing you around town perhaps," she said. "Say hello to Caroline for me."

She hung up, and it was a good thing—he doubted he could have kept calm much longer. He felt a hand on his back, more like the brush of a butterfly than touch. Turning, he saw Caroline, her skin the color of skim milk.

"Are you—"

"I'm fine," he interrupted, wanting to storm out of the room and hit something. "Are you sure you don't want to sever all contact with me? Maybe you should think about it. Seriously."

Trevor didn't slap the back of his head this time, and for that, he was grateful. But his brother didn't leave them alone either.

"Is a deserted island looking good again?" Trev asked him, something he'd asked him over and over during the divorce.

"Yes," he admitted. "But it's like we said. We'd be bored after two days."

"And it would be depressingly devoid of beautiful women like Caroline here," Trev said, pulling him in with an arm.

"Actually, a deserted island sounds great right now," Caroline said, trying to inject some humor into her voice again. "I mean, I'm out of work currently. I have the time."

He seriously thought about it for a moment. The family jet could be fueled and ready to leave Denver in a couple hours. They could get away from it all together.

Walk on the beach holding hands. Swim naked amidst schools of tropical fish with turquoise and orange stripes. Make love under a white canopy until they were both spent.

But Cynthia would still find him.

She'd told him he would never escape her, and with her financial resources, he knew she was right.

Besides, the museum was still in jeopardy, and he needed to see this through. Caroline was counting on it—on him—and he didn't want to let down his great-grandfather's legacy either.

"No deserted islands for us today," Trev said. "The closest you're going to get is a fish tank. Strap your breastplate on, J.T., it's time to do battle. We're going to meet with the university's public relations people and get this press release out by the end of the day—even if I have to knock a few heads together to do it."

His brother clapped him on the back and strode back to the stairs.

Caroline stared at his retreating back with wide eyes. "He's...formidable, isn't he?"

"He likes to think he was a gladiator in the Colosseum." He touched her shoulder. "I'm sorry. I know I sound like a broken record, but I don't know what else to say."

She gestured to her front. "Don't you see it?"

"What?" He honestly had no idea what she meant.

"My breastplate," she said quietly.

His mind took a snapshot of her—though her clothes were wrinkled and she looked more bedraggled than usual, her eyes gleamed with conviction. In that moment, she reminded him of his grandma, who'd told her then war hero pen pal, Noah, she would never give up on him either. God, he couldn't wait to give Caroline those letters to read.

"How could I have missed it?" he said softly. If she

could be this brave, surely he could muster his own courage like his forefathers had done. "How's mine?"

She touched his shirt, sending a bolt of heat through him. He laid his hand over hers.

"Not too bad," she said. "Although not as big as your brother's, I would imagine."

"You were the one who called me Big Boy," he said, feeling a smile touch his lips. "Do me a favor and don't say that around Trev. He'd agree with you in a way that might make you blush."

She smiled too, and he was grateful they could share a moment of levity despite Cynthia. Despite the battle ahead.

"Of course, you could hold me for a moment too," she said softly. "That would be nice, I think."

He would send her home afterward, but right now they both needed this. He wrapped his arms around her, marveling again at how they fit together. "It's more than nice. Caroline..."

His throat closed, and he couldn't speak. God, he was getting emotional.

"I know, J.T."

Somehow, that was exactly what needed to be said.

CHAPTER 14

HER MOTHER DID CLUCK LIKE A HEN WHEN J.T. dropped her off later that morning, but Caroline decided to bask in the attention. Natalie swung by on her lunch hour to give her a hug and a pep talk, only once calling her Carlita. Even Andy and Matt stopped by to check on her. And then there was Moira...

She simply texted. *Hope you're good, Carlita. Tequila is the devil.*

Oh, it was nice to feel so supported even though she was twiddling her thumbs today. She hadn't been jobless since the summer after college ended, and the rest of the afternoon loomed large in front of her. With nothing pressing to do, she decided to take a walk in the mountains to consider her next steps.

It struck her that she didn't want to go back to Denver. Sure, she had an apartment there, and it wouldn't make sense for a newly unemployed woman to take on a second lease, but everyone she loved lived here. While she liked staying with her mother, it didn't seem like a long-term solution.

Her siblings had all offered her a place to stay, but they had their own lives, and she understood the need for privacy.

Later that afternoon, after she'd returned from her walk, someone rang the doorbell at her mom's house. Her mom was off getting her hair cut, so Caroline went to answer it.

"Hey, Caroline," her brother-in-law said to her. "I wanted to come by. Natalie filled me in on some stuff, and we have a proposition for you."

"You're going to pick me as your baby's godmother?"

He laughed. "I appreciate the strategy, but no. We wanted to invite you to stay in our guesthouse. It's mostly furnished finally, and I checked to make sure the paint smell was gone."

"I didn't know it was finished yet," she said, shock rolling through her. Her own place...

"We've been pushing to get it finished since my Once Upon a Dare guys plan to visit after the baby is born. It's best they don't bunk with us, especially after last time, what with the boa constrictor and someone hanging my underwear in a tree."

Caroline had heard the stories about his antics with his NFL-player friends. "I'm...speechless. I mean, I love Mom, but..."

"She has her own life," Blake said. "Plus, she's dating again."

Caroline was really happy about that—her mother deserved the best—but Blake was right. Her mom might have gentleman callers. Her brain threatened to overheat at the mere thought. "Good point."

"I know how important it is to feel like you have a place to get away to when things are in transition," Blake said. "What do you say?"

"I say yes!" She threw her arms around him. "You always were my favorite brother-in-law."

"When Moira marries Chase, you might have to change your tune so his feelings won't get hurt. What else do you need? I mean, we all want to do something, but everyone feels so helpless."

Leave it to Blake to call it out. Everyone said he excelled at the game because he played with pure emotion. "I'm asking myself that. Do you want to come in for a minute?"

He dug out a key and handed it to her. "Sure. Here you go. If you need anything, you're always welcome next door. Touchdown will be happy to see you."

Their dog was a sweetheart. "Thanks. What would you like to drink?"

"I hear tequila is probably out," he said, putting his arm around her. "You Hale women. I think Jill is the only one who can hold her liquor."

"Natalie said she was bright-eyed and bushy-tailed today when she called, except for Jill's ongoing campaign to get Chef T to poison J.T.'s ex."

Blake's arm tensed around her. "If she weren't a woman, I'd have my guys pay her a visit with me."

"I wish brute force would work," she said sadly. "Blake, I'm scared. For J.T. and for me."

He pulled her into his arms. "Of course you are. You haven't dealt with anyone this...evil. Do you want your job back? There are things you could do legally. Matt would be able to tell you better, of course."

He'd already mentioned it on his earlier visit.

"I don't want to work for Kendra anymore," she said. "I wasn't right in some ways, and neither was she, but it's over. My biggest concern is what's next. I mean, Cynthia seems dead set on stopping the museum."

"Yes, that's what I heard from Natalie," he said. "You're just going to have to let J.T. and his brother handle things. They strike me as very capable people. Chase told me he and Evan are locked and loaded if needed, and it seems Uncle Arthur and his crew have also put themselves in the fight. You've gotta trust them to handle her."

But that entailed putting her future in other people's

hands. "Now we're getting to my problem. I feel helpless. J.T. feels so guilty about what happened to me, and there's nothing I can do to reassure him. It's...hurting our relationship some." He hadn't touched her like he had during their one night together, and his hesitation spoke volumes.

Of course, it hadn't been more than forty-eight hours, but still, it felt like a lifetime.

"It's only natural for a man to want to protect the woman he loves, especially when an attack is coming from his camp, so to speak."

"So what should I do?" she asked. "Part of me wants to confront Cynthia, but it seems like that would only make things worse. When I met her, I...knew she wasn't... well, reasonable. She called J.T. again this morning. He didn't give me a rundown of what they talked about, but I know she mentioned me."

Blake smiled wryly. "Well, you did announce to everyone at the bar last night that you were sleeping with J.T."

She made a face. "Yes, in the light of day, that seems like a stupid move." But J.T. hadn't taken her to task about it, for which she was grateful.

"Might be good to get it out there in public," Blake said with a shrug. "I've found that things like that tend to get out eventually anyway."

Indeed. "I suppose I'm sad and scared, but I'm also... excited, I guess. Blake, J.T. is really wonderful. And the museum... I'll be the curator for a top-notch museum if everything goes to plan."

"I'm glad for you," he said. "For all of it. And I like what I've seen so far of J.T. We all do."

But her even-keel brother-in-law looked uncharacteristically worried. Join the club. "How about I leave Mom a note, and we trek on up to my new digs?"

"Where's your suitcase?" he asked.

She pointed to the spare room, and he headed down the hall to fetch it. It felt slightly surreal that she was, temporarily at least, moving to Dare Valley. But it also felt right.

Perhaps it was her bridge to a better life.

CHAPTER 15

J.T. COULDN'T BELIEVE WHAT HE WAS HEARING.

Emmits Merriam University President David Matthau had earned himself a new nickname if you asked J.T.: Dr. Slimeball. Sure, the man might have a PhD and a bunch of academic awards, but he should have been wearing gold chains and an open shirt and hocking Pintos at a used car dealership.

How had he and Trevor not seen the man's greasy demeanor before? Perhaps because they hadn't interacted with him much. There had been an introductory phone call, sure, followed by a brief lunch when he'd arrived in Dare Valley two weeks ago, but that was it.

"I'm sure you understand our family is eager to share the wonderful news of the museum with the world," Trev was saying, his ankle on his knee.

His brother looked casual, but a funny thing about Trev was that he looked the most relaxed when he was gathering energy for an attack. Yeah, they both knew they were being stonewalled. The university's head of public relations had struggled to smile when they'd appeared in the doorway of her office. She'd immediate called up to the president's office, saying he was the person to speak with.

J.T.'s stomach had started to churn the moment he saw the look on her face.

Dr. Slimeball had made them wait twenty minutes, which was totally rude, and then they'd started this bullshit dance.

"Let's get down to brass tacks, shall we?" J.T. finally said.

The man had the audacity to smile at them from behind his massive desk. He had on a three-thousand-dollar suit, something that seemed out of the norm for a man in his position. It didn't bode well.

"My ex-wife is in town with an axe to grind against me, and she tells me you took a meeting with her," he said.

"She's so unhinged she's still calling him, if you can believe it." Trev unbuttoned his suit jacket. "You can imagine our surprise, hearing such folderol. The board recognized the importance of bringing the Merriam art collection back to the university our great-grandfather founded. When J.T. spoke with you, he felt you were on the same page—that you recognized how the Merriam Art Museum would add to the university's already impressive offerings. I mean, who isn't impressed with Evan Michaels' Artemis Institute?"

J.T. had to admire the way Trevor worked. They used to joke Trev had three levels of negotiation. Playing nice kicked things off. No need to make things hard or contentious. If that didn't work, Trevor would remind the person sitting across from them of their common interests or friends. God help the person if that tactic didn't soften them. Then the gloves were off, and he'd hit them hard with what the consequences would be. So far, they were still at level two.

"Of course, Evan's institute is a feather in our cap, but I'm still new at this position and the details of his offering are more...complete than yours. I'm only doing my due diligence."

Bullshit. "I provided your art experts and the board with everything they requested, including the provenance, which is why they approved it."

He let the silence grow, locking eyes with Dr. Slimeball. *Yeah, I know what kind of an ass you are.*

"I've made a lot of changes in my professional life to make this my number one priority," J.T. pressed. "I moved here, expecting to make the public announcement and get started on the museum right away. Now you not only want to delay what you and this university have agreed upon, but you also are meeting with my ex-wife, whose only intent is to stir up trouble and malign my character."

Dr. Slimeball kicked back in his chair, mimicking Trev. "If your character is what you've said it is, J.T., there's nothing to malign."

He ground his teeth. "That sounds like an unpleasant characterization of this situation. You're better versed in the law than I am, Trev. Meeting with my ex-wife seems like a conflict of interest, doesn't it?"

"It does indeed," Trev said. "President Matthau, like I alluded to earlier, Ms. Newhouse has displayed obsessive tendencies toward my brother. She isn't the kind of person a new university president wants to be aquatinted with, least of all influenced by."

Way to go, Trev, J.T. thought.

"Ms. Newhouse's concern is for the university and the art community," Dr. Slimeball volleyed back. "She's a respected member of said community, from a fine family, and is in the best position to inform us of your character. It's said behind every great man is an even greater woman."

God help him if that was the saying. "That's drivel, Dr. Matthau. Sometimes people simply make a mistake when they marry someone. That was my situation. Case closed. I would appreciate it if you'd keep my private business out of our dealings. If you must know, my ex-wife is bent on revenge because I had the gall to leave her. That's it. She's a bully."

Trev leaned forward. "Our family name is on this university for a reason. We believe in what it was created to do and want to continue to support that."

"Yet no one in your family has been affiliated with this university for some time," Dr. Slimeball fired back. "Don't threaten me or this university. Just because your name is Merriam doesn't mean you can waltz in here and tell me how to do my job."

Trevor's mouth flattened. "Your job is to meet the commitments of the university board and be professional. You're currently in breach of that. I don't imagine the board will be very happy hearing about it."

Dr. Slimeball's eyebrows rose. "I've talked to some board members. They know I'm still realigning this university in compliance with my priorities."

God, that sounded ominous. Who the hell did he think he was? A king?

"They also understand Ms. Newhouse's concerns about the art you're proposing to bring here," he continued. "No one wants this university to be on the front page of *The New York Times* for housing stolen Nazi art in their museum."

Ah, so they were finally to the crux of it. Good. "There was one instance of a painting like this some years ago, and the moment we discovered that fact, I had our lawyers find the family and return the piece. We have established the provenance of the rest of the collection, and it's all completely above board."

The man only smirked. "Of course you would say that."

"Surely, Dr. Matthau," Trev said, "you would recognize that a family who owns multiple billion-dollar companies would conduct the most thorough inspection.

The collection is ready to be shown to the world. It's time to put out the press release."

And so they continued their dance. Circle around. Throw a few punches. Get back to the gist of it.

Thank God for Trev's persistence.

"We want to rebuild some of the trust that has been lost with this situation," J.T. said. "Sharing the press release and moving forward with the museum will be a solid first step."

The man smiled—a fake one. He wasn't going to capitulate. Shit.

"Trust goes both ways, and frankly, some of the things Ms. Newhouse shared about you are quite concerning, J.T. I'm not sure this university wants to have you represent it."

An anger three years in the making flared through him, making him see red. "Cynthia would say just about anything to make my life difficult. That doesn't make anything she says true."

"So you don't pay bribes to officials in various African and Middle Eastern countries to do business?" he asked, folding his hands on his desk.

Damn Cynthia. Sure, there were times when they were asked to give what officials called a gift or a donation. J.T. didn't like it, but it was the way that part of the world did things. Otherwise there would be no business.

"We're getting off point here," Trevor said, "but to answer your question, there have never been any such allegations against J.T. or Merriam Oil & Gas. Be careful, Dr. Matthau. We've thought about suing Cynthia for defamation. We'd hate to see you fall into bad company. I can't imagine that would be good for a new president."

The man stood up and buttoned his suit jacket. "I don't like where this conversation is headed. I know what the board decided, but the execution of all university plans ultimately falls to me. It's called veto power. Look it up. Right now, I'd like some more time to look into this before we take any further steps. As you said, we all want to make sure the university's reputation remains top-notch."

What a dick. This was getting them nowhere. Frustration bloomed inside him, and suddenly he wanted more than anything to escape this room and its pompous occupant. "That's your prerogative, I suppose."

"But you won't have the final say," Trev said, standing as well. "Despite what you said about veto power, although that's not exactly the word for it. You know, universities are funny institutions. Since the first one was founded in 859 A.D., I believe—the University of Karueein in Fez, Morocco—there have been assholes like you who thought you could play god in an academic playground. Progress won't wait for you. I can promise you this: nothing will stop the truth from winning out. This museum will be built here as agreed upon by the university board. With or without your support."

J.T. wanted to applaud as he stood from his chair, but that would be really unprofessional. He'd leave the bad cop bit to J.T. "Good day."

The man only turned his back on them as they walked out.

He had to lengthen his stride to catch up to Trevor. They all but marched out of the university president's main offices. When they left the building, Trevor took a deep breath.

"Sometimes I miss smoking," he said, striding fast toward the parking lot. "He's a huge problem."

"He met with Cynthia," J.T. said. "He'd already shown his spots."

Trev stopped and turned to him. "Enough with the leopard analogy. I wonder how leopards feel about that indignity. I mean, it's not their fault their spots don't change."

J.T. laughed. "Okay, so what do we do now?"

"We start wining and dining the board members," he said. "Can we hire Chef T to cater private dinners?"

"I expect so. I'll make sure we put out our best china."

"Haha," Trev said. "Cynthia has to have something else up her sleeve. That guy might be eating out of her hands, but she would know the board has already approved the museum. So would he. There has to be some inducement we don't know about."

Yes, she would have thought of that. "She has to have more cards to play. She told me she was several steps ahead of me on the chessboard."

"You know what I always say about chessboards when the game isn't going your way," Trev said.

"Burn the board."

"You got it," Trev said, clapping him on the back. "Let's find out what Uncle Arthur has scared up."

The thought of Uncle Arthur led his mind straight to Caroline, and to how pale she'd looked after his call with Cynthia. He really needed to do something romantic for her. Today. Hell, he *wanted* to do something romantic for her. His grandparents' letters couldn't arrive fast enough.

Tendrils of depression tried to reach up and twine around his limbs. God, he was so tried of fighting for what he wanted. Of fighting to have a life.

"I need a blowtorch," he mumbled.

Trev turned. "For what?"

"For the board," he said. "Come on." If a blowtorch didn't work, he'd set fire to the whole goddamn room if it came down to it.

This endless battle had to end, one way or another.

CHAPTER 16

ARTHUR HATED SNIVELING, BACKPEDALING COWARDS.
According to his count, President Matthau had one-third of the university board reconsidering the Merriam Art Museum based on recent revelations about J.T. Merriam's character, unethical business practices, and potentially stolen Nazi art. Talk about unfounded pieces of claptrap.

He wanted to throw something. How could people be so stupid? Everyone knew President Matthau's source was a vicious ex-wife. Arthur would never have published an article on such a flimsy foundation.

But board trustees were politicians, and this new president knew how to wheel and deal. Some were being promised select appointments on key university committees. Graft. Patronage.

It didn't matter if a university was supposed to educate young people, it was still governed by politics.

"Grandpa, you look about ready to explode," Meredith said, appearing in the doorway of his office.

"I'm thinking about telling the new university president that I'd like to revoke my name from the Arthur Hale School of Journalism," he said.

"That bad, huh?" she asked.

"Yes, and J.T. just called and asked if I could meet him and Trevor tonight. They didn't have a good meeting with Dr. Slimeball. That's J.T.'s new name for Matthau, by the way. Can't say I blame him. The man's a turd."

Meredith's lips twitched. "Do you want me and Tanner to get a babysitter? I have lots of volunteers. Just the other day, Rhett told me he'd be happy to take Jared to The Grand while he played poker. Thought our son could get started early."

"A good poker face is essential to any gentleman," Arthur said. "If it's easy for you to find a place to park my great-grandson, then sure, do it."

Three hours later, they arrived at J.T.'s house and congregated in the den. As the first order of business, Arthur handed everyone a red hot.

"Won't go too well with my bourbon," Trevor said, holding up his tumbler.

"Might make it taste better." Arthur tossed him one. "For later. Now, let's get down to it. Dr. Slimeball, as J.T. calls him, has managed to turn about one-third of the board."

"Shit," Trev said. "No wonder he was so cocky. He didn't respond well to the threats I dished out after he refused to play nice."

Arthur glanced over at him. "Your smile would terrify small children, Trevor. What kind of threats did you make?"

"Mostly legal ones," Trevor said. "I wasn't ready to pull out the Big Kahuna."

Arthur snorted at the turn of phrase.

"What's the Big Kahuna?" Meredith asked, shifting on the small loveseat she shared with Tanner. "Asking the board to replace the president?"

Silence descended on the room for a beat, and Arthur leaned forward in his chair, following the scent of a good story.

"We pull the museum due to breach of contract," he said. "It's not like there aren't hundreds of universities that would give their right arm to house the Merriam collection. You know how hot art museums are with universities right now. Everyone wants to have one. Unless you're Brandeis University, and you try to sell the art in your museum to handle a budget deficit."

Even Arthur had heard about that bum move. Thank goodness a group of alumni and university patrons had gotten together and sued the university to stop them.

"But this is Grandpa Emmits' university," J.T. said, staring at his brother. "Our family's art should go here! And I want it to be here. That isn't an option."

Trevor threw back his bourbon. "Then we're in a less powerful position. Come on, J.T. You're a businessman. You know you have to be willing to walk away in situations like this one. Otherwise, they're going to have you over a barrel."

Meredith nodded. "J.T., everyone understands why you'd like to keep the museum here. We all want that, and we'll do what we can to help make that happen. Grandpa, I think we should run a story on the delay. This is big news."

Arthur had been wondering when his granddaughter would talk next steps. So far, they'd all been gathering information. "I can get some trustees to go on record about the delay. It's going to get ugly fast. People are going to give their reasons for the delay, which will cast a shadow on you, J.T. The paper can balance that with quotes from you and others, for example, but—"

"People around town will be gossiping about stolen Nazi art and potentially shady business deals and me being a son of a bitch," J.T. finished for him.

"What potentially shady deals?" Arthur asked. "This is new."

J.T. stood and went over to the bar. "I need a bourbon. Anyone else?"

Arthur fought the urge to tap his cane on the floor in impatience, but he could feel the emotion rolling off the young man. He needed something to calm him down. "None for me. It will mess up my red hot."

Trevor laughed. "I'll have another."

"He drinks like a fish with no apparent side effects," J.T. said. "It's a little scary. I shared a womb with him."

"I'll have a bourbon too," Tanner said. "Meredith?"

"Haha," she said. "I'm still nursing. How about sparkling water? Grandpa, would you like one?"

Damnation, these young people. "If I'd known this would be a cocktail hour, I'd have brought my martini shaker. Pour the drinks and let's get on with it. I'm aging as we speak, and this talk about potential shady business deals isn't making me any younger."

"I'll help," Tanner said. "So tell us about this allegation, J.T."

"Allegations like this are a dime a dozen," J.T. said. "When you work in countries where bribes are a way of doing business, it's inevitable that someone will try spinning it this way."

Which wasn't really a direct answer at all.

Tanner poured the rest of the drinks while J.T. sipped his bourbon, still standing by the bar as though he wanted to be close should he need a refill. Arthur watched the kid, taking in his gestures, his expression. His color was still that of a washed-out dishrag, but the angles of his face were a little too rigid. He knew a poker face when he saw it.

"You're talking to a seasoned reporter and a good friend," Arthur said. "Let's cut the crap. So, in the course of business, you sometimes pay bribes. How many people know this and would go on record if questioned?"

Trevor glanced over at his brother, their silent communication reminding him of the way people who'd been married for decades could talk without words.

"I don't think this is something we want to focus on," Trevor said.

Arthur brought his cane down hard on the floor and then pointed to the painting above the hearth. "If you don't trust me now, I don't know why the Hales and the Merriams still speak. You're insulting me in front of Emmits' visage."

J.T. flinched. "We're trying to protect the company and the people involved. It's not about trusting you."

"Bullshit!" Arthur said. "For the first time, you're looking at me and seeing only a reporter. Is all this talk about bribes coming from your ex-wife? Does she have any evidence?"

"No," J.T. said immediately, waving Trevor off when the man started to speak. "Look, I never imagined she'd use something like this. She never did during the divorce."

Tanner sipped his bourbon. "Perhaps she's been saving it. Seems like she had enough leverage during the divorce proceedings."

"Plus, threatening us with crap like this wouldn't have worked well with the judge associated with our case," Trevor said. "He was a by-the-books kind of guy. J.T., other than her saying she thinks this might be possible, does she have any proof?"

J.T. downed his drink, and the deliberation with which he did so told Arthur everything he needed. He cursed, and Meredith looked over at him, her frame as tense as his.

"I might have mentioned in a jet-lagged haze one time that our counterparts in Angola wanted a hell of a lot more side money than I'd ever paid out before. You remember that trip?" This last question was posed to his brother.

"I was in Moscow," Trevor said, his mouth turning into an outright snarl. "You said you could handle it."

"And I did," J.T. replied testily.

"Yet you told Sin City about it? Dammit, J.T. What in the hell were you thinking? Connor and Flynn are going to shit a brick when they hear this, and they're not the only ones."

J.T. slammed his drink down on the bar. "I was thinking I could tell *my wife* that I was sick to death of all the greed."

Trevor stood, mowing down the space between him and his brother. "You trusted her with inside corporate dealings that could hurt our family and the company. Why didn't you tell me about this?"

"Because it never came up," J.T. said. "Besides, it's hearsay. And she was my wife. She couldn't testify against me if it came down to it."

"Shit! Like that's the only issue here. Our reputation is at stake."

Trevor was getting in J.T.'s face, and Arthur knew it was time to intercede.

"You'll have to work this out later," he said. "We need to focus on getting this museum moving forward. You have your ways, and we have ours. I agree with Meredith about running a story on the delay. Tanner?"

He nodded. "Then I can run a follow-up article on the issue of stolen Nazi art and hope that shuts it down. I'll need to interview you, the lawyer who returned the painting to the family, and any more art experts you used to certify the provenance of the collection."

J.T. and Trevor were still standing off like two bulls in the pasture. For a moment, Arthur could see Emmits' resemblance in both boys, from the way they set their jaws to their firm stance. For a moment, his worry left him—if these boys had his friend's resilience, they'd be all right. He could almost feel Emmits standing beside him, poised to fight another battle.

"You'll have everything you need," J.T. said, rubbing his jaw.

"Good," Arthur said. "Then we'll head home. I'll start my interviews when I get back."

"You should leave it for the morning, Grandpa," Meredith said, rising as he struggled to stand with his cane. "You look tired."

"I'm almost eighty, Meredith," he told her, pushing her hands away when she tried to steady him. "Everyone looks tired at this age."

"One last thing," Trevor said, still gripping the back of the couch like he planned to toss it across the room. "I thought boyo here and my jolly self should start inviting trustees over to remind them we're not ogres. Well, at least I'm not."

J.T.'s green-eyed stare could have started a fire.

"Should we forget the Martha Stewart entertaining?" Trev asked.

"You couldn't pull it off anyway," J.T. said dryly. "You eat with your hands."

Trevor simply shook his head. The tension was escalating in the room, and Arthur felt exhausted by it. He would never admit it, but maybe Meredith was right. He should wait to make those calls. Right now, he needed to go home and fall into his favorite chair.

"I don't think it would be a bad idea to make nice with a few key people," Arthur said. "I assume you have a list of who's on the executive committee."

"I do," J.T. said. "This buffoon can probably read it."

You could have heard a pin drop.

"If you need anything else," Meredith said, crossing to J.T. and kissing his cheek, "let us know."

She did the same with Trevor, who stood there stiffly.

Tanner didn't bother to shake their hands, and Arthur had to agree it was best to leave them alone. They'd need to settle this on their own.

"We'll be in touch," Arthur simply said. "Trevor, could you walk me to the car?"

He hated to use the ruse of needing help, but age had to have some privileges. After waving to J.T., he followed Meredith and Tanner out.

"You two head on home," he said when they were outside. "Kiss my great-grandson for me."

They said their good-byes—Tanner's poker smile was much more convincing than Meredith's—then got into their SUV and drove off.

Arthur turned to Trevor. "I don't need to tell you to button this up."

"No, you don't," he said. "I'll get the right people on it."

"And get your brother's head in the game," he said. "Although it galls me to say it. You might be right about needing to threaten to pull the museum, but we'll cross that bridge—"

"If I don't burn it down first," Trevor said. "Let me see you to your car."

Arthur shoved away his hand. "I was only bullshitting you to get you alone. I can manage."

"Still, I'd prefer to do it. It'll give me a few more minutes to clear my head before I go in and have it out with J.T."

Arthur grunted. The young man walked beside him, the cold March air wrapping around them.

"I still can't understand how J.T. could fall for a woman like her," Arthur said when Trevor opened the car door for him.

"Neither can I," the man said, shutting the door behind Arthur.

As he drove home, he decided that even the wisdom of age couldn't unravel the mysteries of the human heart.

CHAPTER 17

THE MINUTE TREVOR WALKED BACK IN, J.T. SHOVED HIM in the chest.

"Do you want to take a swing at me?" he asked.

His brother pulled on his shirt, like J.T. had left wrinkles. "Honestly, yeah. I've had your back through all of this shit, and you didn't tell me this? Knowing what it could do to you and our family? Our business! How dare you put us in jeopardy over a piece of ass!"

"That piece of ass was my wife!"

Trevor waved a hand. "Whatever. I'm calling our lawyers to brief them. Something you should have done a long time ago. Then I'm going to have to call our brothers. Unless you want to pull your head out of your ass for one minute and do it yourself."

He held out his chrome phone, and J.T. knocked it out of his hand, needing to hit something. To *do* something. It flew across the floor. The sound did nothing to satisfy him. It only deepened his shame.

"Take a swing at me!" he shouted.

Shaking his head, Trevor walked over and picked up his phone. "You want me to hit you because you want to hit yourself for being so stupid. I'm going to save my knuckles."

He stormed over, his throat full of bile. "Hit me!"

Trevor's eyes narrowed. "No. That's too easy. I want you to suffer a little more."

J.T. saw red. Suffer? What the hell else had he done for the last three years? He rushed Trevor, his arms wrapping around his brother's barrel chest. Trevor stopped mid-stride and used his elbows to knock him back.

"I am so not fighting you! Dammit, don't you know how hard this is for me?"

He planted his feet. "What about me? Am I going to pay for one mistake for the rest of my life?"

"It would seem so right now," Trevor said, running his hand through his hair. "Do you know why I'm around all the time?"

Even when they were apart, Trevor always called or texted to check up on him. If he hadn't needed someone in his camp as badly as he did, he might have told his brother he was laying it on too thick. Instead, he curled his lip at him. "Because you're a masochist."

This time Trevor pushed him back. "No. It's because I love you! We all love you. During your divorce proceedings, Mom used to cry at night."

And his mother was tough as nails. "Stop it." He couldn't take this new level of suffering.

"Dad would pace the floors for hours. Michaela got an ulcer, and the guys all wanted to punch someone. Why do you think they don't reach out as much? They've used me as the go-between because they can't control their emotions, and they don't want you to worry about their feelings. You've had enough on your plate."

The fight went out of him. "What? I thought they all stepped back because... Oh, shit...because they were disappointed with me. Like you are."

Trevor sighed deeply and was silent a moment. "You think you've had it bad, and I'm not saying you haven't, but do you think it's easy to stand by and watch someone hurt and punish someone you love—over and over again? It's fucking hard! I hate every moment of it, and so do they. So I told them I'd look out for you until this was over. The only thing is it's not over. It's hard to know when it will be. *If* it will be."

His throat closed up, and for a moment he couldn't speak. He thought about all of the awkward visits he'd had with his parents and siblings since this whole thing started. He'd felt like someone with a communicable disease. Only Trevor had been a constant, always there with his sly wit and brotherly grit.

"I didn't realize. I'm sorry!"

"I know," his brother said quietly. "So am I. What galls me is that you didn't listen to me—or anyone else for that matter. I told you Cynthia wasn't who you thought she was when you first started dating."

He remembered that day. They'd argued, a rarity for them. He'd visited his family after returning from a long weekend with Cynthia in St. Barts. Full of romantic vigor and vim, he'd announced that he'd met "The One." Trev had shocked him by telling him Cynthia wasn't right for him, and everyone else had followed suit. He'd felt ganged up on, like they were against him and Cynthia from the start.

At the time, it had almost made their love seem more romantic.

"I'm sorry I didn't listen," he said softly. "I loved her."

"You loved the idea of her and all her talk about art and doing good in the world. What still pisses me off is that you didn't trust me! Me of all people! Don't I know you best of anyone?"

His shout echoed in the house, and J.T. felt tears spurt into his eyes. "I don't know what to say to make you forgive me. You've been holding on to this for a long time."

"Do you blame me?" Trevor asked. "Here I am, taking time off from my day job and our family company to help you out of another mess. Dammit, J.T., I'm tired of this shit too."

"Then go back to Dublin! Or wherever the hell you need to be. I don't need you here." At least he didn't *want* to need him. Just like he didn't want to feel like he was drowning at the mere thought of being in the thick of this without Trev.

Hurt had him stalking past his brother toward the stairs, but Trevor grabbed his arm. He swung out in response, a reflex born of years of pent-up rage, and his brother ducked.

"Are you really going to take a swing at me?" Trev shouted. "Man, I'm your *brother*."

When J.T. looked at his brother, he almost staggered back in shock. Trev's eyes were wet too. Shit. Trev never cried.

He lowered his head, shame washing over him. "I don't want you to go. I appreciate you being here. You know I do. No one else has been."

His brother's arm came around his shoulders. "I know. I'm sorry for what I said."

"It was true, wasn't it?" He met Trev's gaze. "If I had listened to you and everyone else, I wouldn't be in this mess."

"But you are, and you don't deserve it," Trev said. "That was a low blow."

"You've never pulled punches before," J.T. said, trying to shake it off. "And you're right. I've put everyone at risk. How do you think it feels? Fucking awful, let me tell you. I've walked around for the last three years with my gut twisted in knots, looking over my shoulder, wondering if I'm ever going to be free of her. Now it seems like she's never going to back off."

"So we have to find a way to stop her," Trevor said.

"Short of killing her, of course."

J.T. snorted. "She wouldn't die. She's like Rasputin. She just keeps coming back over and over again."

"So you do have experience with necrophilia," Trev said, marching over to the bar. "I always thought so. Sick, bro."

It was a miracle he could laugh. "Don't judge."

Trev poured himself another bourbon. "Want one?"

"God, no," he said. "I almost bawled like a baby just now."

Trev downed the bourbon. "Me too. All the more reason for bourbon."

Shit, was there any wonder he loved his brother? "I should go see Caroline tonight. Then again, maybe I really should stay away. I mean, she put on her breastplate and keeps hanging in there, but—"

"If you say what I think you're going to say, I really am going to hit you. Before you check your phone to see if your sweet little dove called or texted, I need a few things from you."

He gave him his full attention. "Anything."

"It's time to tell me everything you remember about Cynthia's philanthropic dealings or former sexual partners. Anything we can use."

They'd discussed it before, and he'd always said he wouldn't fight dirty. She'd been his wife, and somehow, even after everything she'd done, he'd never wanted to go that low. As he looked at Trev, he knew those days were over.

"What do you want to know?"

CHAPTER 18

CAROLINE WAS WAITING FOR J.T. OUTSIDE HER NEW digs when he drove up.

She'd unpacked her suitcase and made herself familiar with the guesthouse. While she couldn't see Blake and Natalie's house, it was comforting to know it was close by on their property. She was going to have the privacy she craved.

"Wow!" J.T. said when he exited his car, a paper bag in his hands. "From mom's to a modern two-story guesthouse made mostly out of glass. You must get incredible views of the valley from here. Looks like your luck is improving."

She sure as heck hoped so. As he drew closer to the front porch lights, she noticed his face looked haggard.

"Blake and Natalie were sweethearts to let me stay here."

The mere thought of their kindness brought tears to her eyes. Natalie had come over after work with dinner since Caroline hadn't gone grocery shopping yet. They'd eaten together while Blake went on a run with Touchdown. Her sister had teased her some more about being a lightweight, saying there was no question they had the same blood. Still, she'd felt the weight of her sister's concern. Natalie had kept looking at her when she didn't think she was looking.

"It's nice to have family," J.T. said in an odd voice.

She drew him inside, and the moment he shut the door, he set the bag aside and took her in his arms. They didn't speak. She pressed her face into his chest and felt him inhale a ragged breath. Yeah, they were both walking on emotional eggshells. He'd clearly had a bad day, and she'd spent the last couple of hours struggling to stay positive.

"I brought some more hazelnut gelato," he said. "It's not up to Rome standards, but I hear it's just the ticket for tough days."

Funny how hazelnut gelato only reminded her of better days, but she appreciated the gesture. "Good thing since I'm off tequila. That bad, huh? Who would have thought I'd have the better day of the two of us?"

He grunted. "Yeah. I have to tell you something."

Fear coiled in her belly.

"The museum looks to be in serious trouble," he said, "and I could be as well."

"What happened?" she asked.

"Let me fill you in," he said. "Can we sit outside? I know it's crisp, but I need the air."

Perhaps that would keep her head clear as well. It was starting to spin with bad scenarios. What would she do if the museum didn't come to fruition? She'd have to find another job for sure, but could she really hope to find one in Denver after Kendra had fired her for cause? And where did that leave her and J.T.? If the museum wasn't going to happen, he wouldn't have a reason to stay. Would she follow him somewhere? Oh, she just didn't know right now.

"Let me grab a blanket," she said, rushing to the couch, where a few blankets were folded over the arms, so new the packaging creases were visible. She took one for each of them. "There's a nice deck out back."

"Do you want the gelato now or later?" he asked.

"Later," she said, not wanting to mix it with bad news. "Let's put it in the freezer."

They finally settled in on the wooden bench lining the deck, blankets overlapping as they snuggled up to each other. The mountain air was cold but dry, and the million stars above were well worth the chill on her face. She could breathe out here.

He took her hand. "The situation isn't pretty."

As he told her about his meeting with Dr. Slimeball and the chat he'd had afterward with Uncle Arthur and her cousins, she was glad for the dark. Surely he would have seen the tension in her face otherwise.

"We're going to get this museum up and running," he said, rubbing her arms in assurance. "I don't know how yet, but we'll find a way."

The mountain before them seemed colossal right now, but she said, "I know you will."

"You don't have to worry about a job either. I'd like to bring you on board as an art consultant. You can start working on the collection as if the museum's a go."

"But that would be on your own dime, and I—"

"That doesn't matter," he said. "What's important is making sure we're moving forward on some fronts even though it feels like we're moving backward on others."

That was one way of putting it. "What I meant was… It felt like we were crossing some lines anyway—working together and being together—but somehow it seemed like less of a conflict since you wouldn't be directly… well, you know…paying my salary."

"I can see how you might think that, but I'd feel better if we could agree to this. It'll be like staying in this guesthouse. Temporary. Besides, maybe working on the museum would be fun for you right now."

She heard another argument he didn't make—he

wouldn't have the time. No, he would be out fighting Goliath while she organized which paintings they'd display in their Impressionist wing.

"Okay, but I'm going to have Moira...ah...negotiate everything for me then," she said. "No one is more professional, and I don't want you and me to have to talk about a salary and such."

Not when they were sleeping together.

"Let's go a step further," he said, taking her hand. "I'll have Trev negotiate with Moira. That way, we're both out of it."

Suddenly she could breathe easier. Talking about money had never been comfortable for her, and the prospect of discussing such a thing with J.T. was even more intimidating. "Fine. It will be nice to have something to do while—"

"We herd the board back onto the museum tour bus, so to speak?"

Now all that was left to discuss was the trouble he seemed to be in personally. "Yes. Ah...J.T., how serious are Cynthia's accusations of bribery and the like? Does she have evidence?"

"No," he said after a pause. "But she might have people looking. It's hard to say. Of course, her family has a lot of influence, so the right whispers could trigger an investigation."

What would happen to him then? This sounded serious. Like go-to-jail kind of serious. It might be common practice to offer "gifts" like that, but that didn't mean it couldn't get him in trouble, especially if the right people started asking questions.

"I still don't understand this kind of revenge," she said. "J.T., I'm scared for you."

"Me too," he said, putting his arm around her under the blankets. "I'm more worried about my family and the company. And you. When I left Merriam Gas & Oil,

I thought... God, I gave up everything hoping it would keep everyone I cared about safe. Now..."

"What does Trevor say about all this?" she asked.

"Well, we had a horrible row, and I tried to bait him into taking a swing at me. Not my finest moment."

Her brothers had gone hard at each other before, but they'd never gotten that physical. "Did you work it out?"

"Yeah, mostly," he said. "I can't do anything about his anger, and certainly it's justified." His tone was harsh, but she could tell it was directed at himself, not Trev.

Sometimes it took time to work things like that out. Natalie had pushed them all away in her grief over losing Andy's wife, her best friend. She'd even broken up with Blake, though they'd made up, thank God. It had been hard on all of them. But time had restored Natalie to herself, and to all of them too.

"You'll find a way to work things out. He's your brother."

"I know, and I'm so grateful he's by my side. Caroline, my life is a total mess right now, and here I thought I had a clean state for a new beginning. Are you sure you want—"

"Shut up," she snapped. Her mouth dropped open into an 'o' when she realized what she'd said and how she'd said it. "Oh my God, that was harsh. Sorry. What I meant was...I'm scared too, but I still love you. And I don't like hearing you talk about yourself like that."

"You're right," he said. "I need to shake this off. I haven't even asked how you're doing. Your world has been turned upside down. I never want you to think it's all about me. I might be feeling bogged down right now, but you matter. I want to support you. Give you what you need."

A part of her belly ignited at that thought. Maybe what they needed right now was to stop thinking for a while and just be together. Yes, that was it.

"Come with me," she said, taking his hand.

He followed her inside. "Are you sure this is a good idea? I'm pretty emotional right now, and you're—"

"Shhh..."

She led him to the bedroom she'd chosen for herself. It was bigger than her room in Denver, and it smelled of wood smoke from the fire Blake had started earlier to cover up the last of the fresh paint smell. Somehow that made the house feel more grounded, and she realized she needed that right now. She felt like she was walking a tightrope with her life.

"I love you, J.T.," she said simply. "We're both a little lost right now, but when I see you, my heart still lights up."

He looked off, like he was at war with all the emotion inside him. She stepped closer to him and put her hand on his chest.

"And when you touch me, I want you to keep on touching me. J.T., I want to hear you laugh again, like when we were in Rome together eating at that quiet trattoria."

"We will laugh again," he said. "I promise you that, Caroline. I love you too. It means a lot that you're willing to stick by me."

What a funny thing to say—had he expected her to turn tail and run? Then she remembered how the rest of his family had stepped back, whatever their reasons. "That's not who I am. It's not like you deserve this kind of treatment."

He coughed to clear his throat. "The bribery stuff... I need you to know that the money I paid out was always to someone's pet project, like a hospital or a school. I need to be clear on that. I never just gave out cash. Our company decided that in Emmits' time, and it's continued on that way. It's important you know I'm not a crook."

"I would never think that." She took his hand and squeezed it. "J.T., it's time to be quiet."

His mind was spinning, and hers wasn't much better.

Well, she had a solution for that. He hesitated, almost as though he was struggling again with whether he deserved to be with her, so she pressed herself against him and took over. Helped him shrug out of his jacket and unbuttoned his shirt.

Eager now, his moment of hesitation behind him, he peeled off her top, his hands quickly finding her breasts. She sighed in pure delight, leaning in to his touch, and let the noise in her mind fade as he stroked her bare skin. The knots in her belly turned to languid flutters. Yes, this was what they needed. To simply be. Together.

When he kissed the side of her neck, she raised her face to find his lips. He took her mouth gently at first, and then his control snapped. He fed on her, gripping her hips to bring her closer yet. She let her hands clench his back as she met his force with her own. There was power here now. And urgency. She wanted it all, she realized.

He stripped off the rest of her clothes and removed his own. His naked body was a delight, and tonight her belly was burning with want for him. She lay back on the bed with her hand extended to him, beckoning to him, and he came toward her and pressed his full length against her.

She released a moan, savoring the skin contact, and then fisted her hands in his hair as he kissed her again. The slide of his tongue was pure magic, the press of his knee to her core totally hot and welcome. She opened her legs and felt him leave the bed for a condom before he returned.

Connecting their hands, he slid inside her. Gently at first. And then with more force. Their eyes met, and she could see a new glimmer in his gaze. She was his light, and he was hers. Their hearts thundered with the knowledge as he started to thrust.

She wrapped her legs around him, urging him on, and

he levered back and began to take her harder—exactly as she wanted. Their hands still gripped together, she pressed her head back into the pillow, feeling the build, knowing she was about to come.

Then he pressed hard and deep, and she cried out. He followed her over the edge, breathing hard in her ear. She floated on a sea of sweat and heat, trusting everything she felt between them. Whatever came, she would be with him. That she knew.

They would get through it together.

When he rolled away from her, she gave him a moment to clean up, but within moments she was nestled against him. They lay that way for a long time.

"I love you," he finally whispered. "So much."

"Me too," she said.

There was nothing else to say.

CHAPTER 19

CHASE AND EVAN SHOWED UP THE NEXT MORNING WITH matching scowls on their faces.

J.T. had spent the night with Caroline, and he'd barely arrived at the rental before they did. Evan had texted him about the meeting, which was the only reason he'd left Caroline. Despite all the trouble surrounding them, their relationship felt solid. In her arms, he found a sense of peaceful calm, oddly similar to how he felt when he walked through a breathtaking museum. They still had so much to learn about each other, but somehow it felt like he'd known her his whole life.

"Sounds like you're in boiling water right now," Evan said. "Why is it that I had to hear about it from Trevor last night?"

Trevor closed his computer as they walked into the den. His brother inclined his chin as if deferring to him.

"I was with Caroline."

"Tough to keep a relationship going in a crisis," Chase said.

"We're managing," he said. "Trev has been helping on the crisis front." After their harsh words, he wanted his brother to know he was still grateful for his help.

"Your brother shouldn't be allowed to drink with

normal humans," Evan said, rubbing his temples. "I had to ask Chase to drive me home last night."

"I was with Moira," Chase explained as they all migrated to the kitchen.

Trevor poured everyone an espresso, and they took seats around the table—he and Trev sitting across from the two men. "I'm guessing we all need the extra kick today. Especially Evan."

"Your brother is funny even if he is a drinking mutant," Evan commented. "If I could clone him—"

"Stay the hell away, mad inventor," Trevor said with a laugh.

J.T. was ready to get down to business. "Please tell me Cynthia hasn't struck at Infinity Energy. I can't take much more bad news."

"No, actually," Chase said, adding a sugar cube to his espresso from the bowl on the table.

"No offense to the environment or your vision for clean energy," Trev said, "but Sin City knows J.T. cares a hell of a lot more about art."

Evan held up a hand. "No offense taken."

"I'm damn glad of that actually," Chase said. "No offense."

"All right," J.T. said. "So why are you here?"

"One word," Evan said, then paused to sip his espresso. "Artemis."

Ah, now he understood why Trev had invited Evan over after their drinking session last night. "I don't think it's in jeopardy. You have offices on campus and are fully recognized by the university."

"That could change," Evan said, nudging Chase. "Your turn. We had a pow-wow after I talked to Trevor last night."

"He mostly made sense, but I'm used to deciphering his gibberish. Evan and I are going to pay a call to the new university president and let him know we're concerned he's not following through on projects the board of trustees has already agreed to. We'll do the dance and note that if this can happen to you—"

"Our good friend," Evan said, toasting him with his cup.

"Then it could happen to us and any number of other donors or groups," Chase finished. "We'll see if that rattles him."

J.T. was overwhelmed by the gesture. It struck him that he was nowhere near as alone as he sometimes felt. First, Uncle Arthur and his crew had offered to help, and now Evan and Chase were stepping up too. "Thank you. I've been fighting Cynthia for so long that I sometimes forget there are other people who can help—besides Trev."

They hadn't done much more than grunt at each other since he'd returned this morning, but his brother hadn't given him the silent treatment either. Caroline was right. They would work it out.

"Sounds like Dr. Matthau is a problem," Chase said. "I'm looking forward to taking him down a peg."

"Wish I could be a fly on the wall," Trev said.

"I could record it," Evan said, giving his brother what J.T. thought was a leading nod. "I have this special little device James Bond would sell his Aston Martin for. You pin it on your lapel, and it records perfect video and audio. Mine is in the shape of a fleur-de-lis."

Of course it was. Evan was a Paris lover through and through. The two of them had debated Rome versus Paris many times in their meetings.

"In fact, along those lines, Trev said your ex has been calling you." He looked him straight in the eye. "Have you thought about recording those conversations?"

Trev kicked back in his chair, acting as if he hadn't a care in the world, and J.T. wanted to snarl at him for encouraging Evan to do his dirty work. "We talked about it when I first filed for divorce. I didn't want to do it then, and I don't want to do it now."

Chase drummed his fingers on the table. "Not even if it gives you leverage?"

"In what?" He wanted to kick Trev's chair back. "The he-said-she-said game doesn't hold up in court, especially between people who were married. I would think you of all people would know that, Chase." The man had been taken to the cleaners and then some by his ex-wife.

"It was only a suggestion," Evan said, turning his espresso cup in a circle.

J.T. shot Trev a dirty look. "Next time ask me yourself."

"Fine." His brother sat up and crossed his arms.

"Let's move on then," Chase said after a tense moment. "Trevor told Evan you plan on entertaining a select group of trustees from the board, and I thought it might be helpful if Evan and I showed up at your dinner parties too. You know, since you donated so much money to Infinite Energy, which could certainly benefit from the genius inventors to come out of the Artemis Institute, the university's new pride and joy."

J.T. liked where he was headed with this. "I'd love that. Thank you."

"Good," Evan said. "While you're feeling warm and fuzzy toward us, I have to ask. What about the bribery accusations?"

J.T. nodded. "I'd want to know too in your place. Cynthia has no evidence."

"I'm making sure she isn't stirring the pot anywhere, so to speak." Trev cracked his knuckles. "I've got my people on it."

"You mean ours," J.T. said. He didn't want to know what their older brothers had said. It likely had involved a lot of bad words.

"No, I mean mine. You forget. I work in even more dangerous and corrupt parts of the world than you did."

He wasn't going to argue that, although Transparency International's annual corruption report might show otherwise.

"That's reassuring," Chase said. "We want to make sure none of this blows onto Infinite Energy."

Shit. He'd been so caught up in his anger and guilt, he hadn't thought that far ahead. Clearly Trevor had.

"Right. If my name is sullied, people might think I'm bringing my shady business practices to your new enterprise."

It struck him that the joint dinner parties weren't just a show of solidarity—they were damage control. Trev stared him down. Ah, his brother was ahead of him. He really needed to get his head into the game.

"We'll start with Bruce Frenshaw and his wife," Trevor said. "They're long-time art lovers who live in the valley. From what I know, Bruce has ambitions to be on the executive council. I expect Dr. Slimeball is dangling that carrot to him in return for his support."

"I thought it might be nice to have Moira and Margie join us—even though it will likely go past Margie's bedtime," Evan said. "Baking hours really suck. I feel like a farmer sometimes."

Trev laughed, but J.T. laid his arms on the table. They hadn't mentioned someone he considered essential.

"You didn't mention Caroline."

Silence descended, and the tension between J.T.'s shoulder blades grew. He looked at Trev and then Chase. Both had their poker faces on. Evan, however, lowered his eyes.

"What?" he asked, an edge to his voice. Something else had been discussed without him, and he didn't like it.

Trev pushed his espresso cup aside. "It's like this.

Right now, there are university people questioning the provenance of the art collection. Caroline was one of the people who confirmed the provenance."

"It was already done—"

"Hear me out," Trevor said. "Some might say that it's a conflict of interest for her to comment on the provenance at all."

He wasn't following. "I don't understand. She's an art expert."

More silence, and Evan fidgeted in his seat.

"You're sleeping with her," Chase said. "I say this with the greatest respect... She's my family, and I hate having to agree with Trevor here, but she can't be part of the wining and dining. It could raise more questions about the collection, and it might also hurt her reputation. Moira agrees with me. I asked her in confidence and had her put on her human resources hat."

"We were both concerned about starting a personal relationship, but it's separate," he insisted. Even as he said the words, he knew they weren't true. When she'd helped him in Rome and Napa, it had been only as a kindness to Uncle Arthur. He'd changed that by agreeing to hire her on as an art consultant.

And he knew what they weren't saying. If they didn't want him and Caroline to act like a couple at a few dinner parties, then they likely didn't want them to go public with their relationship at all.

"People don't see things that way," Trev said, kicking him under the table. "You need to think here. Perception can be more damaging than truth, and in this case, it's not clear-cut. You know how people like to talk about what goes on in the front office and under the sheets."

This was too much. J.T. stood so fast his chair toppled over. "I fucking love her, man."

"I'm not saying you don't," Trev said, holding up his hand like a stop sign. "I'm only saying we need to be careful. It could look bad and create more problems."

"None of us likes saying this," Chase said. "Perhaps me least of all. Moira freaking got tears in her eyes after we talked about it."

He hadn't thought he could feel worse. "Shit! First, she gets fired because of me and now this…"

"It's only temporary," Trev said. "Until we can turn the tide against you and the museum."

"But—"

"No buts, bro," Trev said, coming to stand in front of him. "If I thought there were a better way, you know I'd propose it."

"But I just agreed to hire her last night as a consultant and have her work on the museum."

All of them looked at him like he was a moron.

"While your heart is in the right place," Trevor said, "you can't do this right now."

How was he supposed to tell her that? "Do you know how shitty that is?"

"Yes," his brother said in a hard tone. "But it'll protect her reputation until we can get beyond this."

Chase nodded, his face hard with tension.

"No one says it doesn't suck balls," Evan said to him.

There weren't curse words vile enough to describe this situation. "So I'm guessing you want us to keep our relationship in the shadows completely?"

"She might have announced it to the town, but yes," Trevor said. "No public dates or hanging out. We need to make a show of professionalism and objectivity."

Anger spurted up, and he wanted to shout, *Fuck that*.

"I know you want to hit something," Trev said. "Me too. I ordered us a punching bag after you left last night. Until then, have another espresso. We need to make some calls."

J.T. took the piece of paper he handed him, counting the minutes until he could give the punching bag a go.

Coming to Dare Valley, he'd thought he'd escaped the past.

He hadn't escaped anything.

CHAPTER 20

WHEN J.T. CAME OVER LATER IN THE AFTERNOON, Caroline noticed the wooden box under his arm right away.

"What do we have here?" she said, kissing him lightly on the lips and reaching for the box. "It's too small for a clown."

"I'm never going to live that down," he said, running his free hand through his hair.

Then she noticed his bruised knuckles. "Oh, my God. What happened?" Had he finally let anger get the better of him and punched Trevor?

"We got a punching bag," he said, "and it saw some serious action today."

Something had clearly happened. "I hate to ask, but how was your meeting?"

"Let's go inside," he said. "I can tell you're chilly."

Despite her worry, she couldn't help but smile. He was so thoughtful, so solicitous of her.

As they walked into the house, he set the box he was carrying on the coffee table. "I was wondering... Would you mind if I brought over some things? Razor. Change of clothes. Cologne. Stuff like that."

She stopped short. They were having *this* kind of

conversation now? "You didn't mention shoes. Or socks. It's still cold out."

"*Shoes*," he said slowly. "Did I make you uncomfortable?"

Until he posed the question, she hadn't realized her chest had gone a little tight. "I've never had a man leave things at my place," she admitted, "although this isn't technically my place."

"I'm not saying I'll spend every night here," he said. "You might want some space, and I have to prance around in a dog-and-pony show for the trustees. Um... That brings me to the reason I needed to punch something."

Every time they parted, he came back with bad news. Keeping her spirits up was proving difficult, and the worry...

She was fretting non-stop. Maybe she needed to take up meditation or something.

"You're a barrel of laughs," she said, dropping into the leather loveseat. "Shoot."

He remained standing. "I'm not sure how to start. Remember how I mentioned Trev and I were planning on doing some entertaining with the university trustees?"

"Yes." Where was he headed with this and how did the box enter into it?

"Well, I hate this, but it's been decided it might be better for you not to be my plus one."

She hadn't even thought that far ahead. "You mean because my role with the museum isn't public yet?"

He unbuttoned his jacket. "No, because we're an item."

Her brow wrinkled. "I don't follow."

"Seems I underestimated the power of perception." He shoved his hands into his pockets. "With Cynthia's so-called accusations about the provenance..."

The problem hit her square in the gut. "People might say I fudged something because... Oh, shit. Because we're sleeping together. Oh, my God. And I announced it to the whole town. J.T., I'm so sorry."

Tequila was never going to touch her lips again.

"Normally this wouldn't be a problem," he said, coming over and sinking to his knees in front of her.

"Bull," she said. "I can't believe I didn't think about the professional implications. Moira should have kicked my butt."

He looked away, and she sensed he still had more to tell her. "Actually, Chase talked to Moira confidentially to get her take on your involvement," he said.

Of course he had. Chase was a forward-thinking kind of guy. Before he and Moira had started seeing each other, they'd had a very honest discussion about becoming involved and the professional issues. Both of them worked for Evan, but not at the same company. Which was why Moira would be the perfect person to negotiate her consultancy.

"So Chase is advising you on things?" she asked. "That's good. He's crazy smart."

"He and Evan might be a little worried that my shit is going to hurt their new company. It's damage control. They'll be...ah...doing the dog-and-pony show with me."

She narrowed her eyes. "Does that mean Moira will be there?"

Nodding, he took her hands. "I know it's shitty. Your sister will be a plus one, but not you. I wasn't sure how to tell you. And that's not even the worst of it."

Had Moira planned on mentioning any of this? Or was she waiting for J.T. to do it? It made sense for Moira to accompany Chase, but being excluded made her feel a little tawdry.

"Better get it all out," she said. "I can't imagine worse right now."

He stood and took a deep breath, saying, "Out of

concern for your reputation, it might be better if we wait to formalize your art consultancy."

"Don't talk like a lawyer," she said. "Talk to me."

"My reputation might take a major hit, and yours might tank with it," he said, his voice hard. "What I'd like to do instead is have you work for me informally. I'd compensate you for everything after this is all done."

She grabbed the cashmere throw near her and clutched it, almost like it was a shield. "I can't believe this. First, I'm not your plus one. Now, I can't even work on the museum." Her laugh was bitter. "Did anyone suggest we stop seeing each other until this blows over? I mean, maybe we can't even be Facebook friends without someone or something getting hurt."

Her outburst might have embarrassed her if the situation were different, but not today.

J.T. didn't respond for a moment. "We seem doomed, don't we? First, you think you're a liability to me, and now I appear to be one to you. That's why I asked you first if I could keep some things here."

She looked over at him. His weight shifted to one leg as if the news he'd brought had stolen all his energy. She knew the feeling.

"I wanted to make sure you knew what was important. You. Me. That's why I brought the— Everything else might be falling apart, but what I felt with you last night..."

He finally sat down on the loveseat next to her. "What I feel for you...it's bigger than all the shitty politics. Caroline, I... This time, I'm asking you to hang on with me."

Before he'd told her he wouldn't blame her if she bowed out, and now he was asking her to stay. She clutched the throw to her chest as the difference hit her.

"I don't ever want to hurt what we have, the museum..." she said quietly, her throat feeling scratchy now. *Our future.*

He uncurled her hand from the throw and squeezed it. "Me either. I know this is hard, but I...need to trust Trev's judgment right now. I...didn't before, and it cost me. With Evan and Chase agreeing with him, it's..."

He didn't need to finish the sentence.

"I understand," she said, wanting to lower her head in defeat.

"We just need to keep our relationship...more private right now," he said.

"What exactly does that mean?" Hadn't she announced to a full bar of people they were sleeping together?

"No, ah...public outings for the moment," he said, looking down. "Like dates. You can't know how much I hate this."

"Me too." She wanted her hand back suddenly. The tenuous connection hammered home that they were being forced to keep each other at arm's length. "Maybe I should go back to Denver for a while." What was she supposed to do otherwise? Twiddle her thumbs?

"No!"

She jerked back at his tone.

"Sorry I yelled. I got freaked out. Caroline Hale, we most certainly are not going to have you turn tail because Cynthia is in town. I want you here. With me. You can work on the museum."

In private. Like everything else.

"We'll figure things out," he said, urgency making him lean closer.

Too close right now. She edged back.

"Please bear with me a little longer. We're going to turn this around."

And if they didn't? God, she couldn't bear the thought. Not only had she gotten fired, but it now seemed she'd inadvertently hurt her reputation by being associated with him. She couldn't think about her career right now. She might just break down.

"Why don't you go and pick up some things to bring over here? We can meet up later tonight." She knew it would hurt him if she said she needed some space.

He held her gaze for an awkward moment before releasing her hand and standing up. "Sure."

She rose too, her body heavy with sadness. They'd been so in sync last night. Right now, it felt like they were walking in two different directions on the same tightrope.

"What about the box?" she asked, gesturing to it.

He swallowed thickly when he glanced at it. "Open it when you want. I should go."

At the door, he kissed her cheek as perfunctorily as he'd done when he'd arrived. She couldn't bring herself to change the energy between them.

"I'll...ah...call you," he said, and after one last look, he headed to his car.

She went inside. The box he'd left caught her gaze, and she felt tears rising up. It was likely something romantic, if she knew him. But romance was the last thing on her mind just now. God, she'd pulled herself up by the freaking bootstraps to start working on a museum that might never happen. She'd believed in her dream job despite everything. And she'd believed in her and J.T.

Was she a fool?

She didn't want to cry, but if she didn't find some sort of distraction, she'd go crazy otherwise. All her siblings were at work right now or she'd have headed over to talk with them. Blake was at home next door, but this conversation was delicate, and her mother...might try and give her a pep talk, which she couldn't take.

Maybe she could clean. Except the house was practically sparkling, it was so new. She started to wander through the rooms, looking for imperfections. The angle of one of the paintings on the wall was off, so she righted it. She felt elation at finding dust bunnies under two of the beds and in the corner closets. She decided to make her bed, something she never did. Yeah, it was that bad. After refolding the blanket on her bed in a mathematically perfect square, she sat down. God, this was pathetic.

She was pathetic.

Tears popped into her eyes, and she couldn't stop them. She couldn't reconcile how things had gotten to be so upside down. When she'd first met J.T., she'd jumped on the happy and spontaneous ride. He'd flown her to Rome and then Napa. Their attraction had been instantaneous and palpable.

For a while, she'd thought she'd end up with her dream job and her dream man, but love wasn't supposed to feel like this. All she felt was fear and dread—and yeah, a little shame too. She lay on the bed for a while, stewing on it, and then made herself get up. It was time to be more proactive, and she had two people she wanted to talk to.

Trevor picked up on the second ring. "Hey! My brother is moping around upstairs but won't say why. I assume he told you about laying low for a while, and it didn't go well. Can't say I blame you. I thought the letters might help, but fuck it. Who wants romance when your career is in jeopardy?"

Had she ever met a more direct man? Right now she was too tired to be anything less than equally direct. She'd deal with whatever these letters were later. "Do you think I should leave and go to Denver?"

There was silence for at least thirty seconds. "It might be helpful, but you've already announced your relationship publicly. Short of you two breaking up— which I don't want to see—I don't think a change of location will help."

"So out of sight out of mind doesn't work anymore?" she asked.

"Not in our modern world, no," he said. "Unless you're living in Siberia, but even then you'd be surprised how well connected they are these days."

Her heart, her career, was in tatters, and he was talking about Siberia?

"Will you tell me if you change your mind? I mean... if you *do* need me to go. I don't think J.T. would be... able to..."

Her throat felt like a cold was coming on suddenly, and she cleared her throat.

"Yes," he said. "I really like you, but I'm always going to put my brother and our family first."

"I totally understand." Family was supposed to be like that.

"Don't underestimate me though," he said. "I think we'll get ahead of this. The law might have sided with Sin City in the divorce, but this is something different. I excel at damage control and influencing people."

"You're a regular Dale Carnegie, I imagine," she said dryly. "Don't tell him we talked."

She hated to keep anything from him, but she didn't want him to feel she'd gone behind his back.

"I won't," he said. "If you need a sounding board, I'm here. Thanks for taking a backseat for a while."

As she hung up, she felt defeated. Yep, that was her. The backseat. Could her life be in worse shape? Well, now it was time to talk things out with Moira.

She waited until she thought Chase and Moira would be home from work and then simply swung by. Moira was holding two glasses of red wine. She extended one to her.

"I thought I might see you," her sister said. "Come on in. I know you're upset."

The sight of the wine only made her stomach turn. "None for me. Moira—"

"Will you get in here? I'm not having this discussion

with the door open. Besides, Barney might run out."

She reluctantly followed her sister inside, mostly out of deference to the cat. It would be just her luck if it escaped and got run over. Chase was sitting on the couch and started to rise.

"I'll just—"

"No, you stay put," Caroline said to him, crossing her arms. "I understand why you didn't tell me about this, Moira, but it still sucks." She wouldn't mention she'd planned to have her sister be her negotiator. None of that mattered now.

"It was my fault," Chase said, holding up a hand. "I wanted a second opinion. I should have handled it better."

"What was there to handle?" she asked. "Announcing our relationship like that last night was a stupid mistake. I'm more mad at myself than anyone...which I realized today while I tidied a guesthouse no one has ever slept in."

"Not that!" Moira said, her lips twitching. "You and Natalie. She cleans like a madwoman when she's upset."

"The place is so clean I had to resort to making my bed," she said, noticing even the cat wasn't coming out to greet her. "Never mind that. I want to know how bad things are for J.T. And the museum. Honestly. Chase, I know you have a sense of these things."

He glanced at Moira. Already you could see their unity as a couple, and if things weren't so bad just now, she might have been heartened by it.

"Well, it's mostly a lot of dirt slinging, and from J.T.'s ex-wife... Normal people would understand she has an axe to grind."

"She seems to keep sharpening it," Caroline said dryly, "and important people don't appear to notice she's carrying it in her Grace Kelly purse."

"Wait!" Moira said, standing up straighter. "Not to be a girl, but Sin City has a Hermès Kelly Bag?"

"Yes. Focus, Moira!"

Her sister playfully slapped her own cheek. "Okay, girl moment over."

"Thank God," Chase said. "I was about to break off our engagement."

"Har-de-har-har," her sister said, sticking her tongue out. "Just because I'm tough doesn't mean I'm not a girl."

"I'd never dispute that you're a girl," Chase said. "Never mind. All right, do you want my balls-to-the-walls personal opinion?"

"Yes, I want the complete truth." She took the chair next to where he was sitting on the couch, and Moira joined them.

Chase poked his fiancée as if he was expecting her to make another joke, but his gaze was on Caroline. "The Newhouse name carries a lot of weight. Cynthia alone wouldn't be as formidable, but her family is loaded—and respected. The Merriam name lays claim to the same respect, of course; it's going to come down to who slings the mud the best. Right now, Cynthia is winning, especially with the bribery and Nazi stolen art accusations. I hate to say this because it's going to piss you ladies off, but..."

Moira nudged him in the chest. "Go ahead. Piss us off. I think I know what you're going to say anyway."

He sighed. "If you tell anyone I said this, I will deny it to my dying day. Cynthia is a charming, beautiful woman, and she's using every tool in her arsenal here on..."

"What?" she asked.

"Men like President Matthau," Chase said. "Some of us are susceptible to such forms of flattery."

"Maybe I need to bat my eyelashes more," Moira said, mimicking the gesture.

"So you think Dr. Slimeball is more susceptible to her claims because of her 'charms'?" Caroline asked.

"Not completely," Chase said. "From what I can tell, Cynthia is holding a carrot in front of Dr. Matthau."

"What's the carrot?" she asked.

He shrugged. "We don't know yet. But I imagine we'll find out soon enough. No use worrying about it now."

She pulled on her hair. "Not worry? I'm out of a job and have just been informed I'm a liability to J.T. both personally and professionally. Hell, I called Trevor before I came over and asked him if I should go back to Denver for a while."

Chase's eyes immediately shuttered. "What did he say?"

It concerned her that the man had to ask. "Not right now. But he promised he'd tell me if that changed. Seriously, I'm in limbo-land. I hate this! I'm out of work. *Fired!* The job I wanted is in jeopardy. The way I was hoping to keep occupied is no longer an option."

"As an art consultant," Moira said. "Chase told me."

"Great, that saves time. Of course, J.T. told me today that I could keep working *informally* and he'd pay me later..."

Moira's brows slammed together. "Usually I would advise against that. Okay, let's talk brass tacks. Here's the thing. Caro, you *are* in limbo. The main question is: do you still want to work with J.T. at the museum?"

"Of course! Haven't you been listening?"

"Then you'll have to keep *waiting* until the job comes open," Moira said. "I hate to sound like a human resource person—"

"But she is," Chase said, "and a really good one."

"Thank you, darling," she said, kissing his cheek. "Caroline, it's not uncommon for jobs to take a while to firm up."

She threw out her hands. "I understand all that. I just don't have anything to do, and I'm...shit...I'm scared. How's that for honest?"

Moira rose and wrapped her arms around her. She soaked in her sister's nearness, letting herself take comfort in her embrace.

"It's okay to be afraid," Moira said in a quiet voice. "I would be if I were you, but you need to let J.T. and the rest of us do our part to get things back on track. Heck, Uncle Arthur has his boxing gloves on, and with Meredith and Tanner—"

"But you didn't see the way that woman walked into the gallery," she interrupted.

Moira pulled back and knelt by her chair. "Tell me."

"She walked around like she owned the place and everything—and everyone—in it. I know you mentioned her beauty, Chase, and there's no denying it. I can't comment on her charm—she had none for me—but she's also scary smart. I mean, how smart are J.T. and Trev, and she has them spinning like tops. Then there's the fact that her viciousness springs from a place of real hurt. I mean, when she talked about J.T. leaving her, even a blind man would have seen her broken heart."

"Heartbreak makes people react all sorts of ways," Chase said.

"Prison is full of them," Moira quipped.

"That's not funny," Caroline insisted, even as she barked out a laugh.

"Do we need to find a picture of Cynthia and superimpose an orange jumpsuit on her?" her sister asked. "Would that make you feel better?"

J.T. had boxed as a coping mechanism. Maybe she needed one too. "Probably. That makes me a horrible person, doesn't it?"

"Terrible," Moira said and made a face. "If so, I'm the worst."

Chase, who'd been shaking his head, started laughing. "A jumpsuit...Moira, no wonder I love you."

"You know, you were a serious fuddy duddy before

you met me," she said, rejoining him on the loveseat and leaning her head against his shoulder. "Thank God you're done with that."

As Caroline watched, Chase put his hand on her sister's thigh and stroked it sweetly. The gesture made her feel a pang of longing for J.T.

"I'm glad you're joining our family, Chase," she said.

"Me too," he answered, looking at Moira a moment longer. "Okay, what more can we do to help?"

"Besides your plan to wine and dine the trustees with J.T. and Trevor?" she asked. "Nothing."

"I meant for you," he said, leaning forward. "If you're bored, you could help us unpack files for the new company."

"I'm not that bored." She wasn't going to mention she'd been organizing her own files for the museum this morning. No siree.

Moira laughed. "Caroline hates that crap. That's why she's in the art world. You could paint the ceiling of our dining room. Two figures touching fingers might look nice above the chandelier."

"Ha. Ha. Very funny."

"Maybe you should keep working on the museum informally like you mentioned," Moira said.

She wanted to kick something. Nothing had been accomplished—she was back where she'd been a couple of hours ago. "You know, I was going to have you negotiate my rate and everything."

"Consider it done," Moira said.

"Things are going to start changing in our favor," Chase said as she left.

She sure as hell hoped so.

When Caroline returned home, she faced down the box J.T. had left her. Inside were a stack of yellowed letters with a note. She opened it with a tight heart.

I asked my mom to send the love letters my

grandparents wrote each other during WWII. I realized the other day you remind me of my grandma. She was strong and courageous and had one of the biggest hearts I've ever come across—until I met you. I hope you'll see what I see when you read them. They were a couple who hung tight during tough times because they loved each other.

She sank onto the chair, holding the box in her lap, fighting tears again. Just when she was so frustrated and defeated, he'd found the perfect way to tell her to hang on a little while longer. In the end, the decision was simple, she realized, as she traced his bold signature.

She would hang on for love, no matter what.

CHAPTER 21

ARTHUR WAS PRETTY PLEASED WITH HIS OP-ED ON THE new museum.

He might be old as dirt, but there was nothing wrong with his pen, so to speak. J.T. and Caroline had been surfing wild emotions all week, and the rest of his family hadn't been faring much better. Even Meredith had popped off about Sin City being one of the meanest bitches she'd ever come across, and she'd been married to a prize dick before Tanner.

While Arthur agreed, he'd reminded her to keep her eye on the prize. Tuck away the emotion and help him deliver the best pieces of journalism they could in response to Sin City's bullshit. First, they'd put out his Op-Ed this morning about the Merriam collection finally coming to the university Emmits founded and why this was so important not only for Dare Valley but art lovers everywhere. Next, Tanner was going to print a piece on J.T.'s vision for bringing the museum to Dare Valley and the process he'd used to establish each painting's provenance, noting his return of the stolen Nazi art in one instance. That should stave off some of the president's fear-mongering.

It was a good plan, and yet he'd crunched on so many

red hots this week, his teeth hurt. His dentist—who was as old as him if not a few years senior—was going to have a field day when he went in for his next checkup.

His Sunday looked pretty promising despite it all. Every Sunday there was a family get-together. Nowadays, there were plenty of babies, and he'd already set out a shirt they could drool and spit up on. Jared was a prize barfer, and if you asked him, Meredith probably overfed the poor kid. But was he going to say anything about that? Not in a million years. Men didn't school women about breastfeeding. He might as well go into witness protection if he tried to put out any pearls of wisdom on that subject.

His house phone rang, and he almost sighed at the prospect of hurrying to his home office to answer it. He rather liked the convenience of carrying his cell phone with him. Grabbing his cane, he moved as quickly as he could—which these days would make a turtle feel accomplished—and picked up the call.

"Hale residence," he said into the receiver. Of course, as a greeting it was stupid. He wasn't the only Hale in town, but he'd been the first, so he figured he was entitled.

"Arthur Hale," a woman said. "I'm so glad I caught you. I wanted to commend you on that prize work of journalistic objectivity in *The Western Independent* today."

"Who is this?" he barked, although part of him already knew. Hard to mistake that tony voice for a local from Dare Valley.

"Cynthia Newhouse," the reply came as he'd expected. "We've never met, but after what I read in the paper this morning, I felt we should."

Her spider web might be spun with gold thread, but it was still a web. He'd seen plenty of keen talkers in his day. "Many people have felt that way about my Op-Eds over the years. I tend to disagree with the sentiment. My opinion is my own. That's what the op part of the ed means, in case you didn't know, young lady."

Her laughter tinkled like a bell, and Arthur wondered if J.T. had been charmed by it. God help them from the power a woman's laughter had over a man's dick. It had brought down many a man throughout history. He'd always wondered about Cleopatra's laugh. She must have had a doozy to bring first Caesar and then Mark Anthony to their knees.

"Oh, I've heard you were cantankerous and crafty," she said. "My father usually appreciates your Op-Ed pieces, but as you might imagine, it gave him indigestion this morning. My breakfast didn't sit well either, of course. We're a very tight family."

She'd mentioned her powerful father to intimidate him, no doubt, but he wasn't the type to care about pissing off someone powerful. If he had been, he would have shuttered the newspaper long ago. "Good for you. Now, I don't mean to be rude, Ms. Newhouse, but it's Sunday. My day off. If you have a comment on the Op-Ed, you can go the comments section online. You can thank my granddaughter for that. But you should know. I don't read them. I'm old-fashioned that way."

"Indeed," she drawled out, her silky voice evocative of money and fur coats. "Well, we've been introduced, and I've noted my complaint."

"Taken. Goodbye, Ms. Newhouse."

"No, Mr. Hale," she said. "Do you know French?"

"What am I, a cretin? Of course I know some French."

She laughed again, and this time the sound set his already sensitive teeth on edge.

"Well, then you'll understand this saying: **à bientôt**."

She hung up, and he rubbed his chest, surprised at the tightness there. *See you soon.* Coming from that viper's mouth, it didn't bode well. But hell, he'd known what he was doing. The fact that he'd pissed off Ms. Newhouse and her powerful father meant he'd done his job well.

He cracked his neck. God, he liked the challenge of it. But he probably shouldn't tell J.T. about her call. The kid's nerves were at the breaking point as it were. He sure as hell wasn't going to tell poor Caroline.

Meredith and Tanner, however, would need to know. Meredith was still working on her piece while Tanner had mostly finished his. The last thing he needed to do was interview Sin City herself, and based on her call, Tanner was going to have his hands full. He probably shouldn't go alone, Arthur thought.

Sitting in the chair behind his desk, he picked up the phone again and dialed them. Meredith picked up on the third ring.

"Hey, Grandpa," she said. "Your Op-Ed looked great when I opened the paper this morning."

He puffed out his chest. Sure, she'd already read it, but his granddaughter was a Hale through and through. An article always looked its best in the newspaper itself. It was like the difference between seeing a dress on a mannequin in a store and then on some beautiful woman.

"I just had a call from Cynthia Newhouse," he said. "I need to brief you and Tanner. Are you going to today's shindig?"

"At Rhett and Abbie's, yes," she said. "Grandpa, that woman *called* you? Are you okay?"

"Well, I'm not dead or anything," he shot back. "Good God, child, what did you think it would do to me?"

"I'm sorry, Grandpa," she said softly. "I got worried."

He knew she worried more the older he got. He tried to be understanding. He really did. But it hurt his pride to be treated like he couldn't handle himself anymore.

"I know you did," he said. "Don't do it again. We exchanged pleasantries and the like. I'll tell you more later. How about I brief you at the shindig? That way, you can park my great-grandson on someone's lap."

"Good idea," she said. "See you soon."

He harrumphed. That damn phrase again. Coming from his granddaughter, it didn't have any malice, of course. But the reminder made his chest tighten up again. He pumped his chest with one fist. "We're fine in there. Settle down."

Grabbing another red hot, he crunched as he let his mind stew on a subject he'd been mulling over for a few days now. Calling Clara Merriam. J.T. had claimed it wasn't worth it, but Arthur wasn't convinced. She had nearly two hundred paintings from the Merriam collection. If she decided to donate them to the museum, surely that would make news, and it would make the museum a more coveted prize. Plus, she ran in similar social circles as Cynthia's family—or at least she used to. Hell, he didn't know. She was seventy-six now, if his memory served him.

Oh, what the hell. He was going to call her. Hadn't he thought about calling and checking up on her after her husband died? Bah! An old man's lunacy, he'd decided then. But now, he had a reason. If she made a fuss and J.T. found out, he'd blame old age. It had to be good for something.

He rang her house after sifting through the ancient Rolodex in his home office.

"Allerton residence," a British male voice answered.

Her married name surprised him for a moment. Then he wondered about the voice. Good God, she couldn't have the same butler? Hell, he'd be as old as Arthur. No, this man had to be another in a long line of upper-crust servants. Clara had always had a thing for London.

"Arthur Hale for Ms. Allerton," he said.

"If you'll hold the line, I'll see if she's available," the man said.

He laid his cane aside. Clara Merriam had been a bit of a brat, no question. Still, they'd spent a fair bit of time together in New York City, back in the day. She might have fancied him, and he might have fancied her a bit too, but hell...that might be age talking. But even after all these years, he still remembered how beautiful she'd looked in an evening gown. Until her, he'd never seen a woman in one, and it had redefined the feminine form for him. And the way she used to take off those long gloves of hers... She'd gotten him hot under the collar every time, and she'd known it, dammit.

"Arthur Hale, you old blaggard," a woman's voice sounded on the line.

"Clara Merriam," he said, a smile touching his face. "Damn but you sound the same."

"You sound old," she said. "Aren't you turning eighty in May?"

He was surprised she remembered, but then again, she'd always been sharp as a tack. "Yes, and that makes you pretty old yourself."

"You're flattering me," she quipped. "I saw your Op-Ed in the paper this morning. I imagine you're calling for J.T. to ask me if I'm willing to give up my part of my grandpa's collection to this new museum. Your timing ruins any hopes I'd had that you still have a thing for me after all these years."

He tapped his finger on her card in his Rolodex, not knowing how to respond to that comment. Did she really read his paper? He'd never imagined it. "J.T. didn't think it was worth asking."

"And yet you disagreed," she said, irony lacing her tone. "How quaint. But he's right. Why would I do that?"

"Because it's the right thing to do," Arthur said. "I still can't believe you waltzed into the house in the Hamptons and took all that art right after your mother died."

"I had my reasons," she said. "I thought you knew me better than that."

He had, but she wasn't getting off the hook. "Clara, the boy needs your help," Arthur said, not giving her a chance to hang up. "I wouldn't be calling otherwise."

"Don't I know it," she said. "We haven't seen each other since my wedding day. You have some gall."

He'd never understood her choice in husbands, but if she had any regrets, she'd never shown it. She'd stayed married to the man until he'd died last year. "Gall is my middle name. I sent a card when your husband passed." Like she'd done when he was grieving Harriet.

"Do you expect a thank you? Maybe I was silly for thinking you might call instead."

Damn, she was going to make him confess it. "I did think about it, but decided against it. We haven't seen each other since Kennedy was president."

There was a pause on the line. "And yet you're still calling me about my paintings. Arthur, the Merriams pretty much disowned me. Why should I care about their problems?"

"I know," he said. "I tried to talk them out of it. It saddened me."

"Water under the bridge, as they say. If J.T. wants to ask me, he should do so himself. In person."

Oh, she was still infuriating, but she wasn't wrong. He'd always believed the person needing a favor should be the one to ask. "What would your answer be if I can convince him to approach you?"

"Like I'd tell you."

"After this conversation, I wish I'd called for a different reason. You're still a brat."

"You know there were times over the years when I actually missed hearing you call me that."

Brat had been his pet name for her. She protested, of course, but it had always made her smile. Like that time she'd dragged him to an art gallery in Soho and brought the artist over, telling the confused man Arthur had volunteered to be painted nude. God, what a fireball she'd been. Infuriating as hell, of course, but only two people had ever been able to make him laugh like that. Harriet and Clara.

"Then let me say it again. Brat." Dear God, was he flirting?

"Oh, you odious man! Goodbye, Arthur."

The phone went dead, and he frowned. Spinning the Rolodex for good measure, he grabbed another red hot and crunched. Hard. What was he supposed to make of that exchange? At their age, people might put them in a rest home for flirting. He eyed the phone again. She'd hung up, upset, but what was he supposed to do? Call and try and make it better? No one could do that with Clara. And yet...he'd liked sparring with her again like old times.

Old times. You'd think he'd know better at his age.

Well, he'd tried on the painting front. Perhaps he'd mention it to J.T. Then again, perhaps he wouldn't. It wouldn't surprise him if Clara slammed her door in J.T.'s face if he came calling. Waste of time, particularly given what they were up against on the home front.

When he arrived at Rhett and Abbie's house hours later, he wondered how he could have thought briefing Meredith and Tanner would be possible in such a zoo. Kids were everywhere, yelling like banshees as they zipped across the room. Adults were laughing raucously and stuffing their faces from the community buffet. It would be like trying to have a serious business meeting at a circus.

"Arthur!" he heard Rhett drawl in greeting. "What can I get you to drink?"

"A bourbon, neat," he responded. Clara Merriam made a man want to dial up a stiff drink. Stiff. God, he was turning loony after a little flirting. In his time, they'd have said he was hard up. And the jokes continued, he thought.

Rhett slapped his knee. "Whooee, that's a tall drink order for a Sunday afternoon. You sure you want to go that hard this early? We have wine—"

"If I wanted wine, I would have asked for it," he barked. "Damnation, will everyone stop treating me like I'm elderly? I'm old. Not elderly."

Abbie came up beside Rhett, her face knit with concern. "I'm sure Rhett didn't mean it like that, Arthur. Please, come with me. I'll get you a bourbon. Everyone will be so happy to see you."

He allowed her to link arms with him. Oh, he knew it was a ploy to help him walk easier, but the help, while not welcome, was somewhat needed. Trying not to grind his teeth, he couldn't help but say, "I always come to the Sunday shindig. Can't understand why people would be any happier today than they were last Sunday."

"Because we just love you so much, Grandpa," Jill said, appearing out of nowhere. She kissed his cheek noisily.

"Do you have to leave a mark, Jillie?"

"Oh, stop being a poo. I heard you bark at Rhett from across the room. He was only trying to be nice."

He harrumphed, his go-to response when words just wouldn't do.

Abbie led him over to the bar, and her brother, Mac Maven, proprietor of The Grand Mountain Hotel, greeted him with a warm smile.

"Buffalo Trace okay?" he asked.

"I need to go see Clara," Abbie said. "I think Violet is undressing her."

Another Clara? God help him, he'd almost forgotten the name Abbie and Rhett had chosen for their daughter. Nothing against the baby, but he'd had his fill of women by that name today.

He followed her with his gaze and saw his little great-granddaughter undressing the baby like she was a doll or something.

"Jill did crap like that all the time growing up," he said, shaking his head. "She once talked Brian into sticking pebbles up his nose."

Mac laughed. "Her little girls are always fun to watch."

"From afar," Arthur said. "They put half-eaten Cheerios in my shoes when they visited last time. I told Jill they can't be left alone for a minute."

"Something she well knows," Peggy McBride said, joining Mac at the bar. "Can I have a tonic water?"

"You sick?" Arthur asked. "Fighting crime in Dare Valley running you down?"

She laughed and shared a look with Mac.

Oh, he'd lay odds on what that look meant... Looked like Jared would have another little cousin soon. He would have been elated—hell, who was he kidding, he *was*—except it meant he'd had it wrong about Jane being the next woman in their circle to end up pregnant. Well, it was early yet.

"I've never felt better. Of course, I hear a particular woman staying at Mac's hotel is giving a lot of people in town heartburn."

"*Peggy*," her husband said.

"Do I work for you? Besides, everyone here knows she's a bitch. The only reason she's staying at your hotel is that it's still a free country and you can't kick her out."

He rolled his eyes. "J.T. just arrived with Caroline. Here's your bourbon, Arthur. Maybe you should go talk to them."

"I spoke with him last night as the paper went to print," he said. "Can't I enjoy my drink?"

"From the look on J.T.'s face, no," Peggy said. "That woman must be stirring up more trouble."

He squinted to see better. Sadly, his glasses didn't give him twenty-twenty these days.

"Yeah, he looks like he had bad milk," he said. "Caroline too. People in love should look all rosy-cheeked. Like they've just gotten laid." He sure as hell wasn't rosy-cheeked anymore.

Mac and Peggy started guffawing.

Abbie, the poor innocent girl, gasped, looking over her shoulder at them as she redressed her daughter.

"What? I said 'laid'? You'd think it was a capital offense. Thanks for the bourbon, Mac."

"Always a pleasure, Arthur," the man said to his back. Arthur was already hobbling across the room with his cane.

Andy's boy ran circles around him, evading Jill's other girl, Mia. It was too bad the weather was so shitty, or they could push the kids outside to give them more space to play.

Arthur met J.T. and Caroline in the middle of the Blaylocks' large den. "You look like hell."

"Cynthia called me earlier," J.T. said. "She didn't much like your Op-Ed."

Like he hadn't already heard that from the horse's mouth, but he still didn't want to upset the boy more.

Caroline leaned in to kiss his cheek. "I'm going to find Moira and get a drink. J.T., what do you want?"

"Is that bourbon?" he asked, gesturing to Arthur's drink.

"Yep. Just catch Mac's eye and point to my drink. He'll pour you one."

"I'll go for the wine Jane brought," Caroline said with forced cheerfulness. "I hear it's from a new vineyard in the south of France." Another strike against his theory about Jane.

As she left, J.T. let out a breath. "She's a trooper, but waking up hearing 'Gold Digger' this morning didn't start us off on a great note."

"Cut into the cuddles, I imagine," Arthur said. "Funny, I thought those love letters from your mom's parents would give you more of a boost."

"Who told you about that?"

"Trevor," Arthur said, scanning the room for him and not seeing him. "He thinks you're a certified romantic."

"He's a dead man," J.T. said. "And Caroline and I haven't talked about the letters. It's been a little tense, to be honest. We're sticking to movies and other forms of entertainment to keep our minds off what's going on."

Sounded like a good plan given the situation. "So what did Sin City say?" he asked, wondering if she'd called before or after she'd spoken to him.

"She said she was impressed that I'd brought you into it," he said, rubbing the bridge of his nose. "The rest of it was pretty much same-ol', same-ol'."

"Honey-toned threats and the like?" Arthur asked before taking a healthy sip of his drink.

"Yes," J.T. said. "But you shouldn't worry or anything. You're a well-respected journalist."

He pressed on his cane and drew to his full height. Of course, he'd shrunk a few inches, but he still had bearing and that made a difference. "I know who the hell I am, boy. No need to tell me."

"Sorry," he said. "She makes me..."

"Crazy," Arthur said, deciding it was *really* for the best the kid didn't know his ex had called him. Or that he'd made an unproductive call to the boy's estranged aunt. "Go get your bourbon."

J.T. put his hand on his shoulder and looked him straight in the eye. "Thank you again. For the Op-Ed. For everything."

"Dammit, I want this museum here as much as you do," he told him. "It's not right what Dr. Slimeball and his minion trustees are doing. I'd write about it even if I didn't know you."

His shoulders visibly relaxed. "Thank you."

"Pull yourself together, J.T. This is a party. Give my great-niece a smile."

"Right," he said and then took off.

Arthur made the rounds, sipping on his bourbon. Chef T told him he'd like to drop off some food for Arthur to sample, saying he wanted to make sure it was better than his competition. Arthur didn't believe for a moment he was trying to outdo Brian and his restaurant, one everyone knew Arthur himself had financially backed. No, Chef T was trying to feed him. He decided to let him. What moron turned down five-star Meals on Wheels?

He caught up with his great-nephew Matt and they talked local politics for a while. The new stoplight at the edge of town was causing a ruckus. Somehow people didn't understand Dare Valley needed to change to meet the needs of its expanding population.

He excused himself when he caught sight of Meredith and Tanner by the door. His great-grandson was rubbing his eyes.

"Did the young man have a nap?" he asked when he reached them.

Jared held out his arms to him immediately, which blew a blast of warmth into his heart. Oh, this new generation. Every time he looked at them he wondered how many years he'd have to watch them grow.

"Let me take your bourbon, Arthur," Tanner said.

"Maybe you should sit down, Grandpa," Meredith said, clucking like a mother hen as Arthur traded off his drink for the baby. "He weighs as much as a bowling ball."

"Your grandfather can handle him," Tanner said.

Arthur kissed the top of the boy's head and leaned more heavily on his cane. His grandson did remind him of his old bowling days, but he wasn't going to say anything. He held him for a few minutes, taking in everything that was good about a baby. That special smell. The trust they conveyed in merely allowing someone to hold them. The warmth from their little bodies.

"Okay, I'm good," he said. "We should find somewhere private to chat before you get pulled away."

Meredith nodded as Tanner took Jared from him. "I'll see if Lucy might want to hold him," she said.

"You could parade through the center of the room with the boy and simply ask for volunteers," Arthur suggested.

Meredith shook her head, "Oh, Grandpa," and took off.

Tanner's lips twitched. "She has grand notions of being a good mom."

"She is a good mom," Arthur said. "I wasn't implying otherwise."

Soon Meredith was back with Lucy, whom he hadn't brought into the Newhouse series, as he was calling it. The paper's budget didn't usually allow for them to use a professional photographer of Lucy's caliber, so she only did important photos for the paper. Oh, and that Calendar Girls calendar everyone in town had bought.

Tanner led them to Rhett's office in the back of the house, if you could call it such. Poker trophies lined the glass case at the back of the room, alongside pictures of Rhett wearing some of his most famous game-day outfits. Thank God the man had given up wearing fur. It wasn't a good look on him if you asked Arthur.

"All right, so Sin City called you," Meredith said the minute the door closed. "The nerve! What did she say?"

"What you might expect," Arthur said. "She was as sweet as a debutante with an ice pick. Played to my vanity at first, noting how Newhouse senior usually loved my Op-Eds. Except not today, of course."

Tanner whistled. "So she brought Albert Newhouse's name into it. From what J.T. and Trevor have said, she hasn't gone there before."

"Yes," Arthur said. "She said she thought we should be acquainted now. Apparently she called J.T. as well. Made a comment about being surprised he'd brought me into it. Like I wouldn't have done it if I didn't know him."

Meredith made a face. "That bitch. She threatened you."

"Not surprising from what we know about her," he said. "My biggest concern is you interviewing her, Tanner. I think you should have someone go with you. Someone junior. We can say it's your protégée or something. I want a witness."

Tanner didn't blink, but Meredith immediately narrowed her eyes.

"Do you think she's going to come on to Tanner?" she asked.

"As a way to discredit him?" Arthur shrugged. "I wouldn't put it past her. We need to be on our toes from now on. We struck first. She's given me every reason to believe she'll strike back."

"Albert Newhouse could make a few comments about the issue, given his connections in business and politics," Tanner said, "but would he? It's not his fight, and he might look ridiculous."

Arthur expected Cynthia would know that. "If she asks her daddy to do something, I doubt it will be public. We'll see. In the meantime, we document everything. I want a full transcript of your interview with her."

"Assuming she grants me one," Tanner said. "I'm not sure she'll want to go on the record."

"True," Arthur said. "Still, it gives her an opportunity to bash her ex-husband publically, and that's what we want. Show with her own words how crazy she is." It would be a fine line, but if anyone could write on it, it was Tanner.

"Assuming she says anything," Meredith said. "She's

like the trustees who changed their minds. They won't say boo to J.T.'s face, but I can guarantee you they're talking plenty behind his back."

Meredith's article was going to be about the board of trustees—how some of them had changed their minds after approving the museum. "I don't know who has the harder job in terms of getting someone to go on record."

Tanner laughed. "Perhaps we need a side bet, sweetheart."

Meredith waggled her brows at her husband.

"Oh, get a room!" Arthur groaned. "Am I the only person around here not getting laid?"

He heard them clear their throats before Tanner said, "We should get back to the party. I'm clear on my marching orders."

Of course, he could have just told them all of this tomorrow morning at the office, but they didn't work like that. They were a team. Their trust meant the world to him, and Meredith would have been angry if he'd seen them socially and neglected to mention the call. Clara, however, was another matter. Her he would keep to himself.

When they walked back down the hall, Trevor was lollygagging in the hallway, a tumbler of bourbon in his hand.

"I'll catch up to you," Arthur told Meredith and Tanner. "Hello, Young Trevor. I looked for you earlier."

"Uncle," he said, lifting his glass in a toast. "I was late due to a call. Rhett told me you were using his office to talk to Meredith and Tanner privately. I got to figuring Sin City might have called you today."

He hoped the grim set of his mouth conveyed his feelings on the matter. "Yes. I was just briefing them on it."

"Anything I should know?" he asked, his body casual but his eyes almost predatory.

Young Trevor could be downright scary when the situation called for it.

"I don't plan on telling J.T.," Arthur said, "so if that's a moral dilemma..."

"It's not," he said. "I don't like keeping things from him, but when it's for the best, I sleep like a baby."

"Glad you think so," Arthur said "since I also called your Aunt Clara and asked her to give her portion of the Merriam collection to the museum."

Trevor didn't even blink. "Did she hang up on you?"

"Not quite," he said. "Of course, this stays between us. No need to mention another probable dead-end to J.T."

"I couldn't agree more," Trevor said. "So what did Sin City say when she called?"

He gave him a succinct recitation, and at the end, Trevor let out a curse word Arthur hadn't heard since Vietnam.

"I don't like her mentioning her daddy," Trevor said.

"Neither do I."

Trevor was silent. "I hope we didn't get you into more hot water than you can handle."

He slapped the young buck on the back. "One thing about getting old is your skin gets a heck of a lot tougher," he said.

CHAPTER 22

J.T. CLOSED THE DOOR BEHIND THE THIRD TRUSTEE THEY'D entertained, just barely restraining the urge to slam it.

"This is bullshit!" he declared to his fellow welcoming committee, who'd gathered in the foyer to bid their guests adieu.

Trevor gave him a bored stare. Evan fidgeted alongside Margie, who took his hand. Chase's poker face was intact. At least Moira seemed to agree with him, somewhat—though she was usually as cool and collected as Chase, today her cheeks were the color of red poppies.

"We're encouraging them to believe Caroline has a conflict of interest by not including her, and I don't like it one bit! How are they going to have faith in me and her unless they see how smart and professional she is?"

Every day, she briefed him on her progress with the new museum as if it were happening, and every day, he tried to keep his spirits up. For both of them. Dammit, this couldn't all be for naught.

"I know I thought it was best to keep her out of it," Moira said, "but I've changed my mind. The Op-Ed Arthur wrote has helped, but it hasn't addressed one of the elephants in the room. Why else would Professor Hockswelter make that comment tonight? *Your sister's recent firing from Leggett Gallery is a serious concern, you understand.* We all know Cynthia was the one who orchestrated that in the first place! I wanted to hit him."

"You can use our punching bag anytime," Trev told her.

"Calm down," Chase said. "I'm as angry as everyone else here, but we need to think carefully. We can't prove Cynthia was behind it."

"Then let her defend herself at least," J.T. said, clenching his fists. "I tried to, but Trevor cut me off."

His brother didn't acknowledge his glare. "I was in a better position to defend her. If you'd done it, it would have looked self-serving, and the same is true of Moira as her sister."

Moira put her hands on her hips. "I hate this!"

"Welcome to political wining and dining," Chase said in a tight voice.

"I love you," she said, "but if you think I'm going to spend the rest of our married life spending my time with horrible people like that, you're crazy. They aren't even interested in art! That jerk just wanted to throw his weight around."

"I agree with Moira," Margie said. "My family used to host these kinds of dinner parties. I don't like watching one of my friends get lambasted like that."

"No one likes it," Evan said, raising her hand to his lips. "I'm sorry. This is why I let Chase do all the entertaining."

Chase set his feet. "Trevor and I are the only ones with the stomach for it, but frankly, we're not the most effective players here. I thought unity would help, but it seems to me there's something we don't know. It's like the three trustees we've had dinner with are—"

"Smug," Trev said. "I agree. Sin City has something else going on. I think it's time to change tactics."

This wasn't what J.T. wanted to hear. He'd spent

three evenings in the last week biting his tongue as he listened to carefully worded slights about himself and the woman he loved. Now they were going to try something else? Terrific!

"What exactly do you have in mind?" he asked his brother. "Is it time to hire an assassin?"

"I'm all for it," Moira said. "God, I never thought I could get this mad. I mean, I've seen crap in human resources, but this kind of steamrolling is a whole new level of shit."

Trevor walked over and slapped Chase on the back. "J.T. and I really appreciate all of you stepping forward in solidarity to help, but I think your service is up. They know you aren't going to pull the Artemis Institute from the university, and our strategy isn't working. J.T. and I need to do some more digging. We need to figure out what's going on behind the scenes."

There was a knock on the door. At another time, J.T. might have been amused by the way everyone's faces scrunched into twin looks of disgust, but he was too busy feeling his own disgust to muster any humor about it.

"Please tell me they didn't forget anything," Moira whispered. "I can't fake smile anymore."

"Me either," Margie said.

Trevor opened the hall closet and started handing out coats. "Why don't the rest of you head out? We'll handle this."

The person knocked louder this time, and J.T. made himself cross to the door.

"Think of England," Trevor quipped in an undertone.

"Yeah, right," he said, opening the door.

Uncle Arthur and Tanner were waiting on the other side, looking grim.

"Not who I was expecting, but... Come in."

Trevor got behind their guests and started herding them out as though they were a bunch of Canadian geese.

"Seriously, you guys go home. It's been a long night, and we all know Margie has to wake up in a few hours."

"Tell me about it," Uncle Arthur said. "I'd kiss and shake hands but I don't have the energy. I'm supposed to turn into a pumpkin at nine o'clock."

Moira still kissed his cheek on the way out, her brow knit with worry. After Trevor closed the door, he took Uncle Arthur's and Tanner's coats.

"Well, I know when someone's died," Trev said. "What happened?"

"Best sit down," Uncle Arthur said, leaning heavily on his cane. "We just blew things wide open."

Tanner's article had gone out yesterday. Cynthia had refused to be interviewed, and Uncle Arthur had been trying to figure out how to wheedle her into going on the record ever since. Even Trev had thought the piece was a solid for them. Perhaps that was why the trustee had gone after Caroline? Dammit, he just didn't know.

"If you have a bourbon, Young Trevor," Uncle Arthur added, "I could sure use it. You might pour one for yourself and your brother too."

J.T. unbuttoned his jacket and joined their visitors on the couch in the den. "I find I'm more afraid to hear what you have to say than of being stuck in an elevator."

"And he's claustrophobic," Trev said, bringing over the bottle of bourbon and four highball glasses. He doled out four healthy pours. "All right, best rip it off like a Band-Aid."

Uncle Arthur gestured to Tanner. "Your source. Your show."

"Right," the man said, reaching for his bourbon. "A little background. You might not know this, but I teach a journalism class at Emmits Merriam and have since I first arrived in Dare Valley."

"A damn good class too," Arthur muttered. "Kids think he's the second coming of journalism."

"Anyway, I'm always telling them to keep their ears open for a story, and it seems one of my students took that to heart. He cleans President Matthau's office as part of a work study program."

J.T. sat forward on the edge of his seat. "And I take it he heard something."

"Yes," Tanner said, his mouth tipping up. "Anyway, this student said the former president always made a point of talking to him, asking about his studies, that sort of thing, but Dr. Matthau doesn't even know he's alive. He might even think he's employed by a cleaning service. Today, Cynthia Newhouse was meeting with the president, after office hours, when my student was cleaning. For whatever reason, President Matthau didn't close the door."

"And your student heard something," J.T. said. "What's she up to?" *Please don't let them be having sex*, he thought but didn't say.

"She's planning on giving the university a three-hundred-million-dollar gift for cancer research," Tanner said.

J.T. felt like someone had hit him in the head. "*Cancer research?*"

"Matthau has a PhD in microbiology, and this is a pet interest of his," Arthur said. "Plus, his mother died of breast cancer at fifty."

His brain started to work. The media was going to love this. "And let me guess—the gift is conditional."

"My student didn't know," Tanner said, "but I think we can assume as much."

"And cancer research wins over art any day," J.T. said, feeling deflated. She'd outplayed him again.

"It's still a breach of the agreement the board made for the museum," Trevor said.

"Also, it's illegal to leverage one gift to knock out another," Tanner said. "If you can prove it, of course, and I don't think we can."

J.T. couldn't sit down anymore. "Doesn't matter. We'll look like dicks if we try and fight it. After all, cancer research is more important."

Arthur growled and grabbed his tumbler, taking a healthy swig of bourbon. "That's not the tack to take. I hate to say this, J.T., but you have a decision before you. Tanner needs to get someone on the record about this gift."

"Not the student?" Trevor asked.

"If he does, he could lose his work study and get kicked out of school," he said. "Also, going up against the president of the university—"

"Dr. Slimeball could and likely would say he lied," J.T. said. "Leave the kid out of it. I don't want anyone to lose their university education out of this." Of course, he wouldn't let that happen regardless. He'd sooner give the kid a scholarship himself.

"I plan to show up at a few trustees' offices tomorrow and ask for confirmation. There are a few people who might be willing to go on record."

"You think other people know about this?" Trevor said.

"About the Newhouse gift, yes," Tanner said. "If it's conditional, they wouldn't be open about that. Only a few people would know."

"She's one smart cookie," Arthur said. "The CIA could have used her to take down the Berlin Wall."

The whole thing was a lot to take in. J.T. rubbed his aching head. "So what happens if you get trustees to go on record?"

"I need to get two people minimum or—"

"We won't run the story," Arthur finished. "But Tanner will get his sources and write a damn good article because he's a damn good journalist. The problem is where that leaves you, J.T."

Over a barrel holding his ankles, like old times. "Any ideas?"

Arthur sighed. "Well, you could issue a press release

saying you welcome this gift by the Newhouse family for cancer research and that you don't see a conflict with the museum. You're divorced and don't hold any ill feelings against Ms. Newhouse."

He'd choke on those last words if he ever had to speak them aloud. Right now he couldn't trust himself around her. He wanted to rage at her for messing with his life. For attempting to destroy his future.

"Trev?" J.T. asked.

His brother was staring into his bourbon and swirling the amber liquid. "I need to think this one through. I can see a gift of this size earning Sin City a seat on the Board of Trustees."

"So can I," Arthur said, tapping his cane on the ground.

Wasn't that a kick in the teeth. "The old president had suggested giving me a board seat so I can represent the Merriam family again." He'd been excited to follow in the family footsteps.

"If that still goes through, you might find yourself dealing with Sin City for the foreseeable future. There would be ongoing power struggles—"

And he'd never be free of her. Exactly like she'd promised him.

"Want to pull the museum yet?" Arthur asked. "Because you look like you're considering it."

He found he couldn't deny it.

"Look, we lost our biggest advertiser for the newspaper today, so I don't have it in me to sweet-talk you."

Trevor leaned forward. "Is there anything we can do, Uncle?"

"Bah, no," Arthur said. "I've managed to keep the paper solid for almost sixty years. We'll weather it. But that's not why I brought it up. Sometimes shit happens. Do you want to hear what I think your great granddaddy would do if he were here, J.T.?" Arthur pointed to the painting where Emmits Merriam stood in all his young glory.

"I'm all ears," he said.

"You find a way not to look like a dick and stand your ground."

J.T. stared up at that painting, taking in the flash of determination the artist had captured. His great grandfather had faced incredible challenges in his day, everything from digging his first oil well to shipping it out of Oklahoma. He wasn't going to be the first Merriam in the history of the family to give up his dream without a whimper. He certainly wasn't going to let Caroline down either.

"Then let's find a way."

CHAPTER 23

WHEN J.T. FINALLY FELL ASLEEP, CAROLINE SLIPPED out of bed.

She thought about reading some more of his grandparents' love letters—she'd stretched them out, savoring the slow unfurling of their romance—but she didn't have the heart. The enormity of his gesture wasn't lost on her. She'd thanked him for lending the letters to her, but the words "thank you" didn't feel big enough. She was showing him how she felt by hanging with him, just like he'd asked, and hopefully that was enough for now.

Still, she couldn't sugarcoat what he'd told her tonight. They had a big problem on their hands, and the museum was more than a little in trouble. If that woman got her way, she'd soon be on the board of the university.

Retreating to the kitchen, she boiled a kettle of water for a pot of chamomile tea, turning the problem over and over in her mind. It was about time she contributed more than moral support, outrage, and art consultancy.

The question before her was terrible, if she were being honest. What about art could be more important or exciting than a huge new cancer research institute?

The first thing that came to mind—the recovery of

a stolen painting—like Marc Chagall's painting "Othello and Desdemona," which had recently been found by the FBI after being stolen thirty years ago from a couple in New York.

That wasn't going to work. Tanner had already mentioned that in his article, and it was old news. Besides, it wasn't like that work was a Chagall.

She tapped her temple. What else got people in the art world excited?

The answer came to her at once: a lost painting by a great master. Something they didn't have.

"What are you doing?"

She jumped and looked over her shoulder. J.T. was tying his full-length navy robe as he padded into the kitchen.

"I...ah..."

The teakettle whistled, making her jump again. J.T. walked over to the stove and turned off the burner. Pouring the water into the waiting teapot, he brought it over to where she was sitting.

"I couldn't sleep," she admitted.

"I'm sorry about before," he said, setting the pot down and going to the cabinet for two mugs.

"What do you mean?" But they both already knew, didn't they? The awkwardness between them was back in spades.

"I had the weight of the world on my shoulders when I arrived, and I pretty much checked out during Jimmy Fallon. Not very romantic."

She went for honesty. "Truthfully, I checked out too. My mind kind of exploded when you told me about the cancer research gift. It was a shock."

"Yeah," he said, sitting down and taking her hand. "Sometimes I feel like we should run off to some private island."

She remembered Trevor teasing him about that.

Right now, it didn't feel very funny. "Me too, but this is... our home. Your grandparents stayed tough and made a home against odds greater than these." There, she'd said it.

"You've been reading the letters," he whispered. "I'm glad."

Crossing the room, she opened her arms and engulfed him in a hug. For a moment, they simply stayed that way, swaying a little from side to side.

Home. That's what I thought when I was coming back here. Then I met you, and everything clicked. I felt like I had everything I wanted."

He was talking about big love, the kind to build a life on. "You still have me," she said, squeezing his hand for emphasis. "Like your grandma writes in her letters, I'm learning what it means to love someone no matter what happens."

He was shaking his head. "That might be the most wonderful thing anyone has ever said to me. That's what I want for us. What I've wanted from the beginning."

"Do you think about us getting married someday when all this is over? Like Noah and Anna? Sorry, they aren't your grandparents to me when I'm reading the letters. They're young people in love like I am even if their odds are so much greater. I mean, what tops war?"

"Not even Cynthia tops that," he said with a harsh laugh. "I love you. And I'd hoped we might make this permanent at some point. Living in the same house. Getting a dog or cat. Maybe kids if you're up for it. But I'm still having PTSD or something about the marriage, and I'm not sure I want to do it again."

"Oh," she said, trying not to sound deflated.

He grabbed her by the shoulders. "It's not like that. A relationship doesn't need to be official to be permanent. Plenty of couples in Europe live together forever without getting married. I guess what I'm saying is that I don't need a piece of paper to tell me how I feel about you."

She knew what he meant, and yet... "Marriage has always been an obvious equation to me. Two people who love each other and want to be together forever get married. But I can see your point. And given your ex, some divorce PTSD seems pretty inevitable."

"I don't want you to feel bad," he said, looking directly into her eyes. "It doesn't mean I don't want our relationship to grow. I'm just not so sure I want it to be sanctioned by the law."

His explanation was honest and it made sense. She inched her chair closer and leaned her head on his shoulder. "I'll open my mind up since it's so important to you. I don't need a piece of paper to tell me how I feel about you either."

"I've watched my parents support each other through thick and thin. I've always wanted that, and with you, I think I've finally found it."

Those words warmed her heart. "I love you."

He kissed her sweetly on the lips. "I love you. Now, let's get you some tea. You're cold. What kind is this?"

She went for more humor. "Raspberry leaves."

He gave her a blank look as he reached out to pour.

"Women's herbs."

Watching him snatch his hand back, she laughed so hard tears leaked out of her eyes. Man, it felt good to laugh like that. "Oh, your face. Just kidding. It's chamomile. To calm the nerves."

"Whew, good thing you're the only one having any," he said, swiping at his forehead playfully. "All I could hear was Trev having a go at me for drinking women's tea. What were you thinking about when I walked in? Your brows were delightfully scrunched like they are whenever you're trying to figure out how to work the entertainment system."

"Blake is insane! I've never seen a system so complicated."

He laughed as he set her tea in front of her. "You don't like technology. Admit it."

"I've never denied it. I'm an art person," she said, cocking an eyebrow. "I'd be happy to buy leather-bound books and handwrite everything. As for what I was thinking, I was trying to puzzle out what kind of art thingamabob would top a cancer research gift."

"Art thingamabob? Is that a technical term? Sounds like we need some gelato."

She socked him. "Yes. I've ruled out the recovery of a stolen painting."

"Right. Been there, done that." He took a sip of her tea. "This tastes terrible. I need that gelato." He rose and grabbed the carton from the freezer along with two spoons.

"I love this," she said when he served her a spoonful of gelato. "Yum. It struck me that what we need is a lost work of art by an old master. But I've catalogued your whole collection, and nothing quite hits that mark."

His spoon clattered to the table, and he grabbed her face and kissed her on the mouth. Before she could properly enjoy it, he broke away and leapt to his feet.

"Caroline Hale! You are a genius!"

"I am? What did I do?"

"You gave me an idea," he said, pacing in the kitchen. "Of course, it won't be easy. She'll probably slam the door in my face, but I've got to find a way to convince her. Of course, assuming the story is true."

Caroline lurched out of her chair and grabbed the front of his robe. "You're speaking in code!"

He set his hands on her shoulders. "You remember what I told you about my horrible aunt who has the other half of the Merriam art collection?"

"You mean the one I've been trying to get you to call?" she asked with some sauciness.

He tapped her on the nose. "Yep, that one. One of those paintings might just fit the bill."

"Really?" She bounced in place. "You have a lost painting! Why didn't you tell me about this ages ago?"

He started laughing, but she thought she detected a little bounce in his step too. "According to family lore, it's a Rembrandt—something he painted right before 'Night Watch.'"

"I think I have to sit back down." Her ears were ringing as she lowered back into the chair. "*A Rembrandt.*"

"You sound like you do when we're in bed, and I'm—"

"J.T. Merriam, you'd better tell me everything. Right this minute."

He saluted her. "Yes, ma'am. The story goes that Emmits' wife, Joanne, was the one who saw it in an old antique shop in a small town in the Netherlands. She was touring the tulips and they'd stopped for a bite to eat—"

Was he crazy? "Forget the tulips! Cut to the painting!"

"I've never see it, but I've heard—"

"What do you mean you've never seen it?"

"Caroline, do you want to hear this story or not?" he asked, sitting next to her.

"Fine, I won't interrupt." She mimed zipping her lips.

"We never went to the Hamptons where it was stored," he said. "My parents preferred...other places. Anyway, from what my dad told me, Great Grandma Joanne had a keen eye for detail, and the painting first drew her eye because of the mood and subject."

She grabbed his robe when he paused again. "Keep going."

"It was a biblical scene—of Mary—done in Rembrandt's trademark light and shadow. It's a nude, which is a little surprising perhaps, but he also painted Bathsheba nude—"

"Because the Bible characterizes her as an adulteress," she finished for him. "He painted Mary, the mother of God, nude?" That was...crazy or...inspired. She didn't know which right now.

"Maybe that's why it got lost," J.T. said. "The fact that half of his signature was scraped off might also have contributed to it disappearing."

"A nude Mary would have been scandalous in the 1600s in the Netherlands," she said. "J.T., this is huge!"

"Don't get so excited," he said, holding up a hand. "We have some obstacles. First, there's my aunt. When I tell you she's a bitch, I'm not mincing words. Second, the painting hasn't undergone any of the new tests, so I can't be sure it's a Rembrandt until we test—"

"But you just said—"

"Given Cynthia's accusations, I'll need more than family stories to bolster my confidence."

Right. "Okay, so we need to see the painting. No use asking your aunt for it back unless there's a strong indication it might be the real deal. You know the Dutch masters are a specialty of mine."

He waggled his brows. "I do, but we have some challenges. Dad says she's purposely refused to have it authenticated because she likes the allure of it being a potential Rembrandt. Kinda like how those churches in Seville and Santo Domingo in Spain both claimed Columbus was buried there until they finally consented to a DNA testing of the bones."

"And Seville won," she said. "I remember that. That story broke right before my high school graduation. I remember Andy yelling at me for dawdling over something so dumb."

His eyes sparkling, he leaned in to brush a kiss on her mouth. "It was like we were meant to be. It happened right before my college graduation at Stanford, and Trev pulled the newspaper out of my hands to get me out the door."

Golly, it *was* like they were two soul mates who'd found each other.

"Anyway, this won't be a walk in the park," he said, rubbing her hand. "But it's the best idea we have right now. I still can't guarantee she'll see me."

"You have to try!" she said. "But we'll need to move fast if Tanner's trying to confirm Cynthia's gift for a news story."

The smile he gave her reminded her of the J.T. of old, the one who'd walked into the gallery and bought a painting for thousands of dollars and talked her into going to Rome on a whim.

"Good thing I specialize in fast," he said, his lips twitching as he dug into the carton and came up with a huge spoonful of gelato.

Her mind flashed to the dreams he'd shared while they ate gelato on Palatine Hill in Rome. Then, like now, he'd seemed larger than life.

"I seem to recall you saying something to me in the gallery like, 'Welcome to my world, Caroline Hale,'" she repeated, to remind him who he was as much as to punctuate the moment.

"Damn right," he said. "*My* world."

CHAPTER 24

BY TWO A.M., J.T. HAD ALREADY CHECKED THE ART LOSS register, the well-known international database for stolen art, as well as various websites from dedicated Rembrandt lovers. Of course, Caroline was by his side, and at one point, she took over the computer when he wasn't typing fast enough.

There was no record of the painting, but that wasn't a surprise. It was supposedly lost.

"We'll need to dig deeper," Caroline said, cracking her knuckles. "And I know just where to look."

Together they combed through articles from the world's most recognized Rembrandt scholar.

"This is going to take a while," J.T. said, trying not to get depressed.

Caroline thrust out her cup. "Get some more tea."

"Yes, ma'am," he said, and as soon as he prepared the two steaming cups, he hunkered back down.

It took another hour for them to come across a short note saying there was some confusion about whether or not the great master had, in fact, painted Mary the Mother of God nude. The master hadn't claimed to have done so, but one of his rivals insisted he had. The scholar went on to note that regardless, the painting in question seemed to have disappeared from history.

J.T. whooped into the air, and Caroline gripped his hand. "I'm feeling those weird tingles again," she said.

"Yeah, I was starting to worry we wouldn't find anything. God knows, Trev would think we're being foolish."

His brother wasn't an art fan to begin with, and even if he made it through an explanation of the situation without falling asleep, he'd have guffawed at J.T.'s description of the painting. Yeah, a lost Rembrandt. Of Mary. Naked.

Was it lost because it was a fake? Or a practical joke on the master? Who knew? It certainly wasn't the solution to his problem with Cynthia if any of those were true.

The mystery thing was almost as compelling as the possible benefits of finding a lost Rembrandt. And if it *was* real...

For his future—and Caroline's—he would beg his aunt on bended knee if it came down to it.

After stopping their research for the night, he and Caroline made love, filled with the shared excitement of the painting as well as the evolution of their partnership. He stared into her eyes as he rocked into her, and she held his gaze until they both found their release. Wrapping their arms around each other, they fell asleep—the first peaceful sleep they'd had since that first night together.

They had hope, and hope changed everything.

After a short catnap, he ordered up the family jet to meet them in Denver at eight o'clock that morning, figuring it should give him enough time to put things in motion. He called Trev, who was glad to sit out on this trip with the horrible Aunt Clara, and then Uncle Arthur and Tanner, who listened with the rapt interest of a reporter with a lead on a good story. Uncle Arthur had followed up with a cryptic piece of advice. "She might consider it if you show up at her doorstep. Don't take no for an answer."

Right.

Next he called his forensic art consultant, Bartholomew Farnsworth, and asked him to meet him in New York City, where his aunt lived, and be on call. Assuming his aunt surprised him with her generosity, he could have it tested by one of the world's leading experts the same day.

By early afternoon, he and Caroline arrived outside his aunt's townhouse in the Upper East Side.

"Are you as nervous as I am?" she asked him.

Likely more so since he wasn't sure they'd get through the front door. This wasn't the time to mention that his aunt had slammed the door in his mother's face when she'd visited her in the hopes of getting the art back for the family. His mom hadn't been too happy about that. "It's going to be fine."

He rang the dignified bell and winced when a wizened butler more apt for the retirement home than service opened the door. Composing his face took effort. Seeing this butler made Aunt Clara seem even more eccentric. Maybe she'd gone mad. Perish the thought.

"May I help you, sir?"

Sure enough, the man had a British accent. "Hello, my name is J.T. Merriam, and I'm here to see my aunt. Kindly inform her I'm here."

He hated to be so declarative, but he'd learned in London how important it was to clearly state your intentions. Otherwise, you'd never gain entry anywhere.

"And the lady?" the butler asked.

"Caroline Hale," she responded before he could. "Arthur Hale's niece."

The butler's expression stayed as flat as though he were one of the guards at Buckingham Palace. "I'll see if she's available."

He motioned for them to step into the foyer and made sure to close the door. J.T. was glad the man considered it rude to leave them wait on the doorstep on a cold New York day.

"Arthur Hale's niece, eh?" J.T. whispered, taking in the grand staircase and the oodles of art on the walls. It was so *silent*. Like museum-quality silence.

"I thought it might help," she said, shrugging, "although I hate having to name drop. I figure people should just meet with you of their own accord." She paused, surveying the walls with a hungry expression. "She likes the Impressionists, I see."

"Yeah, she got most of those paintings from the collection," he said. "I couldn't bear to tell you. Someone thought they were a better fit for the beach house. Although the house in the Hamptons isn't really what I'd call a beach house." In reality, it was a large estate on the ocean.

"I'm rather mad at your uncle," a stern female voice said.

They turned to see a short woman wearing all black and dripping in diamonds. Clara Allerton had gone gray and wore it long. Somehow, it looked regal on her. She was seventy-six, he knew, but those cheekbones made her look years younger. Standing there at the edge of the foyer, her presence made a statement.

"My uncle?" he asked, confused.

She pointed an elegant finger at Caroline. "No, hers. That rapscallion called me a short time ago after not speaking to me for decades. Much like your father, Julian."

God, he hated when people called him Julian. It reminded him of Cynthia, who'd made a point of calling him something other people didn't. He might have corrected her, except he was reeling from surprise. "Arthur Hale called you?"

Caroline turned toward him, her mouth parted. "He didn't mention it."

"He wouldn't have," Clara said, walking toward them, her gait still finishing-school perfect. "He told me to give you all my paintings because it was the right thing to do. The gall of that man is unmatched."

Goodness, Uncle Arthur, J.T. thought. *Nice of you to make this a walk in the park.*

Caroline coughed. "Uncle Arthur does have a way with words. Thank you for meeting with us, Mrs. Allerton."

"I haven't agreed to meet with you, Ms. Hale," she said, drawing nearer.

For some reason it surprised J.T. to see how much she resembled his father. Those blue eyes were the same shade, the bottom lip fuller than the top. "Well, Uncle Arthur wasn't wrong," he said, "even if he was rather indelicate. I'd love to take the whole collection off your hands."

She smacked her fist into her hand. "You're impertinent. Like your father. Perhaps you should be more humble since you're having problems at the university Emmits himself founded. That doesn't bode well for the family legacy, does it?"

Her eyes gleamed like an eagle sighting prey.

"No, frankly, it doesn't. I'm having some trouble with—"

"That Newhouse spawn you married," she said. "Yes, I know. Arthur told me all about it. Why in the world did you marry a woman like that?"

He rocked back on his heels, feeling every bit of awkwardness loaded into that question. Caroline shifted beside him, the movement reminding him he had to say something. "I fell in love with her. My mistake."

"Then you're as blind as all men," she said, "including my Reinhold. He was fooled by mistress after mistress until he fell over dead from a heart attack in the sauna with one of them."

Caroline uttered some inarticulate response, and he couldn't blame her. That was something his dad hadn't told him.

"I hadn't heard the particulars," he said, wondering what the appropriate response was. *I'm sorry?*

"He wasn't the person I thought he was either, when I married him, so I have some sympathy for you," she said. "But that doesn't mean I'm just going to give you all my art."

He cocked his head to the side. She was studying him and Caroline, and while she hadn't agreed to sit down and chat—or even offer them a drink, which was rude— she also hadn't kicked them out. Had Uncle Arthur gotten under her skin? Or was something else going on here?

"How about a proposition then? I understand you may have a lost Rembrandt. I'd like to authenticate it."

She raised her pointer finger and slowly shook it back and forth. "I've purposely left that painting undocumented just to piss your father off. He always liked the Dutch masters, although I think their work is too dark and depressing."

His dad liked the Dutch masters? "I'm sure you're mistaken. My dad isn't much of an art fan."

She swatted his arm. "Oh, don't be ridiculous. He's a huge art fan. Why do you think I took all the Hamptons paintings? I knew it would break his heart."

But his father didn't have anything to do with the collection. In fact, he never talked about it. Whenever J.T. mentioned the paintings, his face glazed over. "You're mistaken."

"Do you think your father would have paid to insure and protect all those paintings if he didn't love them? Or have your mother show up here and beg me to give them back? Goodness, it's easy to pull the wool over your eyes, isn't it?"

"Aunt Clara—"

"Oh, please don't call me that, boy," she said with a hearty sigh. "I haven't seen you since you were a snotty five-year-old, crying beside a grave you didn't understand. Seems my brother pretended to lose his interest in art after I took my revenge."

"And does that make you feel good, Mrs. Allerton?" Caroline asked.

Her tone was polite, but the woman's face scrunched as though she'd tasted a lemon. "You're as impertinent as your uncle. Well, if you're going to insult me, you might as well stay for tea."

She executed a spin a ballet dancer would have envied and sailed through a door opposite the one she'd used to enter the foyer.

"That was interesting," J.T. said quietly, still reeling. "I suppose we should follow her."

Caroline took his arm in a hard grip. "You don't think she'd poison us, do you? Goodness, she's tough. I can't imagine what Uncle Arthur must have said to stir her up."

He agreed, but his mind was still reeling from Clara's revelation about his father. Why hadn't either of his parents ever said anything? Perhaps he should have realized the truth. After all, his dad had kept part of the collection at their home in Napa.

The butler was hovering over a table set with a gold-painted teapot and table service for three. A four-tiered sterling silver tray held an array of sandwiches and small cakes. So, she'd planned to let them stay before she met them at the door.

After pulling out first his aunt's chair and then Caroline's, he settled into the third chair at the round table decked out in a fine white tablecloth. "Thank you for this lovely spread. Everything looks wonderful. And is that Earl Grey tea I smell?"

"Oh, don't butter my bread, Julian," she said, motioning for the butler to pour out the tea. "I'm way too old for your charms, but I do know a lost Rembrandt would help you defeat that Newhouse woman."

He was glad they weren't beating around the bush.

"Are you familiar with the Newhouse family, Mrs. Allerton?" Caroline asked, nodding her thanks to the butler when he finished pouring her tea.

"Anyone who's anyone is familiar with them, of course," she said. "Don't be impertinent."

Apparently that was his aunt's favorite word. "She didn't mean to be. She's only—"

"Trying to get a sense of how much I loathe them," his aunt said and then launched into a cackle. "By all means, let us be straightforward with one another. I don't like them much. Constance, your former mother-in-law, has ice in her veins so cold it would rival arctic ice. She slighted me once at the Met, and I've never forgotten it."

J.T. wanted to dance for joy. "Constance wasn't my favorite."

"And yet you married her daughter," she said, turning her teacup toward her. "Did you not meet that horrible woman's parents beforehand?"

He shifted again in his seat, looking at Caroline. Was it weird talking about your old life with your ex-wife in front of the new love of your life? Hell, yes, it was. But he still needed to do it. "They were…pleasant. I mean, I wasn't expecting to meet Ward and June Cleaver from *Leave It to Beaver*."

"No, I expect not," she said, drawing a cucumber and cream cheese sandwich onto her plate.

When was the last time he'd had one of those? He grabbed a few to be polite.

"Arthur Hale wants me to help you fight this Newhouse woman by giving you the whole collection," she said. "Like I said, he has gall to call asking for a favor after not talking to me since my wedding day."

He wasn't sure what to make of that. "Honestly, we're at an impasse. More paintings might not turn the tide. She's talking about giving the university three hundred million dollars for cancer research."

Her brows shot to her hairline. "She's a smart bitch, isn't she? Art or cancer? There's no question what normal people would choose."

He almost laughed at the way she said 'normal' people. Art aficionados like them were definitely not 'normal' if you asked him.

"Hence your interest in the Rembrandt," she continued. "Well, I don't see that I have a choice, do I?"

Caroline's teacup clattered to its plate. "I beg your pardon?"

"You heard me," his aunt said, thumping the table. "Without the Rembrandt, you're…what do you young people say so baldly? Screwed? Is that right?"

"Yes," he said, trying to hold back his smile. "Are you serious? You're not pulling my leg?"

"I couldn't pull that hard at my age," she said, dramatically sighing.

He shot out of his chair and kissed her on the cheek.

"Oh, do pull yourself together, Julian," she said, swatting at him. "For heaven's sake. We barely know each other."

Unable to contain his glee, he circled the table and kissed Caroline square on the mouth before he returned to his own chair. "You're incredible!"

"I suspected you two were canoodling," his aunt said, rearranging her napkin in her lap. "Grandpa Emmits must be smiling in heaven. A Merriam and a Hale in love. God, it makes me believe in poetry."

"Does it really, Mrs. Allerton?" Caroline asked, taking J.T.'s hand under the table.

"God, no," she scoffed. "Do *I* strike you as a romantic?"

J.T. sat back in his chair and relaxed for the first time in weeks. They weren't in the clear yet—for all he knew, the painting was a fake—but it was a victory, and victories should be celebrated.

"Maybe you've just gotten used to hiding it."

"And you might be as impertinent as my grandfather himself," Clara said, taking a sip of tea.

"If that's true, I take it as a compliment," he said. "So Aunt Clara…"

He waited to how she'd react to the name and caught Caroline putting her napkin over her mouth, likely to cover a smile. Since his aunt didn't remark, limiting her response to a stately glare, he felt like they were making progress.

"This is a personal question," he said, "and you don't have to answer it."

"Now, let's not get carried away. I'll have my butler toss you out if you become too familiar, Julian." She turned her head to the side like the debutante she'd been.

Like that old man could physically throw him out. "Noted. What have you been doing all these years? I mean, you alluded to a difficult marriage—something I sympathize with—but it's been a year since he passed. Correct?"

"Yes, although I wish he'd croaked years ago, if you want to know the truth," she said, pouring herself another cup of tea without waiting for the butler. "I married young, and I made a bad choice. Women from my generation didn't leave their husbands. We made the best of things, so when your father… Oh, never mind."

Now they were getting to the heart of it. He found he

wasn't willing to let it slide. Too many things were left unsaid in his family, he realized, and he wanted to put a stop to that now. "What about my father?"

She went completely still, and he watched her throat ripple for a moment before she sat up straighter in her chair. Pride. She had it in spades. Like all the Merriams.

"Your father didn't like my choice of husband, and he told me so. I wish I had listened."

J.T. thought of his recent fight with Trevor. "I know how that feels, Aunt Clara."

"Then Reinhold got greedy and entitled like he was prone to do, and my mother and brother stood against him. Rightfully so, perhaps, but still, it left me...on the outs. Back in those days, there was no easy way for a wife to go against her husband's wishes, and Reinhold forbade me to speak to them. I was young and angry, and I lashed out in ways I now regret."

Like taking those paintings. "How did you keep Reinhold from selling the paintings, Aunt Clara?"

She rubbed the tip of her nose. "I threatened to tell all his mistresses he had syphilis."

Caroline muffled her laugh. "That's—"

"Effective, let me tell you," she said with a regal nod. "We had plenty of money. He'd been raised with art on the walls. Frankly, he gave the paintings about as much attention as he did me after a few years of marriage."

J.T. felt something shift in his heart. Most of his life he'd been told how horrible this woman was, and now he was seeing the truth. She'd been trapped in a marriage she hadn't thought she could leave. Her family had stood against her husband, and she'd felt included in their disdain. Yeah, he could understand that.

"I don't tell you this so you'll pity me," she said, pointing at him. "I made my own choices, but the older

I get, the more it weighs on me. It was a grace I couldn't have children with that man, but the silence in this house is growing. I don't like it."

Hadn't he noticed it?

Caroline reached for the woman's hand, and wonder of wonders, the regal woman took it. He watched them share a moment before Aunt Clara released her hand.

"I've been waiting for you to show up, J.T." She wiped her mouth with her napkin. "After Arthur called…"

He'd have to thank the old man—after he swatted him for not saying a word about the call.

"I may be late, but I'm no less earnest for it," he said, putting his hand over his heart.

"Oh, you're full of it, aren't you?" Her blue eyes softened. "You're more charming than your father."

His lips twitched. "I suppose so. Dad still believes in knocking heads together when its called for. My twin brother favors him more."

"Yes, Trevor," she said. "He handles the oil and gas negotiations and any sticky items that arise. Of course, I would have thought Connor and Flynn were cut from the same cloth too, given their positions in the company."

"For someone who's stayed out of family dealings for decades, you're well informed," he said, taking a bite of one of the triangle sandwiches to cover his surprise.

"Not much left to do but read these days," she said. "I loathe television."

"It's the agent of the devil, haven't you heard?" J.T. said.

She laughed. She actually laughed. Then she coughed, as if the sound was foreign to her throat. "And how *is* Arthur Hale really these days? Other than being an interfering bastard?"

He gestured for Caroline to take that volley. "He's up to his old tricks," she said. "Working non-stop. Fighting for justice. You know…"

The touch of a smile appeared on Clara's face. "I had a crush on him once, you know. Of course, he pretended not to see it, moron that he is."

"*No...*" J.T. leaned forward. Hadn't she said Arthur had stopped talking to her after her wedding? What was the story there?

"Yes," she said in the same dramatic tone. "I wasn't always seventy-six, boy, but he thought I was a brat, and then he got married in Dare Valley...and I got married too, of course. Arthur tried to mediate a truce between your father and Reinhold, you know, but neither man was interested. I was always grateful for that even though nothing came of it. His heart is in the right place." Clara leaned forward, smiling conspiratorially. "Don't tell him that last part. His head is big enough as it is, I imagine."

"Of course," Caroline said.

"Mum's the word," J.T. said. "So can we circle back to the Rembrandt?"

She adjusted her napkin in her lap. "As you like."

Oh, she was playing hard to get, but he knew she was on board. "I have a Rembrandt expert and a forensic consultant on call to start the authentication process."

This time she scratched her lip, and oh, if that secret smile didn't appear. "The painting has already been authenticated, Julian."

He jumped to his feet, and so did Caroline.

"What?" they said in tandem.

"I never touched the painting while Reinhold was alive. Even a man not interested in art would have had his heart race over a lost Rembrandt."

J.T. felt his own heart beating hard in his chest. "And?"

"I brought it out of storage the day after he died, and had it authenticated confidentially," she said, fiddling with her diamond bracelet, pleased with herself, no doubt.

The world slowed down. "Is it real?"

She stroked those sparkling diamonds encircling her wrist. "Yes, it most certainly is."

CHAPTER 25

J.T. WAS THE ONLY MAN ON EARTH WHO COULD TALK HIS seventy-six-year-old *estranged* aunt into hopping on a plane with him the day they met.

Perhaps Caroline should drop the estranged part. Aunt Clara was on her second gin and tonic, artfully crafted by her butler, Hargreaves, whom she'd insisted on bringing to Dare Valley. Still decked out in his butler's uniform, he had yet to crack a smile. Caroline had struggled not to laugh at the stares people had given them at the airport. What a picture the four of them must have made.

"Your father isn't going to like our little reunion," Clara was telling J.T. as she clinked her ice cubes around in her glass.

"Honestly, I'm not too concerned about it," J.T. said, touching their glasses together again.

"He didn't approve of your choice, right?" She patted his hand, her diamond bracelet winking in the sunlight streaming in through the plane's oval window. "It was the same way with me. I disappointed him, you see. It's hard to overcome that, but at least you and I understand each other. Let's have another drink."

Another? Caroline had stopped at one. After her

incident at Hairy's Bar, she was on a self-imposed one-drink limit.

"You must have Trevor's gift," J.T. said as Hargreaves stepped over to the tiny bar area on the plane. "He can drink like a fish too."

"My dear boy," she said, "since I'm older, he has *my* gift."

"Touché, Aunt," J.T. said, his lips twitching.

"*Aunt,*" she drew out. "Now that's something I never expected to hear again. I'm glad you finally got the balls to come and visit me."

"Me too, Aunt Clara," he said, grabbing her hand affectionately. "Well, Caroline, how's it going over there? Is the authentication report a must-read?"

As the future curator of the museum, she was reviewing the report on the lost Rembrandt.

"It's thorough," she said.

"Of course it is!" Clara said. "Do I look dense? I might be old, but I'm not stupid. Good God, do you know how much trouble a person could get into if they told the world they had a lost Rembrandt and it turned out they really didn't? I might have been egged on the street on my way to Central Park."

"I would have protected you, madam," Hargreaves said in his dry British accent.

"Did I mention Hargreaves is my bodyguard too?" she asked.

"I'm proficient in martial arts," Hargreaves told them.

She found the urge to laugh. Somehow the image of him making a karate chop in his butler's uniform tickled her. "I can't fault the people Clara brought in to authenticate the piece. I mean, her lawyers even tracked down the store owner in the remote Dutch town where Joanne Merriam bought it and learned it had been picked up in an estate sale."

Clara cackled. "Can you imagine? The poor man died without any heirs and didn't tell anyone about the painting, so it was sold alongside his china and silver. Thank God, we tracked down information in the family journals. I love the bit about how the painting was so scandalous Rembrandt denied he'd painted it."

"I wonder what possessed him to paint the Mother of God nude," J.T. said, taking his third gin and tonic from Hargreaves. He shrugged and then lifted his drink. "Whatever the reason, to the Rembrandt. I can't wait to see it."

"You want to see it?" Clara asked, clinking her glass with his.

Caroline lowered the report. When J.T. had asked about the collection, Clara had told them most of it was in a secure storage facility. They'd agreed to leave the paintings there for now. It wasn't like the museum was open for business. Besides, they would need to arrange for packing and shipping and the like. Plus, she'd wanted to read the report...

"What do you mean, 'see it'?" Caroline asked.

"I brought it with us, of course," Clara said, taking another healthy swallow of her drink.

J.T. gripped the edge of the small table between them, his knuckles white, and Caroline felt her own hands ball into fists.

"Don't tease me, Aunt," J.T. said.

"Boy, I haven't had this much fun in years. Do you really want to see it?"

"Yes!" they both shouted.

She wiggled in her chair. "Who's the belle of the ball now? Hargreaves, bring me the painting."

J.T.'s face went black with shock. "I can't believe you really brought it."

"It's in my carry-on."

"Your carry-on!" My God, did the woman not know

priceless paintings needed to be handled with care?

"Oh, don't worry, my dear," she said, chuckling. "It's well protected."

"But anyone might have stolen it," Caroline said.

"Who? It's not like anyone knew I had it on me. Not even you knew until now."

Oh, she *was* having fun with them. At another time, Caroline would have teased back, but her stomach was jumping. This was a lost Rembrandt. This was a miracle. *Their* miracle.

Hargreaves brought forward a black carry-on and opened it on the adjoining sofa. Sure enough, the painting he drew out was packed to Caroline's specifications.

"I told you I wasn't stupid," Clara said.

Caroline barely heard her. She'd left her seat to get a better view, and it didn't surprise her one bit when J.T. did the same.

"You know, madam, I'll just have to re-pack it," Hargreaves said in a tired voice.

"Oh, what else do you have to do?" Clara said flippantly. "It's not like it's a hardship. Come on, man. Open it up."

"I am, madam," he said.

The front packaging came off, and the painting was revealed. "Ohhhhh! It's—"

"Beautiful," J.T. said, edging closer and putting a hand around her back to draw her nearer. "I know it might be scandalous, but she's stunning."

Indeed she was, Caroline thought. Mary was lying on her side on a white mat in front of an open window. Her hand was resting on her rounded belly and—

"Oh my God! I know why he painted her like this. She's—"

"Pregnant!" J.T. exclaimed.

"Didn't you know?" Clara said.

J.T. looked over his shoulder at her. "No! I had no

idea. The signature is slightly scratched off like I was told."

"I imagine Rembrandt had enough pride in his work that he couldn't bring himself to erase his signature completely," Caroline said. "How horrible that something this beautiful could be considered scandalous."

Of course, people across the ages had strong opinions about how biblical characters were represented in art. People would still have strong opinions about the piece—that was what made it so priceless.

"She's happy," J.T. said, tracing the lines of Mary's face inches above the actual painting.

"She's having the Son of God, if you subscribe to *The Bible* and Christian beliefs," Clara said. "I'd like to think she's just happy because she's having a baby. I always imagined it would be a wondrous thing. Minus the diapers and adolescence."

"This is going to be huge," Caroline said, feeling almost in a trance. "We need to—"

"Go out with this fast," J.T. said. "I can't be sure when Cynthia or the university will announce her gift for cancer research."

"Who cares? We need to do this right, J.T. Have a proper unveiling. Invite the right people. Make sure the press is there in force."

"That stuff can catch up," J.T. said, finally peeling his eyes away from the painting. "We need to go out with this tomorrow."

"Tomorrow? I won't have everything in place in time. I need to prepare a one-pager for the press on the painting, plus give them a snapshot of the authentication process. Otherwise, this will come off as a stunt."

He squared his shoulders like he was preparing to argue with her, and she lifted her chin. He was being reckless, and they couldn't afford any more dust-ups. They couldn't afford for their find to be treated as a fake.

Glass clinked, and they both looked over to Clara, who was tapping her spoon against her drink. "Sit down. Both of you. We'll talk about this tomorrow. Caroline, finish reading the report. J.T., drink your gin like a good boy."

His gaze didn't waver. Neither did hers. When he turned away from her, she knew she'd won this round, but at a steep price. The feeling of joint discovery, of being a team, had faded. She was right, dammit, but that didn't make her feel any better about the hurt look in his eyes.

Caroline looked back at the Rembrandt. The painter's use of light to capture the details of the woman's body was masterful. It had to be revealed to the public and the greater art community with the greatest forethought and preparation. The press would go mad for the one-of-a-kind finding, enough so to wash away the gossip about J.T. Enough so to make her reputation as a curator.

And he wanted to throw all that away with a quick reveal.

Oh, they were so going to have it out.

Chapter 26

J.T. knew Caroline was stewing when they landed, and frankly, so was he.

She didn't understand Cynthia, and so she didn't understand his urgency. Besides, her insistence on doing things "right" implied she thought he was wrong, didn't it?

After they landed. Aunt Clara insisted they use the limo she'd rented to drive to Dare Valley.

"When did you have time to rent a limo?" he asked.

"What do you think Hargreaves was doing in between making us drinks?"

"But I have a car here," he protested.

"Your Ferrari wouldn't hold four people comfortably," Caroline said like he was a moron. "Why don't you drive it back? I'll go with Clara and Hargreaves."

She was avoiding him now? He didn't like that. He thought about getting someone else to drive his car back, but it would take too long. Maybe it would give them a chance to cool off.

"Fine."

"Hargreaves can go along with you if you'd like company," Aunt Clara said, her brow arched.

He couldn't tell if she was messing with him or trying

to reassure him. It had to be obvious to her that he and Caroline were having a tiff.

"I'd be happy to navigate for you, sir," Hargreaves said.

Like he needed that old windbag to help him find Dare Valley. "I know the way."

"Very good, sir," he replied.

He caught Caroline fighting laughter. "Great. I guess I'll see you in Dare Valley then."

On the ride back to Denver, he kept an eye on the limousine, but at some point he lost sight of it. How in the hell could anyone lose sight of a car like that? He looked for it, but he didn't see it again. Since he was driving, he used his Bluetooth to call Caroline. She didn't pick up.

Where in the world were they?

Aunt Clara was like a horse released from the barn in spring after a long winter. For all he knew, she might have suggested they stop at a casino or day spa. Although she'd looked completely sober, she'd been on her fourth gin and tonic. God, he couldn't wait to see her and Trevor drink together.

Speaking of whom.

He called Trevor next. "Did you get my text?" he asked when his brother answered.

"You mean the one that said, 'Got the lost Rembrandt and the whole collection. Coming home'?"

Why was everyone giving him a hard time? Wasn't this exactly what they needed? "Aunt Clara is on her way to Dare Valley with me." He paused, then amended the word to "us."

"You're kidding," Trev said. "The old battle-axe? Dad won't be happy."

"Seems it takes two to tango, and Dad played his part. You'll like her. She could out-drink you."

"In your dreams. I got news too. Get your ass back here fast."

"Can't you just tell me now?" he asked. "I'm twiddling my thumbs, driving back to Dare Valley."

"I hate phone calls," he said. "Punch it."

"What if I get a speeding ticket?"

"We'll pay it. Get a move on."

His brother hung up before he could tell him that he'd meant Aunt Clara was coming *now*. Oh well. He punched the gas.

The sun was setting when he entered Sardine Canyon. The Dare Valley sign welcomed him back, and it struck him anew that he *did* feel welcome here. Always had. Suddenly, he was looking forward to being home.

When he arrived at his house, the limo wasn't in sight. "Shit."

Tromping up to the front door, he let himself in. Trev was on his laptop in front of the roaring fireplace.

"I take it the others haven't shown up yet?" he asked, shrugging out of his coat.

"They didn't come with you? Right, the Ferrari. Maybe they're taking their time. Look, we have a problem. I'm still not sure what it means yet, but my gut is telling me Cynthia is behind it."

Some of his excitement about the painting faded. Trev's gut was never wrong. "What is it?"

"Cynthia moved all of her money and a significant portion of Newhouse senior's over to a new bank today."

He tilted his head to the side. "What bank is it?"

"Carlyle's," Trevor said.

He knew it by name, of course, but it didn't ring any bells for him otherwise. "Do we have any dealings with this bank?"

"No," Trev said. "I checked. But it's a big move."

Yeah, changing banks with that much cash would be a total pain in the ass. "What about the safe deposit boxes?" he asked Trev.

The Newhouses had several of them, full of priceless

jewels and important papers. But what could this have to do with him?

Trev pursed his lips. "I hadn't thought of that. Good point. I'm wracking my brain here, but I can't make sense of it. My sources don't have any ideas either."

Which meant the ceiling was likely going to drop on them any moment now.

They needed to tell the world about the lost Rembrandt ASAP, regardless of what Caroline said. He tried her cell again and got her voicemail. Dammit.

He texted her. *I need to see you. Urgently.*

In the meantime, he could write the press release himself and send it out tonight. If she didn't get back to him, that was her fault. *She* was the one avoiding *him*.

Meanwhile, he had to make a move before Cynthia put another noose around his neck. If he didn't, not even the Rembrandt could save them.

CHAPTER 27

ARTHUR STARED AT THE SPREADSHEET FOR THE HUNdredth time. He was fretting over the paper's numbers, what with the stupid loan he'd taken out and the loss of advertising dollars from their number one client. He still didn't buy the department store chain's reasoning, but they hadn't changed their mind despite his follow-up calls. He hadn't had a month this tight since the early days of the paper. Looking for a new client at that level was giving him chest pain, but they'd find someone, by God.

He heard a knock at the door and wanted to snarl. Who the hell was paying him a visit? Crap, at the rate he was going, it had to signal more trouble.

When he opened the door, he found himself staring at trouble with a capital T. The woman standing before Arthur was just as beautiful as she'd been in 1962. She'd aged, of course, but she hadn't lost her regal bearing or her sparkle.

"Clara Merriam," he said slowly. "What a surprise."

She drew her long silver hair over her right shoulder and fixed her blue eyes on him, as if taking in all the changes in him as well. "Arthur Hale. You're old. You even have a cane, I see."

He laughed and executed a Fred Astaire move with it. "Yes, and you're still a brat."

"I don't think you can call a woman my age a brat," she said.

"A bitch then?"

She stepped forward and kissed him on the mouth before he could blink—and then she slapped his face.

"What was that for?" he asked.

"The kiss or the slap?" Her eyes crinkled at the corners.

"Either. Both." He was too old for this aggravation. His ticker couldn't take it.

"The kiss was because you *never* had the courage to kiss me when you were in New York, and I didn't have the courage to press you. The slap was because we haven't seen each other in fifty-six years."

He growled. She'd always been a handful. "I didn't *want* to kiss you before—"

"Liar! You took me out when you lived in New York City."

"As a friend," he reasoned, although she was right. He *was* lying. But she was also the granddaughter of his best friend and mentor. The man whom he'd owed everything.

She ran her hands over her white fur coat. "Will you please let me inside?"

"You could get assaulted with eggs or red paint by some environmentalists for wearing a coat like that around here," he said, stepping aside.

He was about to shut the door behind her when another man appeared in the doorway.

"Who the hell are you?" he asked.

"You remember Hargreaves, don't you?" Clara called, shrugging out of her coat. "God, you haven't gotten that forgetful, have you?"

He'd thought it impossible, but Hargreaves was the same man who'd been her butler in the late fifties.

"I'm sharper than ever, honey," he said. "How in

the hell was I supposed to recognize Hargreaves? He's a barrel of bones."

"You look good too, sir," the butler said, bringing in two suitcases. "Where should I put these?"

"What?" he asked.

"I'm staying with you," Clara said. "I never stay in a hotel when I know someone in town. The least you could do after not seeing me for *fifty-six years* is to put me up. After all, I'm only here because you called."

"Bullshit," he barked. "I called you to help the boy, which you didn't seem eager to do, not so you could come to Dare Valley and shack up with me."

"Such a crude term," she drawled out. "I'm only staying for a few days. To help the boy, as you say. Besides, Hargreaves cleans and cooks. From the looks of you, you could use a good meal. What are you eating these days? Spam?"

"I happen to have a grandson-in-law who's a chef, and I'm a backer of his restaurant," he told her.

She waved her hand as if unimpressed. "Arthur, I'm not leaving."

Part of him wanted to jump for joy, he realized. Dammit, but he'd missed her. "You've gotten more stubborn, Clara. I didn't know it was possible."

"I'd like to say you got better looking, but I can't tell a lie."

He fought a smile. She was still a brat, all right, but heck, he liked brats. Even old ones like her.

"Fine, you can stay," he said. "For the boy's sake. I'm glad you got your head out of your ass and decided to help him."

"Hargreaves, please select two rooms upstairs," Clara said, fidgeting with her diamonds, something she used to do to annoy him. "You might lay out my clothing for tomorrow."

Good Lord. What was this, *Downton Abbey?*

"Very good, madam," he said, taking off for the stairs.

Arthur thought about offering to help him with the suitcases, but Hargreaves managed them just fine.

When the man disappeared from view, he asked, "My God, how old is he now?"

"He's seventy-nine," she said. "A few months younger than you."

"Nice of you to point out."

"Well, you don't look too bad for your age," she said, walking in a circle around him. "You're still lean and have your hair. Good bone structure helps."

"So does drinking milk and clean living," he quipped. "Clara, you're a pain in the ass. What are you *really* doing here?"

"I thought we'd catch up," she said. "It's been a long time, and I'm tired of my weekly bridge game. Arthur, when you called, I got to thinking about old times."

Dammit, she'd gone for his soft spot. The Merriams had a way of bringing back good memories for him. "Me too. It's an affliction of age to think of times past."

"If you still have those infernal red hots, I'll take one," she said. "It was a long trip."

He rolled his eyes and crossed to the table by the armchair for the crystal bowl holding his favorite candy. "You came in a private plane. How bad could it be?"

She laughed, taking a red hot. "These are still atrocious. You gave me one for the first time after we went to a party at the Met."

"I'd just come to New York City to go to Columbia," he said. "You were…"

She'd been a vision with her raven black hair, porcelain skin, and direct blue eyes. No woman up until that point had given him such shit or stirred him up. But she'd also been young and a bit entitled. Unlike Emmits, her grandfather, she'd been born with a silver spoon in her mouth.

He'd known all along they weren't suited—their interests could hardly have been more different, and then there was the class distinction between them. Back in the fifties, that kind of thing was a big deal. He'd made sure not to take things beyond friendship. Then he'd left New York for Dare Valley, like he'd planned all along, and met Harriet. Two years later, Clara had married someone as rich as her. He'd always thought things had turned out exactly as they were meant to.

"I was what?" she asked, her mouth moving as she sucked on her red hot.

"Never boring," he said instead.

Her shoulders seemed to sag, and he finally took in her attire. The black dress she wore fit her slender body nicely even if the neckline and hemline had been popular a hundred years ago.

"Words to flatter any woman," she said. "Have you eaten? I'm starving."

He thought of the dinner he'd been late to start. "I have tomato soup warming on the stove."

"No wonder you're as skinny as a rail," she said. "Hargreaves! I need you."

Footsteps sounded upstairs and soon the man appeared on the steps. "Yes, madam," he said as he climbed down the final steps.

"Mr. Hale has bachelor cooking tendencies, and they won't do."

The man had the audacity to cluck his tongue.

"I'll see to it, madam," he said, walking in the general direction of the kitchen.

"How did he know where to go?" Arthur asked.

"In a house this small, it's not hard," she said, rolling her eyes at him. "You simply start walking."

It was exactly the kind of comment she used to make as a brash young woman—and he found he still rather liked her attitude, her spunk.

"You did the right thing, helping J.T.," he said. "Emmits would have been proud of you."

She teared up, alarming him. "That's kind of you to say. I'm already fond of the boy. I haven't felt any kind of...connection to my family for decades before today."

"I hated to see what happened between you," he said, buttoning his sweater vest.

"Is that why you tried to mediate a truce between me and my brother?" she asked. "I was grateful you tried even if...it failed."

The regret in her voice pinched his heart. "Was your marriage not easy?"

"No, but his mistresses made it more bearable." She waved a hand. "Let's talk of happier things. Do you have fixings for a gin and tonic by chance?"

After the bomb she'd just dropped, he had the odd impulse to comfort her. "No, I stopped drinking those after Nixon resigned," he said. "Brandy?"

"You and your historical life markers," she said, walking over to the bar caddy with him.

He realized he hadn't reached for his cane, but he wasn't about to ask her to get it for him. Besides, his feet seemed to be solid under him. Be a shame to fall on his face in front of her, but at least Hargreaves could help him up. Ha!

"I remember you telling me you'd stopped wearing undershirts after seeing that Clark Gable didn't wear them in *It Happened One Night*. Of course, that was crap because that movie came out in 1934."

"But I didn't see it until 1955." He didn't bat an eyelash at that prevarication. He was having way too much fun.

"You're still a big fibber. I can't believe you've made such a successful career as a journalist—where you're supposed to tell the truth."

He laughed. "It's one of life's mysteries. Speaking of

another... Is that lost Rembrandt the boy is after really a Rembrandt?"

She veiled her eyes. "Hmm... How would little old me know something like that?"

Handing her a brandy, he poured one for himself. "Little old you? *Please.* There is no way the Clara Merriam I knew would be able to stand not knowing. I don't buy that you kept it in your collection all these years without checking."

"You're right," she said. "I suspected it was real, but I had to wait until Reinhold died to go through the proper authentication process."

Reinhold. What a jerk. He'd only met the man at her wedding, and even then, he'd smelled trouble. Besides, the man had a flaccid handshake.

"He would have sold it?"

"I couldn't be sure," she said. "I had to make sure he didn't think I wanted anything to do with it."

That was telling.

"I'm glad he's dead then."

"Yes, I got your card," she said, dryly. "Your condolences were much kinder."

"Do you want me to blow smoke up your ass?" he asked. She never had before.

Turning to the side, she looked at said ass. "You seem to be obsessed with this particular part of my body."

He dipped his gaze to it and let it hover. "It's not bad."

She laughed and extended her snifter to him. "Oh, Arthur, I've missed you. To fresh, new times."

He paused, meeting her eyes. She looked years younger in that moment, and he was transported to their last toast, the day before his return to Dare Valley. They'd been drinking champagne in her parents' townhouse on Park Avenue. She'd said, "To your return to New York."

Of course, he hadn't gone back to stay.

"What are you remembering?" she asked.

"Your last toast," he answered honestly. "Or *our* last toast."

"In 1960," she said, deadpan.

He laughed.

"I'd hoped you would return to New York," she said in a soft tone.

"I never planned to," he said, "you know that. Although I don't blame you for doubting. The only person who thought I could make it out here with a national newspaper was your grandfather."

"Yes, and I'm sorry I wasn't one of the believers. Maybe you should be the one to toast then since my toasts don't come true."

He looked into her eyes again. "To fresh, new times."

Chapter 28

Caroline knew it was petty not to call J.T. back right away, but she couldn't help it.

She was mad.

He hadn't respected her professional opinion. Why keep her around as his art consultant if he wasn't going to seriously consider what she had to say? Let him stew. For a few hours, she was going to set all of this *serious* stuff aside and have a little fun at a late impromptu dinner at Brasserie Dare with some of her girls. Moira and Lucy had both been available, and besides her honest desire to see them, she thought the latter might be able to help her with the Rembrandt situation.

They couldn't talk about the painting in public, of course, but they could at least talk about Clara.

"So Clara told you she was staying at Uncle Arthur's house?" Moira asked, practically leaning across their table. "Just like that?"

"I'd love to have been a fly on the wall," Lucy said, popping a French fry in her mouth after dipping it in the pepper sauce that came with her steak. "Few people tell Arthur what to do. I wonder if she convinced him."

"We could call The Grand Mountain Hotel and ask

to be connected to her room," Moira said, grabbing one of Lucy's French fries.

"Hey! Get your own." Lucy put her hands over her plate.

"I didn't want the steak," Moira said.

"Clara said they hadn't seen each other since her wedding in 1962," Caroline told them, snagging one of the fries while Lucy's attention was on Moira. "After a tense build-up, turns out she's a pretty fun lady who can drink like a fish. Unlike me."

She still couldn't believe how many gin and tonics that woman had polished off, all without a single slurred word or stumble.

"Maybe we should go by Uncle Arthur's house," Moira said, "and see if her limo is parked there."

"No way," Lucy said. "I'm not getting caught spying on Arthur's property. I work for the man from time to time."

"Yes," Caroline said, "and that's a nice segue to a little business I wanted to ask you about. I would really love for you to shoot some of the you-know-what."

There was no way she was going to say *lost Rembrandt* out loud. For all she knew, Cynthia had spies everywhere. She'd briefed them in the car on the way over.

Lucy's mouth parted. "I'd love to. Goodness. What a subject. I might have to pinch myself."

"Time is of the essence," Caroline said, thinking about J.T.'s urgency.

"I can make some time in the morning before my class starts."

"Thank you," she said. *Take that, J.T. We're doing this the right way. With photos for the press and everything.* She would tell him after dinner when she called him back.

"I'll call Clara and set it all up," Caroline said. "Where do you want to do the shoot?"

"I think my studio space at the university would be best," Lucy said, her face lighting up now that she'd agreed. No doubt she was already planning how best to do the shoot. Although Caroline favored paintings to photographs, she loved the artistry of her future sister-in-law's work.

"That's settled, so let's circle back to your personal front, Caro. I say you should let J.T. stew a bit. He probably would never have gotten in touch with his aunt if not for you."

She smiled. "I really love you, Mo." Her sister made a gesture for her to continue and she heaved out a sigh. "When we're alone and block out the world, we do great. I can't tell you how exciting this last day was for us, until he blocked me out. I hate that he brought me into this whole thing because of my experience, and now he won't listen to me."

"Word," Moira said. "I hate it when Chase does that. It's like the dog house for you tonight unless you get your head out of your ass and listen to me. Not just nod like you did."

"Speaking of 'outside circumstances,'" Lucy whispered, leaning forward. "His ex just walked in."

Caroline immediately turned in her chair. Sure enough, Sin City had just walked in, decked out in all her glory, from her glossy blond hair to her cream floor-length winter coat. An older well-dressed man with patrician features was with her. Caroline didn't recognize him. Was he a trustee for the university?

"Shit," she said, immediately facing forward. "I haven't seen her since she walked into the gallery."

All she wanted to do was hide, but that seemed cowardly. *Buck up!* This was her home town, and that woman wasn't going to make her feel afraid or weird.

Or so she told herself.

"There's no reason for you two to interact," Lucy said. "You're here having dinner, and so is she."

"Exactly," she said, feeling all the muscles in her

body tighten with nerves despite the personal lecture she'd given herself.

"I'd like to pop her in that perfect face of hers," Moira said, her face flushing with anger.

"Simmer down," Lucy said. "Eat another one of my fries."

Moira stuck her tongue out.

"I want to pop her even more," Caroline added, "but I know it will only make things worse."

In that moment, though, she wondered. Would it really? Why not take one of the whipped cream desserts Brian served and squash it in her face? How composed would she look then? Okay, she needed to get a grip.

"Caroline."

She'd never forget the way that woman said her name. It was like she was saying the word "herpes" or something equally vile.

The cream coat was suddenly at her side—cashmere, she thought—and when she looked up Cynthia Newhouse was fake-smiling the crap out of her.

"Cynthia," she responded, choosing not to introduce anyone else.

"This is Ferdinand Rollins," she said, "our family lawyer. He just arrived to handle some business for me when I heard the incredible news about the lost Rembrandt. You and J.T. must have sold a kidney for Clara Allerton to bring forth that painting and the rest of her collection. Well, I suppose Ferdinand and I will simply have to readjust our plan."

She knew? Suddenly Caroline felt lightheaded. "I beg your pardon."

The woman pulled off her leather gloves slowly, like she was preparing to torture an uncooperative lover. "I mean, there will be questions, of course."

"What?"

Slapping her gloves against that two-million-dollar

purse of hers, Cynthia said, "About why Clara would have kept such an important work of art in secret for so long. I mean, it's almost criminal. Art lovers everywhere are going to be up in arms. You and J.T. are going to have your hands full explaining things."

She felt Moira grab her forearm under the table like she was trying to help ground her spinning brain. "But how—"

"Ferdinand and I will leave you to your dinner," she said in that same dismissive, upper-crust tone.

Caroline watched as she and her lawyer were shown to a table a few feet away. Moira and Lucy were watching her with wide eyes.

"Are you okay?" her sister asked.

All she could do was wave a hand. She needed to talk to J.T. right away.

"I need—"

"To go," Moira said immediately, signaling the server. "In all my days..."

"Not now," she whispered, acutely aware of the proximity of her nemesis.

Grabbing her purse, she pulled out her phone. Her phone had blown up. She had dozens of text messages and phone calls from people she knew in the art community. She scrolled through the texts first, and there was one common theme that had her blood boiling.

Saw the press release. Heard about the lost Rembrandt. OMG!

J.T. had texted her again over an hour ago, she saw at the end of her messages, likely right as they'd sat down at their table. There was a voicemail from him as well. She read the transcript of the call. Nothing about him sending out the press release tonight. He'd only said it was urgent she call him. That bastard.

He'd told the world about the lost Rembrandt without her.

CHAPTER 29

J.T. WAS ON THE PHONE WITH ONE OF HIS GO-TO ART consultants in Rome when he heard a knock on his bedroom door.

He wanted to growl. Why in the hell was Trevor bothering him? He knew he was making calls. Vincento was going crazy about the lost Rembrandt, and he'd barely managed to get a word in edgewise.

Crawling off the bed, he walked to the door and opened it, taken aback to see Caroline. Glaring at him. She'd heard about the press release. Terrific.

The rapid-fire Italian continued to flow into his ear as he let her inside, pointing to his phone. She crossed her arms as he walked back to the bed and sat down.

"Vincento," he interrupted. "*Scusi.*"

It took a few more tries, but he finally got Vincento to pause so he could tell him he'd call him back later with more information.

"To be fair," he said, setting his phone aside finally, "you left without saying anything and I texted and called you before I sent out the press release."

"That's your defense?" she asked, walking toward him. "You only told me it was urgent that I call you back, not that you were going to publicize this to the entire world before we spoke. Did it ever dawn on you that I might be out to dinner?"

He could play hardball. "Did it ever dawn on you that I was serious? So serious that it might have been worth keeping your phone on during dinner?"

She shook her head slowly like she was having none of it. "You know I turn off my ringer while I'm eating."

He stood up slowly, anger surging through him again. "You were ignoring me! You purposely went with Aunt Clara—"

"She invited me—"

"When you *knew* how strongly I felt about this," he continued. "I told you we had to get the word out right away."

"And I told you that we needed to plan this and do it right," she said, flinging her hands into the air in frustration.

"You weren't listening to me," he said.

"Ditto! We need to move smartly. Or needed to. That's out of the bag now, isn't it?"

While he wasn't surprised at her reaction, he still found himself crossing his arms in defense. "Caroline, this is my museum. I'm the one who decides what's best for it, and in this case, getting the word out fast was the best move."

Silence descended between them.

"Then why ask my opinion?" she finally asked. "Heck, why even have me as your art consultant if you'd prefer to be a museum of one."

Her voice broke at the end, and he realized he'd gone too far. "I didn't mean it like that. Of course I value you. I wouldn't have hired you otherwise."

She shook her finger at him, her whole body trembling with emotion. "No, you don't get to have it both ways. First, you say it's *your* museum and *you* know what's best. Fine. But you don't get to take that tack and then pretend to care about my opinion. I just saw your ex-wife at Brasserie Dare with her lawyer, and she told me there are going to be questions about why your aunt has been sitting on an art discovery of this magnitude."

Shit.

"What? You didn't see that coming? Well, I did."

"You didn't say—"

"You didn't let me," she said. "I tried to explain how I felt, but you cut me off. Your obsession with beating Cynthia to the next attack has clouded your judgment. Honestly, J.T., I don't know what's more important to you right now. The museum or getting a leg up on your ex. Frankly, I'm sick of it. We found a lost Rembrandt—*a lost Rembrandt*—and somehow you've made this all about her."

He felt a burning sensation in his chest. He'd made this all about Cynthia? All he wanted to do was escape her!

"If Cynthia's lawyer is in town, it means she's planning something," he shot back, "exactly like I thought. Hell, even Trev told me something was up when I got home."

"And what was that?" she asked.

He worried his lip. "We aren't sure yet. She moved her money to a new bank."

"That's it? That's your reasoning here?"

Even to him it sounded weak, but he'd been going with his gut for three years. She was new to the Cynthia Newhouse game. She didn't fully get it. "Please understand. I had to send out the press release when I did."

"Then you're going to have to answer those questions yourself because I don't want any part of it." She walked over to the door, and he didn't have it in him to try and convince her not to leave. "I got fired because of your ex-wife and my name is currently dog shit in the art community. Another stunt like this, and I'm done. If this blows up in our faces, I'll look stupid and reckless. The fact that you didn't even take that into consideration says a lot."

"Will you two stop shouting?" Trevor yelled out of the blue.

J.T. looked over to see his brother standing in the doorway. He'd been so intent on Caroline he hadn't even noticed him.

"This is exactly what she wants," Trev said, "and I'll be damned if I'm going to stand by and let her win. Let me cut to the chase here since I heard your entire conversation downstairs. Caroline, you're first."

She pointed to herself. "Me?"

"Yes, you. You come in here railing about not having your opinion valued. Well, that's bullshit. J.T. tried to reach out to you. He was upset you were avoiding him. If you'd gotten your head out of your ass—thank you, Uncle Arthur, for that phrase—and called him back, he would have sent you the press release for your review."

"But I didn't agree—"

"To the press release," he said in the same hard-ass tone. "I know, but my bro is right. Regardless of your personal or professional relationship, he's in charge here. Deal with it. He's been fighting Sin City for three years now. No one knows her strategy better than he does. Not even me."

Hearing Trev say those things clogged J.T.'s throat. In spite of the lapse in judgment that had cost their family so much, his brother still trusted him. Caroline looked like she'd swallowed a bug.

"Cynthia moving her money around does mean something—even if we don't understand it yet. You waltz in acting like this lost Rembrandt is some completely separate issue from the larger problem with the university, when in fact, the museum is in serious trouble. You haven't been at those ill-fated dinners with the trustees. Well, I have, and it's bad. Time was an issue. If something didn't turn around quick, the museum would have been dead in the water. With the Rembrandt, you have a fighting chance."

J.T. thought about stopping his brother. He *was* being hard on Caroline. But before he could even open his mouth to say anything, Trev turned and looked at him. His eyes were scorching, and J.T. knew he was about to get a verbal whipping. Great.

"Your turn, boyo," he said, walking forward and stopping inches in front of him. "You want to deck me afterward, you go ahead, but I'm finally going to get this off my chest." He stuck his chin out. "It's long overdue."

The burning sensation in his heart spread, but he kept his face devoid of emotion.

"Caroline is right. You *have* lost sight of your priorities. You're not just letting Cynthia control your life, you're also putting someone you care about— someone who does technically work for you—at risk."

That burning sensation in J.T.'s chest hurt like hell, but he couldn't talk. Couldn't move. Couldn't speak.

"Look, this museum would be welcomed by any university in the country, and you damn well know it. Does it suck that the university Grandpa Emmits founded might not want it? Yeah. But is it worth all this? Caroline's reputation being called into question? Aunt Clara being seen as a greedy art hoarder or a senile old bird who forgot she had a Rembrandt in the attic? People are going to start asking questions, like why would an ex-wife come at someone like this without a good reason or what could he have done to her. Dammit, J.T., I'm sick to death of this mess too."

He made himself stand tall at his brother's words. Anything less would have hurt his pride.

"I know you're tired too, but you're hell bent on

doing things the hard way. Releasing the press release like this is the hard way, and God…"

When he trailed off, J.T. gathered himself enough to drill his finger in his chest. "What?"

Trev stepped back. "No, that's enough."

J.T. got in his face. "No, you started this. You finish it."

"You're fucking up the relationship of a lifetime with this awesome woman over here." He gestured to Caroline. "Stop spending your life fighting Cynthia. She's taken enough from us."

His brother never called her by her real name, and his point was stronger for it. J.T. looked over at Caroline and watched her swipe away tears and turn her head away. He swallowed thickly. God, he'd hurt her and his brother again, and that was the last thing he wanted to do.

"You're right. I'm sorry."

He walked past both of them and left the house.

He had some thinking to do.

CHAPTER 30

CAROLINE WAS IN HER ROBE WHEN SHE HEARD THE knock on her front door.

Her nerves were stretched taut as she walked to it and looked through the peephole. J.T. was standing on the other side, as she'd both feared and hoped. God, what a fight they'd had. How could they have said those awful things to each other? When he'd marched out and left the house, she and Trevor had been speechless. Then Trevor had asked if she wanted a drink, and she'd declined. For once, he'd seemed grateful to see the back of her.

After coming home, she'd made a fire and sat in front of it, going over her actions in the last twenty-four hours. It galled her to admit that Trev was right—both she and J.T. had been out of line, good intentions aside, and they were letting Cynthia mess with their relationship.

"I'm sorry," she said the moment she opened the door.

"That was my line," he said, putting a hand over his heart. "Sorry isn't good enough—"

"You already said it," she said, covering her bare feet with her robe as much as possible. Cold wind was sweeping in around her.

"Yeah, but I wish there was something more I could say," he said, pausing for a moment. "I'm sorry I walked out on you and Trev. I needed some air, and I thought a drive would help."

So that's where he'd gone.

"Ah...can I come in? I have some other things I need to say."

Her muscles tightened again. "I don't want to rehash things, J.T. I love you. I...don't want us to keep fighting like this. Trev nailed it—this is exactly what Cynthia wants."

He stepped toward her, his eyes searching hers. "Can I...hold you?"

His earnest gaze pulled her to him like a magnet. Going into his arms, she pressed her face to his chest. His arms were tight around her at first, and she realized hers had cinched around him too. It was almost like they both were afraid to let go now that they'd come back together again. She made herself relax, and felt him do the same.

Pulling him inside, she shut the door behind them, then returned to his embrace.

"I was wrong to imply you were just some employee who should listen to me," he said. "I've never thought that or acted like that before. It's not going to happen again."

She wanted to believe him, but his ex had a way of influencing him.

"This is screwing up everything," he whispered.

"What is?" she asked, wanting to be sure she understood.

"When I had the idea for the museum, I was so excited about coming back to Dare Valley to reclaim our family's place here." He edged back so he could see her. "Have I ever told you how nostalgic I've always been about this town? I used to say it had a sky of endless blue, like nowhere else in the world. I'd hike to the top of one of the mountains around here and feel like the king of the mountain. Trev used to make fun of me, but those summers here were some of the best of my life."

Childhood memories were often viewed in a rosy light, she knew, as if they all took place beneath a glorious sunset. "I have feelings like that about the snow picnics we used to have when I was a kid. My mom would pack up submarine sandwiches and load us into her old van. We'd go to Black Lake on a sunny day and build snowmen and have snowball fights and giggle."

"I miss those days sometimes," he said. "The simplicity of them. Growing up has its perks, but my life didn't turn out like I thought it would. I got married hoping to create a family of my own. Happy moments like going hiking with my family or slinging mud at my girl."

He was referring to the famous mud incident when they were kids. Normally, it would have made her smile, but she found herself thinking about that little girl she'd seen in her mind, holding both their hands. Part of her still wondered what it meant. The other part hoped it was a vision of their future.

"I hate how weak this whole thing makes me feel, but I don't know how to fix it. I feel like I'm paying for one mistake over and over again."

Seeing the havoc Cynthia had already caused, she could well understand that point of view, but Trev was right. They couldn't give in. They couldn't let her win. "Your life isn't finished yet, J.T."

"No," he said, "but it's a constant battle. If I ever stop fighting, she'll take everything. That's why I needed to get the press release out tonight."

"I know you believe that," she said with a sigh, stepping away from him. "How about some tea?"

"I'll make an espresso, if that's okay," he said, following her to the kitchen.

Usually he didn't ask. He just made one. When he didn't move toward the espresso machine he'd brought from her place in Denver, her solar plexus tightened. The awkward tension was intense. Making coffee had been such a simple task before.

"Please," she said, gesturing to the machine.

She made her way to the cabinet, taking her time to select an herbal tea even though there were only three choices. It struck her viscerally that their ease with each other was gone.

Oh, she wouldn't let that slide. They needed to understand each other—and for that to happen, they needed to talk openly.

"J.T.," she said, turning around. "I know how precious this museum and coming back to Dare Valley is to you, but I need you to know the stakes are different for us. You have limitless things you could do and a financial safety net in place to do it. You're well known in business and now philanthropy…"

He walked over to the edge of the counter as she searched for the right words.

"What I'm trying to say is… Art has been my passion since I was a child. Some kids were reading *Harry Potter*, but I was combing through art books and those high-gloss coffee table books museums put out. This is the *only* thing I've ever wanted to do, and I figured out how to have a career doing it, which wasn't easy. I even managed to make a name for myself in Denver and the Western art community. But right now, it feels like all of that is in jeopardy. I don't have anything else to fall back on."

She watched him swallow thickly.

"More so, I don't *want* anything else to fall back on," she added, fingering the corners of the tea box as they stared at each other.

"I hear what you're saying," he said, extending his

hand to her and then letting it fall before she could decide whether to take it. "I'll be more careful to consider how my actions impact you and your career going forward."

He shifted on his feet and looked down. She still hadn't pulled the tea box out of the cabinet.

"Maybe I should go," he said. "It's late, and I have a lot of calls to return. Europe is already awake, and there is a lot of interest in our lost Rembrandt."

He wanted to leave? Now? She'd wanted to make things better, but it felt like all the eggshells they were walking on had given way completely.

"Of course," she said, shutting the cabinet. "I've had some calls as well from people I know from Leggett. I wasn't sure what to say, so I haven't called them back. By the way, thank you...for putting me in the press release. I...didn't know—"

She'd finally read it after their fight, and it had brought tears to her eyes.

"Of course you're in the press release," he said, shaking his head at her. "You're the museum's curator, after all. I wanted you to have your due, Caroline. Even though we've rushed things, we're still going to do them right. I promise."

That reassured her. She had to admit the press release had been thorough and professional. She'd realized Sin City's comments in the restaurant had influenced her perspective. No one could manipulate like that woman could.

"Before you go...I forgot to mention earlier, but I asked Lucy to photograph the Rembrandt tomorrow. We need pictures for the press."

He took his time buttoning his suit jacket. "Good idea."

"As you said...we need them fast." *Yes, I understood the urgency*, she wanted to say, *even though we disagreed*.

His eyes flickered to hers, and she could almost feel his guilt.

"I called Clara about it when I got home," she said, "and she's...ah...fine with it."

If the woman had suspected she was upset, she hadn't said anything. She'd merely agreed to the arrangement, saying she'd be there bright-eyed and bushy-tailed with the Rembrandt. And perhaps a gin and tonic, God help them.

"Did you tell her about the press release?" he asked.

She clutched the ties of her robe. "No. I thought it best if you did."

He nodded. "What time tomorrow?"

"I can confirm the exact time with Lucy in the morning and let you know."

"Good," he said, not meeting her eyes. "Good."

Silence grew in the kitchen.

"Well, I should let you..."

He walked out of the kitchen, and she followed him to the door, her chest still heavy with regret.

"I have some ideas about how to handle the next couple of days," he said. "I thought a press conference might be helpful. Aunt Clara can talk about the Rembrandt and why she chose to keep it hidden."

Caroline rubbed the back of her head. "I've been thinking about that too. We'll need to be proactive to address the comments."

He shrugged. "We'll have to get everyone so excited about the painting that little details like that don't matter."

He was being a little naïve. Art was about *details* when it came to things like history and provenance. But she didn't want to say anything right now. She couldn't bear another disagreement between them.

"Of course."

He kissed her cheek, his lips barely brushing her

skin. She leaned forward, but he was already stepping back.

"Goodnight," he said softly, opening and closing the door behind him.

She sank against the wood and listened to his car pull off. Should she have asked him to stay? Right now, she wasn't sure how she was supposed to react. Or even how she wanted to react.

They might have apologized to each other, but they were a long way from being reconciled.

CHAPTER 31

J.T. COULDN'T BELIEVE HE WAS HAULING A PRICELESS painting across town without an iota of security.

To his mind, Hargreaves didn't count—even though Aunt Clara had said he was proficient in the martial arts. The man was ancient, for Christ's sake. A good wind would likely blow him over.

"Hargreaves," his aunt said from the back of the limo, "if it snows, we'll need to find another form of transportation."

Heaven save him, the man also doubled as a chauffeur. "Yes, Aunt, a limo isn't really practical in winter." Or in a small town like Dare Valley, he wanted to add. This wasn't Manhattan.

"Don't be a fuddy duddy, dear. You should have seen the look on Arthur Hale's face when I showed up on his doorstep last night and had my way."

He wanted to plug his ears. Had she phrased it that way on purpose? God, the images. "Yes, I can imagine his surprise. Aunt Clara, you really must let me store this painting somewhere safer. Trevor has a safe—"

"Safer than under my bed at Arthur Hale's house? Julian Thomas, there is no safer place on earth. Trust me."

Under her bed? She had to be kidding. Except he knew she wasn't. If it weren't for this comic distraction, he'd be fretting more over where things stood with Caroline. Even thinking about seeing her this morning had his gut clenching. He'd asked her if she wanted to ride to the university with them in the limo, but she'd insisted on meeting them there. It felt like she was avoiding him, and he couldn't blame her. His apology hadn't gone as well as he'd hoped even though he'd rehearsed it in his car.

He'd hoped to reassure her—instead, she'd hammered through his thick skull how important this museum was to her and her career. She was right. He had something to fall back on and a bank account to pad his way. Part of him had wanted to say she had that same safety net—that what was his was also hers—but it hadn't been the time. The last thing he wanted to do was insult her.

"You're in a mood this morning, aren't you?" Aunt Clara commented, slapping him on the thigh. "You and Caroline didn't kiss and make up, I gather."

Not even close. His glancing kiss on her cheek had left him frustrated and sad, but he'd thought it best not to push her. She hadn't wanted him to be there last night. Hadn't he seen her fiddling with the three tea boxes in the cabinet to avoid looking at him?

"That's none of your business, Aunt," he said. "Now I'd like to talk about the press conference for the Rembrandt."

"Evasion is a coward's tool, Julian," she said.

"Will you please not call me that?" he asked.

She turned her head and studied him. "The coward part or your given name?"

Both pretty much sucked. "Let's focus on the latter right now."

"Why ever not? It's your name, isn't it?"

"My ex-wife called me that, and it leaves—"

"A sour taste in your mouth," she said, playing with the diamonds at her wrist. "Fine, I'll call you by those appalling two letters then. You know, punctuating them with a couple of periods doesn't make them anything more than a couple of letters in the alphabet."

He was going to bash his head against the window if she kept it up. "Aunt, about the press conference... We need to come up with a story about why the Rembrandt remained hidden for so long."

She cackled so hard she fell back against the seat of the limo. "You mean, you don't want to tell them I was protecting it from my dead husband's money-grubbing hands? Oh, J.T., give me more respect. I know we'll need to come up with something better than, 'I forgot I had it.'"

"Maybe we can discuss it after the photo shoot."

"Photo shoot," she scoffed. "If Caroline hadn't felt it necessary, I would have vetoed it. It's a painting. Not some skinny model showcasing a bikini."

He fought for patience. "People all around the world—including the art community—are going to want to see this painting, Aunt. Until the museum opens, this is the best we can give them."

"Other than displaying it at the press conference, I expect," she said. "You can hire security for that event, J.T. A public event calls for a different approach. Hargreaves can stop a few *banditos* but not an entire audience."

"Thank you, madam," the man said from his position in the driver's seat.

Banditos? He should be grateful for small favors, he supposed.

"Do you have any thoughts on where you'd like to hold the press conference?" she asked.

He smiled. "Oh, yes. I called President Matthau last

night after the press release went out to ask for his help in hosting what should be a global media event."

"A global media event? Speak English, boy."

He struggled for patience. It *was* technically her painting. Trevor had wanted him to ask her to officially sign over the Rembrandt and the whole collection, but he hadn't felt it was right yet.

"Yes. Press and art lovers are going to want to be there," he said, "but we're going to have to limit the invitations."

He'd already compiled a solid list of art luminaries. After going home last night, he'd emailed it to Caroline. When he woke up alone in bed at five a.m., her comments and suggestions were waiting for him in his inbox.

She clearly hadn't slept any better than he had.

They were *emailing*.

How had it come to this?

"You should buy her flowers," Aunt Clara was saying. "Groveling wouldn't hurt either."

"Aunt—"

"Not that I'd know what a male apology looks like," she said, tapping the window. "Do you know that no man has ever apologized to me? Not once in my whole life."

That did sound rather incredible. "I seem to be apologizing all the time."

"Too much apologizing means something is out of balance," she said, reaching over to tap his knee. "You need to strike the right tone, J.T. Admit when you're wrong. Then don't do it again. Women hate repeat offenders."

Uncle Arthur was already brushing off on her. Or maybe she'd always been this way. After all, he'd only just met the woman. Perhaps she'd always been a hard ass.

His opinion of Aunt Clara wavered when he brought her up to Lucy's studio. She kissed them both on the cheek and embraced them like old friends. Hargreaves took up his sentry position at the door after laying the still-covered painting on the table.

"Arthur showed me some of your photos over breakfast, my dear," Clara said to Lucy. "Grudgingly, of course, but his bark has always been worse than his bite. I particularly love the one of the mother nursing the child by the ocean. Where was it taken again?"

"In Ghana," Lucy said. "It's such an honor to photograph a painting of this stature. And a Rembrandt! I have to admit, this is a first for me. I'm a little nervous."

"Don't be," Aunt Clara said. "Caroline tells me you've photographed naked women before."

Caroline laughed, and normally J.T. would have joined in, but it stuck in his throat. She hadn't glanced at him to include him in the joke, the way she normally would have.

"I brought you a copy of the calendar, Clara," she said. "Like you asked."

"Good! I can't wait to put it up in my bedroom. That's sure to raise Arthur's blood pressure."

Good God. He didn't want to ask why.

"I still can't believe Uncle Arthur agreed to let you stay with him," Caroline said, keeping her eyes fixed on his aunt.

While J.T. didn't feel like she was ignoring him, he could tell she was glad for the other people in the room. They were a buffer.

"Did Caroline tell me correctly that you hadn't seen Arthur since 1962?" Lucy asked, adjusting the velvet folds of the black cloth she'd set up for the backdrop.

"Yes, the day of my wedding," she said. "It was a horrid affair. A word to the wise, ladies... If you aren't happy on your wedding day, odds are pretty low you'll be happy during your marriage."

The comment reminded him about the conversation

he and Caroline had had about marriage. Was he selling her short? Didn't most women want to have a wedding day? His sisters had talked about it, he recalled, even before they met their first boyfriends. Heck, his mother still said her wedding was one of the best memories of her life. But it was only a single day, right?

He thought back on his wedding to Cynthia. Had he been happy? Mostly, he remembered it being a zoo. Had it been a bellwether for his marriage, the way Aunt Clara had said? Yes, he could see that it had been. He hadn't known the majority of the people Cynthia had invited. She'd spent more time talking to them than she did him.

But if people in a long-term relationship didn't have "a day," how did they start their life together off on the right foot? His parents always celebrated their anniversary with a big romantic gesture—a week-long sail around the Greek isles or hiking seaside trails in the Galapagos, something they both enjoyed. What would he and Caroline do? She was more special to him than any piece of artwork.

But did she know that? It struck him that he'd never told her, not really.

"Caroline?" he asked, taking his hands out of his pockets. "Can I speak to you? Privately?"

She finally looked at him. A deer in headlights came to mind. "Ah...Lucy, do you need me to help?"

"No," the woman said after taking a long, measuring glance at him. "I can manage."

"It's not hard," Aunt Clara said, crossing to Caroline and nudging her toward him. "You set up. You point the camera. You hit the button."

Lucy laughed. "Don't tell my students that, Mrs. Allerton."

"Please, call me Clara, my dear," she said. "Caroline tells me you're marrying her brother, Dr. Andy. I hear he's a nice boy. I made Arthur guide me through his whole family tree over the nasty oatmeal he insisted on having for breakfast. He complained it was cold by the time he'd finished, but I was delighted to hear about everyone."

Oh, she was going to drive Uncle Arthur and him both mad.

"Caroline, you and J.T. step out for a bit for your talk. I don't want Lucy to be distracted."

Okay, now he wanted to kiss the meddling old woman. Caroline crossed the room to join him, still not looking him in the eyes.

"You can use my office," Lucy called.

"Where—"

"I know the way," Caroline said, smiling at Hargreaves as they left the room.

She walked down the hall and opened another door, gesturing for him to go inside.

His spine straightened. Did she think his basic manners had disappeared? "Ladies first."

She sighed as she went by, as if he'd irritated her by fighting her on something so simple. Like being a gentleman was foolish. Heck, he wished women would decide what they wanted sometimes. He closed the door behind him. She turned to face him, her hands behind her back.

"What did you want—"

He grabbed her to him. "This," he said and then pressed his mouth to hers.

She tensed, as he'd expected she might, and he gentled the kiss. She could step away any time, and he made sure she knew it by dropping his hands. When she lifted her face to give them a better connection, his heart started to race in his chest.

"I hated leaving you last night," he whispered in between short kisses. "In fact, I hate all of this. I just... want you."

Aunt Clara was right. The time for groveling was past. He needed to be honest with her—to let her know how much she meant to him.

She fisted her hands on the back of his jacket in response, kissing him harder, and he gave up the fight to keep things gentle. Gripping her hips, he opened his mouth and gave in to the heat radiating through him. She uttered a short moan. He nipped the bottom of her lip. Another moan sounded from her lips, and he fought the urge to lift her onto the nearest surface, lift her dress, and take her right there.

"I hate this too," she said, breaking their connection for a moment.

Then her mouth was back on his, and her leg twined around his calf, fitting their hips more intimately together. He gave her what they both wanted, rubbing slowly against her.

"I love you," he said, taking her face between his hands. "Do you want me to give up the Rembrandt?"

"Good God, no," she said, her eyes horrified. "I only want this to be easier."

He pressed his forehead to hers, fighting a surge of emotion. "I want that too. You're more precious than any painting."

"I love you, J.T.," she whispered.

They stayed like that for a moment, and then she ran a comforting hand down his spine and stepped back.

"We shouldn't..." Her sigh was audible. "This is Lucy's office, and it's not professional."

He nodded and wiped her lipstick from his lips with a tissue he procured from Lucy's desk. He caught sight of a photo of her, Andy, and Andy's young son, Danny. Caroline's brother had lost the love of his life only to find love again with his childhood best friend. Hope shot through his heart. If Andy could overcome such an unimaginable tragedy, J.T. could begin a wonderful new life too.

The tones of "Gold Digger" chimed suddenly, tamping down that surge of hope.

Caroline clenched her hands. "I'll...let you take that."

He watched helplessly as she left the office and closed the door. Pulling out his phone, he stared at it for a moment, listening to the music. He imagined ignoring the call, hurling the phone against the wall. In the end, he clicked it on. No other course of action seemed possible right now.

"Cynthia," he said. "I'd like to say it's a pleasure to hear from you, but it's anything but." He'd actually thought he'd hear from her last night, and he'd wondered at the delay.

"You've been a naughty boy, Julian," she said in what she probably intended to be a playful tone. "Finding a long-lost Rembrandt. And right before I was going to announce to the world I was giving three hundred million dollars to the university for cancer research. I even flew in the family lawyer to finalize everything. That was a nice move, darling. I underestimated you."

Score one for him. "I'm sure you won't let it happen again. What do you want?"

"Like I told your new arm piece last night at the refreshing French bistro in town, you're going to have to do some fancy dancing to explain why your aunt kept this painting under wraps."

He wasn't going to be baited. "So you say. Look, I have to go."

"I'm a little hurt you never mentioned this Rembrandt to me while we were married."

There was a trap here. If he claimed he hadn't known about it, she'd call him a liar. If he admitted he had, she'd make him look greedy or use it as proof he'd known about it and hadn't said anything. "As I said, I have pressing concerns. Goodbye, Cynthia."

"*Julian*," she said as he was poised to press the button to cut her off.

The glee in her voice was unmistakable. This was how she'd sounded when he bought her a hundred-thousand-dollar emerald and diamond necklace in London.

He didn't hit the button, but he didn't say anything either. She'd know he was listening.

"Wait until you see what I have planned next," she said. "It might be my ultimate *coup de grâce*."

The call ended, and he stood there, thinking about the words she'd used. Fear swept through his body.

Coup de grâce was French for death blow.

CHAPTER 32

ARTHUR CAME HOME TO HEAR ELLA FITZGERALD SINGING her heart out to "Dream a Little Dream Of Me" with Louis Armstrong.

He paused in the doorway. It had been a long time since he'd come home to the lights on and music playing with a beautiful woman present. He could get used to this, especially after the day he'd had. Man, he hated kissing the asses of potential new advertising clients. But if he was going to make his loan payment in full this month—pride wouldn't let him do otherwise—he would kiss whatever ass it took.

"Is that you, Arthur?" he heard Clara call as he hung up his winter coat.

He followed her voice to the family room, sniffing the whole way. What was that smell? It was as if a spice market had exploded in his house. God knew what that sack of bones Hargreaves was cooking. He'd dug his feet in about having oatmeal this morning, but Clara had made him pay for it by peppering him with dozens of questions about his family. God, she was relentless—though he had to admit she'd looked stunning, sitting in the kitchen chair across from him with her silver hair streaming over her shoulder.

He found her sitting on his couch with her feet up, a highball in her hand. The navy dress she had on today had a lower neckline and a higher hemline.

Oh, Clara was trouble with a capital T, all right.

And part of him couldn't be more tickled.

"Who the hell else would it be? It's my house, although you seem to be making yourself right at home."

She slid off the couch in a way he wouldn't normally notice, something amazing for a woman her age because it actually looked sexy. "Did you have a bad day?"

"Not particularly," he replied, watching as she went over to *his* bar caddy and made him a martini. Where had the olives come from? he wondered as she added a few with panache.

"Oh, I thought for sure you had since you were barking like a dog," she said, smiling at him as she brought him the drink.

"You didn't get dolled up for me, did you?" he asked, noting the mauve touch of lipstick.

She winked. "You noticed, didn't you?"

He growled. "What *is* that infernal smell?"

She linked her arm through his and led him to the couch. "Dinner."

"You're kidding," he said, sitting beside her. "You're trying to kill me in punishment for not talking to you since 1962."

Of course, her response was to cozy up to him like they were going steady. He decided he'd enjoy it.

"I told you Hargreaves was a proficient cook," she said, sipping her drink. "He's taken courses at Le Cordon Bleu in Paris."

"Good for him, but I know what French food smells like." He pointed in the direction of the kitchen. "That is not it."

She settled back against the couch, rubbing up

against it like she was a kitten. Oh, good gracious. He was too old for this kind of stimulation.

"It's Indian food," she said. "He makes the best naan you'll ever have."

"I haven't had Indian food since—"

"Gandhi's funeral in 1948," she said with a sly smile.

Oh, she thought she had his number, did she? "I was ten years old in 1948, so it's unlikely I was there. But you get points for cheekiness."

She leaned her face briefly against his arm. "I meant to ask you if there's a woman in town who might not like me staying here."

He shifted slightly so he could see her better. Two could play this game. "More than one might get bent out of shape."

Her eyebrow rose slowly. "Looking as you do, I can see you still breaking hearts."

"Better than hips at this age," he said, laughing. "There's a woman I used to go out with every once in a while, but she's still in love with her dead husband. We're more companionable."

"Meaning you haven't slept with her?" Clara asked.

"I'm old. Not dead," he said, giving her his best glower. "But we haven't seen much of each other lately if that's what you're asking."

"Are you still in love with your wife?" she asked.

"You're nosy." He took a healthy swig of his drink. "Egad, you made this strong."

"Part of my plan," she said. "I was hoping you'd tell me all your secrets."

"Oh, good Lord, Clara," he said, shifting on the couch. "You're still a brat. But I'll answer your question. Harriet was the only woman I loved while we were together. But when she died, I grieved her. I can't go about telling the young generation to move on from loss and tragedy if I don't do it. Besides, I know Harriet wouldn't want me to hole up with her old sweaters and cry myself to sleep for the rest of my life."

"I burned all of Reinhold's clothing in the garden when he died," she said, swirling her drink in her hand. "Then I had cake and champagne. I probably had more fun that day than I did at my wedding."

Yeah, he remembered she'd had none of her usual sass that day, and it had saddened him. Every detail she shared about her marriage painted a bleak picture, and he felt for her. No one deserved a lifetime of misery. No one so full of life deserved to be shackled to a human mannequin like Reinhold.

"I'm sorry you had such a bad time of it."

"It was my partly my fault, which is why I understand Julian," she said.

Ah. He'd wondered why she'd been so quick to help the boy.

"I didn't see Reinhold for what he was until it was too late, and convention kept me from divorcing him. We lived separate lives, which was the best I could hope for."

"So you had an understanding?"

She socked him in the arm. "Is that your indelicate way of asking if I took lovers too during our marriage? Well, Arthur Hale, you can go stuff yourself."

Standing, she put her hands on her hips, and he thought about grabbing her by those curves. Oh, sod it. Why the heck not?

He pulled her onto his lap none too gracefully, and his cane clattered to the ground. "Yes, you're a brat, but I still like you. And your legs aren't bad."

She snorted, extending one of the legs he'd complimented. "Did you notice the shortened hemline? Hargreaves stuck me a few times in the hemming process after we got home from the Rembrandt photo shoot."

She'd shortened her clothing today? God, she was batty. Like he cared about a dress.

"I can't wait to see those pictures," he said, feeling like he'd somehow cajoled a wild gazelle onto his lap. "You're the only woman who would keep a Rembrandt hidden."

"I had good cause, but J.T. is twisted up pretty good about whether the world will understand. He and Caroline haven't been seeing eye-to-eye, but I think they made up in Lucy's office today."

He covered his ears. "Don't tell me things like that."

"Do you really want to see the Rembrandt?" she asked, swaying on his lap.

Okay, he'd heard that. "Of course. Clara, stop that. You're going to make me seasick."

"I was trying to be seductive."

He laughed. "Your routine needs some work."

She socked him again, and he had to be losing it because he found he rather liked it. "You're one to talk. Here I dress up for you and shorten my hemline—"

"And lower your *neckline,*" he said, letting his eyes dip to the slight cleavage exposed.

Both her hands twined in the hair at the back of his head. "You *really* did notice. And here I was worried you might be dead in that department."

He pecked her solidly on the lips to prove he wasn't. She held him in place when he went to draw back, and soon he was kissing Clara Merriam for the first time, and damn, it was really good.

When she finally released him, her blue eyes were sparkling. In them, he could see the young woman he used to take to the ballet or for a walk through Central Park. But both of them had changed, honed by life, and she'd acquired a wisdom he found more attractive than that snarky young girl.

"You're more beautiful now, you know," he said softly.

She traced his cheekbone, her lips twitching. "You aren't."

He scoffed. "Well, thank you very much."

"Oh, but I like this new you in some ways," she said. "You were so...driven and serious when I knew you."

"I had a lot I wanted to do," he said, shrugging. "And I haven't done half bad."

"Yet you haven't slowed down one bit," she said, tapping his cheek. "You're just like Grandpa Emmits. He was working a full day when he dropped dead."

Arthur remembered receiving that phone call. He wasn't ashamed to say he'd hung his head and cried. "It was how he would have wanted it. Not a bad way to go if you ask me."

"I'd rather go in the sack with a man I was in love with," she said, looking him directly in the eye.

He didn't blink. Was she teasing him? Or was she trying to tell him something? After a moment, he decided she was serious.

"If you keep things up, you never know," he said carefully. "It could lead that way."

She leaned forward and kissed him gently on the lips, and dammit if he didn't feel a warm glow in his chest.

"You know," he said finally, caressing her incredible cheekbones, "I imagined a hell of a lot of things for my so-called golden years, but I didn't see this coming."

"If you'd called me after my husband died, we'd have gotten to this earlier."

He rolled his eyes. "Brat. You could have called *me*."

She made a rude sound. "Women from my generation do not call up men, Arthur."

She was full of shit, but this wasn't the moment to point it out.

"I'm feeling better than I have in years," she said, lowering her voice, "and I'm old enough to know how precious it is. Just promise me something."

He put his arms around her. "What?"

"You're supposed to say, 'anything, Clara.'"

He barked out a laugh. "You've got to be kidding. I

would never agree to something carte blanche like that. You know me better than to expect otherwise."

She gave a decided huff. "Fine. I was only going to... Oh, never mind."

Before he knew it, she was sliding off his lap. He watched as she started to walk off.

"I don't remember you ever running away," he said to stop her. He was too old to chase after her.

"I was going to check on that revolting dinner you smell," she said, throwing out her arms in a dramatic gesture. "You want to know what I was going to say? Okay, here goes. I was going to ask you to promise not to break my heart like you did in 1960. How's that for one of your timeline markers?"

He stood and felt none too steady without his cane. "I didn't break your heart."

"I know my own heart," she said, laying her hand over it. "I cried when you left, Arthur, and I *never* cry."

He had to cough to clear his throat. "Clara! Oh, dagnabbit."

"As I said, I'm going to check on dinner, although perhaps I'll have Hargreaves open a can of your *boring* tomato soup instead. Then I'll show you the Rembrandt."

She turned the music off, and he grabbed his cane and walked toward her.

"I'm sorry I hurt you," he said, coming to a stop in front of her. "I cared for you too, but the people we were then... Clara, you know as well as I do that we weren't meant for each other."

"And now?" she asked, those blue eyes searching.

He extended his hand to her and was glad when she clasped it. "It's early yet, but things look promising."

Her chest lifted as she took a deep breath. "I must be going senile to think about falling in love at my age, and with someone as stubborn as you are."

"You're stubborn too," he pointed out, bringing her hand to his mouth and kissing it.

"You haven't forgotten all your moves," she said, tapping him on the chest. "And if I'm stubborn, it's only because you like it and need it."

His mouth twitched. "I do indeed. Don't stop."

She fought a smile, but it finally won out. "I won't. I know you better than you think, even after all these years."

Truer words had never been spoken. And she'd lit up his life in a way he'd never expected—and didn't want to lose. He'd never thought he was lonely, but perhaps his life outside the office had gotten stale. "About the Rembrandt... Did you really say you were going to show it to me?"

"Yes," she said, keeping his hand and leading him back to the couch.

They sat down together, and she took his cane and set it out of reach. He decided not to comment.

"Clara, are you telling me there's a priceless painting here in my house?" he asked instead.

She put her hand on his knee and left it there. He rather liked that.

"J.T. had trouble with the idea too, but I told him there was no safer place than under my bed. Besides, Hargreaves would handle any thieves, but seriously, who would break into this house? You're a legend, after all."

He stared at her. "Under your bed? Woman, you're insane to think Hargreaves could handle anything. You call J.T. and ask him to come and get the Rembrandt right now. I don't want that kind of responsibility. That painting's priceless."

"You're overreacting," she said in a bored tone, "but I'll call him tomorrow and talk to him about this safe Trevor seems to have. I can't have you both on my back."

"You're too much," he said, shaking his head and laughing. "Under your bed!"

His phone rang, and he wanted to snarl. Of course the phone would ring when he was sitting beside a beautiful woman on his couch.

"Go ahead and answer it," she said, flicking a hand toward the sound. "I know your work is important."

That response had him stepping even lighter to the phone, and without his cane, he realized. Young Clara hadn't truly understood or respected his work. That had clearly changed, much to his delight.

"Would you make me another drink?" he asked. "I plan to let you wrangle out a few more secrets after I take this call."

Her smile was like quicksilver. "Oh, Arthur, I'm so happy."

He was too. Picking up the phone, he watched her saunter back to the bar.

"Arthur Hale," he answered.

"Hello, Arthur. It's Franklin Gerhardt. I'm sorry to be calling you at home."

His blood pressure rose. Why would the bank be calling him after hours?

"What can I do for you, Franklin?"

"Arthur, this is a very difficult call for me to make, but the decision came from the executive office."

His stomach sunk. "What decision?"

Franklin coughed. "The bank has decided to call your loan in. You have thirty days to pay it, or we'll have to take possession."

That place was his second home, his legacy. He turned his back on Clara, feeling his chest tighten. "Why would you call in the loan? I pay the monthly balance on time and—"

"Like I said, Arthur, this came from the executive office."

Something was wrong here, especially on the tail of losing their largest advertiser. He could feel it in his gut, and his gut had never failed him. He did a mental computation of what he still owed. "You expect me to pull together three million in thirty days? Franklin, that's impossible! This isn't what we agreed to. This is bullshit, and you know it!" His heart pounded in his ears, and he started sweating.

"The loan agreement says very clearly it's at the bank's discretion to call in the final balance at any time, thus giving the loanee thirty days to pay the full balance."

Now he was giving him legalese? Yeah, something was wrong for sure. He'd gotten the runaround from the advertiser that had left too.

"What happens if I can't pay the full amount?" he asked, hoping the man wouldn't voice his greatest fear.

"The bank takes over the paper if you default," Franklin said.

His chest got tight, and suddenly it was hard to breathe.

"I'm sorry, Arthur. We've known each other a long time, and this wasn't a call I ever expected to make."

"You're damn right it isn't!" Arthur barked.

He could lose the paper? It wasn't possible. The thought made him lightheaded.

"Goodbye, Arthur." He barely heard the man's brush-off over the roaring in his ears.

He lowered the phone and stared out the window, rubbing his chest. How was he supposed to find three million dollars in thirty days? Everything he worked for was in danger.

Pain shot through his chest like a lightning bolt, and he clutched it. "Argh."

"Arthur!" Clara called.

The pressure increased, and he felt himself tip and then crash to the floor. He landed hard. More pain radiated from his bad hip. Jesus!

"Arthur, what's wrong?" Clara asked, bent over him.

"Can't breathe," he hissed out, his fist over his heart.

He smacked it for good measure, but it didn't stop the pain or help him breathe. The pain shot down his arm, and it went numb. God, he was having a heart attack.

"Dammit! Arthur Hale, you listen to me."

Strong hands gripped his face, and for a moment, he focused on her. There were tears in her eyes.

"You aren't going to die on me. Not when I've only just found you again. Do you hear me? Hargreaves!"

He heard someone stomping across the wooden floors. A cold hand touched his face.

Then the pain in his chest surged again, and he felt nothing.

CHAPTER 33

CAROLINE WAS HUMMING AWAY AS SHE PREPARED DINNER for her and J.T.

When she'd suggested it—saying it wouldn't be anything fancy, only taco salad—he'd eagerly accepted her invitation. Today in Lucy's office, she'd felt cherished. She'd felt heard. And J.T. had confirmed that he was as scared of losing her as she was of losing him. Outside forces were pulling them apart, and she didn't like that one bit, but Cynthia would only succeed if they let her.

Fortunately, Clara was cooperating regarding the lost Rembrandt. Well, mostly. She had strong opinions about what she planned to tell the media. J.T. had made some suggestions, but she'd remained firm. Honesty was the best policy, she'd said, and she'd kept the supposed Rembrandt under wraps to protect it from her husband. If his family didn't like that, Clara had said, they could put it where the sun didn't shine.

God, that woman had spunk.

When she heard a knock on the door, she untied her apron and hung it over a kitchen chair. Adjusting her skirt and blouse, she walked swiftly to the door and opened it. Trevor stood on the other side, his expression grim.

"Oh, hello," she said, leaning forward and kissing his cheek. "If you're looking for J.T., he's not here yet."

"I know," he said. "I tracked his phone. He drove to Aspen to buy you all twenty-four flavors of Paradise Bakery's famous gelato for dinner."

One of her sisters must have told him Cappuccino Toffee Crunch was her favorite. Ah...

"You haven't checked your phone, have you?"

Tension filled her. That look. Something had happened. "No, I turned the ringer off when I started dinner. It's been a day. People have been calling nonstop about the Rembrandt, and I'm ignoring them like J.T. suggested."

She didn't like that approach, but he wasn't wrong. It wasn't like they could give out more details about the Rembrandt in advance of the press conference.

"Has something happened?" she asked.

"Yes," he said gravely. "Uncle Arthur appears to have had a heart attack."

She gripped his jacket. "What?"

He took her arm and led her inside, closing the door. "Meredith called me from the hospital."

"Oh, God, not this!" she said, rushing to where she'd left her phone. "They called me, and I missed it."

She noted the calls and texts from various family members and felt tears gather in her eyes. One in particular from Andy caught her eye. *Come quickly. He's not well.*

Andy was a doctor. This was terrible news. She had to get moving.

"How could this have happened? That man is invincible." To her, he always had been—no matter how old he'd become.

Trevor came and put his arms around her. "Look, I know you're upset, but we have a serious situation on our hands in addition to that wonderful man being in the hospital."

What could be more important than that? "I need

to go to the hospital," she said, pushing away from him. "Have you reached J.T.?"

"No, I told Meredith to instruct everyone not to call him," Trevor said.

"Why would you do that?" she asked, staring at him in confusion. "J.T. would want to be there."

He sliced his hand through the air. "Don't you think I know that? Listen, I talked to Aunt Clara. She was with him when he had the attack."

Her heart started to pound in her ears. "What did she say?"

"From what she could hear, he got a call from his banker. It seems that someone in the front office decided to call in his loan. Caroline, he has thirty days to pay three million dollars."

Oh, no. It couldn't be. "You don't think it's Cynthia?" Surely the woman wouldn't stoop this low.

He cursed under his breath. "Remember what J.T. told you about Cynthia and her father switching banks? It didn't feel right."

She nodded, feeling short of breath.

"It's the same bank," he continued. "Carlyle's. And they're going down for this. Hard."

She watched him in shock as Trevor pressed the bridge of his nose. That woman had intentionally gone after a wonderful old man. How could she?

"There's more... Uncle Arthur mentioned in passing that the paper lost its biggest advertiser, and when I heard about his heart attack, I realized it happened the day after the Op-Ed was published. I looked up the company before I came here, and the president is close friends with Cynthia's father."

This couldn't be happening. "I can't believe it."

"I want to kick myself for not putting it together earlier, but now it doesn't matter. The damage is done. You know what this means, right?" he asked her, dropping his hand.

"Cynthia's going to pay for this—like you said," she said, heat raging through her system. "She went too far."

Trevor walked over to her and put his hands on her shoulders. "Yes, she's going to pay, but I need your help."

"Do you need me to drive the getaway car?"

His laugh was harsh. "No, I need you to help me with J.T."

Suddenly, it all crashed into place in her mind. Fresh horror flooded her. "He's going to blame himself for this."

"Yes," Trevor said, "and I'm not sure he can come back from this one."

Neither was she.

CHAPTER 34

THE LAST THING J.T. EXPECTED TO SEE WAS CAROLINE'S stricken face when she opened the door.

He slowly lowered the Sub-Zero cooler filled with the gelato he'd made a special trip for. "What's wrong?"

"You should come in," she said simply and let him enter.

His first thought was that she was going to break up with him. Then he smelled Mexican food and thought, nah. She wouldn't have invited him over for dinner, and actually cooked, to break his heart.

"Caroline, what's going on?" he asked, following her into the kitchen and setting the cooler down.

When he looked up and saw his brother, he stopped short. He'd known Trev his whole life, and he'd never seen his face such a sickly shade of gray.

"What is it?" he asked his twin.

Trev walked toward him slowly, and he felt Caroline wrap her arms around his waist. His whole body froze up, sensing the need to protect himself from whatever they were about to say.

"Uncle Arthur had a heart attack tonight," Trev told him. "Aunt Clara and her butler managed to give him an aspirin and call an ambulance, but he's in critical condition."

His own heart turned to stone in his chest. No, not his idol. Not Uncle Arthur. He'd only just gotten him back in his life. He'd thought there'd be more time. "We need to go to the hospital."

He realized they'd been waiting for him, and gratitude filled him. It must have been hard for them to stay here when all they wanted to do was to be with the man they all loved.

He pulled away, but Caroline clung to him, refusing to let him go. She was taking it hard, and he put his arms around her. Then he met his Trevor's gaze, and he knew there was more to it. He wanted to throw off the arms holding him in place and bury his head in the sand. He couldn't take it.

"There's no easy way to say this," Trev said, "so I'm saying it straight out. Carlyle Bank phoned Uncle Arthur tonight and called in his loan. He has thirty days to pay back a sizeable amount or the bank takes over *The Western Independent*. Not that we're going to let that happen, of course."

His mind went blank, like when he entered a room and couldn't remember why he'd gone there. Then his brain fixated on one word—Carlyle—and he put the puzzle pieces together.

"*Cynthia.*"

He would have stumbled backward if their hands hadn't been on him.

"And the paper's biggest advertiser—the one Uncle Arthur mentioned losing the other day—is connected to Newhouse Senior. J.T., I'm sorry I didn't make the connection earlier."

Who could have? This was a whole new level of revenge. A huge well of pain surged up, crashing through him like a category three hurricane.

"No!" he cried out.

He shoved them away and took a few shaky steps. He needed space. He couldn't breathe.

Cynthia's last words came to mind. *Coup de grâce.* She'd delivered a death blow to a man he loved and admired, a man who'd helped him fight for the museum.

Now Arthur Hale was in danger of losing his life.

"It's all my fault," he said softly. "I did this—"

"No, J.T.," Caroline said, coming over to him. "It's not. It's hers. She's a horrible, horrible woman."

God, he couldn't believe she could be this cruel. "She couldn't have come up with a worse punishment," he said, feeling lightheaded. "No one is safe around me."

"Stop this!" Trev shouted, stalking over to him. "I mean it, J.T. We need you to focus."

"I hurt everyone I love," he said, a strange numbness coating him now.

"You stop talking like this," Trev shouted. "Dammit! Don't you see? You're falling into her hands again."

Right, Cynthia. She'd wanted him to crawl, to hurt, to give up.

She'd finally gotten her wish.

He stalked to the front door and heard Caroline and Trevor behind him. Fumbling with his keys, he managed to get into his car and lock the door before they reached him. Trev beat on the window, Caroline crying beside him.

"Don't do this, J.T.," Caroline called, putting her hand on the glass.

She didn't understand. He had to protect her now, before it was too late. What he wanted didn't matter anymore. This was the only thing he could do for her. He turned the car on and sped off.

His first stop was the hospital. He had to see Uncle Arthur. Make sure he remembered just how much of a liability he was. The corridor was crowded with the family he'd come to love when he arrived on the second floor.

Jill was crying when she hugged him, and so were her two small daughters.

"Thank God your aunt was with him, J.T.," she told him. "Andy says so much damage was prevented because she gave him that aspirin right away."

Brian was beside her, rubbing away his own tears. "He's strong, Jillie. He's going to make it and yell at us all for making such a fuss."

"I'm sorry," he whispered as he walked past them. "I'm so sorry."

God, there was such pain here, and he'd caused it.

Caroline's mother kissed him on the cheek, muttering something he couldn't make out. Then Moira and Natalie were putting their arms around him, but he pressed on to the door of Arthur's hospital room. Aunt Clara saw him and stood up from her position in the corner.

She came to him, and he felt her hand on his arm as he looked at his beloved mentor. Tubes were in his nose, winding around him like vines. IVs were strapped to his arms. He was hooked to machines beeping and wheezing, as if he needed them to keep going. His normally ruddy color was sallow green now, and the wrinkles on his face seemed to have fallen inches more from the stress. The great Arthur Hale looked nothing like the vibrant man he knew and loved.

This is what he'd done. He'd been the one to bring this disaster home to Dare Valley. If he'd never come here, Cynthia would have had no reason to target these people.

Meredith and Tanner were holding Uncle Arthur's hands, one on each side. Their faces were etched with worry.

"I'm sorry," he said softly. "Please tell him."

God, he hoped Uncle Arthur would wake to hear

those words. His mind spun. What if he didn't? He could die. People did die from heart attacks, especially when they were elderly. How could he live with that? The answer was simple. He couldn't.

Aunt Clara tightened her hold on him. "Don't you dare go blaming yourself for this."

He untangled himself from her grasp. "It's too late."

He'd tried everything else to thwart Cynthia. Walked away from his career and his family's company. Given away the bulk of his money. And it still hadn't kept the people he loved safe.

The only thing left for him to do was disappear.

Chapter 35

When Caroline reached the hospital with Trevor, they discovered J.T. was already gone.

She tried his cell again, but he didn't answer it. Trev was doing the same, cursing under his breath.

"I don't like this," Trev said. "He's never looked..."

Caroline heard his voice break and put her arm around him. She knew what he meant. The young, vital man she'd come to love had seemed to fade away before her eyes. He'd looked haunted...no, *broken*.

Moira found her and pulled her aside, Chase hovering with concern. "Are you okay?"

"No," she said, letting her phone finally fall back into her purse. It was useless. He wouldn't answer them. "This is horrible! I hate that woman! I hate her!"

A nurse shushed her, but she didn't care. That woman was out there, walking around in her furs or sipping champagne after devastating two men Caroline loved dearly. It wasn't right. How could one person dish out so much hate and punishment?

Natalie and Blake appeared by her side, and Matt and Jane and Andy and Lucy closed in around her too. Everyone was trying to comfort her, but as much as she loved them, she doubted anything could help.

"Find her somewhere quiet, Moira," Trevor said. "Chase, I need to speak with you."

Her siblings drew her toward the hospital chapel, and then her mother was easing her into a chair. April Hale sat beside her and wrapped her up in a tight hug.

"Oh, Mom," she said, and the simple warmth of her mother's embrace broke the dam of her sorrow.

She sobbed her heart out. Every now and then, someone would press a tissue in her hands. All the while she thought of Uncle Arthur and J.T. and all the pain Cynthia Newhouse had wrought on the world in a hollow attempt to cure her own broken heart.

"I just don't understand it," she cried.

Then a strong hand touched her knee, and she felt her mother shift to the side. Sniffling, she looked down to see Chase kneeling in front of her. His face was drawn like everyone else's, but the fire in his eyes told her he knew the whole tale. While tears rolled down her face, he told the rest of her family what had happened.

"We've got Arthur covered financially, of course," he said softly, "although his pride won't like it. Meredith and Tanner told him so. It's well known people who are unconscious can hear. Caroline, he's going to get well. Arthur Hale wouldn't let anyone or anything put him down like this. Right?"

She nodded, wiping her nose. "He'd be all the more determined to recover."

Chase simply said, "And we'll talk some sense into J.T. It's a huge shock. Of course he feels awful."

She wanted to agree, but... "You didn't see him. Chase, he—"

"I'll talk to him again," Trevor said, coming up behind Chase. "I always get through to him—even if it takes a while. Besides, I have you as my ally now."

Even so, she wasn't sure it would be enough.

"He's awake," she heard Andy announce from the doorway.

"Thank God!" she cried, feeling more tears well.

"See," Moira said with a nudge, "it's like Chase said. Nothing will get him down."

"He's one of the toughest men you'll ever meet," her mom said. "We can count on that."

She could only nod as she went to see Uncle Arthur with the rest of the family.

His eyes were barely open, and his mouth was slack, but Uncle Arthur scanned the room as she and the rest of them crowded in, something Andy said he'd allow only for a few minutes.

"You look like you're attending my funeral," he rasped. "Trust me, this isn't going to finish me off."

"Dad and Mom are driving up from Arizona and want you to know how much they love you," Meredith said, kneeling beside the bed.

Caroline imagined Uncle Alan and Aunt Linda were breaking all the speed limits. Her uncle had suffered a heart attack a few years ago, so he had to be especially worried about his father.

"My boy knows what I'm going through."

"Save your strength, Grandpa."

"I have reserves," he said in that same voice. "Besides, I have to stay around. Can't let the bank have my baby."

"No one is going to take our paper," Meredith said in a harsh tone.

"They sure as hell won't," Tanner said, putting his hand on his wife's shoulder. "You have our word on that."

"Dammit, Grandpa," Jill said, coming over to where Meredith was standing. "You're all making me wish I had black ink in my veins."

"Ah, Jillie," he said with a slow smile, "you make me laugh. That's more than enough."

Their solidarity prompted more tears in the room,

and Caroline watched as Clara came to the other side of the bed. She sat in the chair Meredith had vacated and took Uncle Arthur's hand.

"The paper isn't in jeopardy," she told him, "because you're going to let me give you the money. I'm pulling rank on you, Trevor, as your elder."

Caroline watched as his mouth tipped up. "We'll talk it over later, Aunt."

He grunted and then coughed loudly. "Like I'd take money from the woman I fancy—or any of you, for that matter. God, do you not know me? No, we'll figure something out."

"That's the kind of lunacy that landed you in here from all the stress," Clara said, putting her hands on her hips. "I'm not going to argue with you."

"Enough. I'm too tired, but I will tell you this. Cynthia Newhouse messed with the wrong person—and so did Carlyle Bank. I don't care how much money someone has, they can't use their influence to make the bank call in someone's loan. It's a crime, and I'll see her in jail if not hell for this. And if that department store asshole pulled his advertising—"

"Trevor thinks so," Tanner said. "We'll have to see what we can do to him."

"Oh, we'll do something all right," Trevor said. "Don't you worry."

"Where is your brother? Didn't my heart attack rate a visit?"

"He was here, Grandpa," Meredith said. "Now you should rest. Andy..."

Her brother waved his arms like he was shooing swans. "All right, it's time for most of you to go. Uncle Arthur should be okay, but he needs to rest."

"That's not what your text said," Natalie told him, her hands framing her pregnant belly. "Even the baby got scared."

"Well, he's not out of the woods just yet," Andy said. "He's showing extreme stress and exhaustion. His heart isn't too bad for his age, thank God, but he's going to need to make some changes."

"Stop talking about me like I'm not here," Uncle Arthur barked.

Her brother turned to face him. "Bottom line. You're overdoing it for a man of your age, and this is a wake-up call."

"Balderdash," he scoffed. "It's just stress."

"Dad had a heart attack in his *fifties*," Meredith pointed out. "It runs in the family."

"I'm a superior species of Hale, and I'll tell your father as much when he gets here," Uncle Arthur said. "Fine, so I'll eat kale and go to Elizabeth's Latin dance class and exercise more."

This time Andy laughed. "If only... We'll talk about proposed life adjustments with you tomorrow. Right now, it's late. You really do need to sleep."

"Sleep is for dead people," he said. "I hate being here in this see-through gown, hooked up to all these machines."

"I'll stay with you," Meredith said.

"Me too," Jill echoed.

"No, you both go home to your kids," he said. "Clara can stay with me. It's not like she has anything else to do."

A few of their relatives looked shocked speechless, but Clara just laughed, and Caroline found her smiling for the first time since hearing the news.

"Glad to see this heart attack hasn't affected your common sense, Arthur," Clara said, pulling her chair closer to his bedside. "I can have Hargreaves bring you anything you want from home."

"Finally, your butler has a purpose," Arthur said. "Caroline, dear, come here for a minute. You too, Trevor.

Everyone else can skedaddle. Except you, my dear." He said that last bit looking Clara in the eyes.

It was clear to Caroline that things had changed between them.

Clara nodded firmly, holding Arthur's hand as people kissed him on the cheek and said their goodbyes. When everyone else had left, Caroline felt the urge to take Trevor's hand. He looked so defeated, unlike his usually bullish self.

"Where is J.T. really?" her uncle asked.

Caroline looked at Trevor, who sighed. "I don't know. He's not answering his phone, and I haven't heard from him."

"What about you?" her uncle asked.

God, he looked so tired. She felt guilty for keeping him up any longer than needed.

"Let me look," she said, pulling her phone out of her purse. "I've tried calling and texting him too, but it's been a while. Wait, I have a text."

She opened it, and her heart stopped.

"Well, what does it say?" her uncle prodded.

Trevor reached for her phone and then lowered his hand. "You read it."

She would have given anything for the words to be different. For them and for her.

Caroline, I'm sorry to do this, but after what Cynthia did to Uncle Arthur, I can't bear for anyone else to get hurt. Trev used to joke about the deserted island, and maybe he had it right all along. I'm disappearing for a while and won't be back to start the museum. I'll text Trev to handle the particulars.

There's no reason the museum can't go forward without me now that you and Aunt Clara have the Rembrandt. Please continue on like we planned. I like knowing you're living your dream, even if I can't live mine with you. Again, I'm sorry it came to this. I love you, but I just can't risk hurting you or anyone else again.

Tears streamed down her face. He'd left. Just like that. Part of her understood. The other part wanted to beat her hands against his chest and make him see reason.

"That little shit," Trevor muttered under his breath. "A deserted island... I can't believe it."

"You'll have to find him, Trevor," her uncle said, his voice thin. "I won't have this on my conscience."

"Nor I," Clara said, standing up. "A Merriam doesn't disappear. I've never heard of anything so ridiculous."

"He's been kicked down too many times," Caroline said, grabbing a tissue. "He couldn't handle any more."

"Bullshit," Uncle Arthur rasped. "When you can't keep going, you let the people you love carry you. Trev. Caroline. It's your time. I would go, but I'm tied up to all these damn machines."

"I'll find him and drag him back by a chain if I have to," Trevor said in a hard tone.

Caroline noted his fighting stance and decided to voice her fear. "What if you can't find him?"

"Don't insult me," Trev said.

"I didn't mean to," she said. "What if he won't come back?" Chains weren't going to work, and they all knew it. He'd only return if he was willing.

"Then you do everything you can to convince him," her uncle said. "Even if it means fighting a little dirty."

"Can you do that, Caroline?" Clara asked. "Because I believe we've found ourselves at a decisive moment."

They all looked at her, even Trevor. She thought about J.T. and how much she loved his sense of adventure and the way he gazed at her right before he kissed her, like she was his entire world. Then she thought about the letters his grandparents had exchanged from across the sea. They'd weathered so many challenges to build a beautiful life together after the war.

"How dirty are we talking?"

Chapter 36

Evading Trevor wasn't going to be easy, J.T. knew, but to protect him and everyone else, he'd pull out all the stops.

God, he'd never expected Cynthia's grudge against him would end like this—with someone he loved being physically harmed to the point of almost death.

He texted his brother his instructions with an apology he could only hope Trev would accept. Leaving Caroline and his new life behind was the worst thing imaginable, but in many ways, so was leaving his twin. They'd always had each other's backs.

Now, he had to go it alone. The aching feeling of loss was like a void inside him.

As he drove to Denver, he called his credit card concierge service and asked for their assistance. He was glad for something to focus on other than the tightness in his chest. There was no way he could take the family jet, so he bought six first class tickets to different locations around the world: Rome, Buenos Aires, Casablanca, Rio de Janeiro, Bangkok, and Hong Kong.

He only planned to use one of the tickets, and that was to Bangkok. Once there, he would have to find way of making sure his passport wasn't entered into the Thai system, which would keep Trev guessing. From there, he would rent a charter plane under another name and have them drop him off at an island airport with loose security.

His phone continued to ring as he made the arrangements, and his car dashboard showed him who the callers were. Caroline. Trevor. Again and again. Even Evan and Chase called. So far no one else in his direct family, but Trev might be keeping the situation under wraps, hoping he'd find J.T. and talk some sense into him. He knew his brother would want to save them from worrying.

When Cynthia showed up on his caller ID while he was finalizing the tickets, he asked if he could call the sales agent back. This was one call he planned to take.

"How do you feel about almost killing an old man?" he asked without preamble.

He heard a humming sound. "Oh, is that what you think I did? J.T., you give me too much credit."

Strangling her would be too merciful. "I never thought you'd stoop this low. You've become completely morally corrupt. I was the one who left. You want to make me suffer? Come at me, not anyone else."

And yet she'd also targeted his family business and Caroline, he thought. She had never played fair.

"That *old* man came at me. You were the one who brought him into our little game."

He wanted to kick something. "This isn't a game. This is life, and you're hurting people who don't deserve it. I don't want you around anymore. Don't you get it? This is why I left you! Why can't you get that through your thick skull?"

Silence reigned for thirty seconds, and he knew he'd struck a vein.

"Oh, Julian is upset," she practically purred. "That's what I've wanted all along. You keep evading me so I have to keep upping the stakes. Walking away from your career and your family legacy. Then giving away all that money. What's up this time? Because I don't think the Rembrandt is a fake."

"Of course it's not a fake," he said. "I would never leave myself or anyone else open to your arrows. Cynthia, I want this to stop. Right now. You won. Is that what you want to hear?"

"No," she said with an edge in her voice. "I told you that you'd pay for that for the rest of your life, and I meant it."

"You're sick," he said sadly. "All that time spent in therapy as a child didn't help you one bit."

"How dare you!"

He glanced over to see Caroline was calling him on the other line, and his remaining heartstrings broke. He was never going to see her again, and he didn't know how he could accept that.

"You bet I dare," he said, letting the force of his rage out. It didn't matter now.

"Well, you'll keep paying."

"No, I won't," he said, his tone hard. "I'm done being nice. You crossed the line. I'm going to find evidence you influenced the bank to call in Arthur's loan, and I'm going to take you down. And if I can prove your father was involved in the newspaper losing its top advertiser, I'm going to fry him too."

Of course, Trevor might beat him to it, but he didn't care so long as it forced her to stop.

"I don't know what you're talking about, Julian," she said.

"We'll see," he said. "Get ready to wear orange, Cynthia."

Her outraged exclamation was the last thing he heard before he disconnected the call. He thought about finding evidence of her guilt. How long would it take?

And would it really stop her? If he sent her to prison, or her father for that matter—a heartening thought—would it put an end to her harassment? They had money, and they wouldn't be in jail forever.

None of that could matter. She would finally be held accountable for her actions, and her father too, if he were involved. He'd never liked the man anyway.

Good thing he had a focus.

Otherwise, being on a deserted island away from everything he loved was going to drive him crazy.

CHAPTER 37

ARTHUR WAS A CRAFTY SON OF A BITCH, IF HE DIDN'T SAY so himself. Even holed up in a hospital bed.

No vicious rich bitch was going to do him in. No siree. The heart attack had scared the bejesus out of him, but it wasn't going to keep him down for long, and it certainly wasn't going to keep him from suggesting a way out of this infernal mess they'd found themselves in.

Of course, Clara and Trevor had insisted on repaying the loan for him, and even Chase and Evan had offered him financial assistance. His pride didn't want to agree, but given the timeframe, he didn't like his options. Why didn't they understand that he didn't want anyone to technically own his paper besides him?

Journalistic integrity was sacred in his business, and even though he knew they wouldn't interfere in the way the paper was run or what stories it pursued, people on the outside might wonder about it. Especially after his Op-Ed and the other articles about the museum. He'd finally drilled that concept through their heads with the help of his son, Alan. Of course, his son would have done anything he'd asked given his condition, and Arthur was glad he would be staying for an extended visit.

Young Trevor had finally suggested another solution.

He would find another bank to give the paper a loan, and at a better interest rate, which would help offset the impact of the loss of their main advertiser until they found new clients, which Tanner had made his primary job in the interim.

That was a solution Arthur could live with, and both he and the crew of people eager to throw millions his way had all breathed a sigh of relief.

With that problem resolved, he'd turned to their other concern. Stopping Sin City for good and getting J.T. back to Dare Valley where he belonged.

The people he'd summoned were hovering around his hospital bed—Caroline, Trevor, and Evan Michaels. Clara was there too, of course. She was justice with her shining sword these days, and he loved it. The brat was mostly gone for the moment, but he hoped she'd be back.

"Andy is going to have our hides for interrupting your rest," Caroline told him, sitting beside Clara in one of the chairs Trevor had hefted over.

"He's a nuisance, but a good doctor," he said, fussing with his gown. "It's so thin you can see through it."

"Good thing you have such a gorgeous body," Clara said with a smirk. "Now, talk."

"Evan, we're going to need something really special tech-wise. You rigged up some tech solutions to stop Chase from working after his fall, so I'm hoping you can put something together for what I have in mind."

Trevor crossed his arms, his whole stance calm. Too calm. His brother's disappearance was weighing on him, and Arthur didn't blame him. No man should ever feel like his only option was to disappear. Of course, Arthur knew Trevor would find J.T. No one could hide from that man for long.

"What exactly do you have in mind, Uncle Arthur?" Trevor asked.

"There's little to do in this bed but think, and since

it's freezing cold and noisy from all the other patients' moaning, I didn't sleep one wink last night."

"Which is why you look like hell today," Clara said, reaching for his hand.

He liked holding hands with her. She'd stayed by his bedside all night, snoring softly in the chair. He'd almost laughed. Imagine purebred Clara Merriam snoring.

"Thank you, my dear," he said. "Now let's get down to it. This Newhouse woman needs to be checkmated, and I have an idea how to go about it."

"I'm already looking into the collusion with the bank and your main advertiser," Trevor said. "I'm going to nail her and her father. Don't worry."

"That's going to take too much time, and who knows what you'll find. I've always found that banks and rich businessmen cover their asses well. Haven't you heard of the savings and loan crisis?"

Evan nodded. "Good point. What do you have in mind?"

"What's the one thing Sin City has in her repertoire?" he asked.

Everyone was silent, and then Clara met his gaze. He knew she'd guessed his plan.

"Her reputation," Clara said.

"Righto," he said, reaching for the plastic cup filled with water. "Excuse me. Throat is dry."

Caroline stood and rushed to help him, and he waved her away. Dammit, he wasn't that much of an invalid.

"I'm getting out of here in a jiffy," he told them.

Clara simply raised her eyebrows. Andy and his cardiologist had agreed he'd be in the hospital for another four days given his age and condition. That pissed him off, but he'd thought it might be worse. Of course, he knew the insurance companies wanted people out as soon as possible, so perhaps that would work in his favor.

"Anyway, I think it's time to visit Sin City and make a video recording of it. That's where you come in, Evan."

"I'm happy to be of help, sir," the young man said.

"I was planning on paying her a call already," Trevor said, his jaw set.

"You're too tough and intimidating," Arthur said. "She won't make a wrong move with you. But with an elderly lady and J.T.'s so-called ex-girlfriend? Play it right, and I think she might say something she wouldn't want to come out later. I would pay her a visit, but I'm not sure she'd lower her guard, what with me being a journalist."

"So you think Clara and I should go?" Caroline asked. "I might deck her."

"Me too," Clara said, grinning now. "I've never wanted to hit another woman before, but I'm feeling very protective of my new boyfriend here."

Arthur didn't correct her, but they'd have to find a different term. He was almost eighty, for heaven's sake.

"I appreciate that, my dear," he said. "I figure between the two of you, you can get her to say something incriminating."

"She does a lot of charity work, right?" Caroline glanced at Trevor. "Has she ever raised money for cancer research and the like?"

He lifted his shoulder. "I don't know, but it's easy enough to check."

Caroline was starting to smile, and it was good to see. She'd been walking around hunched over, like she had nothing to live for, what with J.T. leaving. Poor girl.

"We could get her to say she doesn't care about cancer," Caroline said.

Clara clapped. "Yes, and that she hates the 'little' people. Trevor, we'll need a list of her charities. I've met debutante philanthropists before. Most of them only raise money to make themselves look good. Fundraisers are just excuses for rich people to get together and party and have their pictures in the paper."

"Not mine," Trevor said, acting affronted. "My, you are cynical, Clara. But I like it."

She gave him a cheeky wink.

"I like this idea," Caroline said. "But what about doing this without J.T.'s consent? He never wanted to go this low."

"Caroline, we talked about fighting dirty, and you said—"

"I know," she said softly. "I just don't want him to get...well, mad at me. Us."

"Good point," Evan said, suddenly looking uncomfortable. "He already turned down my suggestion—at Trev's prompting—about recording his calls with her and trying to get her on record saying something incriminating."

"J.T. doesn't get a vote anymore," Trevor all but growled. "He's not here. Plus, the stakes are higher after what she did to Uncle Arthur."

Arthur considered the point. "J.T. might be uncomfortable, but Trev is right. He's sitting this one out on some deserted island. I'm willing to do whatever that takes. Even if he gets a little mad."

"Me too," Trev said.

"Me three," Caroline added like he'd hoped.

"How long before you find J.T.?" he asked Trevor.

He scoffed. "He thought he could stop me by buying six different plane tickets."

"Did he dump his phone?" Evan asked.

"At the Denver airport," Trev said. "I have other ways."

"I can help you with some new tech my company cooked up," Evan said. "You just can't tell anyone. Homeland Security might get upset."

"I'd appreciate any help you can give," Trevor said.

Arthur stared at the two men. "You two would be terrifying if you ever worked together. Okay, so we have a semi-hatched plan. I'll leave it to you to execute it. Meredith and Tanner have banned me from any newspaper work, so I'm stuck here with nothing to do. Trevor, Meredith has a pretty good list of Sin City's charities. When you ask her for a copy, I'd love one as well."

"I'll read it to you while you rest on the sly," Clara said, smiling conspiratorially. "You must be the only man alive the doctors have banned from reading."

"Now the medical community is encouraging ignorance! It's outrageous." He was going to have to write a series of articles on hospitalization and the state of the medical community in this country.

"Calm yourself," Caroline said. "Uncle, do you really think Sin City is going to trip up?"

"That's what happens when you fight dirty," he told her, noting the tension in her face. "You have to go for it."

"Then let's get down to it," Caroline said.

Ah... He loved seeing that Hale spirit in the younger generations.

It was what gave him the strength to keep going.

CHAPTER 38

FIGHTING DIRTY DIDN'T COME NATURALLY TO CAROLINE. It wasn't exactly something she could practice, after all. But Trevor had role-played the meeting with her and Clara. Frankly, the older woman was better at this sort of thing, but she would give it her all.

Usually she liked visiting The Grand. She'd always found the décor breathtaking and the food on Chef T's menu delectable. Today, however, she was all business in her pinstriped Brooks Brothers suit with Clara at her side. The older woman looked polished and poised in an all-black suit punctuated by matching diamond jewelry at her ears, throat, and wrist. The silver fleur-de-lis pin on Caroline's lapel was the primary recording device, but Clara's top button served the same purpose. If one of them didn't get what they needed, hopefully the other would.

They were going to rock it, she told herself as a mantra—if she didn't throw up from nerves first.

"You're going to be fine," Clara told her as they walked through the lobby. "Spending five minutes in this place should help you with your poker face."

Yes, there were always poker players mulling about. It was a boutique poker hotel, after all. When she spotted

Rhett Butler Blaylock, she wasn't surprised. He was a regular.

"Ladies," he said as he approached them. "I hope you're here for what I think you are."

She couldn't form a smile. "Yes, we are."

"Good," he responded, tipping his finger to his forehead. "Give her hell."

"We plan to, young man," Clara said.

They kept walking like a couple of gangsters, but of course, they ran into Jill before they reached the elevators.

"I just wanted to say good luck," her cousin said, brushing aside tears. "I'll see you at the hospital later, Clara. Thank you for being so good to my grandpa. I really like you."

Clara touched her chin lightly. "I'm growing rather fond of you too. I can see why he loves you so. Now go on and let us continue our plan."

Jill nodded and rushed off in the opposite direction.

"I can't believe she hasn't poisoned the woman," Clara said under her breath. "It would be hard, working in the same hotel."

"Most of us Hales aren't that bloodthirsty," Caroline said as they took the elevator, "but this woman is pushing us all to new depths."

Wasn't she about to engage in entrapment? When her conscience niggled her, she thought about everything Cynthia had done. That was enough to straighten her spine. This woman wasn't going to stop on her own.

When they came to a stop outside Sin City's penthouse suite, Clara turned to look Caroline in the eye and took both of her hands. It was like she was trying to imbue all of her strength into Caroline. She appreciated it. But she was going to pull this off. There was no failing here.

At her nod, Clara knocked, and after a few moments, the door opened.

Sin City stood in the open doorway decked out in a

violet cashmere wrap fitted sinuously around her cream knee-length dress like a snake charmer might hold a snake. Uncle Arthur had told them he'd mentioned the snake analogy to J.T. once—that you have to go for the underbelly. *Well, here we go*, she thought.

"I wondered if I might have visitors," she said in her tony accent. "Honestly, I didn't foresee a visit from the two of you."

"May we come in?" Clara asked.

When the woman nodded, Caroline had to contain her surprise—Clara was leaning heavily against her, as if she were an invalid, and she moved far more slowly than normal. Goodness, they hadn't rehearsed this. *Way to go, Clara. Encourage her to underestimate us.*

"Caroline, it's been too long," Sin City said as they walked into her parlor.

The view was incredible. The mountains looked almost blue at this time of year, dotted with snowcaps. Caroline resented this woman living so large when she'd wreaked such destruction. Good thing she was supposed to play bad cop today.

"Has it?" she asked, relaxing her hold on her purse. "You seem bent on hurting any happiness I might have. First, you get me fired, and now J.T. has disappeared."

Cynthia's cool, collected visage cracked for two seconds before she got it back in place. "He's disappeared? Impossible. I spoke with him two days ago. He was upset, of course, about your uncle's heart attack. Well, at his age these things happen."

Caroline wanted to rip the woman's eyes out. "Do they? It's amazing the kind of stress other people can add to things. As for J.T., there will be no more games to play with him."

That stopped Cynthia short. "What *are* you talking about?"

"He's finally done. Don't you understand? You won.

Are you happy now?"

The woman stared at her for a moment as though rendered mute.

"This isn't about happiness, Cynthia, is it?" Clara chimed in on cue, walking over to the gold settee and sitting down like she owned the place. "It's about making someone pay. I had a bad marriage, so I know what I'm talking about. My husband was a known philanderer, and I had fantasies about his penis shriveling and falling off."

Caroline had to close her mouth at that one. Again, this wasn't something they'd rehearsed.

"But you, Cynthia? You've had everything handed to you your whole life. You're beautiful, rich, educated, and accomplished. At least that's what some of the wealthy matrons I know in Manhattan say about you."

Cynthia marched over to a nearby gold-leaf table and picked up her phone. "I don't care what they say. Julian can't be gone. I need him!"

Need him? "You can't be serious," Caroline said, no acting needed. "All you've done is attack and hurt him at every turn. Now you've hurt the man he considers a mentor."

The woman fussed with her phone and then put it to her ear.

"That's what you do when you hope someone might come crawling back to you," Clara said, her tone somber. "You hurt them."

Cynthia's face suddenly crumpled. "It says his number has been disconnected."

For a moment, Caroline saw what Clara had discerned. "Were you really hoping J.T. would come back to you?" she asked in disbelief.

"What?" She looked at the phone, punched some buttons, and put it to her ear again. "There must be some mistake. He can't be gone."

The broken heart Cynthia had revealed to Caroline at the gallery had become twisted and warped. It had given way to a weird obsession.

"We're doing our best to find him, of course," Clara said, crossing her legs and studying the woman.

Cynthia slammed her phone down. "He has to come back."

"Was all the philanthropy work becoming boring, my dear?" Clara asked in a pitying town.

Cynthia glared at her. "I don't want to talk about it. I want to know what you're doing to find Julian. That brother of his should be able to pull it off. He may be a pain in the ass, but he's formidable."

Caroline wanted to shake her, but Clara clearly knew what she was doing so let her remain the focus.

"Tsk. Tsk." Clara buffed her nails. "I remember all my charity work. When I was your age, I wanted adventure and romance. I hated going to tedious parties for this and that cause, smiling at people I didn't know. Did you know I received more birthday presents growing up from people I'd never even heard of than my real friends?"

Caroline suddenly wondered how much of this the older woman was making up.

"You and I are nothing alike," Cynthia said, an edge to her voice.

"No? Well, my family *was* much wealthier, if that's what you mean."

Caroline had to bite her lip to stop herself from smiling. Clara was going for the jugular.

"My family is as good as yours," Cynthia stated, planting a stiletto on the ground for emphasis. "Better, in fact."

Clara laughed. *"Really?* Not as great as the Bentleys or the Caraouches though, surely?"

"Please, those families didn't earn their first million until the 1960s," she said, coming over and standing beside the settee where Clara was lounging. "They couldn't even be considered *nouveau riche,* they're so fresh off the farm."

More brittle laugher from Clara. "Then there are the Westons. I personally never cared for them much."

"They're boorish," Cynthia said, "and breed some of the ugliest children you'll ever see at day events. They'd be wise to stick to nighttime fetes, if you ask me."

"That's a perspective," Clara said. "But the worst ones are—"

"The Farnsworths," Cynthia filled in. "That family marries as if they're turning the institution into some legalized form of job security."

Clara clucked, and Caroline looked away to contain the glee she feared might be showing on her face. Even if they didn't get anything incriminating from Cynthia, surely this would be enough to embarrass her well and good.

"How scandalous," Clara said. "I didn't know that about them. If I'm ever invited to one of their events, I'll be sure to take it into consideration. Now, what are we going to do about Julian? I know this is horrible to ask, but would you be willing to stop this game of yours so he'll come back?"

Cynthia blinked and then shook her head. "I can't."

Clara stood and patted her on the arm. "I thought not. Trevor is still looking for him, and I imagine he'll be successful. My concern is what happens when he finds his brother."

"He has to come back," Cynthia said, her face stricken. She turned Caroline. "*You* should talk to him."

She nodded. "I plan on it, but you're not making that easy. Why would he come back if we find him? Will you back off about the museum? We have the Rembrandt, after all, and tomorrow the whole world is going to be excited to finally see it."

They'd all agreed to reveal it to the world at the press conference. They'd hired the requisite security this time, of course.

Cynthia narrowed her eyes. "I might concede that you won the round on the museum."

That didn't sound like complete capitulation.

Clara playfully swatted Cynthia. "Like you really wanted to give away *three hundred million dollars* for cancer research," she said with a laugh. "There are so many other things to spend the money on, like furs or summers at a villa in Lake Como. I mean, please..."

"But cancer research was the only way I could check the museum," Cynthia told Clara, as though the idea hadn't dawned on her.

"And yet the museum will go forward anyway," Clara said. "Now you can give all of that money to some other university or research institution for cancer research. I mean, it's already known you planned the gift—"

"There's no way I'm giving that kind of money away now," Cynthia said.

"You don't believe in cancer research?" Clara asked, adding a shocked blinking to punctuate her act.

Caroline was going to have to give her a trophy after this performance.

"There's a dozen better things to spend our family money on, like you said," Cynthia said. "If it weren't for the tax benefits..."

Clara waved her hand and made a noncommittal sound. "So you won't let off Julian? Not even a little bit? Even though the museum is going forward?"

Cynthia walked off to the window, her hands clenched at her sides. Caroline knew she was struggling, but she couldn't find any compassion in her heart. No, this woman had hurt too many people.

Clara shot her a wink as she approached the woman, her put-on limp still in place. "If you called the bank and asked them to reverse their position on Arthur's loan, that might be a good show of faith."

Caroline leaned on her toes, waiting to hear the woman's answer. If Clara got her to admit this...

"I want him to come back, but I can't—" she said softly. "Let's speak of something else."

"Banks are such a pain anyway," Clara said. "If we didn't have loads of money, I'd never use them. I'm old-fashioned, I suppose. I'd keep it in a private vault behind the wine cellar or underneath the pool. I still can't believe you moved all your money from one bank to another. Wasn't it a pain?"

"Ah...yes," Cynthia said. "Clara, please tell Julian I'll let up...for a while. That's...all I can promise."

Did spiders stop spinning webs? Caroline clenched her teeth so she wouldn't call the woman out for lying.

"I don't know if that will do," Clara said, taking Cynthia's hand briefly. "But we'll try. Well, I expect we should go. Thank you for seeing us. I thought you should know...about Julian. I remember when someone called on me to tell me about something my husband did. I've never forgotten it."

Even though Clara said it lightly, Caroline knew it couldn't be a pleasant memory.

"Caroline, we should go," she said. "Take my arm. You know how frail I am. Never live to this age unless you have no choice. I tell you, age is hard on beauty and breeding."

Cynthia shook herself. "You'll convince Julian to come back, won't you? Oh, and I'll need his new phone number when you have it."

If Clara hadn't squeezed her arm, Caroline's poker face would have given way. His new number? The woman had to be demented!

They walked to the door slowly. "We'll let ourselves out," Clara said. "Goodbye, my dear."

No response came from inside the room as the door closed behind them. They didn't speak until they walked out of the hotel and situated themselves in the limo.

Clara waggled her eyebrows at Caroline. "I always wanted to be on the stage. How did I do?"

She hugged her. "You were brilliant! I couldn't believe she was telling you all that."

"Rich people tend to speak more openly with other rich people," Clara said with a decided eye roll. "I don't fully understand why. A perceived sense of the same values or some such drivel. And they love to gossip and talk badly about other rich people. I realized our plan was too direct once I got there and saw her in person. She's...stronger in some ways than I imagined and... weaker in others. I didn't expect her to be so upset... about J.T."

Caroline looked down at her lap. "I don't pretend to understand it. How he fell for her and vice versa, but she still loves him in some weird way, doesn't she?"

"Yes," Clara said sadly. "The ties that bind. Marriage is a doozy for that, and I speak as a woman who stayed married to a philandering piece of crap for decades. But that's all in the past."

That much was clear. The aunt J.T. had heard about growing up—covetous and conniving— was nowhere to be seen in this vivacious woman. "Clearly you're in a new cycle of your life, what with Uncle Arthur and this new acting persona. You should join a theater group."

"New acting persona," she said, humming. "I like that. How about Clara the Charismatic?"

It was a horrible name, but she'd never say so. "You're wonderful."

"I *feel* wonderful. It's like I have a purpose in life again."

Now that the museum looked like it was moving forward, Caroline realized her life purpose was back on track too. But somehow she felt a little hollow inside. J.T. was supposed to be here with her, dammit. Well, they were simply going to have to convince him to come back. Once Trevor found him...

Clara opened a panel in the limo, tapping her feet like she was dancing. "I believe we have enough to stop Sin City, Caroline. Sure, it's not anything that'll land her in jail, but I can guarantee you she won't have a full dance card anymore. For her, it might be worse than prison. I think champagne is called for."

Trevor was still pursuing the legal aspects of the situation, but they'd done their job. Now J.T. could come home. "I couldn't agree more."

And when they persuaded J.T. to come back to Dare Valley where he belonged, they'd open another bottle to celebrate his return.

CHAPTER 39

J.T. WAS STARING AT THE BEACH THROUGH THE PATIO WIN-dow when he heard the door click behind him.

He knew who it was before he turned around to confirm his suspicions.

"You couldn't have been more original than Bali?" Trev asked, closing the front door of the bungalow he'd rented under an assumed name. "I wouldn't call it deserted."

"I thought it oddly fitting," J.T. said, standing in his swim trunks. "I was hoping to find myself."

Trev prowled forward and socked him in the jaw. "Find yourself? How's that for finding yourself and leaving me and the rest of us to clean up your shit?"

He fell back a few steps but wouldn't let his brother mow him down. "You have every right to be angry."

"You're damn right I do. What exactly did you expect me to tell our parents and the rest of our siblings if I didn't find you?"

So Trev had kept it to himself. He'd spent hours awake at night wondering about how his family would react. Stewing about Uncle Arthur's health and money problems. And, of course, thinking of Caroline... He was sad she wasn't with his brother, but who could blame her? He'd run out on her. Of course, he'd had a good reason, but he didn't expect her to see it that way.

"I hoped they would understand I was so upset and defeated I didn't see another way," he said. "For the last five days, I've been trying to find a way to take her and her father down so I can leave this place one day..." He didn't know how long it would take or whether Caroline would understand when he returned. It could be years, and he wouldn't ask her to wait. But he couldn't come back until he was sure he had something solid to stop Cynthia—and her father if he'd used his influence as well.

Trev shoved him this time. "You didn't think we could work together on that? That you could trust me to finish this with you?"

"I'm sorry," he said, crossing to the hand-carved chinaberry wood bar. "Drink?"

He hadn't touched any, knowing drunkenness wasn't the way. This time he didn't want to be numb. He wanted to feel the pain so he'd remember the need to stay away. Man, he needed a bonafide hair shirt.

"There's not enough liquor in the world to patch up how I feel," Trev said, sighing heavily. "You scared me, J.T. I never thought..."

His voice broke, and J.T. felt tears come into his own eyes. He pushed them back and walked over to where Trev stood, socking him in the shoulder like they used to do to each other when they were kids.

"I'm sorry I hit you," Trev said, meeting his eyes.

"No, you're not," J.T. said, "but you will be in a few hours, I imagine. So you found me. Is there nothing you can't track?"

Trev snorted. "What can I say? It's a gift. Plus, Evan was helping, and he's even scarier than me. You almost got us with the fake boat rental, though. I was halfway to Raja Ampat before I realized there was no way you'd go there. They don't have Wi-Fi, and you'd want to be connected to keep tabs on Dare Valley and the museum. Plus, based on what you just said, you'd need it to look into Cynthia and her father."

But he hadn't gotten anywhere so far, dammit. "How is Uncle Arthur? I called the hospital under a fake name and got the nurse to tell me, but I want to hear it from you."

"Isn't that against hospital rules?" Trev asked. "Glad you kept a hand on it. He didn't need surgery, thank God, and he's getting out tomorrow, I believe, if things go well. He wants to see you at his house. I think there's a little family shindig."

A pang of longing shuddered through him. He loved sparring with his idol and also hanging out at Hale family parties. "I'm relieved to hear he's doing well. What about the loan? I sent him a check before I left Denver."

This time Trev made a raspberry sound with his mouth. "He didn't mention it until I was leaving. He said to tell you, and I quote, 'Shove that money right up your ass and get said ass back home.' He refused all of us—even Aunt Clara. He's a proud fellow."

Yes, he was, which was why J.T. admired him so much. "I can't imagine that stopped you."

Trev smiled his scary smile. "No, he finally agreed to let me find a bank that would give him the money in the form of a new loan."

"With better terms, of course," J.T. said, feeling like he'd dropped one of the boulders weighing on him. "I'm relieved."

This time Trevor did walk over and pour himself a drink. Bourbon. Straight. Somehow the familiarity choked him up.

"You should have known we'd never let him go down. You should have trusted us, dammit."

"I did trust you to handle that and everything else,"

he said, turning his back so Trev wouldn't see any tears escape. "How could I have left otherwise?"

"Your precious museum is safe too," Trev said. "The press conference—"

"Went well," he said, remembering the pride and heartache he'd felt watching Caroline and Aunt Clara speak their respective pieces alongside President Matthau, who'd looked constipated. "I saw it online—like I imagine you intended."

"I'm devious like that," Trev said, walking to the front door with his drink. "Speaking of which, I brought someone else who wants to give you a tongue lashing."

His pulse leaped. Caroline! He followed his brother's every step, his heart eager, his gaze intent. When Aunt Clara marched forward, he was sure he blinked twice.

"Ah...you didn't expect me!" She stopped a foot away and poked him. "You're an idiot! When has a Merriam ever run from a fight?"

He didn't want to point out he *was* fighting, albeit in isolation. "Someone I love almost died. I didn't see another way."

"I love him too, and even I saw another way."

She loved Uncle Arthur? Well, good for them.

"Give him the good news, Aunt," Trev said, making her a gin and tonic.

"J.T., my boy, we have some good news for you. The woman who loves you is a terrific bad cop and a truly lovely lady. She and I managed to get Sin City on record saying horrible things about some of the wealthiest families in this country."

He cocked his head, thinking he'd misheard her. "You what?"

His aunt smiled, looking years younger. "We also got her to say on record that there are better things to give money to than cancer research."

Holy shit!

Trev brought their aunt her drink, and she patted him on the cheek playfully. Goodness, what a sight.

"Aunt Clara should have had a career on the stage, we've all decided. Wait until you see the video."

He rocked back on his heels as his aunt popped open her purse and pulled out a zip drive. This couldn't be happening.

"She really said all that?" He took out the drive and looked at it. It was ironic that something so small could hold something so powerful.

"I'm still using everything in my arsenal to go after Carlyle Bank," Trev said.

"But it's going to be an uphill battle," J.T. said. "You'd need subpoenas to retrieve emails and files, assuming it wasn't only a verbal agreement." Which he thought it likely had been. Rich people with influence made phone calls to get what they wanted. He'd seen it done time and time again.

"All that will take time," Trev said. "We need to get you back before ten years go by."

That had been his estimate of the wheels of justice. "What about the advertiser?"

"Nothing concrete, which is what I'd expect given they're golf buddies," Trev said. "But Connor and Flynn have plans for that CEO and Newhouse Senior. All legal, of course."

"I thought you hadn't told the family," J.T. said, feeling his gut wrench.

Clara slapped him on the back of his head. "He hasn't. He only said you needed help. We figured they might kick you in the arse otherwise."

True that. "So this video... Do you think it's enough to stop her?"

"I figure Aunt Clara knows a woman's mind better than I do," Trev said, putting his drink down hard on the table.

"She'll be a pariah socially," his aunt said, sitting down on the sofa and patting the seat beside her. "J.T., come sit."

He did as she bid him. "What about Caroline? How is she?"

There was no way he could make things up to her, and he knew it. She'd looked so beautiful at the press conference. Her responses to questions about the Rembrandt were as brilliant as Aunt Clara's tale about why the painting had been kept hidden. From everything he could see, she'd finally achieved what she'd wanted to, professionally speaking. She was at the top of the art world. He only wished he could have been beside her.

"How do you expect her to be?" his aunt asked. "She helped give you the means to check your ex-wife, and it was hard on her to do it. She has the same kind of moral discomfort about it that you seem to. Gads, boy, I wish you'd taped the woman's calls weeks ago. She's been playing with you like a cat might a mouse."

Did no one understand his reasoning? "That's in the past. Where is Caroline now?"

Clara downed her drink, and Trev started making her another. "I talked her into staying in Dare Valley while you made your decision. A number of us—"

"Including Uncle Arthur and me," Trev added, bringing his aunt a gin and tonic.

"Thank you, my dear," she said, taking a sip. "Anyway, as I was saying, after the press conference, we thought it best if you decided what you were going to do without causing her more pain."

"You don't pull any punches."

"You disappeared—or tried to. I think the time for sweet talk is over, don't you?"

She and Uncle Arthur were perfect for each other, he decided. "What decision are you talking about?"

He heard Trevor growl like a wild dog. Great. Was

his brother about to punch him again? His aunt popped him in the shoulder instead.

"Hey!"

"What decision?" she asked. "Seriously? Trevor, you were right. This man could drive anyone to drink."

He lifted his glass to her.

"J.T., it's up to you whether you want to come out of hiding and use this video to stop Cynthia. I could—any of us could—but it isn't our place. Personally, I think it's time for you to live up to your nickname, Mud Slinger."

The very words made him want to cringe. He hadn't wanted it to come to this. But Cynthia hadn't played fair, and she'd hurt a bunch of people he loved.

"This seems like as good a time as any to give you the three notes we brought for you. Would you grab my purse?"

He picked up the navy Coach handbag and brought it over, anticipation building in his gut.

"First one," she said, handing him an envelope the size of a thank-you card.

He opened it.

Young J.T.,

You have the tools to stop Sin City. Use them and get your ass back to your woman, Dare Valley, the museum, and your favorite uncle. Exile is no place for any man, certainly not one as well loved as you.

Uncle Arthur

P.S. They say I'm going to live, but if you don't come back, I'll probably die and then I'll haunt you for the rest of your life. I'd make one scary ghost, don't you think?

He wished he could laugh, but it felt like a wishbone was stuck in his throat.

"The second one?" he asked, his voice raspy.

She handed it to him. It surprised him to see it was from Meredith.

J.T.,

I feel as guilty as you must, knowing my tech improvements at the paper were the reason Grandpa took out the loan in the first place. I want you to know that you're not to blame for any of it. As Tanner reminds me daily, neither am I.

Caroline and your Aunt Clara have given you the means to stop someone you used to love. You may not know, but I had to make a deal with my ex-husband to stop him from hurting someone I loved, namely Tanner. No one knows the confusing emotions marriage—and divorce—can bring up in a person better than you and I. I know you've wanted to fight fair, and I respect that. But it's time to hold her accountable for what she's done. When my ex returned to punish me, I had to decide what kind of new life I wanted and fight for it. You have the same decision ahead.

Love,

Meredith

P.S. Besides, Bali is going to get boring with all those hippies.

He almost laughed at the last line, but the rest of her letter sobered him. Meredith had managed to convey an understanding no one else had, and for that he was grateful.

He held out his hand for the last note, knowing it had to be from Caroline.

Dear J.T.,

At first I wanted to accompany Trevor and your aunt. Then I realized there was no point if you wanted to remain where you are, removed from life altogether. That's not the kind of life I want for myself, and it's certainly not what I want for you either. For half a second, I considered joining you in Bali, but that's bullshit. I'm not giving up a wonderful job, family, town, and life. Neither should you.

Aunt Clara and I worked hard to give you the keys to free yourself. I hope you use them. For us, yes, but for you most of all. Because you deserve to have a wonderful life, free from fear.

I hope you choose that wonderful life because I want to be a part of it.

Love,

Caroline

P.S. If you don't come back, I'm on board for Uncle Arthur haunting you for the rest of your life. Trust me, he's pretty scary alive. Dead, he'd be terrifying.

"If you ask me, I really don't think this is a tough choice, but I'll give you a few moments alone to decide," Aunt Clara said, patting his arm as she stood and walked out to the patio with Trevor, who was still scowling.

He laid the three notes on the sofa in front of him. All of them had been written with love and encouragement. All of them were full of fight. He felt their strength and their support.

Aunt Clara was right. It wasn't a tough choice after what Cynthia had done.

He deserved a wonderful life, like Caroline had said, and he wanted it with her.

CHAPTER 40

MEMORIES OF HAPPIER TIMES PLAYED THROUGH J.T.'S mind as he stood in front of Cynthia's Upper East Side residence in Manhattan. Coming home after late nights at the opera or ballet. Walks to Central Park on a fall day. Private breakfasts on the terrace out back in the spring. Any happiness associated with those memories was gone after everything she'd done.

Trevor had learned Cynthia had left Dare Valley and returned to her main residence. Whether it was permanent or temporary in her mind, J.T. didn't know. Today he planned to make it permanent.

"We'll wait in the car," Trev said, punching him softly in the shoulder.

"You'll do fine," his aunt said from her seat inside the limo. "Take as long as you need. Trevor here and I can play hearts."

"She's a terror with cards," Trev said with a sigh, but he pulled out the deck from his pocket.

Even though his brother and Aunt Clara sparred nonstop, they seemed to like each other. Of course, their aunt had tested that theory when she'd insisted they stop in Paris on the way home so she could buy a few things. Thank God she was a decisive shopper. He and

Trevor had feared they would be delayed a week.

The car door closed behind him. J.T. walked forward, feeling his phone as a burning presence in his pocket. When he rang the bell, the door opened almost immediately. Cynthia's doorman stared at him in shock.

"Mr. Merriam," he said, his tone stiff.

"Donald," he replied. "I'm here to see Cynthia."

"Of course, sir," the man said, allowing him inside.

The black and white squares in the foyer and the sweeping staircase were decorated in Art Deco style. Not a speck of dust or clutter was allowed, and the silver was polished weekly. He'd hated this place, he realized. There wasn't a single comfortable piece of furniture to sit on. Caroline, he realized, didn't mind a little mess. They had the same idea of what home looked like, and they could make a life on that.

"Darling!"

He looked up to see Cynthia rushing down the stairs in a flurry of New York black, her normal comportment gone.

"I knew you'd come back," she said, rushing forward and throwing her arms around him before he could blink. "Those women were horrible to say you'd disappeared on me."

He pried her arms off him as gently as he could. "I did disappear, Cynthia. Or I'd planned to. Can we talk in your study? I have something private to discuss."

She scanned his face. "You look terrible. Julian, you take things too hard."

During the course of their marriage, she'd told him that often. When three people had died in a small gas explosion while repairing a Merriam pipeline, he'd been devastated. Her response had been cold and rational—they'd accepted the risk when they accepted the job, and things like that happened. He'd visited the families without her. She'd claimed she couldn't clear her schedule. Deep down he'd known the truth: she hadn't wanted to.

"The study," he said, waiting for her to precede him.

Instead, she linked arms with him and started walking. "When I couldn't reach you, I was frantic. Don't you ever do that again."

Inside the study, he closed the door behind him, sick at heart. Aunt Clara was right. In her own way, she still loved him. He figured it was time for them to be honest with each other. For the emotions they'd been repressing to finally come out.

"You're speaking to me like a concerned wife," he said, unbuttoning his jacket and sitting in the chair across from the settee she'd chosen.

She fussed with the edge of her Chanel suit. "Can't I be concerned?"

Was she really going to beat around the bush? "Cynthia, are you really hoping this game you're playing with me will lead to some form of a reconciliation?"

Her gaze flickered up, and he caught the stain of red flushing her cheekbones. "I've given this a lot of thought, darling. Perhaps all this animosity between us is the other side of a love-hate relationship? There can't be this much emotion without it meaning something."

Suddenly he knew the truth. "Given your parents' relationship and how you were raised, I can see you might think that. Cynthia, there *is* a lot of emotion. I'll grant you that, but this push-pull of power...this constant quest for revenge... It's not love."

She leaned back in the settee to better display her assets, he knew. "Perhaps it's not, but it's born out of love. We did love each other, Julian."

He nodded. "Yes, but that time is past. Cynthia, it's time for both of us to start over and find new directions apart from each other." He'd used similar words when he'd told her he wanted a divorce.

She sat up and stared at him, her eyes hard now. "You mean my ship should go one way and yours another?"

"Yes."

"No," she said simply, standing up. "That's not how it's going to be."

He rose as well, the familiar tension filling his body. "You've made my life hell for over three years now. It stops today. Let me tell you in no uncertain terms. I don't love you anymore. I'll never come back to you. I don't mean to hurt you saying so, but it's the God's honest truth."

Her chuckle was soft and ever so menacing. "But you have hurt me, darling, which is why I decide when it stops. Not you."

Even though he'd expected her response, it still saddened him. "You're wrong there."

Fishing out his phone, he brought up the video and hit play. He held it up for her to see, but he watched *her*. Emotion played across her face. Shock. Fear. And then ice-cold anger, a look he knew well.

She didn't say anything until the video ended, and neither did he. Pocketing it, he simply sat down again. She sat back down on the settee, her posture picture-perfect.

"Well, well, well, your elderly aunt and your freshly fired girlfriend have teeth," she said in her bored voice. "I expect Trevor thought up this plan."

"It doesn't matter who it was," he said. "You were indiscreet."

She edged closer to his chair. "I was upset over you disappearing! I didn't know what I was saying."

"Bullshit! You knew exactly what you were saying. Cynthia, for three years, I've been trying to get you to call an end to this revenge quest you're hell-bent on. This video gives me a certain leverage, and unfortunately, I don't see any other choice than to use it."

Her mouth parted. "You wouldn't. One of the things I've always loved about you, Julian, is your sense of manners and fair play. Besides, I know your thoughts on a lot of things that wouldn't be favorable for you—"

"But I have you on record," he interrupted. "You can't say the same. Once this video goes public, your reputation will be in the gutter."

Should Trevor discover collusion at Carlyle, well, they'd pursue that too. It went beyond Cynthia, and he'd decided to stop being bullied. He'd leave it up to Connor and Flynn if they wanted to cook up some punishment for Newhouse Senior and his crony.

"No one will believe a word you say after seeing this," he said, driving it home. "They certainly won't want you over for dinner or hosting a charity function. And you know it."

Her hand curled around the edge of his chair like she was a woman desperately trying to hang on in an untenable situation.

"I only want to be free of you," he said, "so I'm here to make you a deal."

She flounced back on the couch like an angry teenager. "Blackmail? Oh, how Borgia of you, darling. You lived in Rome way too long."

Was it Borgia of him? Right now, he didn't care. "I won't publish this video if you'll swear to leave me in peace. Forever."

"You won't ruin me," she cried, pressing her fists into the settee. "It's not in your character."

His mouth lifted as he said, "Disappearing from everyone and everything I love wasn't in my character either, and yet, only a few days ago, that's what I did. Cynthia, this...horrible game has changed us both."

"You broke my heart when you left me," she spat.

He believed her. "And I've apologized. I've asked you to forgive me more than once. I hope in time we can forgive each other. But I promise you that I will make this video public if you so much as contact me or anyone I care about ever again."

She made an anguished sound as he stood.

"Oh, and my brother plans to go after Carlyle and potentially your father for their involvement in your little games," he said. "I would advise you to leave them to their own devices. They're big boys, after all."

He crossed to the door and turned around to face her. In that moment, sadness rolled through him. Yes, he'd once loved her and she him, but that felt like a lifetime ago. After today, he planned to never see her again, and somehow that filled him with peace, a peace he'd longed for. "Goodbye, Cynthia."

She stood up slowly. "Julian, don't go."

He opened the door and walked to the foyer. Donald was there to see him out. When he was outside, he took a couple of cleansing breaths. The lights from Manhattan prevented him from seeing the stars. He thought of Dare Valley and how much he missed the endless sky.

The door to the limo opened.

Aunt Clara stuck her head out. "Is your work here done?"

He nodded, shaking off the last of the sickness in his heart. Cynthia had made her bed with the choices she'd made. That chapter was officially closed finally, and he could feel excitement gathering in his heart. He'd lived with fear for so long, he barely remembered the sensation of living without it. The time had come to savor life again, to have and enjoy everything he wanted.

Trev stepped out. "You ready to blow this joint?"

He put his arm around his brother, glad for his constant rock-solid presence.

"Yes, let's go home."

He had a wonderful woman and a new life to claim.

CHAPTER 41

ARTHUR WAS WAITING BY THE WINDOW FOR CLARA, something very unlike himself. Watched pots and all of that.

"She'll be here soon, sir," Hargreaves drolled in that British accent of his. "You might seat yourself on the sofa. It would be more comfortable for you."

"Seat myself on the sofa," he muttered. "I've been lying in a hospital bed for days, Hargreaves. I'm making sure I don't get bed sores."

"You really should sit, sir," the man said, worse than a mother hen.

He reached for his cane and realized he'd left it somewhere. "Is dinner ready?" he barked, stalking over to the sofa and sitting down. "I want everything to be in place when she arrives."

"Yes, sir," Hargreaves said, pouring him a glass of red wine and bringing it to over. "Like you requested, I have made madam's favorite meal."

It was more than she deserved for leaving him in that infernal hospital and dashing off to Bali. If it had been for any other reason, he might have been miffed. But she and young Trevor had done a fine job convincing J.T. to come back home where he belonged.

She was showing the spunk he remembered, thank God.

"You letting me booze it up, Hargreaves?" he asked, hoping just once his badgering would crack the man's polite visage.

"Yes, sir," he said again, holding out the glass.

"Dammit, Hargreaves! Stop saying that. My name is Arthur. If I know Clara, there's more to you than your infernal manners and British snobbery. Now sit the hell down."

"I thought I might light some candles, sir," Hargreaves said, not sitting down, of course.

"What for? It's plenty light in here." Was the man dense? Or just going blind?

"Candles set a romantic atmosphere, sir," Hargreaves said. "If you take my meaning."

Arthur cleared his throat. "Hargreaves, we're two old guys talking about lighting candles and romantic atmospheres. Either you get yourself a drink and sit down, or I'll take up my place at the window again."

All he received in response was a blank stare, and then Hargreaves finally walked to the bar and poured himself a glass of water. "Since you leave me no choice," he said, returning and sitting down awkwardly on the edge of the adjacent chair.

It wasn't wine, but it was a capitulation somehow. "Finally."

"May I ask what your intentions are toward Mrs. Allerton, sir?" Hargreaves asked. "Since we're having a drink."

Of all the things he'd expected Hargreaves to say, that question hadn't made the list. "Like it's any of your business."

Back ramrod straight, the man said, "I've been with Mrs. Allerton longer than anyone alive—or dead—sir. Since your phone call, she's shown a renewed interest in life. I would hate for that to change if you haven't thought things through."

Well, well, Arthur thought. That was telling him. "Is she that changed then?"

Sure, she'd alluded to her life—married and otherwise—but not in great detail. Even so, the picture she'd painted hadn't sat well with him.

"If I may be bold, sir, I knew her as a bright young woman, as you did. It wasn't easy to see that spark fade."

That was a hell of a way to say she'd had a shitty life, but he understood. "At the risk of sounding ornery, I'd like to tell you to mind your own business, but since you've been good to her, I'll say this—I don't want her new spark to go out either, Hargreaves." In fact, he was experiencing a similar spark himself.

"Then we're agreed, sir," he said, standing. "Does this meet with your conversational requirements?"

"Oh, light the damn candles," he spat.

He'd gotten out of practice with wanting a woman. With waiting for her and missing her when she wasn't around. Checking his watch again, he frowned. Where in the hell was she?

He drank his wine and called out to Hargreaves, "Why are you letting me drink alcohol after a heart attack? Are you trying to finish me off?"

The man looked down his nose at him, something Arthur loved to do to other people when they were talking stupid. Fair play. "Studies have shown alcohol may increase the levels of HDL or good cholesterol, sir. Additionally, it may reduce inflammation and prevent blood clots."

"Aren't you a font of knowledge?" Arthur exclaimed.

"Just looking after your health, sir, like madam asked me to. I'll check on dinner now."

As the man left, Arthur took another sip of wine. He'd bitched and moaned to her about leaving him with her bag of bones butler, sure, but he knew it meant she cared. Family was a renewed force in her life, and Arthur well knew how powerful a force it could be.

"Honey, I'm home," a familiar voice called.

He turned on the sofa, fighting the joy sweeping through him. Grinning like an idiot was not romantic. She sailed in wearing a tailored red designer dress, her long silver hair trailing over her shoulder. He wanted to kiss her straight away, but he decided to play it cool. She got so flustered when she had to work for it.

"Oh, so soon?" he quipped. "I hadn't realized the time."

She shot him a look of pure hell. Oh, yeah, that was the spark he and Hargreaves had been talking about.

"I stopped in Paris to buy what I hope is my trousseau," she said, gesturing to her outfit, "and all you can say is *that*? If you can't come up with something more original, you might be back in the hospital, my dear."

That threat would shrivel most men's balls, but not his. "You should be nicer to me. I just had a heart attack."

She stalked over and sat down beside him. "Another can be arranged if you aren't more pleasant. After all, I was instrumental in bringing J.T. home and killing the wicked witch of the West, so to speak."

He grabbed her and kissed her full on the mouth. She twined her arms around his neck and kissed him back. Then they got to kissing for real until his heart rate started to accelerate.

"Best slow down, or I'll blow a gasket," he said, pulling away but taking hold of her hand. "I had Hargreaves make your favorite meal."

"Oh, you did miss me," she said, cozying up to his side. "Of course, I wondered while I was gone how many of your so-called female friends visited you in the hospital."

Hadn't he always liked a woman who claimed her territory? "A few did pop by to commiserate with me. The one I used to see visited."

She lifted her head and stared at him. "And?"

He pushed her back in place. "I told her I was in a new relationship." She'd been happy for him. They'd only really spent time together for companionship, and they'd both known it. He'd never had the compulsion to wait beside the window for her to arrive, or vice versa.

"That was wise of you," she said, tapping his knee. "I don't want to have to unleash this sly side of mine on anyone else."

"Sin City was enough," Arthur said. "How did it go in New York?"

"J.T. did what he had to," she said, tracing the wrinkle in his pant leg. "He's planning something romantic for Caroline tomorrow."

"He'd better sweet talk her but good," Arthur said with a harrumph. "That boy scared us all."

Clara put her hands on both of his shoulders. "So did you."

Her blue eyes soaked him in, taking their fill, as if she had missed him too.

"Don't do it again," she said softly, resting against his chest.

He put his arms around her. "We're all going to die someday, sweetheart."

She poked him. "Yes, but now that I've found you again, it had better be in twenty or so years, or you'll regret it."

He supposed he could live to a hundred. God knew the younger generation still needed him from time to time, and so would his great-grandchildren. Goodness, he might even live to see Jill and Meredith's children graduate high school. He liked that thought.

"Enough of this age talk. What's this balderdash

about you buying a trousseau in Paris? Good heavens, woman, no one's proposed to you yet."

"I suppose I'm becoming an optimist in my old age," she said, laughing. "Where did you think this was going?"

"I thought we'd live in sin," he said, chuckling when she socked him again. "We're too old to get married. Seems undignified."

She pulled away and stood, facing him down like a termagant. "Undignified? I happen to love you, you stupid, ornery old man. And you love me. I don't want to be sleeping in the spare room for the rest of my life."

He didn't want that either. "What would Hargreaves say?" He knew what the old biddies in town were saying, and it wasn't nice. Of course, the old men he played bingo with thought his ship had come in. Frankly, he thought so too.

"As the only man I've trusted all these years, Hargreaves would give the bride away if I asked him," she said, picking up his wine glass and drinking from it.

"You'll give me your germs," he said with a frown.

She waggled her eyebrows. "Better get used to it. I plan on hanging around here. Oh, and I want to travel more. There's so much out in the world. We don't have to live like fuddy-duddies, and now that you need to retire—"

"Who said anything about retiring?" he barked.

"Dammit, you're nearly eighty years old," she said with indignation in her voice. "This heart attack was a wake-up call. It's time to let Meredith and Tanner run the paper like you planned."

He grumbled. Andy had said his chances of living longer would improve if he cut back on his hours or outright retired. Cutting back would be impossible. Running a newspaper was a full-time job. Which meant the big R word had been churning in his gut.

"You knew the day would come," Clara said softly, sinking onto a knee beside him on the sofa. "Did you ever think maybe I came into your life at the right time? We can start this new chapter together."

"I called *you*," he said, tapping her playfully on the nose.

"Finally, but I was the one who showed up in all my glory," she shot back. "Arthur..."

"Yes?" he said as she cuddled up next to him again.

"I don't want to go through this kind of worry again," she said softly. "Not until I absolutely have to."

She'd hidden her worry well at the hospital, but he remembered her holding his hand and crying as they waited for the ambulance to come. He didn't want to do that to her again. The pain of watching Harriet get sicker and sicker and then die had made an imprint on him. It wasn't something he'd wish on anyone.

"I don't like my career ending like this," he said, "but I'll retire." Of course, he'd write an Op-Ed here and there. The black ink in his veins wasn't simply going to dry up.

She kissed his cheek. "Good, then we can get married and travel the world. Oh, and I might join a theater group too."

"Planning to be Judi Dench?" he asked, delighted to see her so happy.

"No, silly," she said. "Helen Mirren."

He put his arm around her and leaned in to kiss her neck. Ah, she was wearing French perfume. How lucky could a man be?

"I always thought Helen was sexy," he said, standing and extending his hand. "Shall we go to dinner?"

"Does it involve an after-dinner drink?" she asked, batting her eyelashes.

"I was thinking a nightcap in my room might be nice."

Her brow rose. "Didn't you recently have a heart attack?"

"Give me some credit. I talked to my doctor about it." And hadn't that been an embarrassing conversation... Of course, Andy had beamed the whole time, likely because the thought of a man at eighty having sex would make any man happy.

He grabbed her hand and pulled her off the couch, leaving his cane where it was. Darn thing was an inconvenience with a woman. He led her to the dining room, enjoying the feel of her warm hand in his. Sure enough, Hargreaves had lit the candles.

"Oh, how romantic," she breathed.

Hargreaves shot him a knowing look, and he shot him one back.

"Welcome back, madam," the man said, a brief smile touching his lips.

"Hello, Hargreaves," she said. "Thank you for taking care of this infernal man while I was off on important business helping the family."

"Of course," he said with a slight bow. "I'll serve dinner now."

They took their chairs, and Arthur drew her hand to his mouth and kissed it.

"I love you, Clara Merriam," he said, ready to say the words.

"I know, but it's nice to hear it," she said, her lips twitching. *"Every day."*

Leave it to her to instruct him on something so simple. "I'm still not sure about marriage."

"I am."

"Will you let me get a word in edgewise?" he asked. "You're exasperating."

"I always was your brat," she said, placing her napkin on her lap with a fetching grin.

"Yes, you were," he said, groaning as Hargreaves

brought in the first course of Indian food and his famous naan bread, God help him.

Marriage was around the corner, Arthur knew, but he wasn't going to tell Clara just yet or she'd be even more impossible.

CHAPTER 42

THE KNOCK ON THE DOOR WAS A WELCOME DISTRACTION after all of the fretting Caroline had done since Trevor and Clara left for Bali.

She'd told them not to keep her updated. The only thing she wanted to know was whether he was coming back or not.

When she opened the door, the answer was standing in front of her. J.T. smiled at her, but she noted the fatigue in his eyes, somehow more noticeable with his freshly shaved jaw.

"I'm back," he said, holding his hands out as if to announce his presence, "but before you say anything, let me get a few things off my chest. Can I come inside?"

She wasn't going to let him off too easy so she said, "I thought I wasn't supposed to talk."

He looked like he was biting the inside of his cheek. "Right. I can do this here. I've had hours of travel—and hours in Bali—to consider what I could possibly say to convince you that I'll never again disappear, that I'll stand by your side and love you like you deserve."

Now they were getting somewhere.

"First, I was wrong to leave, but honestly, I didn't see any other way. I was hurt and in shock, and all I wanted to do was protect you and everyone else the only way left to me. You getting hurt was bad enough, but Arthur nearly dying...I couldn't take that."

She nodded, but remained silent as he'd asked.

"Second, while I didn't want to live up to my nickname of Mud Slinger, I did what was needed. Cynthia is officially checkmated. I want to thank you for your role in obtaining that video. You and Aunt Clara are two of the strongest and most beautiful women I know, and I'm grateful for you. More than I could ever say."

He coughed to clear his throat, and she could feel the emotion well up in her too. He'd better finish this speech fast. There were things she needed to say as well.

"Third, I know loving me hasn't been the easiest, but I'm expecting that to change now."

Oh, he was so dumb. Loving him wasn't the hard part. The crap surrounding him hadn't been a walk in the park.

"I'm not worried about Cynthia hurting you or anyone else anymore. Well, I'm still a little paranoid, but I'm hoping that will go away with time. And if she does try something, I'll stand my ground and fight her tooth and nail. I won't let her take away my future. What I hope is our future. What I'm trying to say is that I've done some things that require a heck of a lot of forgiveness on your part, and I was wondering if you could forgive me and trust me enough to begin again. I love you, and God, I hope I didn't ruin this."

Talk faster, you moron, and I'll tell you.

He held up a hand and then blew out a long breath. "I'm nervous," he said, laughing briefly. "I was trying so hard to be all cool, but my insides... Never mind. Caroline, I want to show you something that might help prove to you how different things are. How different I feel. Will you come with me?"

"Can I speak now?" she asked, giving him a stern look.

He let out another shaky breath. "Yes, of course.

Sorry that was such a speech. I rehearsed it… Forget I said that. Maybe come with me and then talk. I feel like my surprise might help things."

"You're really calling the shots here, J.T." She crossed her arms for good measure.

He shrugged, his gray suit slightly metallic in the late morning sun. "I know, but this is important. I figure I messed up royally, so the making amends should be equally huge."

Okay, that sounded more like the J.T. she'd fallen in love with. "All right, I'll come with you. Where are we going?"

"How do you feel about surprises?" He pulled a black bandana from his pocket. "Blindfolds?"

"You can't be serious," she said.

"*Please.*"

"Aunt Clara would urge you to get to the point," she said, arching an eyebrow. He was making her seriously consider smacking him.

"I'm not in love with Aunt Clara," he said. "I'm in love with you."

She paused again.

"Not that the old girl doesn't have her charm, but I believe she's got eyes for Uncle Arthur."

"Yes, isn't it wonderful?" she commented. "Fine. Put the darn bandana on me. But this had better be good. I could be doing my nails or something."

He laughed but reached around her and tied the bandana. Without her vision, her other senses kicked into higher gear. She caught the scents of leather, spice, and citrus in his cologne and felt his body heat inches away from her. Then she heard a blast of something off in the distance.

"Whew, thank God that timing worked out," he said cryptically. "Will you take my hand? It would be easier, and I'd really like to hold it right now."

That damn charm of his... She held out her hand, and he clasped it tightly before she felt him raise it upward. His lips planted a gentle kiss on the back of her hand.

"You're beautiful," he said softly. "Thank you for coming with me."

Another strange blast sounded, this one closer than the last. "Did you hear that?"

He led her slowly off the front steps and then down the sidewalk. Because she couldn't see where she was going, she took her time feeling the ground beneath her.

That blast erupted much closer this time, and she shied away. "What is *that*?"

He laughed, leading her forward. "Step up."

She felt the ground change to something different, something she couldn't make out.

"Over here," J.T. said, propelling her forward. "Put your hands out. I'm right behind you."

His presence was comforting somehow. She reached out and touched a thatch of woven material. From the feel of the edges, it was some kind of wicker. Boy, she was confused.

"Hang on," J.T. said close to her ear.

Then she heard that loud whoosh again. Super loud this time, and then her knees bent as everything shifted. A blast of heat surrounded her, and suddenly it felt like she was in an elevator. Her mind filled in the rest.

"Are we in a hot air balloon?" she asked. No one else in the world...

"You sound shocked," he said, his hands resting lightly on her waist for balance. "It seemed like the easiest way to get to where I wanted."

She couldn't begin to imagine what that meant. "You're crazy!"

His soft chuckle sounded in her ear. "Welcome to my world, Caroline Hale."

He sounded like the old J.T. again, and all she wanted

to do was throw off the infernal bandana covering her eyes and see his face. Hope was rising in her as high as they seemed to be climbing in the balloon, and her love for him was firing up her heart.

"Please tell me we aren't going to Rome in this," she said dryly, speaking up to be heard over creaking of the balloon. "You're lucky I'm not afraid of heights."

"I checked with Moira," he said. "I'd never knowingly put you in an uncomfortable or scary situation. Again."

Leaning back against him seemed the best way to communicate her gratitude. Her love. His whole body shook for a moment, and then his arms came hesitantly around her waist.

"You're giving me hope," he whispered. "Thank you."

Tears burned her eyes behind the bandana. His cheek came to rest against hers.

"This is a strange way to have a balloon ride," she commented over the emotion roiling through her. "Usually people go on these for the scenery."

"You'll have plenty of time to take in the view, babe. Don't worry. Just let your senses unfold."

And so she did. The cold wind touched her face, and its freshness seemed to dissolve the worry and fear she'd been stewing in. As they continued their ascent, she felt like they were soaring through the air together, his arms around her.

"If you make a *Titanic* joke right now, I'm going to kill you," she muttered.

He laughed, and she felt a familiar click between them. A new beginning was taking root. She took a moment to think about Cynthia being out of his life for good. God, it was hard to believe after everything that woman had done to them. She could tell he felt lighter too, could hear it as he talked to the balloon operator whose name she learned was Roy.

Then music started to play, and J.T. laughed. "That's Trev, calling to see if we're airborne."

"What's that song?" she asked. "It's familiar..."

"Trev programmed it onto the phone he gave me," he said. "It's Jay-Z's '99 Problems,' and the first verse says, 'Ninety-nine problems, but a bitch ain't one.' His idea of a joke."

"Your brother has a crazy sense of humor," she said, laughing.

"Yeah, but he came to Bali to slap some sense into me—literally—and for that he can pretty much get away with anything. All right, hang on tight."

She felt the balloon shift again. "We're going down?"

"Yes," he said. "I can't wait to show you where."

His hands gripped her waist moments later and then the balloon touched the ground. Her knees dipped, but she was prepared. All motion stopped, and then J.T. was reaching for her hand.

"This way, my lady," he said, leading her onto solid ground again.

"I'm giving you ten seconds to take this bandana off," she said. "Ten, nine, eight—"

"Okay, okay," he said urgently. "You've been more than a good sport."

His hands touched her head and the cloth lifted from her eyes. "Oh, my God."

A purple balloon accented with green and yellow towered over her. Behind it, all she saw were blue sky and mountains. Snowcaps dotted most of them, and she cradled her arms as a cold wind rushed around her.

"Do you know why I brought you here?" he asked, drawing her gaze.

She watched as he stretched his arms out and closed his eyes. His face lifted as if he were basking in the sunlight. Words wouldn't form in response, but her heart expanded in her chest as she watched him.

He looked back at her with a grin. "You've helped me feel like I'm back on a mountaintop again, Caroline."

She remembered his story about how he used climb up to the tallest mountain in Dare Valley and feel like he was the king.

"My life suddenly seems as full of possibility as the blue sky above us," he said. "There's no one I'd like to have by my side more than you. I love you with all my heart, Caroline Hale. And I want to show you just how much."

Sinking to one knee, he reached into his pocket and pulled out a black box. Her mouth dropped open. After the hell he'd been through with Cynthia, she knew just how big a step this was for him. Funny, how it shot a stream of pure electricity through her own veins.

"You're... You're..."

When he opened the box, the diamond ring nestled inside seemed to send out an arc of rainbows. She put her hand over her mouth, feeling the urge to cry and laugh and sing, all at the same time.

"Will you marry me and be my queen of the mountaintop?" he asked. "Because, babe, I've got my groove back."

Her lips twitched. "You told me not to speak while you did all of this." She gestured around them. "What were you going to do if I said no?" She wanted to be able to tell Clara she'd given him somewhat of a tough time.

"Leave you up here until you came to your senses," he said, pursing his lips. "Seriously though. I know it's a lot to ask...after everything."

Everything indeed. He was the one who'd said he wasn't comfortable getting married again. Men! She marched over and poked him in the chest, causing him to lose his balance and sit back in the snow.

"Jeez, that's cold," he cried, balancing her and the ring he was holding.

"Serves you right," Caroline said. "You should have let me get my speech in before you proposed."

"What can I say? I needed to pull out all of the stops to convince you I'm worth forgiving and that I'll never fail you again."

He looked down, and she could sense his vulnerability. Taking his beloved face in her hands, she gazed into his eyes.

"You're forgiven for leaving this once, but if you ever do it again—"

"I got your note," he said, shivering playfully. "You're right. Uncle Arthur would be one scary ghost."

"Yes, he would," she said. "Now, while your butt freezes, I'm going to give you the highlights of my speech."

He barked out a laugh. "If you take too long, I might be frozen to this mountaintop."

"Roy and I will just have to fly off without you," she said, poking him again for good measure.

"Are you enjoying yourself?" he asked.

"Yes," she said, her tone playful. "You?"

"Cold, but amused. All right, give me the highlights. My butt is numb now. I should be able to take it."

She kissed his right cheek. "First, I do understood why you left, but like I said, don't ever do it again."

"A day into it, I wanted to die," he said. "I was missing you and Trev, and hell... It wasn't pretty."

The honesty of his words gripped her heart.

"Second, while you seem to think there's a lot to forgive, there isn't. As far as I'm concerned, most of it is on Cynthia. She made her bed, and I'm glad you tucked her in, so to speak."

She'd do a victory dance with Clara and her sisters at some point. Everyone was happy that bitch was gone for good. She likely wouldn't be going to prison for stalking or for what she'd done to Arthur, but that didn't matter so long as she stayed away.

"Third, I'm glad you're back to feeling like yourself. You've always been king of the mountain in my eyes."

"Does that mean you'll be my queen?" he asked.

She shot him a look. "I'm still giving my speech."

"My ass is getting hypothermia, Caroline," he said, shifting on the cold hard ground.

"Don't whine, honey," she said, unable to contain her smile. "Fourth, yes, I will marry you because I love and adore you, you silly man."

His eyes flashed, first with shock and then joy. Then he grabbed her by the waist and fell back onto the snow. She shrieked.

"What are you doing?" she asked.

"Getting us both cold and freezing," he quipped. "That way we can warm each other up when we get home."

Home.

There was that word again. The rainbow light from the diamond caught her eye as he slipped on the ring, and for a moment, she could see herself holding hands with J.T. and that little girl.

"I love you," he said, sitting up and caressing her cheek.

"I love you too," she whispered back.

"I'm going to make you the happiest woman on earth and be the best husband," he said. "I give you my word."

She pressed a hard kiss to his mouth, her heart dancing in her chest. "You have my word right back."

"Since I seriously am losing feeling in my extremities, can I simply say, 'my queen, your chariot awaits'?"

They stood, and he led her back into the balloon's basket. Linking hands, they walked to the edge and looked out together.

They sailed into the sky of endless blue and their happily ever after.

EPILOGUE

ARTHUR WAS READING WHAT HE WAS CALLING MEREDITH and Tanner's newspaper at the kitchen table with a cup of coffee beside him.

While he'd only been retired a few weeks, it still unnerved him to read the newspaper like a regular person after years of putting it together piece by piece. It really was news to him. Ha. Not that Meredith and Tanner weren't doing a damn good job or anything.

Clara's humming caught his attention, and he watched her walk into the kitchen all gussied up in a teal Chanel dress she'd brought in Paris for her *trousseau*.

"What are you looking at?" she asked, putting a hand on her hip.

Like she didn't know. Since she'd joined him in what she was now calling their *boudoir*—God help him—she'd become even cheekier.

He loved every minute of it.

"Not a thing," he said, turning the page he was on, pretending to read the paper. "You look beautiful, by the way, but don't let an old man's compliment go to your head. Some might say I'm addled at my age."

She smacked him lightly on the back of the head, and he had to fight to contain his grin. She was so easy to rile up, but he knew she was playacting too. This Cary Grant and Rosalind Russell routine was simply their way.

A hefty stack of papers landed on the table beside him, and he looked away from his paper to see her staring at him.

"What's that?" he asked.

"A pre-nup," she said matter-of-factly. "Read it. Make changes to it. Consult your lawyer."

He grumbled. "I haven't even proposed yet."

"But you will," she said, nodding as Hargreaves walked into the kitchen. "We can't live in sin for the rest of our lives in this small town. Besides, we should be role models for your great-grandchildren. Right, Hargreaves?"

"Young children are quite impressionable," the old sack of bones replied in his stiff British accent. "If your father were still living, he wouldn't hear of it."

Neither would Emmits, Arthur knew, but was he going to make this easy? No way. She'd be disappointed. "We won't need a pre-nup, Clara. Presuming I propose, of course. I've recently discovered some things that make me feel we're incompatible. You snore like a field hand, and your feet are cold as ice."

"And you grind your teeth and run into things in the dark on the way to the bathroom and curse like a sailor," she said. "We balance each other out. Hargreaves, do you have the presents?"

"Wait," Arthur said, putting a hand on her arm. "You're coated in diamonds again. Why you need an engagement ring..."

"It is customary, sir," Hargreaves said, coming forward with two parcels.

Surely she hadn't bought an engagement ring. She'd been hinting like a bull in Pamplona hinted, but he was determined to take his time. She'd have a ring in his nose if he didn't do things his own way.

"Customary," he barked playfully, earning him another poke. "Now about this pre-nup... I don't want you thinking you can't trust me."

Clara stared him down but good. "It's not about trust. It's about the infernal laws in this country. You have a newspaper I did nothing to create. Did you know I could lay claim to part of it if we married and then divorced? Or that you could do the same to me with my paintings and fortune?"

Exactly why they both needed to sign over those things to the younger generation. He needed to call his lawyer about transferring ownership next week.

"I know the damn law, and it sucks," he said. "If you pour your blood, sweat, and tears into something, it should be yours—not someone else's simply because you shagged them while you were hitched."

He heard a sound and looked over to see Hargreaves covering his mouth. Had he finally made the old man laugh finally? Incredible.

"You know, I've talked to Meredith and Tanner about this and Jill and Brian too. I'm working my way through the family. Everyone needs to have some legal protections in place. If I'd had that in my marriage, maybe I'd felt comfortable revealing the lost Rembrandt. These young people need some serious schooling, Arthur."

He loved hearing that. She was rapidly becoming an integral part of his family.

"I've told them it's not about a lack of trust or love," Clara said. "This is about respect. It's about making sure the person you love honors the work you do and your accomplishments. And let me tell you something else—"

He pulled her onto his lap and kissed her soundly. She stopped like she usually did and wound her arms around his neck, kissing him back. Arthur heard

Hargreaves leave the room. Thank God the man gave them space, or he'd have to insist on building him a separate living area. Come to think of it...

"Done with your soap box?" he asked, caressing her cheek.

"You're an old bull, but I love you," she said, kissing him lightly and then hugging him.

Hadn't he been thinking that about her? "No woman at your age should complain about bunking with an old bull," he said, letting his hand slip to her butt.

She laughed in that bawdy way of hers—a giddy, tinkling laugh he imagined her old stupid deuce of a husband had never heard, God rot his soul.

"Are you ready to go to your birthday party?" she asked.

He was looking forward to seeing everyone, but he hated the fuss. "No reason to celebrate getting this ancient."

"The pyramids are older than you," she said. "You're far from ancient. Now, I decided to give you my presents beforehand."

He eyed them with suspicion. "Anything going to jump out and give me another heart attack?"

His heart was recovering great, or so his doctors told him, but a man still needed to be careful.

"Nope," she said. "Open this one first," she said, nudging the large silver-wrapped box toward him.

When he tore off the paper and opened it, he looked at the contents. Stunned. The painting was of him as a young man, his head lowered over a scatter of papers at his old desk, the one he'd had in the corner of his apartment in New York. He had what he knew was one of his first red pens in his hands, marking up whatever article he was reading.

"What?" he sputtered, gesturing to the painting. "How?"

"I had it painted," she said, tracing the gold frame. "Before you left New York. I was planning on giving it to you for your birthday, but when you announced you were going back to Dare Valley, I...put it away."

"In a rage, no doubt," he said, his heart hurting.

"Not only rage," she said softly.

He looked up and studied her. No, she'd grieved over his departure. Over what might have been. "You're going to make me a sap with all of this mushy stuff, Clara."

Her blue eyes flashed fire, but he kissed her hard on the mouth and put his arms around her. He felt a riot of powerful emotions, holding her, ones he hadn't felt since Harriet had died. God, he was glad to be feeling them again.

"Clara Marissa Merriam, will you marry me?" he asked softly.

She edged back, her eyes shining with unusual tears. "'Bout time you asked me."

Perhaps it was. "This proposal has a time limit since my leg is starting to fall asleep..."

"Yes!" she said, her voice almost girlish. "Oh, you're odious sometimes, but I love you."

"Keep that in your mind for a moment while I tell you something," he said, patting her fanny. "I love you too, but I don't have a ring yet."

"You proposed to me without a ring?" she asked. "What kind of man are you?"

"Spontaneous."

She snorted.

"Hey, I just got out of the hospital, woman, and the kind of ring you'd like isn't going to be in Dare Valley."

"We'll need to go on a road trip then," she said. "After your party. Speaking of which. Open this present and then let's get going."

This package was smaller, and when he opened it, he laughed. "Red hots?"

"These are dark chocolate-covered ones," she said, pointing to the label. "I figured since I'm living here I should have red hots that represent my unique style and taste."

Cinnamon and chocolate suited her, he thought. He was oddly moved by the gesture, almost as much as he'd been by the painting she'd commissioned all those years ago.

"Have Hargreaves put it in a candy dish alongside mine in the den and my study."

She beamed. "I will. Shall we go celebrate your life?"

He coughed and felt his face turn as red as one of his red hots. "When you put it that way, I'm staying home."

But of course he didn't.

When they arrived at Meredith and Tanner's house, his entire family was fanned out in front of him. He felt tears fill his eyes as they all yelled, "Surprise."

He put his hand to his heart playfully. Smiled when his great-grandchildren ran forward to welcome him. He was hugged and kissed and hugged and kissed some more. God, they were a mushy lot.

"Speech!" he heard a familiar voice call out.

He gave Jill the fisheye for being a busybody, but more people joined in, shouting that word, and soon he felt Clara pushing him to the center of the room.

"All right, I know when I'm licked," he said with a gusty sigh. "I remember telling J.T. and Trevor how family circles the wagons when there's trouble, and God knows we've seen our fair share, but we've weathered it together. What I neglected to mention was that family also circles the wagons to celebrate. Victories. Anniversaries. Graduations. Reunions. And yes, even birthdays for a man as old as I am."

Meredith grabbed Tanner's arm, resting her face against his shoulder. Goodness, he was moved seeing them together, knowing they would continue his legacy.

For a time, he'd thought his son would take over, but Alan had taken his early heart attack as a sign he needed to slow down. He spied his son holding Jared with a smile on his face. Alan had handled retirement well, what with moving to Arizona. Somehow knowing that told Arthur he'd be okay too in this new chapter. Besides, he had Clara. He swiped at the tears in his eyes as he darted a glance at her.

"I've given a lot of you advice over the years, and I'm going to take the opportunity to give you a little more today. I've been fortunate to devote most of my adult years to a profession I love, and it makes me happy to know the paper I created, the one people out East told me was impossible, is in good hands. Many of you have found your passion in life. Keep the fire lit and give it your all."

A few people coughed, and he noted a whole host of people wiping tears, notably a very pregnant Natalie Hale. And, if the rumors were right, both Peggy and Jane would be announcing their pregnancies soon as well. Damn if he hadn't been right about Jane. Neither had been drinking alcohol at family occasions for a few weeks now. Man, he was glad he had the chance to see more babies born into this family.

"I was lucky enough to find a woman to love, one who understood and supported the love I had for my paper. Our family paper," he added. "Somehow I've been fortunate to find another woman to love, which only goes to show you never know what surprises life might send you. When they come, open your arms and thank your lucky stars."

He put his hand in his pocket, fingering a red hot, as he considered the rest of what needed saying.

"I've done a lot in my life, and I hope to do even more in what time I have left. But when I look around this room, I see something truly miraculous."

He swept his arm from right to left, gazing at so many beloved faces.

"In the past few years, this family has grown. Not everyone is blood, but who the hell cares? Family isn't only about blood. It's about finding the people who get you. Who you can call in a pinch. Who want to help you succeed and thrive at everything you do."

A number of people were nodding, including Rhett Butler Blaylock, who didn't share a lick of his DNA but was kin nonetheless.

"I'd like to take responsibility for some of this," he said, making a few people laugh. "Here are some statistics to prove my case. I've seen about ten new couples come together. Four children born. A whole heck of a lot of you—nearly all—have returned to Dare Valley or found us somehow on a map destiny planned for you all along. I like to think more might be coming home."

He pointed at young Trevor, who shook his head slowly, making his brother nudge him with an elbow.

"Emmits Merriam would be happy to have his great grandson back here, opening a museum at the university he founded. What I expect Emmits wouldn't have foreseen was his old friend becoming engaged to his granddaughter only moments before his eightieth birthday party. It sure as hell shocked the heck out of me."

Clara winked at him.

"In the best possible way, of course," he added gruffly.

Jill stepped forward, her mouth open like an eager puppy. "You're engaged?"

"And I'm the one old enough for hearing aids," he said, rolling his eyes heavenward. "Yes, Clara and I are getting married. In fact, we'll be leaving Dare Valley for a while. With all this free time on my hands, we've decided to see the world. Expect a visit in Dublin, young Trevor."

Perhaps he could help more of the Merriam kids find themselves a good companion for life—even if they didn't come home to roost in Dare Valley. Emmits would like that. Clara would be happy to play matchmaker, he imagined. And he could help the Merriams get their heads out of their asses if needed.

"Did you all expect us to live in sin?" he finally joked.

Everyone seemed to be in shock, and he found himself biting his lip to keep from laughing at their faces.

Rhett burst out laughing, and then the tall man was bustling forward and picking him up off the ground. "I want to grow up to be you, Arthur."

"Put me down, you crazy Southerner," he said, trying to contain his mirth.

The moment Rhett heeded him, he was rushed again by people hugging and kissing him and congratulating him on the engagement. In the melee, he managed to look over and see Clara being surrounded by the same eager beavers.

"Get it out of your systems," he said as Jill rushed toward him from the makeshift party queue.

"Oh, I'm so happy for you, Grandpa," she said, hugging him tight. "Grandma would be so happy."

He'd talked to Harriet the other night, his eyes fixed on the star he thought was her in the night sky. That star had winked at him—much like Clara liked to do—and given him a final sense of peace about starting a new life with another woman he loved.

J.T. came forward after the hubbub finally died and held out a small present. Since returning a couple weeks ago, he seemed to be more like his old self. It made his heart happy to see Caroline was ever by his side.

"This is from all of us," he said, taking Caroline's hand when she came forward. "As you said, you're been there for all of us. We wanted to give you something we thought you might enjoy."

He shook the present as Clara joined him. "This had better not be jewelry."

She laughed and leaned into him, making him wish he didn't have his cane. Funny how he didn't seem to need it as much these days.

Opening the box, he frowned at the key. "I almost hate to ask. What's it to?"

J.T. and Caroline walked to the front door and opened it. "Come see."

He took Clara's hand, and together they followed the other couple out, the crowd coming out with them.

The present was unmistakable, what with it being parked smack dab in the driveway.

He fought to breathe. "A 1960 Chevrolet Corvette Convertible? That's my present?"

"We heard from a reliable source that you talked about wanting this car when you first came back to Dare Valley, but you couldn't afford it," J.T. said.

That must have been Clara. Goodness. No, he'd poured all of his money into the paper and his life in Dare Valley.

"You shouldn't have," Arthur said, handing Clara his cane and walking toward it.

She was a beaut, what with her Roman red body and white accents. The black leather interior was in mint condition like the rest of the car.

"Since you plan on traveling, we thought you might want something fun to drive," Caroline said. "It's the least we could do after everything you've done for us."

"Everyone loves you to pieces, Grandpa," Meredith said, leaving her parents and coming to stand beside him. Goodness, she'd been standing beside him ever since her unexpected return to Dare Valley, he realized. They'd become a team.

"I don't know where I'd be if you hadn't come home, sweetheart," Arthur said, sniffing a moment.

Meredith wiped away a few tears. "Me either. I'm going to miss seeing you every day at the paper, but I'm glad you'll be kicking up your heels with Clara."

"Gads, I'm going to be bawling like a baby in a moment," he said, hugging her. "All of you have overwhelmed me. Thank you!"

"Perhaps we should go for a test drive, Arthur," Clara said, opening the passenger door of the Corvette and hopping inside.

Yes, indeed, she'd hopped. Then again, she'd planned this. No doubt, she'd told them about this car strategically. Goodness, she had some memory.

"Good idea, my dear."

He walked around to the driver's side and slid in. The leather seat cupped his body, and after he turned on the engine, he put the car in first but kept his foot on the brake.

"Happy birthday, Grandpa!" Meredith and Jill called.

J.T. and Caroline waved as they drove off, and Arthur couldn't help but smile. He couldn't be prouder of his role in bringing them together.

He took the car toward downtown. Nostalgia was running through his veins, but he figured that was okay since it was his eightieth birthday. Clara shook out her long hair, and it flew behind her as he gathered speed. She held out his cane and then threw it out of the convertible.

He forced his gaze back to the road. "What the hell did you do that for?"

"You don't need it anymore," she said. "I've been watching you. Hargreaves agrees."

He tried not to smile, but couldn't help himself.

"Like either one of you have any medical training," he barked.

"Let's face it, Arthur," she said, putting her hand on

his knee. "You might have had a heart attack, but you're looking and feeling younger than your years. Just think about how great you're going to feel after being married to me for a few years. Who knows? You might run a marathon or something."

"When pigs fly," he spat, but he did feel younger with her, and this car certainly didn't hurt.

"It is a nice town," Clara said. "You did well here, Arthur."

Yes, he had. He slowed down to drive past *The Western Independent*. God, he loved that brick building. But Hales would continue to walk the halls and put out the voice of the West. That was all that mattered.

Jill's first venture, Don't Soy With Me, made him smile as they passed it. He'd never been one for fancy coffee, but she'd done a hell of a job with it. After Matt was finished being mayor, Arthur was going to talk her into running—although he expected it wouldn't be too difficult.

Brian's restaurant caught his eye and then Margie's bakery, the one she'd taken over with such obvious respect for the legacy it held in town. Like Mac Maven, who'd restored The Grand Mountain Hotel, she'd added her own flavor to the business while keeping its old bones. Emmits' university had changed too, but J.T. would ensure his friend's legacy lived on. And now so would Caroline.

As he reached the edge of town, he looked over at Clara, the woman he'd spend the remainder of his days with. Yes, he'd done pretty well.

"You ready to see how fast this baby goes?" he asked her.

She put her hand on his knee. "I was waiting to see if you were up to it. Otherwise, I was going to drive."

He laughed and looked over his shoulder once more before hitting the gas. Dare Valley and its people got to a man, sure as shooting.

Arthur expected his old bones would be visible for some time yet in this town he loved so dearly, and he was glad for that. The younger generation had done a bang up job so far in the changing of the guard, and he knew they would continue to do so.

Dare Valley was in good hands.

This letter is really emotional since it marks the last Dare Valley book, my first series. Honestly when Grandpa Hale said Dare Valley was in good hands at the end, he couldn't have been more correct. Like you, I've loved seeing everyone's journey. Who hasn't looked forward to Jill's new antics or the kind of wackiness Rhett might get up to? But Grandpa Hale felt like he wanted to take his warm fuzzies (haha) on the road with Clara to help the Merriam kids out, and who was I to refuse him? So yes, there's a new Merriam series...keep reading.

When I wrote NORA ROBERTS LAND, the first Dare Valley book, I wanted to create a magical small town everyone wanted to be a part of. All of you have embraced it in ways I'd never imagined, and I can't tell you how grateful and blessed I feel. This town was modeled after ones I knew and loved, but Grandpa Hale was who I imagined my great-great grandfather, George, to be. Like I say in the dedication for this book, he was larger-than-life. He lived in the Old West. Won our family newspaper in a lucky hand of poker (maybe the coolest thing ever). Brought the town embezzler back for justice when he skipped town. Hid in a pickle jar with the town sheriff to learn some local vigilantes' plans and stop them. But one of my favorite stories is about him writing a story exposing a corrupt federal judge and getting himself arrested—with his sheriff friend's help—for urinating at the courthouse, no less, when he was tipped off that said judge was sending his own "guys" to bring grandpa in, likely to muscle him. Talk about an incredible figure! Even better, he worked with my great-great grandmother on the newspaper in pure partnership, a rarity back in those days. She ran the paper after he passed, and it still prints news to this day. What a remarkable story, right?

So yes, while this beloved series is finished, we're not saying goodbye to our treasured Dare Valley friends. I like to think we're taking the best of Dare Valley on the road. And first up will be Trevor kicking things off in Ireland. The book is called WILD IRISH ROSE, and it has an ornery cat, a mischievous Irish setter, and a famous ghost all intent on seeing Trev fail in making a business deal with Becca O'Neill, who not only won't give Trev the time of day but also won't serve him her award-winning scones (and that's *bad* in Trevor's world). Or course, Arthur and Clara show up to help, but their version of helping doesn't match Trevor's. Shock, right? I'm already laughing at their antics. The Merriam series is going to be such a fun journey, and I can't wait to share it with you.

Thanks again for being part of this beautiful family.

Lots of love,

Ava

P.S. Grandpa Hale and the rest of Dare Valley would love to hear what you thought of this book and the series, so please leave a review. Hugs and thanks.

P.P.S. The lost Rembrandt is pure fiction, but wouldn't it have been cool?

ABOUT THE AUTHOR

 International Bestselling Author Ava Miles joined the ranks of beloved storytellers with her powerful messages of healing, mystery, and magic. Millions of readers have discovered her fiction and nonfiction books, praised by *USA TODAY* and *Publisher's Weekly*. *Women's World Magazine* has selected a few of her novels for their book clubs while Southwest Airlines featured the #1 National Bestseller NORA ROBERTS LAND (the name used with Ms. Roberts' blessing) in its in-flight entertainment. Ava's books have been chosen as Best Books of the Year and Top Editor's Picks and are translated into multiple languages.

Made in the USA
Las Vegas, NV
28 December 2021

39704030R00225